ONE THING LEADS TO ANOTHER

DAVID W. ROBERTS

Published in Australia by Sid Harta Publishers Pty Ltd,
ABN: 46 119 415 842
23 Stirling Crescent, Glen Waverley, Victoria 3150 Australia
Telephone: +61 3 9560 9920, Facsimile: +61 3 9545 1742
E-mail: author@sidharta.com.au

First published in Australia 2020
This edition published 2020
Copyright © David W. Roberts 2020
Cover design, typesetting: WorkingType (www.workingtype.com.au)

Roberts, David W.
One Thing Leads to Another
ISBN: 978-1-925707-01-4
pp426

ABOUT THE AUTHOR

David Roberts migrated as a qualified teacher from the United Kingdom. After seventeen years working as a teacher, deputy principal and principal in country New South Wales, he became a university academic. University appointments and consultancies enabled David to travel widely and broaden his horizons. Now retired, he lives with his wife in Adelaide.

To my wife, Joy

CONTENTS

CHAPTER 1

Charles Frederic Allsop

They found him shortly after 2 pm on Monday 7 February 1975. Charles Frederic Allsop lay peacefully on his back in the monstrous waterbed he had purchased for his new wife during May the previous year. Three pairs of anxious eyes surveyed the scene but their owners feared the worst.

The three pairs of eyes belonged to Joanne Ernstein, Charles' daughter; Scott Harris, the manager of The Everglades Retirement Village; and Detective Inspector Mike Johansson, who had recently been assigned to the Missing Persons Department within the South Australian Police. The three had reacted remarkably differently. Joanne's immediate instinct was to rush over to her father but Johansson, who had summed up the situation on entry to the bedroom, shot out a strong constraining arm and held her firmly.

'No, Mrs Ernstein, wait a moment please while I check things first.'

The young manager, Scott, had no idea what to do and stood with a look of horror on his face. Appointed to his first managerial position only a few weeks earlier, he had pondered how he would react when first confronted by the death of one of his residents. He didn't think he knew the elderly gentleman lying in front of him but with approximately 300 residents in the retirement village, and his very recent arrival as manager, this was hardly surprising.

Detective Inspector Johansson's training and extensive police experience kicked in straight away as he moved over to the body, felt for a pulse and finding nothing, gently closed the eyelids. Joanne collapsed on a nearby chair whimpering and in shock whilst the young manager continued to stand gawking and totally overwhelmed by the situation.

The Inspector turned his attention to Mrs Ernstein who had only that morning telephoned the police to express her concerns that she had been trying to contact her father all weekend without success.

Joanne Ernstein was past her best in the looks department, although the Inspector could still recognise a woman who in her prime had probably been most attractive. She had, as they say, let herself go and this was reflected in her somewhat flabby disposition. Crying uncontrollably, it was difficult to decipher what it was she was repeatedly saying. Somewhat impatiently the Inspector managed after a few moments to deduce that Joanne was bemoaning the fact that she had not tried to contact her father earlier in the weekend and that she might then have been with him when he passed away. Meanwhile, Inspector Johansson was anxious to carry out the normal routine checks to satisfy himself that this was a natural death and that nothing untoward had happened in Apartment 77 of The Everglades Retirement Village. Action was needed.

Turning to the young manager, Johansson barked, 'Righto sir, take Mrs Ernstein with you and look after her. See she is offered a hot drink and conveyed back to her home when she's ready. I'll be in touch with you again Mrs Ernstein for some details, either later today or tomorrow. We already have your address and contact number.'

Scott finally snapped out of his catatonic state, nodded unconvincingly and at last demonstrated that he did possess a voice after all. 'Oh yes... yes, yes of course, Inspector. Umm... can I help you up, Mrs Ernstein?'

Mrs Ernstein looked doubtfully at the insipid-looking young manager and surmised that he was quite possibly physically incapable of helping her to her feet and so with one determined heave raised herself up on her own accord. Gathering some composure, she asked the Inspector if she might have a moment alone with her father before leaving.

'I'm sorry, Ma'am. I have to be present until the doctor arrives. Stay for a few minutes by all means, but then I must go out to ring the doctor and you will have to leave.'

Shortly after, the still sobbing Mrs Ernstein and the pale young manager departed together. Inspector Johansson sighed with some relief and followed them out the door ringing the doctor from his patrol car.

¶

It was a pleasant enough day as the Inspector left Apartment 77. The air was still cool and fresh after a southerly change the previous evening that had pleased the gardeners in the retirement village with around twenty millimetres of welcome rain. A pair of spotted turtle doves were cooing and flirting on the rooftop of the apartment across the road as the sun broke through and smiled on the village. He noted that the manager had recovered sufficiently to think of opening the passenger door for Mrs Ernstein who lowered her large frame rather clumsily into position. This operation successfully completed, and Mrs Ernstein safely ensconced in her seatbelt, the manager's car drew slowly away, presumably back to the manager's office for a much needed cup of tea for its occupants.

All appeared quiet in the retirement village. There was no doubt tongues would soon be wagging amongst the residents with the sudden appearance of a police car outside Apartment 77. The retirement village had been open for barely two years and Inspector Johansson suspected the arrival of a police patrol car was regarded as a major event for the retirees. When contact with the doctor was achieved, and a promise that the doctor would arrive at Apartment 77 within the hour, the Inspector was pleased. With any luck he could get home early enough to grab his golf gear and squeeze in nine holes before dark.

Whilst contemplating these quick few holes on his favourite course, he noticed an elderly male resident moving towards the car and flourishing a walking stick around in an aggressive manner. Johansson quickly summed up the approaching man and decided he would be in a better position to engage him if he was standing outside his vehicle. This guy was probably just a harmless nutcase. Grabbing his police cap and placing it on his head, Johansson jumped out and stood leaning on the open door. The policeman, once a rugby union front row forward, was solid and he eyed the advancing man without fear.

'He's a bastard that man, an absolute bastard!' were the first recognisable utterings of the angry male as he neared the policeman. 'What's he gone and done now? I could tell you a few stories about him that you wouldn't believe, copper.' Breathless after hobbling down the street, waving his stick about and mouthing off, the old fellow stopped in front of Johansson and glared. 'They should never have let him into this village, he's done nothing but create trouble for everyone here.'

'Good afternoon sir, and who might I be speaking to?'

'Henry, Henry Childs, I live at the back of this idiot's place in number 82. I tell you he's a pain in the arse. I hope you arrest him and throw him in jail.'

'And why would I want to do that, sir?'

'If you have a spare hour I can spell out everything stupid that Charles has done to upset everyone here, and me in particular. Charles and I go back a long, long way and he's been a constant bloody thorn in my side for over forty years. He's a bloody criminal that man. And next week I've heard Charles plans to bugger-up the village AGM as well.'

'I doubt that he will be doing that sir, because Charles Allsop is dead.'

'You're joking?' exclaimed a wide-eyed Henry Childs.

'We don't joke about death, Mr Childs. I suggest you return to your apartment and calm down.'

'I'm sorry, Officer, I hated his guts, but I never like to hear when someone carks it.'

'I'd appreciate it if you would leave now sir, and let me get on with what has to be done.'

'Yes, of course...' And with that, a far more subdued Henry Childs, the occupant of Apartment 82, turned around, and using his walking stick this time for what it was designed for, hobbled his way back up the street.

Johansson filed this brief encounter away in the back of his mind, slammed the car door shut and ambled back up the path to the entrance of Apartment 77 to await the arrival of the doctor.

He did not have to wait long. A tap at the door revealed a nervous bespectacled man, probably in his fifties, who answered to the name of Dr Peters.

'Thank you for coming so quickly Doctor, routine stuff, need to know cause and approximate time of death please and then if you would kindly arrange for the body's removal ASAP.'

The doctor strode briskly to the side of the bed, plonked his medical bag of implements on the eiderdown and conducted the necessary checks. Doctor Peters was one of the three doctors that the police could call upon at short notice to confirm a death and attest that the cause of death was natural. Occasionally, post-mortems were ordered if suspicious circumstances were detected. Dr Peters was recently appointed, and Johansson had only once before had to call on his services.

'All is well here Inspector, he died of ischaemic heart disease, probably last night. I'll write up the medical report, sign the death certificate, and have it over to you in a day or so. I'll arrange for the body to be removed immediately. What number did you say this is?'

Johansson reminded the doctor that it was number 77. In doing so, he couldn't help noticing once again what an edgy man Dr Peters was. Unusual in a doctor, he thought. Other doctors he had had dealings with, both personally and in the line of duty, always appeared at least outwardly calm and generated an air of self-belief such that you had confidence in their expertise. Not so with Dr Peters; an anxious weed of a man. Johansson made a mental note to never call on Dr Peters if requiring medical assistance for his family in the future.

The doctor hurriedly gathered up his bag, managed a flimsy handshake and with a 'Thank you, Inspector' disappeared through the front door as quickly as he had arrived five minutes before. Inspector Johansson checked his watch. Excellent! The nine holes were now a definite possibility. He locked the front door behind him, delivered the key back to the manager who, he noted, was still endeavouring to persuade Mrs Ernstein that going home would be a good idea. Mrs Ernstein, on the other hand, had found the packet of Tim Tams the manager had proffered sufficient reason not to be too hasty.

Half an hour later Johansson teed off and the doings of the afternoon slipped from his mind as he relished the joys of the great outdoors.

¶

Another glorious summer day was heralded in by a chorus of birds from across the neighbourhood. January in Adelaide was a favourite time for Johansson; coolish nights, and, more often than not, hot, sunny, dry days. He rolled over to look at his wife still blissfully sleeping. They had been married almost twenty years, but Lynda still looked as gorgeous as the day they wed.

Life as a primary school teacher suited her because with the long holidays and short working days, she was able to energetically maintain all her various sporting interests. Not only had she been born with a beautiful dark skin colouring but with her sporting pursuits her body remained firm and lithe. Despite providing them with two fabulous children, Lynda's figure was the envy of many women her age.

Johansson felt a sudden stirring of sexual desire and was about to wake Lynda with a full body cuddle with the intention of encouraging Lynda to make love, when his passionate thoughts were rudely shattered by a yell from somewhere below.

'Dad, Dad, are you awake?'

'No, I'm not Michael, go back to sleep.'

'Good try, lover boy,' Lynda purred as she felt his hardness. 'How about tonight then?'

'That's a date for sure.'

With a quick kiss, Johansson hauled himself out of bed and set about the morning's routines. Within an hour or so they were all breakfasted, the kids in their uniforms and Mum and Dad leaving to go their separate ways; Lynda to her school and Inspector Johansson to the police station.

Arriving at his desk, Johansson thumbed through yesterday's mail, checked his voice mail and phoned Mrs Ernstein. Now that Dr Peters had confirmed a natural death for Charles Frederic Allsop, all that was needed was a routine visit to her home to gather a few more details so the matter could be concluded and filed away. It would be handy to sign off on this matter quickly so that he could commence work on the two new files that had been dropped into his in-tray overnight.

'Thank you, Mrs Ernstein. I'll be at your place by nine-thirty. It shouldn't take long.'

Mrs Ernstein's abode was impressive. Set on the side of a low hill in the newish suburb of Hallett Cove.

It boasted two full storeys with a single attic above. It was mock Tudor-style; white all over with black wooden beams providing a stark contrast. Johansson, who was a lover of the seventeenth century Tudor houses still to be found in parts of the United Kingdom, was quietly disparaging of people who sought to imitate the genuine article. He estimated the house had been completed within the last twelve months which explained why the substantial front garden was still in the throes of extensive landscaping. A picket fence and a winding pathway with assorted recently planted geraniums on either side completed the scene. Admiring the stylish timber front door, he pressed the bell.

'Oh, good morning Inspector,' a slightly out-of-breath Mrs Ernstein welcomed him with the slightest of smiles. 'Do come in.'

Accepting the invitation, Johansson wiped his feet on the mat, returned the smile with a curt nod and ventured into Mrs Ernstein's domain. He was at once taken with the tasteful and not inexpensive furnishings. Chiswell, if he was not mistaken. Everything he set eyes on was mission-brown Chiswell; the dining setting, the easy chairs, display cabinets, the nest of tables and the fine coffee table that occupied centre stage and sported a generous bunch of fresh flowers.

'Please take a seat, Inspector. Can I interest you in a cup of tea or coffee perhaps?'

'No thank you.' It was Johansson's unwritten rule that he never accepted beverages, or anything else for that matter, when visiting homes on official business. Sinking back into a comfortable Chiswell armchair, he hastily jettisoned the large cushion he found there, and then observed Mrs Ernstein's lumbering movements. She was more overweight than he had realised when first meeting her at the apartment belonging to her father, Charles Frederic Allsop. *Why do so many women allow themselves to become overweight or even obese?* he wondered. Thank God his own wife, Lynda, looked after herself so well and, though only a few years younger than Mrs Ernstein, managed to look stunning wherever she went.

'Inspector, this has been a terrible shock to our family. It is all so sudden and quite unexpected. My father was in quite good health for his age. He was eighty-one, you know.'

'Mrs Ernstein, I didn't have a chance to express my condolences yesterday, so please accept them now. I realise what a shock this has been. I won't need to bother you for long. I just need a few more details.'

Mrs Einstein had manoeuvred herself onto a straight-backed Chiswell chair, easier to get up from when the time came. She seemed anxious to talk and Johansson registered this with some alarm. The last thing he wanted was for someone like Mrs Ernstein to tearfully unburden herself and for him to be trapped with no easy means of escape. Realising this potentially dangerous scenario was imminent, Inspector Johansson seized the initiative.

'Let's get this over with Mrs Ernstein. Now, am I correct in understanding that you are the next of kin?'

'Oh no, I don't believe I am. He is... sorry, he was, married.'

This news surprised the Inspector. It was Mrs Ernstein who had contacted the police, it was Mrs Ernstein who had come around to her father's apartment. He had wrongly assumed that Charles Frederic Allsop was not married and that Mrs Ernstein was his closest family member. He made a mental note to be more careful in future. There had been little to indicate the presence of a wife at number 77. So where was this wife? Overseas on a holiday? In a nursing home? Visiting family interstate? Intrigued, the Inspector probed as was his natural instinct as a detective.

'That's interesting, Mrs Ernstein. And where, may I ask, is Mrs Allsop?'

Mrs Ernstein tugged at a rogue bra-strap and looked the policeman straight in the eyes, 'That's anybody's guess, Inspector. She's no wife to him and only married him for his money. Last year it was. She's just a fancy floozy. None of us can stand a bar of her. We tried to tell Dad that she was up to no good but he wouldn't listen. Some men are like that you know, think that because they have a lot of money they can attract a woman half their age. She completely fooled him so that he thought he was in love again and that this woman loved him back. He had the OBE when they married, you know.'

'The OBE?' queried the Inspector, who had considerable respect for those who had been awarded the Order of the British Empire, despite the anachronistic sounding honour.

'Over bloody eighty. He was eighty years old when he married her!'

The Inspector had not encountered this alternative version of the OBE before and gave a wry smile. His own dad was rapidly approaching eighty and he could use this amusing form of the OBE in the speech he was inevitably going to have to give at his eightieth birthday bash.

'That's all most interesting, Mrs Ernstein, but surely you have some idea where Mrs Allsop might be?'

'She doesn't call herself Mrs Allsop. She's kept her own name, Jayne Prescott. Just shows how much she was prepared to put into this marriage,' snorted Mrs Ernstein. 'And if I know Jayne, she will be off with her boyfriend staying in some exotic location. She often disappears for several days and never tells anyone where she's going. It's disgusting!'

Johansson absorbed this additional information with some scepticism. Clearly Mrs Ernstein had no time for Jayne Prescott but he suspected some hyperbole might have crept in.

'Mrs Ernstein, it is important that I make contact with your father's wife because by law she is the next of kin. Presumably Jayne Prescott has yet to hear of her husband's death? Surely you have some inkling as to where she might be?'

'It's anyone's guess, Inspector. Jayne never tells me anything, we are barely on speaking terms. She'd be shacked up with Mark, her boyfriend, somewhere. She's been having an affair with Mark for months now. I don't know how my father put up with it.'

'Very well, Mrs Ernstein. Do you have a surname for this boyfriend Mark then?'

'Yes, it's Mark Stephens. It's an easy name for me to remember because my favourite teacher at primary school was a Mr Stephens.'

'Thank you, Mrs Ernstein. I don't think I need to bother you anymore. I will put out a call on the local radio stations for Jayne Prescott and Mark Stephens to contact police immediately as a matter of urgency.'

Realising their meeting was at an end, Mrs Ernstein hauled herself to her feet and began to lumber slowly towards the front door.

'It's okay, Mrs Ernstein, I can see myself out. Thank you for your assistance.'

Inspector Johansson was at the door promptly and let himself out with a final, 'Thank you' to Mrs Ernstein who was still making painfully slow progress towards her front door.

Within minutes Johansson had arranged for the police liaison officer to contact South Australian radio stations to broadcast announcements that Ms Jayne Prescott and Mr Mark Stephens were to report to their nearest police station as soon as possible. Anyone knowing of their whereabouts were to also contact the police as a matter of urgency. Announcements were to be repeated throughout the day until radio stations were advised otherwise.

Jayne Prescott

Jayne Prescott collapsed onto her back beautifully fulfilled yet again. At forty-nine she marvelled at the heightened libido she still enjoyed so intensely when with a man like Mark. She had lost count. Was it four or five times she had climaxed with him overnight? This last one had been the best when she sat astride him and rode to glory. Glancing at Mark she pondered whether she had finally exhausted him so that he was incapable of any more sexual performances for some time. He had a fine physique, not muscle-bound like those gym maniacs, but strong and wiry without a slither of excess fat. He was tall, athletic and highly creative with his sexual activities. He knew how to surprise and excite a woman. Mark's erection was slowly subsiding, but Jayne knew that with her feminine charms she could seductively coax it back into action whenever she felt the need.

Mark was thirty-nine, ten years her junior. As he rolled onto his side and pulled her towards him, she wondered how much longer he would find her sexually satisfying. It was an increasingly difficult battle to maintain her hourglass figure and she was horrified at times to see an unwelcome wrinkle or to find her breasts sagging slightly.

She ate carefully, always nutritious foods and never too much, imbibed perhaps a trifle more than was wise, but then spent time every day exercising strenuously. She adored running and always selected a route and time when other male runners would be out and about. She positively glowed every time men followed her with their eyes or found an excuse to stop and talk. Jayne lapped up male attention and dreaded ever reaching a time when she was no longer seen as sexually desirable. When not running, she might work out in the gym or complete laps in the pool. Both arenas offered additional opportunities for her to show off her figure and relish male attention.

Sometimes she wondered if she was over-sexed. Most women her age had been married for years and must endure very mundane sex lives being stuck with just the one man. Until last year she had never been married and had enjoyed a never-ending succession of male partners from all walks of life since she was sixteen. Wow! Thirty-three years during which she had rarely slept alone. She mused that if there was a competition to find the ten most sexually experienced women in the country, she would be up there and still climbing up the rankings. It was simple really; she depended on regular and satisfying sexual activity to recharge her batteries. Nothing had changed since her betrothal to Charles, she still enthusiastically pursued multiple sexual liaisons but endeavoured to be a bit more discrete. Charles was an adorable pet and she was loath to upset him in his dotage.

But it wasn't just the sex, it was also the lifestyle. By making herself adorable and irresistible to as many men as possible, she found that her male admirers would allow her to stay with them for weeks at a time entirely at their expense. It was a bit trickier with the married ones. Sexual trysts with them were generally short-term and secretive but still with all expenses paid and usually in a smart hotel or a delightful bed and breakfast. Camping invitations she politely declined but high-quality caravans, yachts and cruises were welcomed. Frequently she found herself in the enviable position of having more than one invitation for a weekend away. On these happy occasions she literally auctioned herself off to the best bidder, thereby increasing the luxuriousness of her stay.

Of course, all this activity demanded a high level of organisational skill. She owned a small apartment, but she never entertained there, or even disclosed its whereabouts for obvious reasons. For many years she had carefully maintained a large annual diary for all her bookings together with her clients' names and contact details. Previous annual diaries were filed away neatly, because she found many of her customers requested her company time and time again, and sometimes she needed to refer back to her comments after each and every encounter.

Some years ago, she had adopted a five-star rating system that covered the three most important considerations for each of her clients; luxuriousness and generosity, likeability and performance in bed. Fifteen stars was almost impossible for it meant millionaire treatment from a man she found totally adorable and great fun to be with, capped off by sensational sex. Her highest score to date was thirteen out of the possible fifteen. She found her rating scheme invaluable when trying to decide with which client she would spend her next week, fortnight or weekend.

Jayne Prescott never thought of herself as a prostitute. That was a lowly profession that she wanted nothing to do with. Perhaps she was a high-class callgirl, but she didn't like that term either. An escort maybe? Again, she felt that the terminology was not appropriate. So she preferred to be just plain, Jayne Prescott, a friend to those that could pay well and refused to be put in a box with a name.

Gradually over the last two or three years it had dawned on Jayne Prescott that she wasn't getting any younger and that her marvellous lifestyle could be threatened as she aged and began to lose some of her sexual vitality. What if men no longer desired her company? The thought of a sexless life without males to support her financially began to seriously haunt her. She needed an insurance policy. So it was that she resolved that she must marry a wealthy man and become "respectable". If she could find the right man, she could look forward to a long life of comfort although she had no intention of abandoning all who were currently on her books if they were still interested in her company.

It needed a special man however, a multi-millionaire prepared to leave his fortune to her, excellent company and not too demanding on her time. Above all, the husband-to-be must be extraordinarily tolerant so that she could continue her highly satisfying dalliances. Of course, she in return would provide sexual favours for her husband, endeavour to be good company at all times and act discreetly whenever visiting her clients so as to avoid any embarrassment for her husband.

The challenge was to find such a man. Jayne had never been one to study seriously. She had dropped out of school at sixteen, but now, she reasoned, her best means of finding a marriageable male was to go back meticulously through her considerable collection of diaries and produce a short-list. This she did using her revised set of criteria; must be a millionaire, excellent company, and exceptionally tolerant of the lifestyle she was determined to maintain during the marriage. She was surprised to discover her well-kept diaries went back almost twenty years and it took her many late nights to work her way through them all and identify the likely starters. Despite the care she had taken to report on every client in some detail, her memory had clouded overtime, and understandably, she had rarely commented on the attribute of tolerance which was to be so fundamental to any lifetime commitment with her chosen husband.

The short-list produced seven names. This was the simplest part of the exercise. Now she had to approach each man on her short-list in turn and confront them with her proposal. After much thought, she resolved that she must be totally honest in her dealings. She wanted to be a kept woman, to inherit the estate and live the life of a totally liberated woman when and with whom she pleased. She would put her cards on the table from the outset.

At the top of her list was Charles Frederic Allsop. He was a delightful old man with a wicked sense of humour who had surprised her in the bedroom with his passion and sexual exploits. Charles had lost his wife to cancer a few years back and had been a regular customer ever since. He was wonderful company and could make her laugh like no one else. Charles had made his money in haulage. Starting with one truck he had steadily expanded his business until he owned over a hundred vehicles. On several occasions Charles had suggested marriage to Jayne but she had always shied away from such an idea seeing it as the end of her exciting and varied lifestyle. But now she was thinking differently. Perhaps Charles could be broad-minded enough to accept her marriage proposal? Charles certainly met her criteria.

Wisely, Jayne waited until the next time Charles invited her to share a few days with him at his new home in a retirement village. Everglades Retirement Village was a shock to Jayne because most of her earlier visits had been to his lavish mansion in the Adelaide Hills. Unexpectedly, Charles had decided he no longer needed an extensive abode with six bedrooms, a library, billiard saloon, three bathrooms, a tennis court, swimming pool and five acres of landscaped garden and bushland. Instead he had opted for inner city living.

Everglades was the most prestigious retirement village in Adelaide. The apartments were spacious with superb fittings, three bedrooms with an office, double garage, Blackwood kitchen and surrounded by high quality manicured gardens. The village facilities were superb. Designed for the wealthy, it was fully gated and offered twenty-four/seven security. Particularly attractive for Charles was the discovery that a couple of his close friends already lived at "The Glades" as it was known. Since he had moved in, the three of them met regularly for bridge evenings, played golf occasionally and simply relished each other's company. Charles was convinced The Glades had been an excellent decision.

From the outset Charles had been very open to Jayne's marriage proposal and could immediately see a number of positives. He adored Jayne and thought it might be considered more acceptable among the conservative villagers of The Glades if he was to marry his lady visitor. He would become the epitome of respectability. Jayne was great company. She was a delightful host and together they would be able to entertain more. In addition, she could accompany him on social outings. A particular benefit was that Jayne could drive him to functions at night. For some time, Charles had avoided night driving as with his advancing age he found it all too difficult.

As for Jayne inheriting his wealth, this was no real problem as his three offspring were now well established financially. He did, however, wish to reserve the right to leave some of his money to the three charities he had already identified as worthy recipients of a small part of his wealth. Charles was perfectly happy to adjust his will accordingly. Instead of a three-way equal split of his estate between his daughter and two sons, his worldly belongings would now be bequeathed to his new wife and next-of-kin, Jayne. Jayne was still relatively young and as far as Charles was concerned could gallivant about as much as she wanted as long as he always had first rights. So, with these minor provisos, Charles was prepared to marry her and become "respectable" again.

They married quietly a few weeks later.

¶

Mark had lapsed into a peaceful sleep. Gently she untangled herself, slid to the side of the bed and pulled the sheet up over her naked partner. Rummaging through her suitcase she found her running gear, remembered to grab the key to their room and crept out without disturbing Mark. As always, she rejected the lift, which she regarded as unhealthy, and skipped down the stairs. Arriving on the ground floor she flashed a smile at the young concierge who greeted her with, 'Good Morning Mrs Stephens, another lovely day.' Momentarily surprised at being called Mrs Stephens, she recollected just in time, that she and Mark had checked in as Mr and Mrs Stephens the night before.

Emerging onto South Terrace, she threaded her way through the already busy traffic to arrive in the lush green parkland on the other side of the road. Colonel Light was a man well ahead of his time when he had laid out his plans for the city of Adelaide with the city centre surrounded by a green belt on all sides. Adelaidians today, fully appreciated his foresight when they relaxed in the verdant surrounds.

It was just past seven am when she selected her path to

run along. Jayne noted, with pleasure, that there were plenty of walkers and runners out this morning relishing the cool early morning air. She sensed her athletic body responding to the inviting environment. Her breathing came easily and she felt strong enough to run for hours. Jayne was wearing a sleek costume that showed off her figure admirably. After a few moments, as she was approaching a signpost, she heard someone yell out her name.

'Hey, Jayne, stop a moment, I've been trying to catch up with you.' Turning quickly, she recognised a familiar face. At some time recently she recollected they had paired up for a weekend on a Farm Stay near Yankalilla, a cute little village south of Adelaide. Terrible with names, 'Hi, how are you?' was all Jayne could manage. The young man quickly put her out of her misery.

'Tom Railings. You remember me, don't you? Down at Yankalilla? Back in June I think it was.'

'Of course, Tom, I couldn't forget you. You had a touch of gout if I remember correctly, but thankfully not where it mattered most.'

'That was a great weekend. We should do it again sometime. Listen, I heard your name on the radio this morning. Six o'clock news on the ABC.'

'Really! What about?'

'Don't know what you've been up to, but the police are after you Jayne. They want you and some other bloke to get in touch ASAP.'

This information put the wind up Jayne. True, she had

lived a life of sexual debauchery but there was nothing illegal about that. Her activities were always with consenting adults. She never intentionally ripped her customers off or took anything that was not hers. One thing she had learnt from her parents was that in the long run it always pays to be honest. So, what could all this be about?

'Are you sure they didn't say why the police want to see me?'

'Yup, one hundred percent.'

'Thanks Tom, I'll check it out as soon as I get back. Here's my card if you ever want to get together again. I've moved to The Everglades, a swanky retirement village in town.'

'What on earth are you doing in a bloody retirement village, Jayne?'

'That's my business. Get in touch if you think you can stand the pace.'

With a smirk, Tom continued on along the track. Jayne turned on her heels and loped back towards their hotel on South Terrace. The morning's run had been ruined.

¶

Jayne almost tripped as she ran up three flights of stairs to the floor where their room was located. She flung open the door and was annoyed to see Mark still in bed. If he was expecting some early morning hanky-panky, he could forget it. She switched on both the radio and the television.

'Good God, what's the big hurry, Jayne?'

'The police want me. I just met a bloke I know and he said the police have put out a call for me to report to them ASAP. I can't think of anything I've done wrong. I'm not a criminal.'

'Well, if you're so worried, ring them. It's probably not you they want anyway. There's been some sort of a mix-up I expect.'

'Yes, good idea.' Jayne moved to the hotel telephone leaving both the radio and television still blaring away in the background.

Within a few minutes the police explained that her husband had died suddenly, and, as next-of-kin, the police had been trying to notify her of this so that appropriate arrangements could be put in place as soon as possible. Jayne's stresses, thinking that she was in trouble with the law, now gave way to the stress of realising that her husband was gone and that she must now face a very different future. She replaced the receiver, sat down, and ashen faced, explained to Mark what had happened.

Mark, who had by now switched off the television and radio, was most sympathetic and appreciating that his sexual activities were now doomed, for the time being at least, offered to drive her back to Everglades. However, always a practical man, he did insist that they have a full breakfast before they left.

Jayne's mind was in turmoil. A thousand thoughts and emotions were crashing about randomly. She supposed that she was in what they called "a state of shock". She found her breakfast uninviting and waited impatiently while Mark gorged himself, ate half of what she had left on her plate, and then went back for even more.

'Okay I'll go and pay the bills, meet you down at the car in fifteen.'

Fifteen had turned into thirty minutes by the time she had packed her things, completed her ablutions, and made it to Mark's car in the hotel carpark. As they drove north along Main South Road, a few ideas began to float to the top of her chaotic thinking. She was Charles' next-of-kin so everything now landed in her lap. She would have to handle the funeral arrangements, notify all Charles' friends and family and deal with the family papers and his last will and testament.

Then it struck her that she was only forty-nine and therefore not eligible to remain in the retirement village. You had to be fifty-five or over to apply to be a resident. All this was going to keep her so busy that she would have to cancel her next few clients. And then she felt ashamed because only now was she thinking about Charles, her devoted husband. The police had only informed her that he had died two days ago of a heart attack. She hadn't been there at his time of need. The poor bugger had died with nobody by his side while she had been romping about with Mark.

And so it was, that a subdued Jayne Prescott returned to Everglades to try and behave more responsibly than she had ever been called upon to do before.

Mrs Joanne Ernstein

Joanne Allsop was born in 1924, the first child from the union of Charles Frederic Allsop and his wife, Wilhelmina. Joanne's father had just purchased his first lorry and was immensely proud of this acquisition. In fact, his wife sometimes teased him that he had had twins, his lorry and his daughter both of whom had arrived about the same time. As an owner-driver, Charles needed to keep the wheels of his lorry rolling so he could fulfil as many contracts as possible every week, thereby bringing in sufficient money to pay off the vehicle and support his young family. Of necessity, he was away from home for long hours driving, picking up loads and delivering. It was not unusual for Charles to work a seventy to eighty-hour week and to be frequently driving through the night.

Despite her workaholic father, Joanne had been born into a loving, supportive home. Both her parents doted over their cute little daughter, and sad to say, overindulged her at times. To say that Joanne was spoilt is perhaps to overstate the matter, but she was certainly quite demanding as is often the case with the firstborn in a family.

She was nearly eight when her parents announced over dinner one evening that Joanne could look forward to a brother or a sister in a few months' time. Joanne really didn't know what to make of this revelation. She wasn't sure she wanted a baby in her house; babies were noisy and demanding things. They couldn't do anything for themselves and had to be fed, dressed, bathed, played with and even burped. No doubt her mother would be doing this all day and she would be ignored. She treasured her position in the family as the only child and now this privileged life would be no more.

Joanne's dire predictions eventuated. Her mother was forever fussing over the baby and she felt neglected. When her mother wasn't caring for the baby, she was trying to catch up with housework, shopping, cooking, darning clothes and had little or no time to devote to her firstborn. Her mother was often tired and cranky too. There was, however, an unexpected upside to all this baby business. Her father was now the proud owner of three trucks and employed three drivers to do the bulk of the work. If things became hectic, he would still take on some of the driving duties, but he spent most of his time managing his business from a small office at the back of their house. And so it was that Joanne found her father far more approachable. She would occasionally visit him in his office, although not too often, because he could become angry when busy. Her great joy was that her father was home and about the house far more. Long nights away driving the highways was almost a thing of the past. As her mother became more and more tied down by domestic duties, it was to her father Joanne turned for company and fun times. A strong and powerful bond developed between father and daughter.

This changed family dynamic was further exacerbated when a third child arrived shortly after Joanne turned ten. Her mother seemed even more absorbed with this new baby and her cantankerous two-year-old toddler. The family fortunes continued to improve however, so that they could now afford to have some domestic help and a lady would come and do the cleaning and washing three times a week. The ten-year-old Joanne had nothing in common with her two much younger brothers and she felt deeply resentful of their presence. More and more she turned to her father for the attention she craved and at the same time began to take an interest in his steadily expanding trucking business. Whenever he had spare time, usually at weekends, he would tell her stories of some of the adventures he had experienced driving about the country. There were tales about flooded roads, bushfires, even snowstorms. Many times, her father had collected a kangaroo and on one occasion had hit a brumby up in the Snowy Mountains.

Joanne loved the stories about the characters he had met at various eating stops, his altercations with police and once when he had apprehended a thief who was attempting to steal hay bales from his truck. The worst story was when her father had fallen asleep one night deep in the outback and overturned the truck on a corner. His first recollection was waking up to find he had only suffered minor injuries but the hundred sheep he had had on board were scattering everywhere. Some were badly injured and he shot those. The truck was a write off and it was too difficult to round up the sheep. It was hours before someone else ventured along the road. He had been picked up and taken to the nearest hospital to be checked over.

Slowly the idea germinated in Joanne's mind that she could perhaps work for her dad. Women never drove trucks or did the maintenance, but she might get a job in the office as a secretary or a receptionist. By the time Joanne was in her early teens her father had set up a new, much larger, depot on the edge of town complete with an office complex. Around fifteen trucks were serviced there, and business was forever expanding. Dad was, of course, the manager and he had a smart office, a full-time secretary and a receptionist to help run the show. Joanne had by this time begun to take an interest in boys and there was no shortage of young men at the depot, either drivers or maintenance crew. She determined to concentrate on secretarial studies and typing at her high school.

The close bond between father and daughter never diminished and at the age of sixteen Joanne commenced work in the office of the headquarters of Allsop Transport Company. Branch offices had by now been set up interstate and the fleet of transports had escalated to over forty. More and more staff were required. There was even a special finance section at headquarters headed up by a fully qualified accountant. Life was good for Joanne even though it was 1940 and World War II was under way.

Most of the young men in the company had been called up and finding replacements was proving increasingly difficult. A few retired drivers and maintenance men came back to fill the vacancies and even a few women were now being trained to be drivers and to work in the service yards. As the war dragged on, and Joanne gained more experience, her father promoted her to be his personal assistant when she turned twenty. This required Joanne to travel interstate with her father to visit branch offices and it was on one of these trips that she met her husband-to-be.

Joanne had matured into a tall, slim woman with striking looks. Romances until now had been few and far between since most eligible young men were away at the war or had returned injured or in a casket. John, her latest boyfriend, was a twenty-four-year old accountant responsible for the financial affairs of the Sydney branch of Allsop Transport Company. Much to John's disgust he had been denied entry into the armed services on health grounds. Doctors had detected a heart murmur and had upheld their decision when John appealed.

There had been an immediate and strong attraction from their first encounter, but a romance seemed out of the question since Joanne was in Adelaide and John in Sydney. Joanne's father had, however, been highly impressed with John's accounting skills, particularly when the Sydney office outperformed the others financially, and John had made some excellent suggestions for the overall financial management of the company. Consequently, her dad offered John a promotion to be one of the senior accountants at the head office in Adelaide. The offer was too good to refuse, and John would also have the opportunity to possibly further develop his relationship with the gorgeous Joanne.

The newly appointed senior accountant took up his Adelaide position late in January 1945 and the romance rapidly blossomed. Joanne's dad continued to be delighted with John's work throughout the year and enjoyed John's company whenever he came to the house to pick his daughter up for a date.

Early in 1946, at a lavish wedding, Joanne and John tied the knot. Allsop Transport Company was so successful by now that Charles promised to have a new house built for the young couple in the developing suburb of Hallett Cove in South Adelaide. Charles promised to pay all expenses initially with the proviso that John and his wife pay back fifty percent gradually over the years. It was a win/win all round. John and Joanne could move into a spanking new home within a few weeks of their marriage and Charles was assured of the services of his daughter and son-in-law in the fortunes of the company well into the future.

The newlyweds soon settled into a life of well-to-do comfort. They wanted for nothing. But, as is often the case when very young adults prosper too early, whilst all around them were still struggling financially, they became somewhat tedious company and slipped into a mundane and boringly predictable lifestyle. Both continued working at Allsop

Transport Company. After five years however, Joanne fell pregnant and became the typical stay-at-home mum. Meanwhile, John continued as a senior accountant but lost much of his zest and drive, so he never made it any higher up the promotion tree. His colleagues passed him by and became chief accountant or a branch manager.

John was not particularly stressed that he was marking time; they were quite well off and he was perfectly happy with his round of golf on Saturday mornings followed by a couple of beers at the nineteenth. He had started a family and expected a couple more children to arrive in due course. They had a holiday on Kangaroo Island a couple of times a year where they had bought a small weatherboard weekender.

Joanne continued to get along well with her dad. Now that she was a mother, she had lost contact with the day-to-day happenings at Allsops, but her husband and father kept her up to date with any major developments. Quite often Joanne and her family would visit her parents for the Sunday roast. Her mother was an accomplished cook and took considerable pride in the meals she served. It was at one of these dinners that her father confided in Joanne and her husband about his last will and testament. As they sipped a port, Charles cleared his throat which was an indication that he had something of importance to announce. Mrs Allsop was still in the kitchen helping the housekeeper with the washing up.

'Now, Joanne and John, while Mum is in the kitchen, I want to fill you in on what I have done with my will. I am over sixty now, so I thought it wise to do this as a precaution. John, as one of my senior accountants, you are aware no doubt that I am now a multi-millionaire. Allsops continues to expand and has recently entered the export business; things are booming.'

'It's a great credit to you,' John responded.

Mr Allsop ignored the compliment and went on. 'There is only one dark cloud on the horizon. Your mother has been diagnosed with cancer, Joanne. She refuses to tell you so I'm telling you now. It's breast cancer and it's serious. She is to have a double mastectomy next week and the long-term prognosis is not good.'

There was a moment of stunned silence as this shocking news registered.

'Oh my God!'

'That's terrible news, I'm so sorry.' exclaimed John.

Charles stumbled on, too afraid that he might break down if he heard any more reactions.

'So, with this ghastly medical prognosis, I called in my solicitor and made sure that everything is in order should your mother die. As the will now stands, should I pre-decease her, then your mother inherits everything. However, her chances of surviving this aggressive cancer are poor at best, so I have taken measures to ensure that once your mother and I have both moved on, then everything I own is to be split three ways equally between my three children.' Joanne and John only half heard what Charles was saying as they both tried desperately to digest the news of Joanne's mother's situation.

The evening wound up on a sombre note. Joanne and John did their best to appear optimistic and supportive but left the house feeling depressed and helpless. Mrs Allsop bravely underwent her surgery, returned home and appeared to be recovering only to die quite suddenly about seven months later.

Charles took it hard. His way of dealing with his grief was to redouble his efforts to further build his transport empire. He virtually shut out all memories of his wife of nearly forty years and worked increasingly long hours. He travelled overseas more as he established further export opportunities. He accepted his new role as a widower and relied more and more on his housekeeper to maintain standards in his home. As a physically fit man in his mid-sixties he craved sexual encounters with women to provide some sort of intimacy in his life. He sought out high-class escort girls in Adelaide and when travelling to some of the Asian cities for business. These liaisons satisfied his sexual urges but did little more.

One Saturday evening he arranged to meet a new, more mature woman, who had been recommended and resided nearby in Adelaide. They hit it off sensationally and a relationship developed that Charles found went way beyond satisfying his sexual desires. He adored this woman, loved her company and always felt amazing after spending time with her. Was he falling in love again?

CHAPTER 4

Henry Childs

Henry Childs was born a country kid on the wrong side of the rails in a small sheep and wheat town in central NSW. Life was tough for Henry from the time he first opened his eyes in a ramshackle old house on one of the nondescript back roads on the edge of town. The house had not seen a lick of paint for many a year and was gradually falling into such a state of disrepair that the local council had placed it on a list of old residences that might have to be condemned as unfit for human habitation.

Windows were cracked or broken and the floorboards along the veranda had collapsed in several places. The yard out the back was so overgrown with weeds and thistles that it was a challenge to make it to the outside toilet. An ancient peppercorn tree afforded some shade on one side of the house but also provided easy access for the possums to climb onto the roof and create bedlam romping about and chasing each other. A broken concrete path led from the unhinged front door to the remnants of a fence beyond which was a dirt road that generated clouds of dust that frequently wafted across the house when traffic went by.

If the house was in a shambolic state, its inhabitants were equally so. No less than eight souls occupied the house together with a variable number of cats and an ancient one-eyed cattle dog. Henry was the youngest of six children. Nobody was sure who the fathers were of any of the children which was the cause of much speculation about town and even some heated arguments. The current eighth occupant of the house was an unemployed vagrant who had somehow inveigled himself into the good books of the mother and been allowed to hang around and lay his head down on any bed he could find about the house. He probably wasn't Henry's father because the good folk who lived across the road didn't remember him visiting until a couple of months back.

Educationalists, sociologists and psychologists had claimed quite rightly for many years that a child born into such abject poverty has little or no chance of ever becoming a high achiever. However, little Henry was to become one of the very few exceptions. He was intelligent and when first despatched to a place called "school" had found himself in an environment he liked. The kids teased him for the dirty clothes he wore and laughed at his bare feet, but he liked the female teacher and found learning phonics, tables and simple spelling came easily. The teacher went out of her way to help him. She always brought an extra sandwich or two and a piece of fruit or perhaps a biscuit to get him through the day.

At the end of the first week Henry walloped one of the

boys in his class who persisted in teasing him and calling him smelly. He walloped the boy so hard, and in front of all his classmates, that an extra-curricular lesson was learnt by the children; don't tease Henry unless you want to be hit hard back. The teasing stopped and Henry had also learnt an important lesson; stick up for yourself!

Henry continued to make the most of the opportunities that school offered him. He was quick to discover that if you are nice to teachers and do as they ask, they will like you and encourage you to do well. Consequently, he was soon one of the brightest in his class and felt great satisfaction at the end of the day when he had performed up to his teacher's expectations. A bonus was that he proved to be athletic.

As the years went by, he established a reputation for being able to bat and bowl better than almost all the other kids at school and to crash through tackles to score tries on the rugby league grounds. Henry showed so much all-round promise that he was awarded a scholarship to attend the state high school. The primary school principal took responsibility for banking the money and ensuring that the scholarship was appropriately used for Henry's transport, uniforms and textbooks.

High school necessitated that he stayed at the boarding house in town during term time, so for the first time in Henry's life, he was completely independent of his ramshackle home and family and all the misery that dwelt therein. It was at high school that he first became interested in a subject called Automotive Engineering. Again, he excelled. On leaving high school he was head-hunted by the local garage, awarded a three-year apprenticeship and became a paid employee.

Henry stayed on at the garage after his apprenticeship ended and continued to expand his expertise in the field of motor mechanics. A couple of years later saw him go into partnership with a colleague and start his own small automotive repair business. The business blossomed but Henry had his sights set on the transport and haulage industry that was rapidly developing across the country. Soon he purchased his first truck and, with uncompromising business acumen, began to steadily build up a haulage company based in central NSW. Rapid expansion saw him become a wealthy man and it was not too long before his haulage vehicles were criss-crossing the country. It was the process of establishing his branch offices interstate that brought Henry into contact with Charles Frederic Allsop, managing director and owner of Allsop Transport Company.

Henry Childs had never forgotten the time he started school so many years back and had walloped a classmate who unwisely persisted in teasing him. Then, when unfairly provoked, Henry had responded aggressively, and this type of reaction had never left him. Throughout his career he had always tried to be tough but fair. He had faithfully adhered to this principle in his dealings with others, in the way he treated his employees and even in his personal relationships. Ninety-five percent of the time he found this approach successful. But just occasionally his dealings with others turned sour and nasty if he considered the other party to be trying unfairly to get the better of him. Henry ruthlessly undermined anyone who did not play fair with him and remained totally unapologetic. The message was, don't mess with me, play fair, or suffer the consequences.

Childs and Allsop were ambitious men and each were chasing recognition as the owner of the nation's leading transport and haulage company during the late 1960s. Both yearned to be "top dog". For years Allsop Transport Company (ATC) and Childs Haulage Company (CHC) were locked in a desperate fight for market dominance. Regrettably, as sometimes happens when two powerful men are in competition, there was a massive falling out. In part this was over Childs' decision to open a major branch office in Adelaide to capture more of the lucrative east-west transport business. Allsop, who was born and bred in Adelaide, had many years earlier established Adelaide as his headquarters and strongly resented Childs' push into what he regarded as "his state". There were numerous other bones of contention too. The upshot of this whole sad saga was that the men no longer communicated, except through a third party, and took every opportunity available to denigrate each other.

Both men eventually ended their days at The Everglades Retirement Village. In an extraordinary move, Henry purchased a unit at Everglades just a few months after Charles had settled into his luxury apartment. True to character, Henry, who felt he had been deeply wronged by Charles over the setting up of his branch office in South Australia, was intent on revenge. It was Henry's plan to live in the Everglades village primarily to make Charles' life hell. As an elderly man, Henry had become totally unforgiving towards anyone by whom he felt wronged and Charles was way out on top of his blacklist. Despite his great wealth, Henry had become a nasty piece of work, bitter and twisted.

There was no end to the unpleasantries Henry dreamt up in his spiteful behaviour towards Charles. He would phone him any time of day and night to abuse him until Charles never answered his phone and left it on Ansa phone and disengaged the phone when he retired to bed. Henry would leave rude messages in Charles' letterbox and never missed a chance to find fault or disagree with Charles at any meetings of the residents of the Glades. He would complain to the manager over ridiculously petty matters such as Charles' bin being put away late or Charles supposedly driving his car through the village too fast. One time, Henry happened to be walking past Charles' unit at the same time a stunningly dressed Jayne Prescott was alighting from a taxi anticipating a more than pleasant evening with Charles. Henry couldn't resist giving her an earful.

'I wouldn't go near him, lady. He's no better than a crim. He couldn't lie straight in bed if he tried…'

Jayne let herself in as quickly as she could with Henry's tirade of rude comments following her all the way.

¶

The heightened antagonism between these two men could also be attributed to their contrasting backgrounds. We have seen how Henry had courageously dragged himself out of the desperate environment he had been born into. Life had never been easy. He had struggled all the way. Anyone who knew about Henry's origins was full of admiration for a man who had made good, despite his humble beginnings.

Charles, on the other hand, had been born on the right side of the railway line. Coming from a stable, middle-class family, he had attended private schools and moved on to Adelaide University where he had completed a respectable Arts degree. His was a comfortable life with rugby union, golf and squash as his physical outlets. Socially he was much in demand and women were naturally attracted to him. He had married well and adored his wife. His politics were conservative. Blessed with a strong education and a supportive family, it was no surprise that with so much drive and business acumen he quickly proved a success in the world of business.

Dealings between the two men were cold and business-like. Perhaps Henry was determined to finally be "top dog"?

CHAPTER 5

Dr Peters

Three years had passed since Charles Allsop's death and Inspector Johansson was gazing out of his office window. Rain trickled down the panes and brooding clouds scudded across the sky. It was one of those rare days in Adelaide's winter when the maximum temperature was forecast to reach only twelve degrees. A cold southerly that seemed to blow in all directions at the same time meant there was no avoiding the chilly blasts.

A comforting mug of black coffee steamed next to him and had already begun to warm and stimulate him to meet the normal Monday morning tasks. For a moment or two he allowed his thoughts to wander back to the round of golf he had enjoyed yesterday before this cold change had arrived. How surprised his playing partner had been when he'd birdied the fifteenth and then–

'Excuse me sir, there is a lady here to see you.'

Johansson reluctantly left the golf course and turned his

attention to the young constable who was now gracing his doorway. 'What did you say?'

'Sorry to disturb you sir, but there's a lady to see you. She's some sort of a reverend. Wearing a dog's collar.'

A twinge of guilt registered with Johansson. His wife was a regular attender at church but he rarely went. Surely the clergy didn't go around nowadays to chastise those that had fallen away from their churchgoing.

'Thank you, Constable. Where is this lady?'

'Interview room three, sir.'

Johansson sniffed, rose to his feet, drained the dregs of his coffee and armed himself with a notepad and pen.

The door to interview room three was open and Johansson was welcomed with a smile from a not unattractive woman probably in her early forties. His trained eye noted that she was conservatively dressed with a dog collar, as the young constable had observed, and a small badge in the lapel of her camel-coloured coat.

'Thank you for agreeing to see me, Inspector. I particularly wanted to meet you, rather than any of the other police at the station. I'm so glad you are still here.'

Intrigued by this opening statement, Johansson returned the smile, pulled out a chair and offered the standard invitation. 'How can I help you?'

'My name is Agnes Motherwell and I'm the assistant minister at the Anglican Parish Church in Cannon Hill. I have come to see you in relation to a Dr Peters who I believe you met briefly about three years ago?'

'I vaguely remember that name but I meet hundreds of people in my line of work so, sorry, I can't put a face to him.'

'I quite understand, Inspector. Perhaps I can elaborate. Dr Peters worked for a short time as an on-call police doctor who would attend deaths that the police had to deal with and sign any death certificates.'

'Okay, I think I remember him now. Very quiet and a rather timid character if my recollection is correct?'

'Yes, I think you have the right person in mind, Inspector. Dr Peters was a fully qualified medical practitioner but apparently sometimes had difficulties relating to people. Being an on-call police doctor suited him because, well, dead people are not good conversationalists as a rule.'

Johansson smiled inwardly at this observation from the Reverend Motherwell.

'Dr Peters attended our church occasionally and I got to know him. Not well, but enough for him to feel he could trust me. Three months ago, he was diagnosed with a particularly aggressive cancer and given six months at best. He didn't make the full term. A few days ago, his wife rang me and asked if I could visit him. By this stage he had been sent home as his death was imminent and passing away in the comfort of your own home and with family and friends around is usually the best option when there is nothing more that can be done medically. He was well dosed up on morphine. We don't have formal confessions at my church, but when I visited Dr Peters it became clear that he wanted to speak to me privately about a matter that was troubling him.'

Interesting as all this was, Johansson wondered where it was leading.

The Reverend Motherwell cleared her throat and continued.

'Dr Peters died yesterday and I am responsible for conducting his funeral service. I'm so glad I spent time with him because what he told me was important. I am now in possession of some alarming facts that the police should know about. However, Dr Peters was at great pains to try and protect his family from any unpleasant repercussions resulting from what he confessed to me.'

Johansson's interest sharpened. He picked up his notepad and turned to a clean page. 'I'm listening, please continue Reverend Motherwell.'

'I need to stress Inspector, that Dr Peters was most anxious that his family and friends should never hear about what he has confessed to me. He wants me to tell you in complete confidence and for you to handle any ramifications with the utmost discretion.'

'Before you continue, Reverend Motherwell, I need to tell you that the withholding of any information that may be of assistance to police in the solving of a crime is, in itself, a crime. So, like it or not, you are now duty bound to tell me what you know. I will certainly do my best not to implicate Dr Peters' relatives and friends, but if they are in some way involved, then they must face the full force of the law.'

'I understand, Inspector. I'm sure that none of Dr Peters' immediate family are implicated in any way. However, their protection from any publicity must be respected.'

'Yes, yes, I'll do everything I can to help you and his family. Now, how about you tell me what it's all about?'

The Reverend Motherwell took a deep breath, settled back into the chair and did her best to compose herself before speaking. Fronting up at a police station was not something she did on a regular basis and she was nervous.

'Dr Peters asked me to speak to you rather than anyone else in the police force because you were present at the time of the crime.'

Johansson immediately bristled and looked as though he was finding it difficult to contain himself. What the hell was this woman on about? 'What crime?' he demanded gruffly.

'I'm sorry, Inspector, I didn't express myself very well. I'm referring to the death of a gentleman called Charles Frederic Allsop about three years ago. He lived in a retirement home called Everglades and you called in Dr Peters to certify that Mr Allsop was in fact deceased and to complete the death certificate.'

Some of the grey cells at the back of Johansson's brain began to align themselves and help him vaguely recall the occasion. A woman, the daughter of Allsop, had called him in a panic one weekend, because she didn't know where her father was. He'd been missing for a couple of days. He'd gone to investigate and found the old boy dead in his bed. Dr Peters was the on-call police medical practitioner who had attended the death. It was a stroke or a massive heart attack. Not wanting to appear forgetful, Johansson replied, 'Yes, of course, I remember it now. Allsop died of natural causes, something to do with his heart. He was an elderly man.'

'Yes, that's what everyone thinks, but it's not true.'

'What do you mean it's not true? I was there. Dr Peters did the assessment in front of me and the old man's daughter. How can it be not true?'

'He didn't die of a heart attack; he was poisoned.'

'Are you trying to tell me that Dr Peters got it wrong and this was a murder case?'

'Yes Inspector, Dr Peters confessed to me that he had deliberately falsified the cause of death.'

Now Johansson had witnessed a number of surprising events during his long career, but a qualified police doctor falsifying the cause of death was a first. 'Right, you had better tell me more. I want any details you can give me please. How do you know that Dr Peters was not making all this up, or perhaps he was delirious?'

The Reverend Motherwell's hands fidgeted nervously in her lap. 'There's quite a lot more, Inspector.'

Johansson was finding it hard to disguise his growing impatience. 'Come on then, come on.' His pen was poised.

'Dr Peters said he had lived with this on his conscience for three years and wanted to confess to his part in the crime before he passed away. It's not unusual, Inspector, for people on their deathbed to want to make a clean breast of something that has been on their conscience. I think they get worried about where they are going to end up after death. Heaven or hell suddenly seem very close. They think they might get a few more brownie points if they own up to something.'

Johansson regarded this as a bit of mumbo-jumbo. Hardened crims were not worried about such niceties. He waited for more.

'Dr Peters was in on the plot. He didn't poison Mr Allsop himself, but he agreed to falsify the documentation to assist the murderer.'

'This is a very serious allegation ma'am. You are telling me that Mr Allsop was poisoned and that one of our police doctors falsified the papers to make it look like a perfectly natural demise?'

'Correct, Inspector.'

'And did Dr Peters tell you who carried out this poisoning?'

'No, Inspector. Dr Peters knew who it was but refused to tell me. He was terrified that if the truth came out this person would kill his family. He was not prepared to take that risk. All he was willing to do was to confess his part in the crime.'

'Yet he wanted you to tell me what had happened. Seems a bit odd. If he was so terrified that there may be repercussions on his family why did he want you to come and tell me about it all? This is now a murder case and we will move heaven and earth to find the murderer.'

'Yes, it does seem a bit inconsistent, Inspector.'

'When's the funeral? I want to be there. Murderers who think they have gotten away with it have an uncanny habit of turning up at funerals. I bet whoever did this came to Allsop's funeral too.'

'2:30 pm Friday afternoon at my church.'

'Thank you for coming to see me, Reverend. You have done the right thing. I will now get a police statement drawn up and I will want you to come back to verify it as a true and accurate account of our conversation. I also want you to leave full contact details with the receptionist as I'm sure I will need to talk with you again.'

The Reverend Motherwell held out a limp hand, gathered up her handbag and did as she had been told. Johansson returned to his office. He slicked a hand over his hair, then rubbed his eyes. A murder had happened on his watch three years ago. He knew it was time to develop strategies.

CHAPTER 6

Inspector Johansson

Fortified by a second mug of strong black coffee, Johansson sat at his desk to review what he had heard from Reverend Motherwell. He never doubted her story, she appeared honest and sincere. As for Dr Peters it seemed inconceivable that he would concoct some cock and bull story as his final act as he lay dying of cancer. Like it or not, he had an unexpected new murder on his hands. But how was he going to approach this case? Who could he find that might shed some further light on the murder? The detective determined that the place to start was the report he had written three years ago when he had travelled to Charles Allsop's apartment at Everglades.

He was pleasantly surprised to find three names included in his report who would now become his initial lines of inquiry. There was Charles' daughter, Mrs Joanne Ernstein, who had first raised the alarm, Charles' wife, Jayne Prescott, and the grumpy old man, Henry Childs, who didn't have a good word to say about Charles. He congratulated himself on writing a sufficiently detailed report which three years later would serve as a useful starting point for his investigations.

On the surface he was off to a promising start. He had a body, although it was either buried somewhere or had been turned into ashes and scattered to the four winds. He also knew how the murder had been carried out; poisoning. Now he needed to find a motive. Who would stand to benefit from Charles' demise? Working against him was the fact that the murder had happened over three years ago and the leads and clues had well and truly run cold.

With a little imagination, Johansson could conjure up likely motives for the three names already on his list. The daughter, Joanne, presumably stood to inherit much of Charles' wealth. Charles had recently re-married and may have been considering changing his last will and testament so that his new wife, as next of kin, would become the sole beneficiary. Certainly a possible motive for Mrs Joanne Ernstein to think bad thoughts. And what of the new young wife, Jayne Prescott? She had led a somewhat debauched life it seemed and behaved like a parasite, seducing men who were willing to spend serious money to maintain her lifestyle in return for sexual favours. At her age she might soon lose her attractiveness to men and need a more long-term source of income such as her new husband's wealth. Why else did she marry him? Finally, there was the elderly Henry Childs and his obvious hatred of Charles. Did this hatred run so deep that murder was the final outcome? Johansson concluded all three were "people of interest" and that he would commence his investigations with a second visit to Mrs Joanne Ernstein.

Johansson remembered the Hallett Cove mock-Tudor house as soon as he parked. In the three years since his first visit the starkness of the then recently completed building had been pleasantly modified. The money spent on the landscaping had paid off. A row of shade trees now thrived along the picket fence giving a relaxing dappled effect of sunlight and shade. The detective's limited knowledge of trees meant he could only be sure of the oak on the corner of the block and several colourful lantana bushes interspersed with some kind of blue gums. Lush lawns now accompanied the visitor along the winding path to the main entrance. A wide selection of roses, that grew so well around Adelaide, ran along the front of the house. Johansson checked the rose nearest the front door for aphids and black spot and was impressed to see neither were present. Perhaps they could afford a gardener?

The doorbell chimed the ubiquitous Big Ben sequence of notes and eventually the heavy wooden door was opened by a smiling but heaving Mrs Joanne Ernstein. The last three years had not been kind to the lady of the house. She was certainly a couple of dress sizes larger and the double chin was threatening to become a triple. Mrs Ernstein held out a podgy hand and offered a limp wet handshake which the Inspector ignored. Handshakes, in the Inspector's thinking, were limited to citizens who were not under consideration for having committed some kind of a demeanour.

'Welcome Inspector, good to see you again although I have to admit to being somewhat surprised that you find it necessary to discuss my father's death a second time and after three years have elapsed.'

'Indeed, Mrs Ernstein, I have to confess to being surprised myself, but something unexpected has arisen that warrants further investigation.'

'Oh dear, Inspector. Before we sit down may I offer you a cup of coffee or tea perhaps?'

'Not for me, thank you.'

The niceties over, Mrs Ernstein wheezed her way over to her favourite upright chair and with a grunt lowered her sizeable posterior onto the seat. 'Now Inspector, what's this all about?'

Johansson employed a technique that had paid dividends before. He would not mention anything to do with murder at this stage as this might frighten people into silence or to concealing part of the truth. Instead he would keep things low-key in the hope that this would elicit more open and free discussion. This was also the reason why he was conducting this interview on his own without a colleague. Two police fronting up at Mrs Ernstein's would have been overkill. Instead he wanted to give the feeling of this being a quiet informal inquiry into some minor matter that had remained unresolved.

'Well, please accept my apologies for having to return to the matter of your father's death, but we need to clear up a couple of concerns in relation to his last will and testament.'

Mrs Ernstein looked distinctly uncomfortable on hearing this and avoided the Inspector's penetrating stare.

'Without going into detail, could you tell me please Mrs Ernstein who inherited Mr Allsop's very considerable wealth?'

'Isn't this private business, Inspector? I believe what happened to my father's assets is confidential. With respect, I don't think I have to answer your question.'

'I can understand how you feel. Of course, I can do things officially and seek out a full disclosure from your solicitors. However, I had hoped not to have to go down that path and that a more friendly discussion with you might prevent the necessity of involving your solicitors. You see, in situations like yours we would normally expect to see the wealth either go to your father's wife or his offspring or be divided up somehow between them. As I said, I don't want you to go into letter and verse, I just want to know broadly how the assets were divided up. Did the money all go to his wife, or to his children or somewhere else? It will help our inquiries if you could answer this question please.'

Mrs Ernstein appeared to wobble, jelly-like, on her chair. She felt trapped. It was her husband, John, who dealt with their money matters and solicitors and all that stuff. He was an experienced accountant and handled legal and financial affairs all the time for Allsop Transport.

She ruffled around for a tissue that normally resided up her sleeve because she felt the tears welling up. The tissue finally located, she blurted out, 'It was awful Inspector, my father let us all down and left everything to that ghastly woman who forced him to change what he was going to do with his money. It's shameful and shouldn't have been allowed.'

Johansson hesitated before responding in case Mrs Ernstein wished to expand on her tearful statement. 'I am sorry for you, Mrs Ernstein, but unless this was done illegally, there is nothing more that can be done.'

'That woman he married is nothing more than a glorified prostitute, Inspector, and she was plainly after his money. Would you please pass me those tissues, this whole thing upsets me so much.' The packet of Kleenex tissues having been safely received, she yanked a tissue out and gave her nose a formidable blast. 'Inspector, if there is nothing more you want to question me about, I would be pleased if you could leave. I have high blood pressure and getting upset like this is not good for me. My doctor–'

'Yes of course, Mrs Ernstein. You have been most helpful and I certainly don't want to pry any further.' He stood to take his leave and in doing so noticed a large, framed photograph of a passenger liner docked at Circular Quay in Sydney Harbour. To ease the tension he remarked, 'What a splendid photograph, which ship is that?'

Recovering quickly, Mrs Ernstein revolved in her chair and became quite animated, 'Oh Inspector, that's the P and O's steamship Oriana. Isn't it a beauty? John and I had twelve months last year cruising around the world. We had a beautiful stateroom and loved every minute. There are so many wonderful places to visit.'

'That sounds amazing Mrs Ernstein, and the Oriana must be one of the world's elite liners?'

'Yes, it's the P and O's flagship vessel. We were so fortunate.'

As the Inspector moved towards the front door to take his leave, he made a mental note to check on the cost of occupying a stateroom for twelve months on one of the world's elite luxury passenger liners. If the Ernsteins had missed out on the spoils left by Charles Allsop, how had they been able to afford such an expensive holiday? This was something to follow up.

Once the Inspector was back in his car, he scribbled down some notes about his visit to Mrs Ernstein, checked his watch and moved slowly off to keep his next appointment at The Everglades Retirement Village where he was due to meet Henry Childs for a second time. The traffic was busy along Main South Road and he arrived ten minutes late at the gated community. After being admitted by Henry, and advised how to find apartment 82, he drove slowly along the lanes, admiring the well-kept lawns and the avenues of jacarandas that flourished on either side of the road. Whoever had planned the landscaping in the village knew what they were doing. Several of the elderly residents were enjoying a game of bowls with a number of spectators watching and lapping up the sunshine.

Pulling up outside Henry Childs' abode, Johansson recalled the vitriolic language the old man had used when speaking about Charles Allsop three years before. Was that aggressive behaviour the norm with Henry or was it reserved only for the hapless Charles? His visit hopefully would throw some light on this.

'Park your vehicle in my driveway, you can't leave it out on the road,' shouted Henry standing at the entrance to his apartment. 'The manager will have a go at me if you leave it out there.' There was no 'please' or 'thank you' offered, it was more like a sergeant major barking out his orders.

Johansson did as requested, ignoring the rude opening salvo, and locked his car. 'Good morning, sir.'

'Morning, Officer.'

Henry Childs was in his early eighties and somewhat fragile physically. His rugged red face sported an even redder pock-marked bulbous nose. Steely blue eyes glared from behind a pair of heavy-rimmed glasses that didn't appear to have been cleaned for weeks. A sparse covering of snowy white hair flopped untidily across his scalp. Childs leant heavily on a sturdy walking stick. The elderly man's clothes reflected a bachelor's existence being generally unkempt. Food stains dotted his shirt. 'What do you want with me, Officer?' demanded Henry Childs in a far from friendly manner. Inspector Johansson wished to find out more about this man so he had determined to remain polite and courteous for as long as possible. He ignored the old man's challenge and moved indoors.

In contrast to the somewhat dishevelled Henry, the apartment was filled with expensive furnishings, luxurious floor coverings and fine works of Australian art. Johansson did not regard himself an expert on Australian paintings but recognised a fine Hans Heysen oil painting on one wall and what was probably a couple of Arthur Streeton's on another. Albert Namatjira was represented on a third wall. No shortage of money in this apartment!

'You have some nice pieces of art here, Mr Childs.'

'And all honestly purchased from legitimate dealers, Officer. Art is a safe investment.'

Johansson assessed his chances of a cup of tea or coffee as almost nil but felt a seat was perhaps on the cards. 'Mind if I sit down, Mr Childs?' Henry sniffed and waived an arm vaguely towards an armchair that the Inspector interpreted as the nearest he would get to being invited to take a seat.

The old man lowered himself gingerly into the other armchair leaving his walking stick conveniently handy.

'Mr Childs, I want to ask you some questions about the late Charles Allsop.'

'He was an ignorant bastard of a man. I had absolutely no bloody time for him.'

'Those are strong words, Mr Childs. Why do you have such a low opinion of him?'

Henry Childs spent the next fifteen minutes or so explaining his own background and that of his rival, Charles Allsop, in Australia's transport industry. He spared the detective nothing and employed plenty of colourful language to embellish his account. The detective was soon wondering whether the hatred displayed by Henry Childs towards Charles was sufficient motivation to lead to murder.

'One final question before I go. In your long career, did you ever, at school or afterwards, study chemistry?'

'What sort of a bloody question is that, Inspector?'

'An important one, Mr Childs. And how do you answer?'

'Wouldn't have a bloody clue about chemistry. I did OK at high school but I concentrated on the tech subjects. Never touched bloody science. Too much like hard work.'

'Well, thank you for your time, sir. I'll be in touch again if need be.'

Within a few minutes Johansson was back in his car making brief notes. Clearly Henry Childs was driven by a deep hatred of Charles Allsop. But was he so fanatical about making amends that he would arrange for the murder of his rival?

¶

Two down and one to go. Of the three names on the Inspector's list only Jayne Prescott remained to be visited. Mrs Ernstein and Henry Childs had not changed their residential addresses over the last three years but tracking down Jayne Prescott was quite a different matter. Although the management of Everglades had been prepared to allow Jayne to remain in her apartment as the legal widow of a deceased owner, even though she was only forty-nine at the time of Charles's departure, Jayne had decided Everglades was not for her anymore. The occupants of the retirement village were essentially old and decrepit and offered no real company for a feisty, fun-loving woman full of the joys of life. Besides, living in a retirement village was hardly the message Jayne wished to send out to her many male admirers. Most importantly, she was now a wealthy woman and had the money to live wherever and however she wanted. Financially, she no longer needed to ply her trade as a top-notch escort but, because she began to miss the intimacy of her sexual liaisons, and the good company that came with many of her clients, she continued on as before but was now more selective in the company she kept.

Inspector Johansson was aware that Jayne Prescott no longer resided at Everglades but annoyingly she had left no forwarding address. The detective put one of his juniors on to the job of discovering Jayne's current whereabouts. Several days later his junior reported that Jayne Prescott had purchased a stunning luxury villa on the south coast of Upolu, the main island of Samoa. This presented a problem. So far, the murder inquiry had been proceeding quietly as a low-key, low-priority investigation with minimal costs budgeted and only Inspector Johansson involved. With the surprise revelation that the third person of interest now lived in Samoa, a visit there was well beyond the money allocated for the inquiry. Additional funding was required. After some days waiting, official approval came through, and Johansson prepared for a short trip to the Pacific.

As the Qantas flight began its approach into the International Airport in Apia, the capital of Samoa, Johansson reflected on his good fortune to be getting an overseas trip, albeit a very short one, as part of his inquiries into the murder of Charles Allsop. He had been doing his research on Jayne

Prescott and had been amazed at the lifestyle she had so successfully led throughout her adult life. He had telegrammed Jayne Prescott with the details of his time of arrival and a message to say he hoped to visit her the day after his arrival. He imagined this would be a fascinating couple of days.

CHAPTER 7

Samoa

The oppressive heat engulfed Inspector Johansson as soon as he approached the aircraft's exit. Almost immediately his clothes began to stick to his body as he broke out in a lather of perspiration. His long pants, socks and black shoes seemed unnecessary and he yearned to get into shorts and sandals with a loose-fitting tropical shirt so much more appropriate for the tropics.

He was struck by the casual friendliness of the folk at the airport. Small as it was by international standards, there was a buzz of excitement as beaming islanders welcomed back relatives with never-ending hugs and kisses. Officialdom took a backseat here. This airport belonged to the people, and annoyances such as customs and passport control were not considered overly important. Detective Johansson felt quite out of place wearing his formal clothes whilst all around him were Samoans wearing colourful clothing and thongs. Nobody was here to welcome him, so he made his way slowly to collect his suitcase and then on to passport control, and with nothing to declare, sailed through customs.

Emerging from customs he was surprised to find a young Samoan man holding up a large piece of white cardboard with his name scribbled across it. The young man had already anticipated that the tall sweaty man dressed in Western clothes was the person he was waiting for. Visitors from cooler climes always looked weirdly dressed and horribly uncomfortable.

'Excuse me sir, are you the inspector?'

'Yes I am.'

'*Talofa*. Welcome to Samoa. I have been sent by Ms Prescott to collect you. She has invited you to stay with her in her villa.'

'Really?'

'Yes sir, I'm Ms Prescott's driver. My name is Luke.'

They shook hands and Luke picked up Johansson's suitcase and headed out into the glaring sunshine. Some fifty metres away stood a near-new Jeep and within a few minutes Luke and the policeman were on their way out of the airport carpark.

'Does Ms Prescott live far away from the airport?'

'The journey will take us about an hour and a half, sir. We have to go into Apia first and then take the road across the central mountain range, past the Bahai temple and on down to the south coast. Ms Prescott owns a beautiful villa there, sir.'

This was Johansson's first visit to what had been known,

until recently, as Western Samoa. The road to Apia was rough but on both sides the villagers had established beautiful lawns and gardens. Set back some way from the road were clusters of fales– open houses where families lived. These fascinated Johansson as they were essentially raised concrete floors on which stood all the family's belongings. There were no walls but thatched roofs provided shade.

In wet weather bamboo blinds could be dropped down on the side of the fale where the rain was entering. In front of the fales were two or three large stone graves on which clothes were drying or children played. In the centre of each large village, stood a substantial church with an impressive spire. The church doors and windows were left wide open to allow the air to circulate. Villagers could be seen sitting in the shade of their fales or under trees. Others were walking slowly along the road carrying wood, cane, fruit or vegetables often escorted by small children and dogs. The lush surrounds and beautiful dark-skinned people reminded Johansson of the Tahitian natives in the paintings of the post-impressionist Gauguin.

The scenery gradually changed as they left the sleepy capital, Apia, and began to wind their way up into the hills and mountains of Upolu. Most of the population lived along the coasts but up here in the hills where it was several degrees cooler some enterprising farmers had established vegetable gardens, coffee and vanilla plantations and were even experimenting with cattle. The mountains were sparsely populated and the children, less used to seeing vehicles, would always wave and smile or laugh.

Soon they were descending to the southern side of the island passing occasional waterfalls as the temperature and humidity steadily increased again. Joining the coastal road, it was only a few more minutes' drive before Luke pulled off onto a driveway well concealed amongst trees and frangipani.

'Welcome to the home of Ms Prescott, sir,' announced Luke as he pulled the Jeep up in the gravel driveway in front of a handsome dazzlingly-white villa with a red tiled roof and fountains playing on both sides of the main entrance. In a flash he was around to the detective's side of the vehicle to open the door. 'I hope you enjoy your stay, sir. I'll be here to take you back to the airport when you are ready to leave.'

'Many thanks, Luke.'

Johansson stood at the front door with his suitcase at his side when, as if by magic, the door opened to reveal a stout, motherly figure wearing a uniform and a generous smile. 'Talofa, Mr Josun.' Clearly the pronunciation of his name was beyond her capabilities, nevertheless she was most welcoming and seizing his suitcase ushered him into a large airy foyer where a roof fan turned slowly. 'Please wait here a moment while I tell Ms Peacock you are here.' Clearly this good lady had trouble with European names.

'Inspector, how nice to meet you.' Johansson turned to see a glamorous, tanned woman scantily dressed in a white bikini and holding a glass of wine. 'I do hope you had an enjoyable journey and feel like joining me for some refreshments by the pool? Perhaps you would like to change into something more comfortable first?'

'That sounds marvellous madam and thank you very much for putting me up in your beautiful villa.'

'My pleasure, I hope Inspector,' Ms Prescott replied, with a bit more than a twinkle in her eye. 'See you shortly. My housekeeper will see you to your room.' She turned and with a coquettish walk left him to it.

Showered, changed into his swimmers, and armed with hat, sunnies, towel and sunscreen, the detective appeared at the outdoor swimming pool some twenty minutes later where he found Jayne relaxing in a deckchair with a book.

'Ahh, Inspector. How nice it is to have you here. You know it is a very rare event for me to be interviewed by a real fair dinkum policeman. And one who has especially flown out from Australia must be no ordinary policeman. I feel so very important.'

'Well my visit reflects the importance of the crime I'm investigating. I can assure you madam, I would not be flying to Samoa unless there had been a serious crime.'

'Oh, how exciting. But if we are to live together for the next two days and nights, I think I should drop all this "Inspector" crap and call you by your Christian name. Please will you drop the ma'am stuff and just call me Jayne? I respond far better to my name, you know.'

Reluctantly, Johansson agreed. 'My name is Mike.'

'Do sit down and join me, Mike. I like nothing better than good male company,' she purred. Reaching down she jingled a small bell which brought a barman scurrying from out of the shadows. 'What would you like to drink, Mike? Or are you still on duty?' She giggled.

'A beer will do fine, thanks.'

'Do have a cool off in the pool while he gets you your beer, Mike.'

Fully aware that Jayne was doing her utmost to be seductive, Mike Johansson decided to take her advice and have a dip. He moved over to the water's edge, checked the depth and executed an almost perfect dive. Jayne was impressed with Mike's physique and athleticism. A fine figure of a man like Mike would be a most welcome addition to her bed for the two days and nights he would be staying with her. She wondered whether she would score tonight or whether it might take another day to entice the detective between the sheets. She always liked a challenge.

Johansson completed two or three laps freestyle then rolled over to do the same backstroke. This allowed him to unobtrusively observe his interviewee. Jayne was going to be difficult. Having researched her background she was, he felt, entirely predictable. She would happily be interviewed only after her sexual appetite had been satiated but was likely to resist any questioning unless she first got what she wanted. Highly attractive as he found her, Johansson was not prepared to accept her terms. Quite apart from being a married man, any evidence gleaned from Jayne would not stand up in a court of law if he had sexual relations with this woman. No, he had to have another strategy. Any information he managed to collect would be the result of his way of doing things and not Jayne's. He resolved to put his plan into operation forthwith. Quite simply his plan was to scare the living daylights out of

Jayne so that in a desperate bid to defend herself she would forget her world of sexual fantasies and tell all.

Johansson clambered out of the pool, quickly dried himself down, had a generous swig of his beer and decided to launch into attack mode.

'Jayne Prescott you are under investigation for the murder of your husband, Charles Frederik Allsop. Unless you supply me with satisfactory answers, I will arrest you and take you back with me to Adelaide to face the full force of the law.'

This opening statement had the desired effect. The colour drained from Jayne's face and she was stunned into silence. She gawked at the detective as if she had already been taken into custody and was up on the murder charge. Before she had recovered sufficiently to speak, the detective opened up again.

'I shall be recording our conversation so that there is no disagreement on what has transpired. It may be used to provide evidence.' Out of his swimming bag the detective produced a small battery-operated recording device which he placed on the table between them and turned on.

'Were you legally married to Charles Allsop?'

'Yes,' Jayne pouted.

'Where were you the day he died, Mrs Allsop?'

'Inspector, I do not use the name Mrs Allsop. My name is Jayne Prescott and always has been.'

'Please answer the question.'

'I was away.'

'Where?'

'Oh, I don't know. I was often away visiting friends. Charles was quite happy about that.'

'I think you need to do better than that. If you were, in fact, *away*, who will vouch for you? Do you have an alibi?'

Jayne recalled the delicious weekend she had spent with Mark at a swanky hotel in Adelaide only to hear the next morning that the police were looking for her. If she had to mention Mark's name, he would not be pleased.

'Inspector, this is a delicate matter. I was actually enjoying a weekend with a lover and I don't wish to reveal his name. He is a prominent businessman in Adelaide.'

'I'm afraid I cannot guarantee that your little liaison will not come out in evidence at a later date. Do you have his contact details here in Samoa?'

Jayne reached into her beach bag and pulled out a well-used red address book. Flicking through, she came to the name she wanted.

'Mark Stephens, Inspector. If you pass me a piece of paper, I can write his contact details down for you.'

'Thank you. Now your husband was about thirty years your senior. Many would argue that you married him for his money. What do you say to that?'

'Well, to be perfectly honest, money was part of the agreement. But we got along famously. Charles was lonely and missed his wife dreadfully. He had invited me to marry him previously. Eventually I relented, but on the understanding that his money would come to me when he died. He was quite happy about it.'

'And has Mr Allsop's wealth come to you?'

'Yes, pretty well all of it. This villa was purchased with some of it.'

'Mr Allsop was in reasonably good health before his sudden death?'

'Yes, I think so.'

'Ms Prescott, did you assist in the killing of Mr Allsop so you could get access to his money earlier?'

'Of course, I didn't. That's an outrageous question. I was very fond of Charles and he adored me. I would never have hurt him. We enjoyed a good life together.'

'Indeed. Yet you went off with this Mark Stephens. This is hardly acceptable behaviour for a married woman, is it? Did Mr Allsop know where you were?'

'Inspector, I enjoy men's company, always have, and I hope I always will. Charles and I had an agreement that I could continue with some of my liaisons after we married. Poor old Charles was eighty-one and hardly a dynamo in bed, you know. We had a perfect understanding.'

'I think you can see why things are not looking good for you, Ms Prescott. You would be wise to tell the truth.'

'Inspector, I resent that comment. I have been more than frank and honest with you.'

'Did you know Dr Peters?'

'No, who is he?'

'Dr Peters attended your husband after he died. We now know he falsified the information on your husband's death certificate stating he died of natural causes when in fact he died of poisoning. Are you absolutely certain you and Dr Peters were not working together to murder your husband?'

'I don't know this Dr Peters so you are barking up the wrong tree, Inspector.'

'Well, perhaps you can tell me if your husband had any enemies? Are you aware of anyone who might have wished to murder him?'

'I was only married to him for less than twelve months. There was that mad idiot Henry Childs who really hated Charles. Perhaps he did it? He never missed a chance to abuse Charles.'

'Anybody else?'

Jayne adjusted her sunnies and stretched out her arms so that her breasts were displayed to full advantage.

'I don't think so. Actually, now I come to think of it, there was another man who wrote abusive letters to Charles. I went into Charles' study one day and found this letter on his desk. It was threatening all kinds of nasty actions. There was very little detail, but it seemed like a blackmail letter to me.'

'Go on,' urged Johansson.

'It was several months after we had married, and I asked Charles about it at the time. He just brushed it aside but I thought it was pretty awful.'

'Do you remember what was in the letter?'

'It was short. It just said he was not going to wait any longer for compensation. He wanted payment now or else Charles would pay with his life. Charles didn't want to talk about it. He just said he had had other letters from this man and the bloke was insane.'

'It is extremely important that we follow this up. Receiving threatening letters is not something we should ever be taking lightly. Where is this letter now?'

'In storage. After Charles died, I had all his office stuff bundled up and stored away in boxes. I thought there could be papers and things from his transport business that might be required one day.'

'That sounds promising. I want the full details of this storage facility and the company running it please. I will also declare the storage facility part of a police investigation and therefore out of bounds to all. This includes you, Ms Prescott.'

Jayne was not used to being spoken to like this. Most men were all over her and she naturally fell into her seductive ways to more fully enjoy their company. But this policeman was something different. She found his gruff domineering behaviour stimulating but also knew that her usual techniques for taming a man would probably not work. She felt uneasy and out of her depth. Her very considerable feminine charms were being ignored. She smiled limply.

'Ms Prescott, is there anything else you would like to tell me with regard to your husband's sudden death?'

'What can I say, Inspector? Regardless of what I tell you, I am suspected of his murder. I can see why you think I could have been involved. Inheriting money is, I suppose, motivation. But please don't forget that I was already legally entitled to his wealth. I might have had to wait for a few years till he died but there was no need for me to hurry the process up by killing him. I was really enjoying life as his wife.'

Johansson declined to answer. He felt he had pushed Jayne Prescott hard enough and had made some progress. He had uncovered another person of interest but certainly Jayne would remain on his suspect list.

'Ms Prescott, in view of the serious nature of this police inquiry, I don't believe it is wise that I accept your invitation to stay. Would you please arrange for your driver to take me back into Apia where I will book myself into a hotel? Perhaps you can recommend somewhere?'

'Aggie Grey's, Inspector. They also have a fabulous live show every evening except Sundays. Would you like to use my phone to book a room?'

¶

Two hours later the inspector checked in at Aggie Grey's and found his room. There he showered before listening to the recording of the interview with Jayne. What a stunning woman she was. He could well understand how men fell for her. Was she just a sex-maniac or was she more? Was she capable of murder? Was there more to Ms Prescott than being a classy escort?

Before he went along to the dining room for the evening meal he re-scheduled his flight home to be a day earlier than originally planned, rang his wife and contacted his junior assistant at the police station. He left instructions for the storage depot to be visited where Charles' belongings had been stowed, and the particular shed declared an area under police investigation. Mark Stephens, the lover that Jayne had provided as her alibi, was officially added to the list of suspects. He wondered whether perhaps the two lovers had planned this together.

CHAPTER 8

Tania

Twenty-five-year-old Tania Markovina parked the police car in the designated parking spot at the Adelaide airport. Being the junior assistant to Detective Inspector Johansson meant she was on a steep learning curve. Police academies could only teach you the theory and basics; it was not until you started working with an experienced officer, such as Johansson, that you began to appreciate what real policing was all about.

It was only six months ago that she had been promoted and assigned to Johansson as his understudy. Much of her time was now spent in research; finding missing persons, tracking down evidence, delving into archives, old newspapers and court cases. Being of an academic inclination, she loved the research although it had its frustrations when nothing useful could be unearthed. She also found herself working as a sort of personal assistant; making bookings, organising meetings and being a listener when Johansson wanted to fire off new ideas and theories. She felt they made a good team.

Meeting Johansson's plane at 8:00 am on a Monday morning did, however, test the friendship. Earlier this morning she had been curled up in the arms of her boyfriend. She and Tony had been an item for the past two years and she was convinced that Tony was the man for her. He possessed almost all the qualities she was looking for in a future life partner. Kind, considerate, a great sense of humour and excellent job prospects were all pluses.

In addition, he was well above average in the looks department, played sport with masses of energy, if not skill, was her intellectual equal, and thrilled her in the bedroom like no other man had come close to. They had never actually talked about marriage, but she felt they both had reached a point in their relationship where this was a natural progression. Reluctantly, Tania stopped thinking about her Tony and channelled her thoughts instead to what she had to do as a policewoman.

One thing they didn't teach you at the police academy in the 1970s was how to present yourself in police uniform when you were a highly attractive looking female. Somehow you had to remain "modest" and hide your good looks but at the same time you wanted to be noticed. Throughout her training, and since joining SA Police, she had found getting the balance right was no easy task. Men would often ogle her when she was trying her best to look professional. At other times she felt she came over as too officious. In the end, she tried to be natural and simply ignore the stares of men and their occasional suggestive remarks. In her haste to get out to the airport on time this morning, she had abandoned all hope of applying any perfume or lipstick and just came au naturel.

Tania had only just got out of the vehicle when a gritty voice broke through her ponderous thoughts, 'Morning Tania. Looks like you only just made it?'

'Oh, good morning, Inspector. Your plane must have landed early. It's only just eight.'

'Correct. An excellent flight with a tail wind.'

'Jump in, sir, all ready to go. Where to? Your home or the station?'

'Station please, Tania.' She eased the car out and headed for Sir Donald Bradman Drive.

'Was it a useful trip, sir?'

'I think so. We now have a fourth suspect. There's the daughter, disgruntled Mrs Ernstein, who feels cheated out of her inheritance, the eccentric old Henry Childs who hated Charles' guts, the sex-machine wife, Jayne Prescott, who was perhaps impatient to get her money and…' Johansson paused to get the full dramatic effect, 'And a new mystery man who apparently sent Charles threatening blackmail letters over many years.'

'And what's your instinct telling you, sir?'

They pulled up at the lights before the detective responded. 'At this stage I have no idea. Whoever it was, persuaded Dr Peters to come in on the act which successfully delayed this inquiry for three years and could have prevented the murder from ever being discovered. If Peters hadn't got scared that he was off to a fiery hell when he carked it, nobody would have ever been the wiser. We have several leads to follow up now Tania. There's Jayne's lover boy from three years ago, Mark Stephens, the mystery blackmailer and I'm also wondering about Mrs Ernstein's family. Perhaps her husband John was involved, or her two brothers? They all missed out on Charles' fortune remember? There's plenty to keep us busy, Tania.'

Tania slowed to 25kph for yet another set of roadworks. Adelaide seemed to be digging up its roads forever. As so often seemed to happen, there were only two council workers actually doing anything, one at each end holding up stop/slow signs and nobody else working in between. 'Are you in need of a coffee, sir?'

Johansson was not addicted, like some, to an early morning kick of coffee but he sensed that Tania was, so he okayed the idea and they pulled in at a service station for takeaways.

'What would you like me to do first, sir?'

'See if you can track down these letters from the blackmailer. I sent you the details of the storage facility. I'll try and chase down lover boy. Let's review progress at 9:00 am tomorrow morning.'

Tania dropped the detective off with his suitcase at the police station and proceeded on to the storage depot in Noarlunga, south of Adelaide.

She had no problem getting access to the shed that held Charles Allsop's belongings, although she had to endure the young man in charge running his eyes up and down her body longingly. He wanted to escort her to the shed but she quickly plugged that idea. 'This is police business only. I'll return the key when I have finished. It could be some time though depending on what's there.' She could feel the young man undressing her as she proceeded towards Shed 15.

Tania was surprised but relieved to discover Shed 15 was largely empty. About half a dozen small sealed cardboard boxes sat in a row on a strong wooden shelf. One at a time she opened the boxes using her Swiss army knife and meticulously examined their contents. She was thankful it was a cool day as sheds could heat up mercilessly in warm sunny weather.

The first box contained nothing but old green files still with their labels attached. Every file contained papers relating to business dealings from the 1960s. Box two was the same but from the 1950s. *Why do people hang on to all this old stuff?* wondered Tania as she moved on to box three.

As she deftly used her Swiss army knife to cut the masking tape, she heard a sound behind her. It was the young storeman again. How long had he been standing there perving? 'I thought you might need some scissors and masking tape to re-seal all the boxes.' He grinned.

Clever bugger, thought Tania, *any excuse to come and gawp at me again.* 'Okay, thanks, leave them by the door please.'

'Want a cuppa?' the young man persisted, delaying his inevitable departure as long as possible.

'No thank you,' Tania replied tersely. The young man finally got the message that he was not welcome and trudged off.

Box three was full of black and white photos possibly taken

with a Kodak box camera. As with many families, Charles and his first wife had never managed to get these hundreds of old family photos sorted and stuck into photo albums. The photos of Charles went back to when he was a baby. There was something rather sad about them as Tania leafed through. Here was someone's life captured visually and lovingly but now just discarded in a cardboard box in Shed 15, no doubt to eventually be destroyed as unwanted rubbish.

Box four cheered Tania up slightly because it contained a dozen full photograph albums. Each album was dated on the spine. These, she surmised, were the best photographs faithfully selected and stuck in with short captions neatly handwritten with a fountain pen underneath every snap. *"Charles at school picnic, March 1902"*, *"Charles playing with Scamp in the backyard, September 1904"*. Intriguing stuff.

Surely, thought Tania, *someone in the family should have these in their possession for safekeeping.* One day somebody might want to do their family history. Putting the albums back tidily she moved on to box five.

This, the penultimate box, housed old personal income tax forms for both Mr and Mrs Allsop together with the Australian Taxation Office's assessments. Nothing of any use.

Tania moved to the final cardboard box. As soon as the box was opened, her spirits lifted. Inside were several large brown envelopes with writing scribbled on their fronts. Here was a collection of Charles' more private papers. She quickly discarded the envelopes labelled "Certificates", "Medical", and "Letters from my wife, Jenny" and focused on the remaining two envelopes both entitled "Personal correspondence". These envelopes possibly contained a letter, or letters, from the mysterious blackmailer. She settled down to peruse their contents thoroughly.

After ten minutes she found what she was looking for, a bunch of folded letters with a rubber band around them. Donning her rubber gloves, Tania carefully removed the rubber band. She counted eight letters in all and they spanned a period of over twenty years with the final letter arriving about a month before Charles died of poisoning. There were a number of obvious similarities across all the letters. They were typed, short, threatening in tone, with no address provided and signed off always by "Hank". Tania placed the letters into her small police evidence bag and began the tedious job of resealing the six boxes and placing them back on the shelves.

By the time she had finished, her stomach was grumbling about having had no food. A glance at her watch revealed it was already 2:00 pm. Tania returned to the uncouth young storeman, thanked him for the masking tape and scissors, handed over the key and slapped a form on his dirty desk.

'I'm removing these eight letters as police evidence. Sign here please. They will be returned eventually but may first be required as evidence in a court case. You need to keep the duplicate form in your records.'

The young man relished another opportunity to be up close and personal with this sexy policewoman. 'What's in them letters then?'

'None of your business.' And with that Tania headed back

to the station to gobble down some sandwiches before examining the letters more closely.

There was no sign of Johansson at the station. Her stomach now pacified, she pulled on a clean pair of gloves and sorted the letters into chronological order. The first letter read as follows:

19th July, 1954

Charles,

Your behaviour last weekend was disgusting and unforgivable. To have taken advantage of me the way you did was criminal.

I know you are a wealthy man so you can pay for what you did. I want twenty thousand pounds in cash. If you pay up, I won't go to the police.

You have until the end of the month to pay me. Place the money in Post Office letterbox 78 at the Adelaide Central Post office.

Remember you have only until the end of the month.

Hank

Tania re-read the letter. What was the criminal behaviour Hank was referring to? How had Charles taken advantage of Hank? Did Charles pay up? The second letter might provide some answers. It was dated over four years later.

8th August, 1958

Charles,

It's me again. I'm in a spot of trouble and need more money. Ten thousand pounds should do it. Same as before; put the money in PO Box 93 at the Adelaide PO. Note I have changed the number.

Make sure you give me the money or I'll spill the beans.
Hank
PS. This is urgent. Get the money to me by August 23 at the latest. Or else…

What had happened after the first letter? It seemed that Charles had decided to pay up and had refrained from going to the police but this she would need to check. Was there a case of blackmail reported to the SA Police shortly after July 19, 1954?

Letters three to seven were similar in tenor and the nature of their demands. Apparently, Charles kept paying up. Every few years another letter would arrive and the money always had to be deposited in cash at an Adelaide PO box. There was, however, an ugly change of tone in letter eight which was dated only four weeks after letter seven was despatched.

18th January, 1975
You are a BASTARD, Charles! You have not given me my money. I will give you one more chance. Put $30,000 in my PO box by January 25 or else.

Don't piss me about. If you don't give me the money, I will tell the police, I will tell your new pussy and if necessary, I will do more.

You know I can ruin you.
Hank

This final letter was particularly malicious. Tania noted that Charles had died on February 6, 1975, not long after he had received this last missive. Had Hank decided "to do more" as he had darkly threatened? Had he teamed up with Dr Peters and somehow poisoned Charles?

Johansson was still not back in his office, so Tania sought out the clerical staff in charge of police records to find out whether there had been any reports of blackmail during the years covered by the letters; July 1954 to February 1975. Her careful searching revealed a couple of small, amateurish episodes of attempted blackmail that had been followed up and dealt with but neither crime was related in any way to the Hank/Charles case.

Apparently Charles had sat tight and paid up in response to the first six demanding letters but for some reason declined to pay when the seventh letter turned up. What had Charles done to Hank back in 1954 that had set off this whole ghastly business? And why, after forking out a total of around $200,000 to keep Hank quiet, had Charles elected not to pay when the seventh letter arrived? Who was this mysterious Hank? How could they track him down? Was Hank even his real name? So many questions!

¶

Tania was at her desk enjoying her takeaway coffee well before the 9:00 am meeting with Johansson the next day. She had much to pass on to the detective from yesterday's work. Johansson arrived in a cheerful mood a few minutes later armed with his own black coffee and they immediately got down to business. The inspector was impressed with Tania's efforts and when she had completed her verbal report, he even offered a rare compliment.

'Lover boy, Mark Stephens, was not difficult to find, although getting a chance to speak with him was less easy. In the end we met at his office after he had flown in from Sydney where he had been exploring possible new deals. He's a nice enough chap but was really annoyed that Jayne had exposed him as one of her clients. I managed to calm him down and get him to try and see things as Jayne obviously saw them. Eventually he understood that Jayne was a murder suspect, and desperately needed Mark to verify that they were an item the weekend her husband had died. So, I challenged him to prove that he was with Jayne during the whole of the February 5th/6th weekend.'

'Is he a married man?' inquired Tania.

'Nope. He seems to lead a very promiscuous existence and has liaisons all over the place. He distinctly remembered this particular weekend with Jayne because he had arranged to spend the weekend with another much younger woman, but she had pulled out at the very last minute. He had already booked an expensive hotel room and was about to collect her when she rang to say she was sick. As a last minute replacement, he rang Jayne Prescott to see if she was free and Jayne was happy to oblige at short notice. It seems that Mark has three or four women at his disposal around Adelaide. Mark also remembered the weekend being somewhat spoilt because the police were trying to contact Jayne and himself. I checked this out with our police records late yesterday and sure enough several police calls had gone out for both of them. So Jayne's alibi certainly stacks up.'

'Not actually being physically present in the unit with Charles does not mean she didn't somehow organise the poisoning,' Tania commented.

'Good point. Regrettably, I doubt whether we will ever know what poison was used since it happened well over three years ago now.'

'So, sir, all we have confirmed so far is that Jayne was away the weekend Charles was poisoned. She has to remain on our list of suspects.'

'Agreed. So where do we go from here?' Johansson paused a moment. 'It is vital that we pursue this Hank guy. He is at the top of my list. Leave the letters with me, I want to read them through before sending them down to forensics. With a little bit of luck, the experts will find fingerprints and be able to work out what kind of typewriter was used. The analysts may even be able to provide other clues too.'

'What would you like me to do next, sir?'

'It's a long shot, and may be a waste of time, but spend the day out at Everglades Retirement Village. Talk to the manager and any residents who remember Charles. Give Henry

Childs in apartment 82 a miss though, otherwise you'll get a ghastly earbashing. Find out if any of the residents recall Charles having visitors on the weekend of February 5th/6th over three years ago? Do they remember anything out of the ordinary? Concentrate on the residents living closest to Charles' place. Let me know if you get anything of interest at 9:00 am tomorrow please.'

It was a pleasant enough day, a cool southerly was blowing and keeping temperatures down, so Tania was happy to make this her task for the day. As she drove out to the retirement village, she planned her tactics. Talk to the manager first and get his or her cooperation before calling on the elderly folk. Keep careful notes.

She arrived at the gates shortly after 10:00 am and pulled up outside the manager's office a few minutes later. The folk she hoped to meet shortly might provide some valuable insights.

The Everglades Retirement Village

Tania pulled into the visitors' carpark, donned her cap and found her notebook. As she alighted, she flashed one of her luscious smiles at the waiting manager.

'Good morning, Officer. My name is Scott Harris and I'm the manager here at The Everglades.'

'Good morning, Scott. If you can spare a few minutes, I'll explain why I'm here, and how you may be able to help.'

'My pleasure. I have a couple of potential new residents coming to see me in about half an hour but until then I'm at your disposal. Shall we go into my office?'

Tania had only been serving in the SA Police for about three years but was proud of her ability to quickly sum up the people she met, together with their environments. This attribute was something she had been deliberately practising. Highly developed powers of observation were crucial in her job. The young man sitting behind his managerial desk was well groomed and smartly dressed in a suit and tie. Even his shoes were well polished. Everything about him exuded professionalism. Scott appeared to be quietly confident as he looked Tania in the eye. She noted that he showed her respect and was pleasant and polite in his manner. Clean-shaven, blond and striking blue eyes made him quite handsome although he did not have the ruggedness of an athlete.

To a lesser extent, Scott Harris was also able to effectively appraise the many folk who came to see him in his role as manager of The Everglades. A stunningly attractive young policewoman was, however, a first for him. Normally his visitors were in their sixties or more, either residents or would-be residents, retired with time and money on their hands. This was indeed a welcome change.

The constable looked as though she was mid-twenties, although he always found ages difficult to predict. Beneath the uniform he envisaged a lithe, athletic body, tanned and as beautiful as the face he looked into. No rings on her fingers he noticed. Quickly suppressing further such thoughts, he smiled in his most professional manner and asked, 'What can I do to help?'

'I'm making some inquiries into an incident that occurred about three years ago. How long have you been the manager here?'

'Coming up to three and a half years now. Time flies when you're having fun.'

'Were you here as the manager on the weekend of February 5th and 6th 1975?'

'I certainly was. I took up my position here on January 5th that year.'

'On that weekend, one of your residents, Charles Frederic Allsop, died. Do you remember this?'

'I most certainly do. It was my first death of a resident, and I hated the whole experience.'

'Why?'

'Well, nobody likes having to deal with death at any time, but this was a really scary time for me because, as the manager, I was supposed to know what to do and to be able to step in and handle things in a professional way. I remember being quite overwhelmed and almost panicking.'

'I can understand that. Describe the scene for me please.'

'There was a lady, I don't remember her name, but she was Mr Allsop's daughter, and she had rung me at home two or three times on the Sunday. Now, I'm only meant to be available to the residents during the working week. Weekends are my time off and I certainly have never encouraged anyone from the Glades to ring me out of hours. This lady was getting increasingly upset because she couldn't contact her father. She had rung him several times and had got no answer. She said it wasn't like him and that he rarely went out. She thought he may have collapsed or something. The wife hadn't answered the phone either. Were they both gassed or something? She was getting panicky, so after her third call, I agreed to come down to the Glades and go over to Mr Allsop's apartment with her. In the meantime, she had rung the police to report Mr Allsop as a missing person. The three of us arrived at the entrance to The Everglades at the same time; me, this panicky lady, and a police inspector.'

'Let me stop you there, Scott. The lady was Mrs Ernstein, and the inspector is now my boss. His name is Detective Inspector Johansson. Go on...'

'Well, we all went up to Mr Allsop's apartment and I knocked and rang a couple of times but there was no sound, so I used my master key and opened the front door. Well, you know the rest. Mr Allsop had died in his sleep. When the doctor came, he filled in all the forms and said he had died of a heart attack. The doctor then arranged everything to do with the body and all I had to do was to complete my own report for the Board of Directors.'

'Tell me about the doctor.'

'There's nothing to say really. He came fairly quickly and determined the cause of death straight away. I was surprised how fast he did it. He knew almost immediately. Hardly had to check anything.'

'Did you speak to the doctor?'

'No, he didn't seem to want to talk and was in a bit of a hurry. I remember thinking that he might have another death to deal with. Not a pleasant job I reckon.'

'Quite. Was there anything odd you remember about the whole incident?'

'No, I think I must have been a bit like a stunned mullet. I wasn't functioning well.'

'Well thank you, Scott. If, on reflection, anything else

comes to mind please contact me.' Tania handed over her business card and went on.

'Do you have a list of the residents who were here when Mr Allsop died?'

'Indeed, every few months we print off an updated list of everyone in The Everglades. With 100 apartments, and most occupied by married couples, at any one time we might have 160 people living here.' Scott opened the filing cabinet nearby and lifted out a folder labelled "Lists of Residents".

'Here we are. This list is for January 15th, 1975 only two or three weeks before Mr Allsop died.

Do you mind me asking, is there something unusual about Mr Allsop's death?'

'Possibly, that's why I'm here. Now I want you to understand, Scott, that I am conducting preliminary inquiries only. I don't want you, or anybody else, running around making up ridiculous stories. I'm sure that in a place like this, rumours spread like wildfire anyway, so don't add fuel to the fire.'

'You are right about the rumour mongering. But what can I tell residents when they start asking me? They will all know by lunchtime that the police have called at the office today.'

'All you can tell them is that the police are making some further inquiries into Mr Allsop's death. Now, tell me, how many of the residents who lived close to Mr Allsop when he died, are still here? I want to interview them.'

Scott stood up and pulled out a laminated map of the entire village. Placing his finger on the apartment once occupied by Mr Allsop, he noted down the numbers of the closest apartments. Because Mr Allsop's apartment was at the end of a short cul-de-sac, there were only four apartments close by that would have been able to see who might be coming and going. Of these, two no longer accommodated residents who were around when Mr Allsop was still alive.

'There are only two apartments that could be of interest to you. In number 62 there is a married couple, Colonel and Mrs Bailey. He is a retired colonel from the British army with a gammy leg and rather deaf. She is a sweetie and serves on a couple of the Everglades social committees. Right opposite to where Mr Allsop lived is a Mrs Snelling. She is a wealthy widow who has a reputation as being the village's greatest gossip. What she doesn't know she makes up. You will have fun with her!'

'Thank you, Scott. Now another question. What did you make of Mr Allsop's wife who lived here, Jayne Prescott?'

'Well, she was here for only about six months from the time I arrived at the start of '75 until mid-July. An intriguing lady to say the least. Certainly out of place in here; she was probably twenty-five years younger than anyone else here and her interests seemed to be outside the village. She and Charles appeared to get along okay, but half the time she was away on business. Dressed to kill, she always gave me a friendly wave as she drove out in her cream-coloured sports car. I asked Mr Allsop once what sort of business she was engaged in but he didn't really answer my question. There were some malicious rumours floating about the village that she was a high-class call girl but I have no evidence of that. Why would she be? She was married to a wealthy man and had all she needed.'

'Thank you. How popular would you say Mr Allsop was in the village?'

'A lot of folk keep to themselves in here. Some are not too mobile or don't like going out after dark. I think Mr Allsop was a bit like that. Occasionally he went out with his wife somewhere. I believe he sometimes came to functions within the village. There was one gentleman who complained about Mr Allsop several times. To be honest, I thought he was usually making a mountain out of a molehill.'

'And who was this gentleman who used to complain?'

'Henry Childs in apartment 82. His place backed onto Mr Allsop's. Mr Childs is still here. He gave me the impression that he really disliked Mr Allsop. He was always demanding that I take action against Mr Allsop about petty things. *He has left his car parked out on the road; he leaves his garbage bins out too long; he waters his garden when it's not necessary.* All that sort of silly stuff.'

'And did you ever take action?'

'No. On one occasion, I saw Mr Childs yelling obscenities at Mr Allsop in his front yard.'

'What did you do?'

'I pulled over and parked, but by the time I got out of the car, Mr Childs was off like a guilty school kid, hobbling back to his own place so I let the incident pass.'

'Okay, would you mind giving the colonel and his wife and Mrs Snelling a ring to warn them a policewoman is about to come and visit them please? I don't want to cause three heart attacks.'

Scott chuckled. While he made the calls, Tania scribbled a few more comments in her notebook, then visited the ladies to freshen up.

'You're in luck they are all home and seem quite excited that they are about to have a visit from the police after I had explained they were not in trouble with the law.'

'Thanks Scott. Don't forget to contact me if you remember anything else you think might be helpful.'

¶

It was very quiet and peaceful in The Everglades Retirement Village. Road signs directed you not to exceed 10kph and the gardens surrounding each apartment were well maintained. The professionally landscaped frontages displayed a variety of natives. Tania recognised melaleucas, grevilleas, banksias and various eucalypts. One day, Tania thought she would love to have her own garden full of natives.

She rang the bell at Colonel and Mrs Bailey's place first. A sign by the side of their door announced, "Friends welcome anytime, relatives by appointment only". Tania was still giggling as the door opened to reveal a small grey-haired bespectacled lady with twinkling blue eyes and a welcoming smile. 'Oh...' she said, surprised, 'You're the lady policeman. Please do come in.'

Standing in the centre of the spacious lounge was the retired British colonel bedecked with a neat moustache, a ruddy face and thinning white hair. Still slim and straight-backed, he held a walking stick in his left hand and extended his right to shake Tania's hand. 'Good Morning, Ma'am,' he said politely in a clipped, Queen's English accent. 'Do take a seat.'

Before Tania could reply, Mrs Bailey jumped in with an invitation to have a cup of tea.

A few minutes later the three of them were comfortably seated with a cup of Earl Grey tea. A grandfather clock ticked its comforting rhythmic beat in one corner of the room. The paintings were portraits of family ancestors or hunting scenes from the old country. It was hard to imagine a more English setting.

The small talk dispensed with; Tania opened up. 'Thank you so much for sparing me some time. I believe you knew the late Mr Allsop and his wife?'

'Oh yes we did,' piped up Mrs Bailey, 'although not well.'

'Do you mind if I smoke my pipe?' interrupted the colonel.

'Of course not.'

While the colonel started going through his pipe-lighting routine, Tania continued with her questions.

'I wonder if you could tell me how well you think Mr Allsop and his wife got along. Were they happy?'

Again, Mrs Bailey took the lead, as the colonel was still busy fixing his pipe. 'I think so, but it was a strange sort of a relationship. She was out much of the time and left poor old Charles on his own. He seemed happy enough though.'

'A bit of a tart if you ask me,' ventured the colonel.

'Oh, darling that's a bit strong. I found her pleasant enough.

She was always dressed up to the nines. Quite a glamorous woman, you know.' Mrs Bailey looked at Tania for assurance.

'Well dear, you may not have seen Mrs Allsop as I saw her. I was at the golf club one evening, having a whiskey with a couple of colleagues, and saw Jayne carrying on with a young man. All over him like a rash she was. She never saw me, too busy flirting, but I watched her and this young fella arm-in-arm go into the lift up to the bedrooms. I don't think they were just going up to visit the toilets.' The colonel at last gave a satisfied first puff on his pipe.

Mrs Bailey looked quite taken aback at this revelation. 'Oh dear,' was all she could offer.

'Did Charles and his wife have many visitors?' Tania inquired.

'I don't think so,' replied Mrs Bailey, seemingly over the shock of hearing about Jayne's dubious escapades.

'That idiot Childs came around sometimes to hurl a few expletives at Charles if he was out the front doing a spot of gardening or sitting on his balcony. Something wrong with that fella. I'd have had him on fatigues until he calmed down a bit. It was only Charles he had a go at, nobody else. Must be a bit of history there I reckon.'

'Someone in a red sports car came around a couple of times just before Charles died,' volunteered Mrs Bailey.

Tania was all ears. 'Do you know who it was?'

'No, I'm sorry I can't help you there. It was a woman though.'

'What kind of a car?'

The colonel chimed in, 'Looked like an Austin Healey Sprite to me but I can't be sure. Flashy looking job.'

'Can you describe the woman you saw please, Mrs Bailey.'

'Oh dear, not really. Middle-aged perhaps, or a bit older. Slimmish.'

Tania looked towards the colonel for any additional observations he might offer.

The colonel shrugged his shoulders, 'Sorry, I think I was more interested in the car than the woman.'

'Well, that's a pleasant change,' Mrs Bailey snorted.

'It would be very helpful if you could contact me if you think of anything else that would assist us to identify the car and/or the lady. Here's my card.'

'Another cup of tea before you go?' urged Mrs Bailey.

Tania politely declined. Thanking them for their help, she rose from her chair. Mrs Bailey jumped up to see her to the door accompanied by another of her radiant smiles.

Tania walked back slowly to her car and scribbled a few more comments in her notebook. The woman and the red sports car sounded promising.

¶

Next on Tania's visiting list was Mrs Snelling, reputed to be the village's chief gossip. Leaving her notebook in the car she walked across to the front door to find Mrs Snelling already there waiting on her welcome mat.

'Good morning Officer, so lovely to meet you. Do you

mind if we sit out here on the porch? I like to keep an eye out for everyone in the village, you know.'

It was a rhetorical question and Tania accepted the seat to which she was ushered.

'Good morning Mrs Snelling, it's good of you to spare me some time.'

'Not at all, Officer. Always pleased to help our police, you know. You do such a good job and–'

Tania politely butted in. She had sensed already that Mrs Snelling was the kind of person who could talk all day with very little prompting, so their conversation would need to be "managed". Tania's boyfriend described the Mrs Snellings of this world rather rudely as "gasbags" or "suffering from verbal diarrhoea".

'Mrs Snelling,' smiled Tania, 'I believe you knew Mr Allsop?'

'Oh yes, of course I did. Such a nice gentleman. He lived over there just across the road, you know.'

Tania did know and continued her line of questioning. 'How well did you know him?'

'Well Officer, I make it my business to get to know everyone here if possible. It's quite a challenge you know because people come and go–' Tania gently brought Mrs Snelling back to the question.

'Very commendable Mrs Snelling, but let's get back to Mr Allsop if you don't mind.'

'Of course, of course. My friends tell me I sometimes ramble on, you know, Officer. I think it's an age thing. Yes, sorry, did I know Charles Allsop well was your question I think?'

Tania nodded as she ran her eyes over Mrs Snelling. Plumpish, she belonged to the purple-rinse set and probably visited her beauty salon every week for a touch up. She wore far too much make-up and rather ornate earrings for a woman her age. Mutton dressed up as lamb. Funny how some elderly women never gave up dreaming that they were still young and attractive. Mrs Snelling began to launch into another set of rambling comments.

'Well, let me see, I don't think we were friends really, just acquaintances more like. He was only here for a few months and then he got married to this woman half his age. It was a strange arrangement. Charles stayed home much of the time, but Jayne was always charging off somewhere. She often stayed away all weekend leaving poor old Charles with a meal or having to get takeaway. I don't think they were really in love or anything, but they got along okay, and I never heard them arguing. A marriage of convenience. Of course, we all reckoned she had married him for his money. He was very rich, you know. I never saw them kiss or cuddle. I went over to their apartment a few times but they never asked me in.'

'What about visitors, Mrs Snelling. Do you remember any visitors?'

'Not many. His daughter and her husband came over sometimes. I don't think Jayne ever had any visitors. I felt a bit sad for Charles because he and his new wife rarely went out together. Goodness knows where she went all the time. I even heard people say she was a prostitute. It was sad he died so suddenly. He was the first one to go, you know, in this half of the village. He was only eighty-one and–'

Tania intervened again. 'Do you remember ever seeing a woman in a red sports car visit?'

'Oh, yes I do. Fancy me forgetting that. I sometimes wonder if I'm starting to lose my marbles, Officer. You know there are people in Everglades who are losing their capacities–'

'Well, I'm glad you are still fully in possession of yours, Mrs Snelling. Now please tell me everything you can remember about this woman and the red car.'

'I remember thinking that perhaps Charles had invited a lady friend over to see him because his wife was away so much. Men do that sometimes you know, Officer. But she didn't stay very long. Perhaps ten minutes. She was about the same age as Jayne, fifty-ish. Nicely dressed but looking very cranky. Perhaps she was an old flame of his? Anyway, she looked even angrier when she left and Charles slammed his front door.'

'Did she only come the one time?'

'No, she was back again a few days later. In the same red car. But this time it was night-time. I remember this because it was a heatwave and I had opened the front door to try and get a breath of cool air into the house. I think it was February but I'm not sure.'

'Can you describe the car in more detail?'

'Not really, Officer. I don't know anything about cars. All I can say is that it was a bright red sports car kind of thing. A bit like a racing car. The sort of vehicle young men like to drive around in when they want to show off to the girls. I think it had the hood down.'

'How long did the lady stay this time?'

'Not long, perhaps ten minutes again.'

'Did you ever see her again?'

'No.'

'You have been a great help, Mrs Snelling. Thank you. I'll get in touch sometime soon if I need to.'

'Can I ask what this is all about, Officer?'

'I'm sorry, Mrs Snelling. Just some routine police investigation work.'

Mrs Snelling looked disappointed. However, having had a visit from the police would provide her an almost endless list of things to tell everybody in the village about for ages and she would be in high demand. Her mind was already working overtime on how this experience might be embellished.

Tania took her leave and recorded a few more notes. On her way out she stopped at the manager's office again to inquire whether they had any closed-circuit TVs that might have picked up the mysterious red car and its occupant. The answer was in the negative. The manager stressed that they were seriously looking into installing a system soon. Tania endorsed the manager's thinking and explained how valuable the police would find such a system in the deterring and solving of future crimes.

'Bring it on, Scott!' was her parting comment.

With that, Tania returned to base.

Lyn Peters

Detective Inspector Johansson and Tania held their usual catch-up and planning meeting at 9.00am the next morning. It was crucial that the lady in the red sports car be found. In all probability she was the person who had administered the poison to Charles. She must have been known to Charles Allsop as he would have opened the gates to allow her to get into the village using his remote. Perhaps Jayne Prescott knew who the lady was? Perhaps the lady was known to the other members of the family?

Johansson resolved to meet, not just Mrs Ernstein this time, but her husband, John, and Mrs Ernstein's two brothers. In addition, Johansson put out a request to the motor registry offices and police headquarters in all states and territories to search their files for red Austin Healey Sprites that were registered for use on Australian roads in 1975. He hoped to assemble a complete list of cars, registration numbers and owners as a starting point.

The eight blackmail letters were already undergoing a full

forensic analysis but the findings would not be available for a few more days. Nothing more could be done with the letters until these results were back.

Another line of inquiry would be Dr Peters' wife and family. Did any of them know about Dr Peters' involvement in the cover up of Charles' poisoning? The minister who had heard Dr Peters' confession and reported it a few days ago seemed to think that it was a closely guarded secret and that the only two people who knew the details were Dr Peters and his accomplice. Still it was worth a try. The matter would need to be tackled with extreme sensitivity since Dr Peters had only just been buried and the family would be deeply grieving. Johansson assigned this task to Tania believing a policewoman would be better able to talk with Lyn Peters and her family.

Inspector Johansson had attended the funeral. Not only was it his duty as a police colleague to be present, because Dr Peters had served as one of the on-call police medicos for several years, but also because he wanted to observe the members of the congregation. Was Dr Peters' accomplice there too? The service, in the Anglican parish church had been well attended. Johansson estimated at least 200 mourners were paying their last respects. Amongst the congregation were a couple dozen family members, officers from the SA Police and a large group from the medical community. In addition, there must have been many friends and neighbours. Eulogies had come from Dr Peters' eldest son Michael, a close friend from the medical fraternity and a life-long friend who had been at school with Dr Peters and had shared a number of amusing adventures over the years. The service was traditional and Johansson formed the impression Dr Peters and his close family were active members of the Anglican church. Disappointingly, Johansson neither saw nor heard anything that might help with their inquiries.

Tania was not looking forward to interviewing Lyn Peters and her three children. When arranging the appointment, she had stressed the need for them all to be present. The thought of having to endure a police interview and for them all to be in attendance had clearly rattled Lyn Peters. She could understand that there may have been a reason for someone to speak to her from the SA Police about her husband's work as a police medical officer, but why did this require the children to be there as well? It didn't make sense.

Tania pondered how she would approach the interview as she drove to the Peters' home. It was a beautiful location in the lush Adelaide Hills. A long driveway snaked its way through an avenue of elderly radiata pines and led to a white gravel courtyard in front of an imposing house. Light rain had just started to spatter the windscreen and Tania inhaled deeply to enjoy the magic aroma of fresh rain falling on vegetation. She rang the brass bell and waited nervously. This was something out of her comfort zone as she recalled her relative inexperience talking with people who had recently lost a loved one.

The door was opened by a pleasant looking young man probably about thirty years old. 'Hello, I'm Michael Peters. Please come in.'

Tania was ushered into a spacious open living area. The rest of the family rose to their feet to welcome her with a handshake and to introduce themselves. Tania felt the tension in the room. This was a family still reeling from Dr Peters' recent death and funeral. The last thing they wanted was a member of the police force turning up having insisted the four of them be present. They wanted to be left alone with their memories and not have to face up to someone they didn't know and who was not invited. Why the police wished to be involved in any way was a mystery to them. Tania was left standing and feeling awkward.

Michael Peters came to her rescue. It had not escaped him that this was a particularly attractive member of the police force who had come to visit. Indeed, his opinion of the SA Police shot up immediately if it was now recruiting pretty young women like Tania. 'Please sit down. Can we get you anything? A cup of tea or coffee perhaps?'

Tania politely declined and sat down on the edge of the vacant armchair. She cleared her throat, smiled rather timidly, and launched into what she had rehearsed along the way.

'May I say how sorry I am to hear of your loss. I do apologise for asking you all to be here for my visit and I can assure you that I would not be here unless we felt it absolutely necessary. This must be very difficult for you all and I can understand your concern.' Tania glanced at the four faces arrayed in front of her that registered various degrees of resignation and impatience as to why they had to be put through this ordeal with a police officer.

In the centre sat Mrs Lyn Peters. First impressions could be misleading but were nevertheless powerful determinants of how you would think of a person later on. Lyn presented as a strong matriarchal figure. *Surely,* Tania thought, *Mrs Peters "wore the pants" in this household.* She was a "no-nonsense" sort of person. Tania envisaged Lyn Peters running the school canteen and getting things done with great efficacy. Business-like, firm, but fair, seemed to sum her up. Mid-fifties perhaps?

Next to Lyn sat Michael Peters, the handsome young man who had ushered Tania into the Peters' abode. Tania was later to discover that Michael was an intern at the Royal Adelaide Hospital having followed in his father's footsteps. He was the eldest and had a pleasant disposition. Tania found him physically attractive and would have been more than happy to test out his bedside manner if ever lying in a hospital somewhere.

On the other side of Lyn Peters sat Nadia, tall and elegant. Nadia, it transpired, was a schoolteacher. She exuded confidence and looked sporty. For a moment, Tania thought she might have come across Nadia at one of her basketball matches. The lass appeared to have inherited the attributes of her mother, determined and forthright.

The baby of the family was the sweet-looking Sylvia. She was the most feminine of the three women and was clad in a pretty skirt and a tight-fitting blouse. Smaller than the other members of the family, she had just turned twenty-one and was at Adelaide University studying an Arts degree. It was Sylvia who seemed most distressed at her dad's passing and she held a tissue at the ready. Perhaps she had held a special place in her father's world?

Mrs Peters took the lead, 'How can we help you, Officer?'

'Mrs Peters, I asked you all to be here today because there is an on-going police inquiry that involves Dr Peters. We felt it sensible to explain this to the four of you together in case any of you can shed any light on the matter.'

There was an expectant hush. Tania had put it well and the members of the Peters' family already sensed that something potentially worrying was about to be revealed.

'I'll try to put this as tactfully as possible. I want to stress that our inquiries are at a very preliminary stage, so please don't jump to any conclusions. Please also be assured that what I'm going to tell you is totally confidential at this stage. It may also come as a bit of a shock.'

The level of concern in the room had risen again. Four sets of eyes were firmly locked on Tania as she went on. 'It has come to the notice of the police that Dr Peters, whilst serving in his capacity as an on-call police medical officer, may have been involved in a fraudulent report.'

'Oh, what utter nonsense. My husband was as honest as anyone can be. He certainly would never knowingly be involved in fraud of any kind.' It was Mrs Lyn Peters who had reacted. The others looked on with disbelief.

Tania knew this news would not be well received. She pushed on.

'Perhaps I can give you some more details, Mrs Peters. Possibly you, or one of your family, may be able to shed some further light on this business. This fraudulent report occurred over three years ago at the death of a Mr Charles Allsop. Dr Peters, as the duty police medical officer, was called in to confirm the death of this eighty-one-year-old gentleman and to complete the necessary death certificate. Dr Peters did this and gave as the cause of death a massive heart attack. Nobody disputed this at the time. However, we now have reason to believe that Mr Allsop was actually poisoned, and that Dr Peters knew this but chose instead to lie about the cause of death.'

'Oh, this is disgraceful. How dare you come to our home and accuse my late husband of such a thing. He would never do anything dishonest. There must be some terrible mistake.' The rest of the family looked on, united behind their mother at Tania's outrageous suggestion. Sylvia, the youngest, broke into tears and reached for a second tissue.

'Please let me continue. We were only made aware of the assertion that Dr Peters had falsified the death certificate very recently.'

Lyn Peters had had enough and she interrupted again. 'Officer, I repeat, my husband would never do such a thing. Where on earth are you getting this information from? Unless you can provide good evidence to support your assertion, I think you should leave.' Mrs Peters was clearly outraged, red in the face, spluttering and barely able to control herself.

'I'm sad to say that the evidence comes from Dr Peters himself. On his deathbed he called in his Anglican Minister to hear his confession. He wanted to tell her what he had done. He confessed to her that he had falsified Mr Allsop's death certificate. The minister asked him why and he said that he had been threatened. If he had refused, he said his family might be killed. He refused all the minister's requests to say who had made him do this.'

This last piece of information was met by stunned silence. Even Lyn Peters was momentarily unable to respond. Sylvia was now openly weeping. Tania felt awful. However she tried to break this news to them, it was going to come as a thunderbolt on top of their misery. She felt so sorry for them. The work of the police was, she now appreciated, not always pleasant or easy. Tania tried to fill the awkward silence, 'I'm so sorry to bring you this information. Perhaps you can see now why it is important that I meet you all to discuss this?' This last comment was met by a couple of grudging nods, but Mrs Peters had recovered enough to speak again.

'If this is true Officer, something awful has been going on and none of us here knew anything about it. Are you sure the minister got it right?'

'The minister has provided a sworn written statement of the interview she had with Chief Inspector Johansson.'

'I just can't believe it. Are we in danger now, Officer?'

'Certainly not, unless one of you knew about this matter all along, and who it was that persuaded Dr Peters to commit this offence, and have kept this secret for over three years?'

The family members exchanged glances but nobody spoke.

'I have to ask again, did any of you have any idea that Dr Peters had been threatened to falsify the documents? Did you even suspect that something was amiss? Did Dr Peters ever say anything that, on reflection, might have suggested he was caught up in all of this?' Tania waited patiently but all she saw were shakes of the head. The family appeared overwhelmed by her disclosures.

It was Michael who finally broke the silence.

'My father had an excellent reputation. In all his years as a doctor and family man he never put a foot wrong. Now, it seems, that under duress he did something that went against all his principles, but he must have done it to protect his family. Surely this cannot be adjudged a crime to defend your family?'

'I hope not, Michael. But matters like this ultimately are ruled upon by the courts. I can assure you, the police will not let this information become public. It will remain private and confidential for as long as possible. However, I cannot promise that some judge in the future may not want this matter opened up in a court of law. If that happens you are going to have to deal with it.'

'Well, Officer, I think you have given us more than enough bad news for today. We need time to digest what you have divulged.' Mrs Peters volunteered, 'I cannot stress strongly enough how important it is to our family for you to keep what you have told us totally confidential.'

Tania responded quickly, 'You have our complete agreement on that. In the meantime, if any of you think of anything that will help in this case, we want to hear from you. Here are my business cards. Please take one.'

Tania had mixed emotions as she took her leave. She felt bad about having to impart such shocking news to the family but was relieved that nobody in the family appeared to have had any idea what Dr Peters had confessed to on his deathbed.

CHAPTER 11

The Ernstein Family

At the same time Tania was interviewing the Peters family, Inspector Johansson was returning to the home of Mrs Ernstein to meet with the good lady yet again, but this time with her family present too. When he had rung to make the appointment, Mrs Ernstein was not impressed and expressed her displeasure in no uncertain terms. Getting the other five members of her family together at this time of day and at such short notice was, apparently, more than inconvenient. As a rule, Johansson never apologised. If it was police business, he had every right to pursue all angles and to keep revisiting places and people as many times as necessary. He dealt with the cantankerous Mrs Ernstein firmly but politely. Once she had let off sufficient steam, she resigned herself to yet another visit from the police.

The Inspector wanted to find out about three matters; how had they found the money to go on a twelve-month round-the-world trip in the State Suite if they had not inherited Mr Allsop's fortune? Could they shed any light on the mysterious woman in the red Austin Healey Sprite that had been seen visiting Mr Allsop at least twice shortly before his death? Finally, could any of them have been involved in the murder, perhaps as an angry revenge killing?

This time the door was opened by Lily, a twenty-something year old who seemed quite excited to be welcoming a real live policeman. She smiled broadly and cheerfully invited Johansson to follow her out to the back porch where they were all having morning tea. As the detective fell in behind Lily, he was saddened to see she was already following her mother's example with an oversized figure. What were young people doing these days with their diets to be overweight so early in life?

The area at the back of the house was somewhat grander than a back porch. There were several outdoor chairs and glass-topped tables surrounded by an array of potted exotic plants. A black cat wound its way around Johansson's legs, asking for sustenance no doubt, while various faces looked up at him expectantly from comfortable armchairs. Beyond, the detective noticed the water in a newish kidney-shaped swimming pool glistening invitingly in the sun. Again, the scene depicted a family that was well cashed-up.

'Inspector...' Mrs Ernstein's husband, John, stood up and extended his hand. Johansson reciprocated. 'Let me do some introductions. You have just met Lily, my daughter, and I believe you know my wife well by now. This is my younger daughter, Freda, the cat is Sooty, and I'm John, the master of the house.' Mrs Ernstein snorted derisively at this last comment. 'And over there helping themselves to coffee are my two brothers-in-law, David Allsop and Chris Allsop. Take a seat, Inspector. Tea or coffee?'

True to form, Johansson declined the offer of victuals and positioned himself where he could see everyone. He ignored the offer to sit down, preferring instead to enjoy the advantage that height gave when directing questions.

'Thank you for seeing me at such short notice. I appreciate that you have other things to do with your time. As Mrs Ernstein has probably already explained to you, we are conducting some inquiries into the death of the elderly Mr Allsop over three years ago.' As the detective spoke the two brothers wandered over and stood opposite him with coffee mugs in hand. 'There have been some further developments which necessitate my coming to speak to you all today.' He was pleased to see he had everyone's attention as he went on. 'The news is not good, I'm afraid. We now believe that Mr Allsop Senior did not die of natural causes.'

There was a moment's silence while the seriousness of Johansson's statement was processed, followed by a chorus of differing exclamations of surprise and disbelief.

'Please let me explain in more detail. We have good reason to believe that Mr Allsop Senior died from poisoning, so we are treating his death as murder. As family members, you have a right to know this, and as the senior investigating officer, I have a duty to question each one of you as potential suspects.'

It was Christopher, one of Mrs Ernstein's brothers, who recovered quickest from this dreadful news. 'I bet my bottom dollar that that tart he lived with is your culprit, Officer.' This blunt statement released a torrent of animated comments, some in support of Christopher and others in disagreement.

Johansson raised his voice, 'I understand that this is not welcome news, however I am asking you all for your help as a group and individually. I have a number of direct questions I want to put to you, and I'd be pleased if you could answer as accurately as possible. Remember that to conceal any facts, or to distort the truth in any way, is a criminal offence.' As order restored, the Inspector continued.

'Mr Ernstein, did you, or any member of your family, inherit anything substantial from Mr Allsop Senior?'

'I have already told you we didn't,' Mrs Ernstein chipped in before her husband could answer the question.

'What say you, Mr Ernstein?'

'My wife is correct. None of the people here received any-thing from Mr Allsop's very considerable estate. We are all very angry about this. My wife received a couple of pieces of her mother's jewellery she had always requested but that's all. Until Jayne Prescott came on the scene, we stood to receive millions, but we ended up with a big fat nothing!'

'What about your two brothers-in-law?' Johansson looked directly at Christopher and John. Both men shook their heads.

'OK, let me ask you a more personal question. Mrs Ern-stein, I would like you to respond to this one first please.' Not surprisingly, the detective had a captive audience.

'If none of you received anything from Mr Allsop's very

considerable estate, how then have you been able to afford to put in a brand-new expensive swimming pool and to go on a world cruise on a luxury ocean liner for a whole year?'

'That's easy Inspector, John and I won $450,000 with a lottery ticket. We won it shortly after Dad died, so it was some sort of consolation prize for being shunned in his will. The rest of the family can vouch for me because we gave them each $10,000.' Mrs Ernstein's answer was seconded by all present in varying ways. The inspector made a mental note to double check this claim with SA Lotteries.

'Thank you, I'm delighted that you had this success. Now, I have one more question which is directed to everyone. Shortly before Mr Allsop died, he was visited at least twice by a slim woman driving a red Austin Healey Sprite. We are most anxious to trace this person. Does anybody here remember seeing a woman driving a red Austin Healey Sprite around that time? Can you shed any light on who this person was?'

'Sounds like Jayne Prescott to me. She's slim. Perhaps she had a rental car or something,' suggested David.

'Mr Allsop's neighbours saw this person coming and going but are sure it wasn't his wife. They should know.'

David wasn't about to give up, 'She could have been wearing a disguise. Nasty bit of work that Jayne. Wriggled her way into Dad's pants and all his money so we got nothing. Why don't you go after her? Hire a car to put everyone off the scent, whack on some disguise, and then go in and poison the old man. Too easy.'

'Except that we know Ms Prescott was somewhere else at the time, so it couldn't have been her,' Johansson responded.

'Then she paid someone else to go and do her dirty work for her. It's got to be her, Inspector.'

'Why do you think she would have wanted to murder her husband?'

'I reckon, once she got Dad to change his will so that she inherited everything, it became important to knock him off quickly. She became a multi-millionaire overnight. She never loved him. She was always off shagging someone else. How can you say you love someone if you are constantly unfaithful?'

Johansson had to agree that what David was suggesting was plausible. It was only a theory though, and he had no evidence to back it up.

'Thank you for that suggestion. Now does anyone else have anything else they would like to add?'

'I have a question for you Inspector.' It was John. 'How do you know Mr Allsop was poisoned? And how come you have only now come up with the idea?'

'I regret that I cannot divulge the source of the information, but I can say it has only come to light in the last few days.' Two or three conversations broke out at this point and Johansson decided that he had achieved as much as he could and that he would end the interview.

'Thank you all for your cooperation. If you think of anything else that may help our inquiries, please get in touch. Here are my business cards.'

The overweight Lily escorted the detective to the door

and he went on his way. He pulled into a cafe on his way back to the police station to grab a coffee. Whilst waiting for his long black, Johansson reflected that the only thing he had really settled was from where their money had suddenly eventuated. He was no closer to finding the mystery woman and her red Austin Healey Sprite or establishing whether any of the family he had just met might have been the murderer or murderers. He dismissed the Ernstein children as being far too young and naive three years ago to have been capable of murderous thoughts, but the four adults should not be eliminated from the list of suspects. They could certainly have been motivated by extreme anger at missing out on their inheritance. He resolved to do some further background research into the lives of Mr and Mrs Ernstein and David and Christopher Allsop. Perhaps there was something in their past that might be of interest?

CHAPTER 12

The Eight Letters

It was a warm Friday morning. The sun was shining and Detective Inspector Johansson was in his office thinking about the round of golf he had arranged for Saturday. He was up against his archrival. He had lost track of the number of rounds they had had together but he was sure that if there was a count back of the results he would still be narrowly ahead. He intended to keep it that way. They were very competitive around the course but always enjoyed a few ales together at the nineteenth.

Tania was in her office too. Her mind was also preoccupied. She, and her long-term boyfriend, Tony, were planning a camping weekend at Deep Creek at the southern tip of the Fleurieu Peninsula. He seemed particularly excited about this venture and Tania wondered if there might be something more to it that he hadn't divulged. Was Tony, at last, going to propose? After two years living together, he must surely know her well enough by now. He had seen her at her best and worst. Long ago Tania had decided she could happily settle down with Tony but had lacked the courage to bring the topic up herself. After all, it was still the expectation that it was the man that made the move and had to propose.

'What are you daydreaming about? Are we meeting or not this morning? It's after 9:00am.'

Tania blushed and apologised. 'Sorry sir, I was just thinking about the camping weekend we have planned.'

'I have received the report back from forensics about the eight letters. Come to the office and let's see if the report helps us in any way to learn more about this guy, Hank. I've ordered two coffees.'

Tania hurriedly grabbed her notebook and trailed after her senior. Looking out of the Inspector's window, she noted the weather looked ideal for the weekend, then dragged her mind back into police mode and sat waiting.

'Okay, now I asked forensics to do a full analysis. They have done well to get it back so fast.' He slit open the envelope marked "CONFIDENTIAL: Attention Detective Inspector Johansson only" with his prized brass letter-opener, sat back and began to read silently. Several minutes later he looked up and made a face that Tania interpreted as signifying that the information therein was promising.

'Here's a quick summary. All the messages appear to have been typed on the one typewriter using a range of different A4, 80 GSM paper. The papers used are very common and available almost anywhere. So that's no help. The specialist in writing styles believes they were all written by the same person using similar phraseology, grammar and sentence structure. Whoever it was appears to be quite well educated as there are no obvious spelling or grammatical errors. Again, that's little help. But the next bit is more interesting.'

Tania waited patiently. She had learnt about these detailed forensic reports during training, but this was the first time she had been actively involved with a real one. 'The good news is that we have plenty of fingerprints. They belong almost entirely to just two people. One we would have to believe is the reader, Charles Allsop, the second set presumably belongs to the person we are trying to find; Hank, the blackmailer. A third set of fingerprints show up on the eighth and final message only. I think we can assume this third set belongs to Jayne Prescott, who told us she had found the letter on her husband's desk and read it. The next piece of information is perhaps the most intriguing. These days forensics can detect any special smells or odours with amazing accuracy. Perfumes are particularly easy to pick up. Two quite strong perfumes were detected on the eighth letter and one of those perfumes can be detected with decreasing strength on the other seven. The older the letter, the fainter the perfume shows up.'

'That's strange, sir. Does this Hank get a woman to type his letters for him? Or does Hank wear perfume? I have heard that there is a small percentage of men who use perfume nowadays. I believe some gay men like to apply perfume too. Perhaps we are dealing with a homosexual who had some connection to Charles Allsop? Could Mr Allsop have been gay?'

'Whoa, steady on Tania. I like your lateral thinking but don't get carried away. Now there's a bit more here. The envelopes were a mess, as regards fingerprints. Too many postmen collecting, sorting and delivering leaving their prints everywhere. Believe it or not, there are traces of perfume on the more recently sent envelopes. What is really interesting though are the postmarks. All the letters were posted from Orange, New South Wales. Unless Hank is very clever, and is trying to throw us off the scent, he probably lived in Orange when he wrote the letters and very likely still lives there today. We may be getting much closer to finding our Hank.'

'I've been to Orange, sir. My grandmother lived there when she was alive and we went to visit her occasionally as part of our holiday trips. It's a very pretty place but bloody cold. It's a good-sized country town with a population of perhaps 30,000. Everybody knows everybody in country towns so I reckon we will easily be able to locate anyone with the name "Hank" that lives there.'

'Righto, that's your next job. Get hold of the electoral roles for the years we are interested in and look for all the Hanks residing in Orange.'

'No problem, sir.'

'There's one more section in this report headed up, "Reason for Threats". Let me have another look. According to forensics, this is inconclusive. Essentially forensics are saying that the blackmailer repeatedly accuses Mr Allsop Senior of a "disgusting or despicable act". It appears to have been one event only, and the blackmailer never says exactly what this act was. The suggestion is that it was sexual in nature and their best guess is that Mr Allsop and Hank had a sexual encounter that was non-consensual as far as Hank was concerned. So this brings us back to the idea that Mr Allsop was gay, or at least bisexual.'

Tania nodded in agreement. This certainly seemed the most likely explanation. 'Is there any way we can check out Mr Allsop's past to find out if he had a history of sexual encounters with men?'

'The obvious place to start would seem to be Orange if we can locate this Hank. Hank may spill the beans when we find him, particularly if he knows we believe he could be a murderer.'

'Do you think we are making good progress, sir?'

'Yes and no. We still have a lot of spadework to do. We are a long way from solving this case.'

The next quarter of an hour was spent exchanging views and discussing the separate interviews they had both conducted the day before. Johansson enjoyed a well-earned reputation in the SA Police for his thoroughness and leaving no stone unturned. One of his ways of ensuring nothing was missed was as simple as making a list which he proceeded to do now with Tania's enthusiastic input. By the time they had finished their second coffees, and were needing to visit the toilets, the list of matters to be followed up looked like this:

- Complete background profile studies of Mr and Mrs Ernstein and David and Christopher Allsop.
- Track down the woman in the red sports car.
- Check the possibility that Mr Charles Allsop was gay and had sexual liaisons with men.

- Focus on Orange as the likely location for "Hank".
- Once Hank is found, spend time discretely working on his background profile BEFORE challenging him.
- Keep Henry Childs on the suspect list and do some more digging.
- Interview Jayne Prescott again and do more digging into her background.

Johansson re-read his list. 'Well Tania, we still have eight people listed. They remain "people of interest" until we can definitely discount them. It's possible someone else could still come up out of the woodwork so let's continue to keep an open mind. I'm going to ask the superintendent to give me a couple of extra staff to start to do some of the background checks.'

'What would you like me to concentrate on, sir?'

'Get on to the electoral rolls for people living in and around Orange and list all the "Hanks". Next, contact the local Orange Police and talk to them about the "Hanks" you have identified. They should be able to shed some light on which ones could be our man. Local police in country towns have their fingers on the pulse and know their residents far better than we could manage here.'

'What about you, sir? Where will you focus your attention?'

'I'm going to do some digging into Charles Allsop's background. Let's meet next on Tuesday morning at the usual time to check progress.'

CHAPTER 13

Hank

Constable Tania Markovina arrived for work a few minutes late on Tuesday morning but still in time for her session with Detective Inspector Mike Johansson. Tony, the boyfriend, had this Tuesday off and seemed to think that that was sufficient reason to delay Tania's departure by being ridiculously amorous. Although she had thoroughly enjoyed the sexual romping they had engaged in, it meant that she only had time for the shortest of showers and had to forego breakfast altogether before dashing out the door. Her stomach complained all the way to work so she had ended up buying a packet of weird-looking sandwiches at the police canteen. She was sure they were leftovers from the day before and when she took a hungry bite out of one of the more respectable looking objects masquerading as a sandwich, this was confirmed.

The weekend had been great fun. She and Tony could see the funny side of anything, which was just as well, since camping always threw up a few unexpected challenges. A night of heavy showers had left them scrambling to stay dry and the next day, whilst bushwalking, Tony had inadvertently sat down on an ants' nest to eat his muesli bar. He leapt up smacking himself all around his nether regions and continued to do so for another half an hour or so as they negotiated a steep incline. The big disappointment for Tania was that no engagement ring was forthcoming, and she had to be patient a bit longer. She wondered what she could do to hasten the proposal that must surely come.

Inspector Mike Johansson had also enjoyed his weekend. His golf was on fire and he had trounced his golfing partner who, after a few holes, had begun to blame his poor form on a sore shoulder. A load of codswallop in Mike's opinion. His friend didn't like losing and that was that. They were enjoying a couple of beers in the clubhouse later when his wife rang to remind him they had friends coming over for dinner and not to be too late. By the time their friends had been generously wined and dined, Mike had consumed rather more alcohol than was wise, resulting in a nasty hangover come Sunday morning. All was well by work time on the Monday morning but Johansson was becoming increasingly aware of his middle-age spread. It seemed to be spreading in all directions at once. He resolved, yet again, that he must do something about it. A fat policeman does not inspire confidence.

Haunted by the need to reduce his creeping middle-age spread, Mike had surprised his wife on Tuesday morning by announcing that he would walk to work. This being a distance of about four kilometres, the detective arrived late for the 9:00am meeting with Tania. He was hot and sweaty and his feet were sore, which resulted in a somewhat grumpy senior policeman fronting up. The perceptive Tania, seeing a stressed Johansson arriving, had a glass of cool water at the ready and a mug of black coffee ordered. Sensibly, she made herself scarce until the detective was ready for action and gave her a call.

Tania had contacted the Australian Electoral Commission's Head Office first thing Monday morning and requested they fax copies of that part of the electoral roll that covered the city of Orange and surrounds and was in use on January 1st, 1954. This was shortly before the first blackmail letter had been sent. She also ordered the same for January 1st, 1975, the year the last letter was mailed. She reasoned that any man with the name Hank appearing in both rolls would need following up.

Half an hour later she was shocked to find over sixty pages of close print ejecting from the fax machine and falling all over the floor. Horrified at the thought of searching for "Hanks" on so many pages, she remembered that there were two Year 10 students in the station on work experience for the week. She grabbed them and set them to work. Unsure whether they were up to the task, she offered to buy them lunch at the canteen if they were halfway through by lunchtime, and lunch again tomorrow if they finished before the end of the day. She was lucky. Both were good students and applied themselves well.

At the end of the day they had found three "Hanks" that

appeared in both the 1954 and 1975 electoral rolls. Tania had stressed to the students that they were engaged in important detective work and that police work was not all action as shown on TV shows, but in reality, often involved countless hours of tedium. By the end of the day the students had certainly got the message. Whether they were now totally repulsed by police work Tania didn't know. She was delighted however, to have three names to investigate further.

Tania was able to contact a detective at the Orange Police Station by the name of Jim Sankey. It transpired that he knew Tania's boss, Mike Johansson, and was more than happy to oblige in undertaking a bit of background research into the three men with the name of Hank residing in or around Orange. Jim wanted to know how Detective Inspector Johansson's golf was progressing these days and Tania was able to tell the detective from Orange that he had dropped his handicap recently. 'Tell your boss to come to Orange sometime. We have two excellent courses here.' The niceties over, Jim Sankey promised to ring later in the day.

The news when it came was a disappointment. Jim reported that he had had little trouble in doing some background checks on the three men. The first was a Hank Arnold Jones who lived at Molong, a village about twenty kilometres from Orange. This Hank was ninety-two years old and had to be looked after at the small Molong Hospital as a dementia patient. He had been admitted about six years ago. There was no possibility that Hank Jones was the man they sought.

Second on the list was a Brendan Hank Sutcliffe. It

seemed most unlikely that he would ever be known by his middle name. In fact, Jim Sankey said he knew him quite well and had even played squash with him a couple of times in the local comp. Brendan was a successful businessman in town, a Rotarian and a strong member of the community. Jim was convinced that this "Hank" was an excellent fellow and would never have engaged in any untoward behaviour.

This left the third and last "Hank". Jim Sankey had found this "Hank" the most difficult to trace. Hank Thomas Williams was an American who had come to Orange to marry an eccentric woman who lived next to a quarry which she believed contained gold deposits left behind by the early miners. Her new husband, Hank Thomas Williams, regarded himself as an expert prospector. The more cynical neighbours viewed Hank Thomas Williams' appearance on the scene as a love of the potential gold find rather than a love of the woman he had married. When no payable gold was unearthed, he moved back to the States and seldom returned to Orange, although he had taken the trouble to be naturalised. Apparently he had died five years ago and nobody had yet reported this to the Australian Electoral Commission. Hence his name still appeared on the electoral roll.

Tania thanked Jim Sankey for his help and contemplated her next move. The three Orange "Hanks" so far identified were clearly not the Hank they were seeking. Perhaps the two girls on work experience had missed one? Even though the girls together had put in over twelve hours studying the lists methodically, it was possible that as they tired, they had become careless. She needed to double-check. Who could she get to do such a joyless task? To do the work properly would need somebody to be paid for two days' work.

A few weeks ago, one of her colleagues had casually mentioned in the staffroom during smoko that the local pathology labs occasionally employed autistic people to take on laborious tasks that nobody else wanted. Apparently some autistic people had an extraordinary gift for completing intensive and detailed analysis work with great accuracy and, amazingly, actually enjoyed the experience. She rang the lab and explained her predicament. They were most helpful. Send the electoral rolls up and they would happily assign the task to one of their autistic employees.

Late the next day the lab rang to say the job was done and could she please come and collect the work. Tania called in and met the shy young man, Fred, who had laboured through the sixty pages of close print. He wouldn't look at her but smiled wanly when she thanked him. The staff assured her that he was verbal but only spoke when something really intrigued him and then he would carry on in an animated way for quite some time until everyone had to try to calm him down. Tania made a mental note to find out more about autism. Perhaps there was a place for an autistic person in the police force to do some of the more onerous tasks?

Fred had even typed up a short report for her. The three "Hanks" that the two girls had found were on Fred's list but to Tania's joy a fourth name now appeared. Number four on the list was a Hank Darcy Henschke. Congratulations

Fred! Within a few minutes Tania had phoned Jim Sankey in Orange and asked him to please investigate one more person.

Jim called back within the hour. This "Hank" looked promising. Hank Darcy Henschke was fifty years old, married and employed in Orange as a bus driver. For over twenty years he had driven school buses and at weekends was a driver/guide taking tourists around some of the vineyards and wineries in the Orange region. The cool climate grapes around Orange were establishing a fine reputation for the quality of their boutique wines and Hank was cashing in on this growing industry.

Jim Sankey wanted to know whether he should dig any deeper and if so, what was he supposed to be looking out for? Without going into great detail, Tania gave a brief outline of the blackmailing of Charles Allsop by a "Hank" from Orange over a period of twenty years. The suspicion was that this "Hank" had been sexually molested by Allsop back in 1954 or earlier. Jim Sankey was asked to explore this possibility and, in addition, whether at any stage, Hank had worked for Allsop Transport. Perhaps this was "Hank" the blackmailer, they were after? Tania went to lunch in a hopeful mood.

Late in the afternoon the anticipated call came. Jim Sankey had spent several hours discreetly researching Hank Henschke's past, much to the increasing annoyance of his boss, who had other ideas about how Jim should be spending his time. Jim's work had been made easier by a fortuitous connection with Hank's former wife during the fifties and early sixties. She was able to categorically deny Hank Henschke had ever worked for a company called Allsop's Transport. During their married life they had been in a joint fruiterer business and she had handled the financials. She had never even heard of this transport company and was one hundred percent certain that they had never had any dealings with Allsop's or any subsidiary company. She had never even heard of a Charles Allsop.

When Jim Sankey inquired as to Hank Henschke's sexual preferences she had laughed outright. She went on to explain that when you are trying to run a fruit and veg business in a small city like Orange, in competition with the big boys like Coles and Woolworths, it is a never-ending commitment. 'You would have no idea how hard we worked. It was ten to twelve hours a day twenty-four/seven. Although we were young newlyweds, we were so exhausted by night-time that we hardly ever managed to have a sex life ourselves. How you think poor old Hank ever managed to find the time and energy to have affairs outside of our marriage beats me. We separated mid-1960s, sold our business for a pittance, and went in different directions. As for Hank having any inclination towards a gay life, I can't think of anyone less likely. He loathed gays.'

Jim had summed up the situation well. Tania thanked him yet again and hoped she could one day do some research for him in Adelaide as pay back.

Tania was flummoxed. She had conscientiously and comprehensively followed up on all her "Hank" leads but the trail had gone cold. Regrettably, she must report no progress at her next meeting with Johansson. She racked her brains to think what else she could do. It was then she recalled one of her lecturers at the Police Academy telling the class that it was common to come to a dead end. Often the trail would go cold. A seemingly good line of investigation would just wither and die and there would appear to be no way forward. This, the lecturer had enthused, is when the truly talented police come to the fore. If they could think "outside the square", think laterally, be creative, try to get into the mind of the criminal, then they might have a breakthrough. Tania was at a dead end now. Hank, the blackmailer from Orange, appeared not to exist. She desperately needed a breakthrough if she was to impress Chief Inspector Johansson.

CHAPTER 14

Exploring Allsop's Past

The more he thought about it, the more Detective Inspector Johansson convinced himself that he had taken on the more difficult mission. Young Tania was to hunt for the missing Hank in Orange, but he had to pry into the private life of a successful businessman who had departed this world over three years ago. Where to start? Should he go back and trouble Mr and Mrs Ernstein yet again and see what he could rake up? He decided against this option on the basis that fathers are most unlikely to impart any dark secrets about their private lives – if in fact there were any secrets – to their daughters or sons. As parents we all wish to preserve a worthy and morally upstanding example for our offspring and, if necessary, will go to great lengths to cover up any serious misdemeanours. Family secrets must stay as such. There are no skeletons rattling around in our cupboards! What Johansson decided he needed was someone outside the family who knew Allsop over many years.

Mike Johansson's ruminations wandered back to the time

in January 1975 when he had been called out by Joanne Ernstein to enter the apartment at The Everglades Retirement
Village to see if Charles Allsop was there. She was frantically
worried that her father had disappeared, or that something
was seriously amiss. Mrs Ernstein's fears were, of course,
realised. Charles Allsop had been murdered.

The detective was doodling on his notepad and started
to scribble down the names of those who had been present
when he had investigated Allsop's supposed disappearance.
There was Joanne Ernstein, the daughter, and a young and
inept retirement village manager whose name escaped him.
Then there was Dr Peters who had falsified the papers. Mike
Johansson had three people on his notepad but had an uneasy
feeling that there was someone else there on that day. Was he
just imagining it? After all, this did happen quite some time
back. Mike's synapses were working overtime. Somebody else
was there on that day. But who was it?

Johansson was deliberating whether to consume the second Tim Tam that sat temptingly on his plate in front of him,
or whether to be strong-willed and stay on his self-imposed
diet when it came to him. There was another person there in
the village that day. It was that cranky old bloke with a limp
and a walking stick who had abused Allsop until he had quietened the old fellow down by telling him that Charles Allsop
had died. He remembered now. The old man had given him
his name and said that he and Allsop went back forty years
or so. Five minutes later the detective had pulled out a folder
marked January 1975 and found the notes he had taken on

that eventful day. There it was; the old guy's name was Henry Childs and he had definitely told him he had known Allsop for forty-odd years. Childs resided, his notes told him, in apartment 82.

It was a promising start. If the old man was still in the retirement village and had his wits about him, he might be a help. The danger was that if Childs did really loathe Charles Allsop, as he had professed in their brief previous encounter, anything Childs might say could be grossly exaggerated or even concocted. As an experienced policeman, Johansson would have to try to sort the truth from the hyperbole.

Henry Childs was not listed in the telephone book. Perhaps he had died? A phone call to the manager at the Glades provided the welcome news that Henry Childs was very much alive but now in a nursing home. Apparently, Henry had not lost his mental capacities at all, and despite being in his eighties, had earned the nickname Casanova at his new residence. Confined to a wheelchair with rheumatoid arthritis, the manager had heard that Mr Henry Childs was the life and soul of the place.

Johansson needed to see Childs so took the liberty of sussing out the nursing home. Johansson was thankful that he had air-conditioning in his car. Afternoons in Adelaide during summer were hot. Today the mercury had sizzled up to thirty-nine degrees and forty-one was predicted for tomorrow. Trees and gardens drooped under the relentless sunshine and the few people out in the open hugged the shade or moved about under umbrellas. The nursing home was a fine old mansion along Fullarton Road surrounded by magnificent shade trees well over a hundred years old. Amazingly there was a parking spot under the ancient branches of an English oak. The detective did not relish a visit to a nursing home. He usually found them depressing, with limp bodies lying about the place waiting to die.

Johansson pushed his way through the revolving door entrance and found himself in a pleasant and cool hall, tastefully furnished with art works covering the walls. A spectacular vase sat on a plinth in the centre of the hall displaying some sort of floral work. To one side was a window with the word "Reception". Johansson moved over to find a young woman smiling up at him. 'May I help you?'

'I'm Detective Inspector Mike Johansson. If it's possible, I would like to spend half an hour or so with one of your patients, Henry Childs, please?'

'I don't think that will be a problem. Does he know you?'

'No, not really. I did meet him very briefly about three years ago. That's all.'

'I'll ring the ward clerk to see where Henry is.'

This done, she flashed another smile and instructed him to sign the Visitors Book before taking the passage to the right and going down to the large Day Room at the end of the corridor. Henry was there watching the cricket on TV.

It was a long passage broken up by the doors into the private rooms on either side. The detective couldn't resist having a peek into the rooms where the door was left open as he went. His father was almost eighty now and may end up in a nursing home one day. Some of the beds were occupied, some of the patients were sitting in their own chairs in their rooms and other rooms appeared to be vacant with the beds neatly made. He noted the rooms were all airy and looked out onto the garden. There was a faint aroma of some sort of disinfectant, necessary no doubt, when some of the patients were incontinent.

The ward clerk was waiting for him when he reached the door to the Day Room. 'Good afternoon Inspector, my name is Adrian. I understand you are coming to see Henry Childs?'

'Correct.'

'Would you mind making sure that this door always remains shut and locked please? We have some wandering dementia patients. There are a couple of patients in the Day Room at the moment who will call out to you when they see you. Just smile and move on. Don't stop to chat because they will never let you go. Henry is the one in the wheelchair wearing an Aussie cricketer's cap and watching the test match. He loves his cricket. He's quite a character with some very strong opinions. When you are leaving please let me know. Any questions?'

'Any chance of a tea or coffee?'

'Yes of course. The patients are not allowed to make tea or coffee in case they burn themselves or burn the kettle dry, so you will need to ask the nurse over there in the small annex to make it for you. She will bring it over for you and even provide a biscuit or two if you chat her up nicely.'

The Inspector thanked the ward clerk and entered the Day Room. It was a huge room with a high ceiling, possibly the ballroom originally. Easy chairs were scattered all over the place. Many were occupied by grey or snowy white heads. There didn't seem to be much activity, most patients apparently happy to just sit and doze slumped in their seats like sacks of potatoes. A couple of the ladies were more upright and knitting while two others were having a natter in the corner. The TV was tuned to the cricket and turned up high. Perhaps Henry was deaf? It was easy to spot him with his cap on, next to a couple of other "cricket tragics".

'Henry Childs?'

'Yup, who are you?'

'I'm Detective Inspector Mike Johansson and I've come to ask you for your help.'

'Jeez, what does the strong arm of the law want with a bloke like me?'

'Well you can start by telling me the score.'

'Ahh, the bloody Poms are getting thrashed. They've no answer to Lillie, Thommo and Max Walker. We're going to be bloody three-nil up very soon now and the Ashes are ours.'

'I'm wondering if you would like a cup of tea or coffee while I ask you a few questions?'

'Bloody good idea. Go and ask that sheila over there to get us a cuppa. They treat us like bloody cripples here, can't even make a tea or coffee. Strong black for me with three sugars and none of that bloody white stuff.'

Johansson felt like an errand boy being ordered to go off and organise smoko. He dutifully returned with the victuals and a plate with an array of biscuits.

'You bloody beauty,' exclaimed Henry on sighting the Arnotts biscuits. He grabbed three and stared up at the policeman with a questioning look. 'Don't often get the pleasure of a bloody policeman coming to see me,' Henry remarked as he dunked his first biscuit.

'And I don't get to come to many nursing homes often either.'

Henry stole a look at his two test cricket colleagues and propelled his wheelchair away into a quiet corner of the room where conversation would be easier. They exchanged niceties for a few more moments before the detective brought up the topic he wished to pursue.

'I believe you knew Charles Allsop?'

'Allsop! Don't tell me you've come here to talk about that stupid bugger?'

Johansson ignored the angry response and pressed on. 'How long did you know him?'

'All me bloody working life. Couldn't help it. We were in the same business, bloody transport and long-distance haulage. He had his company and I had mine.'

'So you were in competition?'

'Too right we bloody were. I always played fair but he was a real mean bastard. Time and time again he would go out of his way to stuff up half my initiatives. Couldn't stand the bugger.'

'So how come you both ended up at The Everglades Retirement Village?'

'I went there deliberately to make his life hell. I wanted to get my own back. He'd gone out of his way to mess me around so when I pulled up sticks, I thought, okay, I'll stuff your retirement up now.'

'And did you?'

'I did for a time but then I got bloody tired of it and he went and married that bitch. Him being married and all that, I thought I'd better lay off the abuse. So, I stopped.'

'Are you aware of how Mr Allsop died?'

'Heart attack, they said.'

'It may surprise you to hear that he was murdered.'

'What! Bloody murdered! I don't believe you. Mind you, there would be a few around who would be quite happy to do that to him. He made a few enemies. I'm not the only one.'

'Do you remember meeting me the day that Mr Allsop died?'

'Ahh, is that where I bloody saw you before? I thought I recognised your face.'

'Let me remind you of the occasion. You came stomping down the street and gave me an earful of what you thought of Mr Allsop. Would it be fair to say that you were still very angry with Mr Allsop?'

'Well yes, I suppose so. You would be too. I'm still angry about what he did to undermine my business even though he's gone.'

'Did you murder Mr Allsop?'

'Good God, no. I hated his guts, but I've got bloody principles you know. Murdering people is not one of 'em.'

'I want to ask you a few questions about Mr Allsop's personal life. He was married to his first wife for many years until she died of cancer. Was Mr Allsop a faithful husband, do you think?'

'Not always, no.'

'That's a strong call to make. How do you know he was not always faithful?'

'Now you're starting to get on bloody dangerous ground Officer. If I tell you what I know are you going to make trouble for me? I don't want to get bloody arrested because I reveal something to you.'

'The only thing I would arrest you for is if you murdered Mr Allsop or assisted in his demise in some way. I will give you a promise here and now that anything else you tell me will be kept strictly confidential. All I'm trying to do is build up a picture of how Mr Allsop behaved in his personal life because this may help us to find his killer. So, what can you tell me?'

'When we were both getting our respective bloody businesses started, we actually got along well. For quite some years we would meet up in one of the capitals as we set up our bloody branches. Believe it or not we cooperated for the first twenty years or so. Allsop was okay back in those days. At one point we even contemplated a bloody merger; Allsop-Childs or Childs-Allsop.'

'Go on,' urged Johansson.

'Well, I'm a single man, always have been, always will be, but that doesn't mean I don't like a bit of female company. When Charles and I used to meet up in the old days, we would usually have a meal and knock over a bottle of red. Afterwards we would go down to a bloody nightclub somewhere and have a couple more drinks. We were young, successful and bloody rolling in dough. Finding nice lasses to come and join us for a few drinks was easy. To cap the night off, I would visit a brothel. At first Charles refused to come with me, but after a couple of years he changed his mind. From then on he never missed out.'

'So, he was cheating on his wife on a regular basis?'

'Too bloody right he was.'

'My next question will surprise you, but I want you to think about it carefully before you answer.'

'Fire away, copper.'

'You have told me that Mr Allsop availed himself of female company at brothels regularly. Did he at any time show any inclination towards having sexual relations with men?'

'Good God, no. He couldn't stand bloody poofters. Once in Sydney we walked into a bloody gay bar by mistake and he was out of there like the bloody clappers. He told me once that if he knew a bloke was queer, he wouldn't bloody employ them. I had no time for Charles the last twenty-five years or so but one thing I can't accuse him of is being a poofter.'

'What made you and Mr Allsop fall out so spectacularly?'

'A couple of bloody things. For some reason he started to get protective towards his transport business. It didn't bloody worry me to begin with, but then he began trying to freeze me out and stop my business growing. There was room for us both to keep expanding but he didn't bloody agree. He wanted to be king pin in Australia and he was worried that I might become the biggest and best in the bloody country.

So he started doing things to undermine my company. It was subtle at first, but it became more and more bloody blatant. I confronted him, we had a massive bloody argument, then we just went our own ways and avoided each other from thereon.'

'Do you remember when you had this falling out?'

'Yes, it was mid-1954. I remember it well because it was the same day it was announced that Melbourne had won the right to hold the Olympics in 1956. There were huge celebrations everywhere.'

'You said there were a couple of things that made you fall out. What was the other one?'

'I'd rather not talk about it, copper.'

'Why?'

'It's personal, it's bloody family business, private.'

'It may be helpful for our inquiries. Please think again. What you have told me so far has been of great assistance. Remember I have promised to keep everything confidential.'

'This is a private family matter and I want it to bloody stay so. I shouldn't have bloody said there were two things in the first place.'

Henry Childs was becoming angry. His face reddened and he pointed his finger aggressively towards the detective. 'Do you understand? I don't want any dirty bloody washing coming out.'

Hearing Henry's furious voice, the ward clerk came hurrying over. 'Please gentlemen, calm down. You are disturbing our other patients and getting stressed is not good for Mr Childs' blood pressure.'

'Bugger my blood pressure,' Henry replied, and slumped back into his wheelchair. He said nothing more and just glared at Johansson.

Realising that the interview was over, the detective extended his hand and apologised, both actions he rarely ever granted to anybody. Henry Childs had been a big help and he did not want to aggravate him further just in case he needed to return at a later date for more information.

Driving back to the station, Mike Johansson replayed the conversation in his mind. So there was a darker side to the life of Charles Allsop after all. Now he felt he understood why Henry Childs had fallen out with Allsop but he would also love to know what the "family" problem was that Henry was so reluctant to divulge. Did it have any bearing on this murder case? He felt this was unfinished business. It was a nut that had to be cracked.

Johansson was still no closer to discovering who the mysterious blackmailer Hank was. He had hypothesised that Hank may have been in some kind of gay relationship with Allsop that had gone seriously wrong, but Henry Child's testimony did not support this theory.

Perhaps he needed to pursue other lines of inquiry.

David Allsop

Back in his office, the detective checked his list of matters to follow up that he had written down on his notepad following his visit to the Ernstein's. Top of the list was undertaking a life profile of the two Allsop boys, David and Christopher. He was not yet prepared to completely eliminate the two men from any involvement. He had only met them briefly a few days ago when he had summoned them to meet with him at the Ernstein's home in Hallett Cove. Did they have much contact with Mr Allsop Senior after they had left home? How well did they know their dad? Did they know about his unfaithfulness? Could they shed any light on Hank? Further digging was necessary and the best way to do this was face to face with the brothers one at a time.

Two days later Mike Johansson's plane touched down at Sydney Airport and he made his way by train to Central Station. He enjoyed the short walk from there to the University of Sydney. The university's prestigious sandstone building, with its eroding gargoyles, always intrigued him. Modelled on the campuses of Oxford and Cambridge; the entrance stood proudly and resplendent surrounded by green lawns. Sadly, his appointment with Dr David Allsop was not in this original building but elsewhere on campus. Using the campus map, the detective eventually found the Faculty of Geology.

Johansson was surprised at the sheer size of the building that housed the Faculty of Geology. Along one side of the entrance foyer were a series of glass frames containing the names and photographs of the academic staff in the faculty together with their floor and office numbers. With around seventy staff, it took him a couple of minutes to locate the name of the doctor he was after. Five minutes later, after traipsing past several smelly laboratories, he arrived at 5L46 the office of Dr David Allsop (Micropalaeontologist). A time-table was appended to the door showing the times during the week when Dr Allsop was lecturing, tutoring, attending meetings and away undertaking research.

Checking his watch, the detective noted he was only a few minutes late, and knocked confidently on the door. 'Come in' was the call, and he entered to find the doctor peering down a microscope with three students looking on. 'Yes, you are correct, these are definitely Cambrian brachiopods. Now, I'll have to ask you to leave as I have a visitor.' The students grabbed their slides, thanked the doctor, and promptly left.

'Good afternoon, Inspector.' Dr David Allsop gave him a hearty handshake, moved a couple of books off a chair and invited him to be seated. Johansson surveyed his interviewee carefully. Early forties, with a mop of hair and a somewhat unkempt black beard and a face that smacked of many hours outdoors on field work without adequate sun protection. He certainly looked the part, scruffily dressed and wearing thick-framed glasses.

The room was typical of any academic's office. Rows of books and folders were arranged along the shelves and stacks of papers sat on the floor in one corner of the room, while a seriously neglected cactus of some description filled another. A large desk occupied much of the office behind which sat the expectant doctor on an executive swivel chair. Next to the microscope sat a photograph that the detective presumed was David's immediate family. The walls were adorned with framed copies of David's degrees and a large stratigraphic map of the Sydney Basin. Daylight streamed in through the only large bay window.

'Thank you Doctor, for sparing me some of your time.'

'Not a problem, Inspector, I have put aside half an hour. I hope that will be sufficient?'

'I didn't have an opportunity to follow up with you when we briefly met at your sister's place in Hallett Cove. I guess the news that your father was murdered came as a shock?'

'You can say that again, Inspector. The family was pretty pissed off about the inheritance money going to Jayne Prescott when dad died, and then to hear that he didn't die from natural causes was another twist of the knife.'

'I have to ask you a number of rather sensitive and personal questions about you and your family as part of our ongoing inquiries. I'd appreciate it if you could be totally honest with me.'

The doctor nodded and kept his eyes on the detective's, inviting him to 'fire away.'

'Let me start with your father. How well did you get on with him?'

'Reasonably, I guess.'

'Only reasonably?'

'Yep. Dad was a clever businessman and built up a nation-wide transport enterprise. As his eldest son he always wanted me to follow him and become the next owner/manager of Allsops Transport. He was not pleased when I chose not to join the company and instead to pursue a career in the Earth Sciences. I think he never really forgave me for that decision when I was still only seventeen years old. He felt I was ungrateful and had let him down. I can understand how he felt. He had worked his guts out all his life and wanted one of the family to take on his legacy. He saw it as a family business.'

'Your experience is one shared by many other people. What about the other members of your family? Did any of them work in the family business?'

'Well, yes and no. My older sister, Joanne Ernstein, joined the company from a young age as a secretary and for a time was even dad's personal secretary but she gave it all away when she had kids. Her husband, John Ernstein, is an accountant and he still works for the company, but he never had the drive to work his way to the top of the tree. Then there's my younger brother, Christopher, who also worked in the company for a time but he fell afoul of the law and has since moved on. The company still trades today as Allsop Transport but it certainly is not run by any Allsops since Dad died.'

So, Johansson concluded, *there was nobody in the immediate family who would have been motivated to knock off Mr Allsop Senior in order to take over the company. But what about others outside the family?*

His next question to David Allsop covered this possibility but it was promptly dismissed as definitely not the case.

'How well did you get along with your father after he had accepted that you were set to be a geologist?'

'It took the old man a bit of a time to get used to what he saw as my rebellious behaviour. He refused to come to my graduation as a geologist. He did attend however, when I was awarded my Ph.D. I think he was proud of me by then. He came to my wedding, a bit grudgingly, I think. Mum made bloody sure he came. Once I had my Ph.D., and had presented him with a couple of grandchildren, he became far more amenable. We would join Mum and Dad at Christmas every second year. We were never close but enjoyed each other's company a bit more as he aged and mellowed.'

'What about the others, Joanne, John and Christopher. How well did they get along with your father?'

'My sister and John were always on friendly terms with dad. Much closer to Dad than I ever was. When Dad cut them out of their inheritance, it was a huge smack in the face for them though. They took it hard and were very angry.'

'Sorry to ask you this, but do you think they were angry enough to consider murder as a means of revenge?'

'They may have felt like it, but I'm sure they wouldn't do anything as drastic. If anyone was likely to get murdered, you'd think it would be that woman Dad married who got everything when he died.'

'What happens to the inheritance once Jayne Prescott dies?'

'Apparently Jayne has no issue. Dad decreed that when Jayne dies anything that remains is to be split three ways equally between us three children. So, we will inherit eventually after all, as long as Jayne Prescott doesn't fritter it all away.'

'Interesting. Now what about your brother, Christopher? Did he get along okay with your dad?'

'My bro, Christopher, is the problem child in our family. My sister and I have always been dependable, reliable and somewhat conservative, some would say plain boring. Christopher, on the other hand, has always been unstable, highly volatile, erratic and troubled. He is the opposite to us.'

'Can you expand on that a bit please, Doctor?'

'Well, it is just as I said. He is totally unpredictable. You never know what he is going to do or say in response to a situation.'

'Can you give me some examples?'

'There are so many. He was twice expelled from school, fooled about with drugs and alcohol so that he never qualified to go to Uni, despite being potentially the cleverest of the lot of us. He is only about forty-three now but has been married and divorced twice. He claims to be passionately in love with every woman he meets. The old man had a soft spot for him though, and kept giving him jobs in the company in the hope that he would become more responsible, but he would always blow it. He's smashed up a couple of cars and has been on the wrong side of the law on a few occasions.'

'Do you know what the offences were?'

'All the usual stuff; drink driving, minor drug offences, drunk and disorderly. He's been locked up for a few nights but has miraculously avoided a full prison sentence to date. You never know where he is or what he's doing.'

'Has he ever been in trouble for domestic violence, GBH or aggressive behaviour?'

'I'm not too sure about that. I don't mix with him unless I have to at some family function.'

'How did he get on with your dad?'

'Well, up and down as you might expect. In the distant past, they were as thick as two thieves, but in the last twenty years or so, up until dad died, the relationship was quite cool. I reckon something bad happened between them about twenty years ago. I never talked to Christopher about what occurred in any detail, but it must have been significant.'

'Can you hazard a guess as to what that might have been, Doctor?'

David Allsop smiled. 'I'm a scientist, I deal in facts not supposition.'

'But you must have some theories, Doctor, surely? Scientific methodology begins with a theory, does it not?'

'True. All I know is that my dad and Christopher used to meet up sometimes here in Sydney for a weekend. They went out nightclubbing. Perhaps they had a falling out back then.'

'Can you be a bit more specific about the time they had this falling out, doctor?'

'Yes, I can. Dad had a flat or an apartment in Glebe somewhere and Christopher and Dad would always bunk down there after they had been out nightclubbing. Christopher rarely ever visited me and my family. But there was a time in July 1954 when he unexpectedly turned up here and crashed. He had never asked to sleep here before. I remember it was early July 1954 because my wife, Eleanor, was due to have our first baby. It was hardly a convenient time for my drunk brother to suddenly front up here. We had Eleanor's bags packed and were ready to fly out the door as soon as her contractions started. Anyway, when I confronted him the next day, once he had sobered up a bit, he was clearly outraged about something Dad had done. I was too worried about Eleanor to pester Christopher about what the problem had been so I just let it drop. I often wondered what had happened that weekend though. I have never seen Christopher so irate. He was calling dad 'a bloody criminal' and a 'sex maniac' and plenty of other less than complimentary terms.'

Bingo! July 1954 was the month that the first blackmail letter had been sent to Charles Allsop. Mike Johansson always felt a quickening of his pulse when two pieces of a puzzle suddenly fell into place. Clearly he was on to something. The first blackmail letter was dated July 19th, 1954. Only a few days earlier there had been a massive falling out between Christopher and his dad. It had to be all connected.

Did this mean that Christopher was the blackmailer and possibly the murderer too? Did Christopher adopt the name Hank as a cover? Perhaps there was no Hank at all? If so, this would explain why Tania had been unable to unearth a person by the name of Hank sending the eight letters from Orange. Johansson decided to try and squeeze a few more details out of the good doctor.

'I'd like you to continue to focus on that eventful weekend in July 1954 when Christopher came to your house. Do you remember your brother making any threats towards your father? Did he talk about what he would do as a result of your dad's behaviour?'

'It was over twenty years ago now, I reckon I've done well to remember anything useful. As I said, I was more worried about my wife's imminent confinement than Christopher's ravings. To be honest, I just wanted my brother out of the house and gone. He did leave after a bit of lunch much to my relief.'

'So, you can't recall any direct or indirect threats against your father?'

'No.'

'Let me change my line of questioning: Christopher called your dad "a sex maniac". Was that fair comment?'

'Well, I think we all suspected that he was doing more than just visiting nightclubs when in town. Dad seemed to have irrepressible energy. He worked hard and played hard.

I don't remember anything untoward happening when I lived at home during my childhood. Mum and Dad got along well enough. Dad was often away building up his business. It was not until I went to Uni that I began to wonder whether he was playing up sometimes when away from home. I never had any proof of this though.'

'Which Uni did you go to?'

'Adelaide.'

'Did you live at home?'

'No. Dad was so angry with me for choosing geology over the family business that I moved into digs with friends at the Uni. This saved all his snide comments when he was home.'

'One last question. Do you think your dad was a homosexual or perhaps bisexual?'

'I doubt it very much. He always gave the impression that he had no time for gays or "poofters" as he called them. He certainly had an eye for the women though. He used to embarrass Mum sometimes by making remarks about "sheilas" and carrying on about some gorgeous woman he had met. I remember once when I was at high school Dad sent me to his office to get a pen off his desk. I couldn't find it, so I looked in his drawers and there I found a couple of copies of Playboy.'

'Doctor, you have been a great help. Thank you for your time. Here's my card if you think of anything else. I want to warn you not to speak to your brother, or indeed any other members of your family, until this unfortunate case is over. Do I make myself clear?'

'You certainly do Inspector. Have a pleasant trip home.'

'Oh, one last thing. Do you have an address for Christopher?'

That afternoon, Detective Inspector Mike Johansson flew back to Adelaide where he was met at the airport by his assistant, Tania Markovina. They had plenty to discuss.

Christopher Allsop

The journey from the airport to the police station was the ideal opportunity for a debrief. There was little Tania could add to the exchange since she had already informed her boss that she had not uncovered any likely "Hanks" in Orange. The Inspector, on the other hand, offloaded the valuable conversation he had had with Dr David Allsop in its entirety.

As they drove into their parking lot at the station, Tania summed up the situation, 'There is no Hank. We suspect that "Hank" is actually a woman who blackmailed Mr Allsop for twenty years following some kind of a sexual encounter that went badly wrong in July 1954. Christopher Allsop is the person most likely to have the answers we are seeking.'

'Correct.'

'So, sir, do we go to interview Christopher Allsop tomorrow?'

'No, not yet. Christopher has had a couple of run-ins with the police over the years. I want to check these out and find out what background profile we can build up of Christopher from past police interviews. Once we have a better understanding of who we are dealing with, then we both go and pay a visit to Christopher. This will be a key meeting with a major suspect, so I want you to be present as well.'

'My pleasure, sir.'

'First thing in the morning, start gathering all the info you can about our friend Christopher. Start with the police reports, then move on to any other sources. Anything that can shed more light on the man. Check out his employment profile, details about his marriages, divorces, girlfriends, any special interests. I want to feel as though we know this man well when we go to visit. Take two days to gather the data if necessary. Let me know when you have everything together.'

'Okay, sir, just as well I enjoy research work.'

¶

Tania spent all Wednesday and Thursday on her allotted task including staying back after hours on Thursday night, much to Tony's annoyance, as it was late night shopping. Come Friday morning she had a dossier ready to present to Johansson. With a coffee in hand and a Tim Tam sitting invitingly in front of her, she outlined her main findings.

~ ~ ~

Christopher Frederic Allsop
Born: August 17th, 1933.
Age: 43

Schooling: Reports show a highly intelligent boy who failed to realise his potential. Expelled from two private high schools initially for smoking and insubordinate behaviour and secondly for the attempted rape of a local girl.

Psychological assessment: Christopher has a history of uncontrolled behaviour patterns leading to disruptive incidences throughout his education. Frequently displayed aggressive tendencies and was disrespectful towards teaching staff. Borderline delinquent.

Home background: Appears to have been a normal and happy environment. Father was a highly successful businessman who was away a lot. Mother was quiet but loving and caring. Two older siblings have done well. Christopher's poor behaviour was a constant concern to his parents who may have spoilt him. Family wanted for nothing materially.

Employment: Christopher left school at fifteen and in 1948 was enrolled at a technical college to study automotive engineering as an apprentice. At the end of the first year he did not sit his tests and dropped out of the course. Re-enrolled at the same college in 1949 to study plumbing. Left both his home and the college midyear. Nobody knows what he did or where he went for the next eighteen months. Early 1951 he showed up again working in a South Australian Government run scheme for the unemployed. Later in 1951 his father gave him a job in his company as a storeman in Adelaide. This lasted for about twelve months. From late 1952 until 1955 Christopher worked as a storeman in his father's Sydney branch. He left suddenly, and without giving notice, in July 1955 and has had a succession of jobs as a storeman mostly in Sydney but also in Melbourne and Adelaide over the next twenty years. For a few months he joined a colleague who owned an antiques business as a part-time worker on weekends only. Currently employed as a senior storeman at Mark Foy's main warehouse in Adelaide. Appears to have been receiving wages for most of the last twenty years indicating he has become far more stable.

Criminal record:
September 19th, 1948 (aged fifteen). Arrested by SA Police for driving without a licence when inebriated. Got off with a strict warning not to offend again and a fine of 200 pounds.

July 7th, 1949 (aged sixteen). Arrested by SA Police for being drunk and disorderly. Fined 300 pounds. Warned that next time he will go to prison.

May 25, 1951 (aged eighteen). Appeared in court on a charge of GBH. Complaint made by his first wife. This event led to divorce and the judge placed Christopher on a good behaviour bond for twelve months.

July 24th, 1955 (aged twenty-two). Arrested by NSW Police for being drunk and disorderly. Got off with a warning and a fine of 300 pounds.

Marriages:
Married Elizabeth Dutton on 13th September, 1950 (aged eighteen). She divorced him mid-1951.

Then married Rochelle Joan Brooks on January 19th, 1953 (aged twenty). They divorced August 1955.

As far as could be ascertained, Christopher had not fathered any children with his wives.

Special interests: Car racing, antiques, pubbing, gambling and nightclubs.

Health: Difficult to assess. Has suffered depression at times and been admitted to hospital twice as a result of car accidents.

Tania Markovina

~ ~ ~

Johansson studied his copy of the dossier intently making ambiguous grunts and mmm sounds as he went. 'Very interesting,' he opined and started reading the dossier a second time, this time without the sound effects. Finally, he looked up and said, 'Bloody good job, Tania.'

Tania flashed one of her dazzling smiles, 'Thank you sir.'

'We need to meet up with Christopher Allsop ASAP. I think the element of surprise would be to our benefit. When we are finished here, ring the manager at Mark Foy's and ask him to provide a private room on the premises for us to interview Mr Allsop at 10:00 am tomorrow morning. Any problems get back to me. In the meantime, what jumps out at you from all this data you have gathered?'

'A couple of things, sir. Clearly Christopher has had a rocky life so far, but there are definite signs that he has matured somewhat with age. He seems to be holding down a job okay now. Something serious happened in his life mid-1955. Around about then he suddenly quit his job working at his father's company in Sydney without giving notice, got into trouble with the law, and divorced. That's a triple whammy! We can pinpoint these events as happening in early July.'

'Good observation. July 1955 was also pinpointed by David Allsop as being the time when Christopher and his dad fell out. And...' the detective paused for effect, 'July 19th was the date of the first blackmail letter sent to Charles Allsop. It all adds up. Somehow, we must find out what happened that July because it seems to have been the trigger for the blackmailing which eventually culminated in murder. Crack this, and I think we will find our blackmailer and murderer.'

9

Worried that Christopher Allsop would leave his workplace in a panic if he knew two police were coming to interview him, Tania executed a little plan with the cooperation of the manager of Mark Foy's. The arrangement was that the manager would call Christopher to his office at 10 am, ostensibly to conduct a review of his work schedule. Detective Inspector

Mike Johansson and Tania would be waiting in the board-room next door and enter once Christopher was seated. The three of them would then retire to the boardroom leaving the manager to his own business. The tape recorder, a necessity for all formal interviews, would already be set up at the end of the long wooden table that graced the boardroom. The manager had even ordered tea and coffee to be available for them.

Arriving quietly, as plain-clothed police, half an hour before the allotted time of the interview, they took the opportunity to briefly question the manager about Christopher Allsop. The manager provided a useful oral report. Christopher had been with the company for about three years now and was employed as a senior storeman in recognition of his experience elsewhere. Generally reliable, although his attendance record indicated a few too many days off sick, he seemed to get along well enough with his workmates although he had "off days" when he was surly. There had been one incident, about three months ago, when he had lost his temper and tried to physically attack a co-worker. The other store-men had quickly intervened and stopped what might have developed into a major fracas. Both men were reprimanded, and no punitive action was taken. The two police thanked the manager and retired to the boardroom to set up and wait.

The plan worked to perfection and shortly after 10 am, a guarded and rather worried Christopher Allsop, was ushered into the boardroom to be confronted by Johansson, whom he had met before at the Einstein's, and the attractive Tania who was someone he had not met before. The manager silently locked the door behind Christopher who quickly resorted to verbal punching.

'So, what's this then? You've set a bloody trap to get me in here. I ain't done nothing wrong. Getting me in here like this isn't right.'

'I'd watch your language if I was you. This is a formal police interview. Sit in this chair and I'll explain why you are here.' As he spoke, Johansson glared menacingly at the younger man who must have noticed that the detective was considerably larger than he was and had a dominating, commanding presence. He glanced briefly at Tania instead who was far more pleasing to the eye.

'Mr Allsop, we are recording this interview, so may I remind you that what you say may be used in evidence at a later date.' Christopher sat awkwardly on the large executive chair he had been assigned. He had never before been in this stately room with its smell of leather upholstery surrounded by darkly panelled walls. He placed his hands on the edge of the shiny, mahogany table that stretched down the centre of the room and felt dwarfed by his surroundings. The detective continued.

'A few days ago, I went to Sydney to interview your brother, David, at his university. As you know, we are investigating two extremely serious crimes; the murder of your father and the blackmailing of your father over a period of around twenty years. Your brother was most cooperative. I trust you will be also?' Christopher fidgeted in his over-sized chair with his eyes averted and offered no comment.

'We have uncovered some interesting facts going all the

way back to your school days. You seem to have had some troubled times?' Still no comment. Christopher began to fiddle with his top shirt button and was clearly uncomfortable.

'So, we already know a lot about you.' Johansson waved the folder containing Christopher's dossier in the air to add emphasis.

'Let's start by talking about your relationship with your father. You and he used to enjoy each other's company when you worked in Sydney as a storeman in Allsop Transport in the early 1950s. Tell me about that time.'

Christopher sniffed and looked even more worried. 'Dad used to come to Sydney for his business and sometimes we would get together at weekends. I was working in the company.'

'And what did you and your dad do when you got together at weekends?'

'We went out sometimes. Sometimes we just stayed at dad's apartment.'

'Come on Mr Allsop, we already know a lot about what you two did. Now open up and get talking.' Johansson leant across the table and eyeballed the suspect.

'Sometimes we went out for a drink at the local or visited a nightclub.'

'It must have been quite a time for you. Did Dad pay all your expenses? Did he buy the drinks?'

'Yep.'

'And what else did Dad pay for, Mr Allsop?'

'Meals, a bit of gambling here and there.'

'Mr Allsop, are you aware that your father was often unfaithful to his wife?'

'Yep.'

'How do you know that, Mr Allsop?'

'Sometimes he brought a woman back to his apartment or he went to a brothel.'

'But how do you know that, Mr Allsop? Did you go with him to the brothels? Did you join in with the goings-on at your dad's apartment?'

'Yep.'

'If it was alright for your dad to play up, it was okay for you I suppose, even though you were a married man?'

'Yep.'

'Okay, so we have established that for a few years you and your dad enjoyed yourselves with prostitutes.'

'That's not against the law. Dad always paid the sheilas well. He gave them drinks and all that. He even paid for them to have a bit of a go on the pokies or at the gambling.'

'Very good of him, I'm sure. And this debauched life continued on until early in July 1955 when something went badly wrong, Mr Allsop. What was that?'

'I don't know.'

'I think you do. What happened in early July 1955 to spoil all the fun you and your dad were having in Sydney?'

'Nothing.'

'I don't believe you, Mr Allsop. You suddenly left your job, you left Sydney shortly after being arrested by the police for being drunk and disorderly, and you got divorced. Quite a busy month, Mr Allsop. What happened? Did you and your dad have a falling out?'

'Yep.'

'Over what?'

'I can't remember.'

'That's not good enough, Mr Allsop. You and your dad have a cosy little arrangement for two or three years and then suddenly, boom, it's all finished. What was the disagreement all about? What made you leave your job, leave Sydney and leave your wife all in the space of a couple of weeks?'

'I told you I don't remember.'

'Mr Allsop, I don't think you understand the seriousness of the position you are in. You are our number one suspect for the murder of your father. If you cooperate with us now, we can put in a good word for you when we have all the evidence to arrest you.'

'See, you haven't got any bloody evidence, have you!' Christopher was clearly rattled. His face had reddened and a nervous tick began in his left eye. He thumped the table with his fists as if to reinforce his assertion beyond all possible doubt. 'You can't keep me here. I've told you everything I can remember. I demand access to a solicitor.'

Johansson realised he had insufficient evidence to hold Christopher Allsop any longer. He had come tantalisingly close to discovering the reason for the split between father and son. Whatever it was, the detective was convinced it was the cause of a chain of events resulting in years of blackmail and finally murder.

'I'll let you go now, Mr Allsop, but let me warn you that we will leave no stone unturned until we can pin this on you. I believe you are guilty of serious criminal behaviour and I intend to prove it. It is only a matter of time. Remember, if you come clean on what went wrong between you and your father, it will make it much better for you in the long run. Good day.'

A relieved Christopher pushed back his chair and marched to the door. Much to his annoyance, he found it locked. Johansson yelled out to the manager to please unlock the door. He must have been eavesdropping as the door opened almost immediately. Christopher only just managed to stop himself from making a crude gesture as he left the room.

Johansson slumped angrily back into his chair. 'He's in this right up to his ears. The trouble is Charles Allsop is dead and now his son won't spill the beans. Unless we can find someone else who witnessed this falling out, we could be stuffed.'

'We don't even know where they argued, let alone whether anybody else was present,' Tania added. 'All we know is that their relationship suddenly broke down whilst they were living in Sydney during July 1955. It must have been a monumental event. One thing we do know though.'

'And what's that?'

'The offence must have been committed by Charles Allsop.'

'How come?'

'Well, he was the one subjected to blackmail. He was the one who ended up in the grave when he refused to cough up any more money. The blackmail letters refer several times to "disgusting and disgraceful behaviour". It all points to Charles being the cause of the friction. Whatever Charles did, it was deeply offensive to Christopher. If this offence was sexual in nature, I can think of three possibilities.'

Tania Markovina's ability to think laterally impressed the detective. She was destined to do well in the police force. 'Go on...' he urged.

'My theory is that whatever happened occurred at the apartment. Christopher says they took women back there for sex. If they had gone to a brothel they would most likely have been in separate rooms and Christopher would not have seen anything abhorrent. Back at the apartment it would be more open. So the three possibilities are, firstly, that Charles engaged in a homosexual relationship in front of Christopher. Secondly, Charles behaved incestuously towards Christopher. Thirdly, Charles had sexual relations with Christopher's wife. Don't forget Christopher was a married man and he divorced shortly after the falling out with his father.'

'Sordid, isn't it?' was Johansson's only comment.

'So, if you agree with this as a working hypothesis, we have two obvious lines of inquiry to explore. We should try to locate the apartment where the sexual encounters occurred and see if any of the neighbours can assist us. My other idea is to track down Christopher's wife way back in 1955 and talk with her.'

'Sounds as good as anything I can think of,' replied the Inspector.

They packed up the recorder, pushed the chairs back into position and headed out. As they left the building, Johansson requested the manager to let him know if Christopher failed to turn up for work. They needed to keep a close eye on his whereabouts as there was unfinished business.

En route back to the station they decided they needed a break from the case. The weekend promised glorious weather in the mid-twenties with welcome cool southerlies blowing. Tania and Tony had a wedding of a close friend to attend up at Hahndorf. Mike and Lynda were off to a B&B to celebrate their wedding anniversary. Mike had selected; there was an eighteen-hole golf course only five minutes away.

Austin Healey Sprites

Monday morning was heating up. A high was moving across the state and the cool southerlies enjoyed over the weekend had moved across to Victoria. Today the air was still and the sun already had a bite to it. The ancient air conditioners at the police station were already grinding away doing their best to keep its occupants cool. 'Expecting 36 degrees today,' observed Johansson as he grabbed the folder that had appeared this morning in his in-tray.

'Oh, for a bit of time off to hit the surf,' bemoaned Tania.

It was after ten-thirty and they were at last seated ready for their 9 am regular meeting. Several unexpected delays had interfered with their usual Monday morning catch-up.

'Great news. I have here the collated report of all the red Austin Healey Sprites registered in the country in 1975. It has taken over two weeks to get it, bloody Northern Territory held up proceedings as usual.'

'It's a long shot sir, but this report might just help us track down the mystery woman who turned up at Charles' apartment twice just before he died of poisoning.'

'According to the executive summary, there were 346 Austin Healey Sprites registered in Australia that year. 287 were red. Obviously if you wanted to show off, red was the preferred colour. 287 red sprites are far too many to try and follow up so let's concentrate initially only on those that were registered here in South Australia. We had the grand total of twelve red Austin Healey Sprites registered here in 1975. So, Tania, your first job today is to get on to these twelve vehicles and find out who the owners were back in July/August 1975. Bring me a list as soon as possible with contact details if possible and rank them in order of likelihood of leading us to the female driver. Can you manage that by late this arvo?'

'I'll do my best, sir.'

¶

Working on the principle that the best way to get a job done is to speak to the person involved face-to-face, Tania jumped into a police patrol car and made her way down to the South Australian Motor Registry Head Office. The smartly dressed policewoman turned heads when she entered the building and the young man who she first spoke to couldn't do enough to assist. She flashed him one of her stunning smiles as a thank you, and within minutes was with the archive's manager in the archives collection down in the basement.

'This should be no problem,' the manager assured the

senior constable, leading the way along a lengthy row of files all labelled with the months and years of car registrations stored within. 'We have alpha listings according to the person who registers a vehicle, listings by registration numbers and also by make and model of car. So, if you follow me down this next aisle, I can find you the list of people who registered Austin Healey Sprites in 1975. You will need to go through the list though because they could be all sorts of colours.'

A few minutes later Tania was comfortably seated at a table with an angle poise light shining onto a photocopied list of 1975 South Australian registered Austin Healey Sprites. Fifteen appeared on the list and twelve were described as red. She crossed out those that were not red and studied the twelve that remained. For each vehicle a number of other basic facts were provided such as engine number, year of manufacture, registration number, registrant, phone number and address of registrant. An additional reference number was provided in case she wished to cross-reference with one of the other files.

The challenge that Tania was now presented with was that the persons who registered each of these vehicles in 1975 would probably not be the only people likely to be driving them. It was the vehicle that was being registered and any number of licensed people were entitled to drive it at any time. So, she was not really any closer to finding out who the lady was that had come to visit Charles Allsop on two occasions just before he died. To take this line of research another step would be tedious. She would have to call on all twelve registrants and quiz them on who else was driving their car in the weeks before Charles died in August 1975. Some registrants may not even remember that far back. It looked like a lengthy process that may be a complete waste of time. Another complication was that the red Austin Healey Sprite they were seeking may not have even been registered in South Australia. There is nothing preventing someone from outside the state visiting Adelaide and driving into The Everglades to see Charles Allsop. This thought made Tania realise that all 287 red Austin Healey Sprites may have conveyed the mysterious lady into the heart of The Everglades Retirement Village and this was not, after all, a fruitful line of inquiry.

Tania could barely raise a smile for the pleasant young man who had welcomed her to the building when she left five minutes later. Johansson agreed with her. Nevertheless, they safely filed the photocopied list just in case it helped in the identification process of the car and its mysterious occupant at a later date.

Only two lines of inquiry now remained; try to locate the apartment that Charles owned in Sydney back in 1955 and question any near neighbours, or try to find Christopher's wife at that time, Rochelle Joan Brooks. Neither prospects sounded hopeful.

Johansson's view was that they should bring Christopher Allsop back in and put more pressure on him to outline what had happened in August 1955. Weeks of careful detective work might be needed to find the apartment and Rochelle

Brooks, and quite frankly, the detective did not have the resources to pay staff to do this laborious spade work.

They were both feeling despondent when a surprise long-distance phone call came in.

The Return of Hank

'Switchboard here. Am I speaking to Detective Inspector Mike Johansson?'

'Yes, you are.'

'I have a long-distance phone call for you from Western Samoa. Do you wish to take the call?'

Johansson's face registered surprise as he answered in the positive.

'Hold the line please and I'll connect you.'

A moment of crackling sounded on the airwaves until a female voice cut across the noise, 'Is that you Mike Johansson?'

'Sure is. Who am I speaking to?' Johansson beckoned to Tania to come closer so she could listen as well.

'This is Jayne Prescott ringing you from Western Samoa.'

'This is a surprise Jayne. How can I help you?'

'Well you are not going to believe this, but I have had a threatening letter from someone calling himself Hank. It must be the same person who wrote to my husband demanding money.'

'What have you done with the letter?'

'It's here, in my hot little hand.'

'Jayne, it is very important that you do as I say. First I want you to describe the letter and then to read it to me.'

'Well, it's got Australian stamps on the envelope and it arrived today. It's dated the 12th of February so it's taken over a week to get here. It's been typed and looks like the letter I found on Charles' desk that I told you about.'

'Does it say where it has been posted from?'

'Yes, but I can't read it. This is the wet season here and the letter looks as though it has been dropped into a puddle or something.'

'Can you decipher any of the letters, Jayne? This is important.'

'I think the last two letters are C and E. It's certainly an E on the end. The C could be a G though. I can't tell. The rest of it is impossible to read.'

'Okay, don't worry about that now. Please read the letter to me slowly and clearly so I can write it down word correct.' Tania had anticipated this and was ready with her notebook and pen poised.

Jayne did as she was bid, and Tania scribbled it down. Johansson then gave the phone to Tania to read her letter back to Jayne to make sure they had the wording a hundred percent correct. After a couple of minor corrections, they had the letter complete.

12th February, 1979

Jayne Prescott,

You were married to Charles Allsop and have inherited all his wealth.

Mr Allsop behaved despicably towards me and for twenty years he paid for his crime. Then he decided to stop paying so I had him murdered. I am still waiting for that last payment of $30,000.

If you pay up, I promise I will make this my final demand.

Take out $30,000 in cash ($100 notes) and leave the money at the top of Mount Canobolas just outside Orange in NSW. There is a road to the top of the mountain where you will find a trig station. Place the money in a cash box and hide it under the loose rocks at the base of the trig station. The money must be in place no later than 1st March.

If you tell anyone about this letter you will go the same way as your husband did. I know where you live!

Hank

'Okay, thank you Jayne. Now listen to me carefully. Have you told anyone else about this letter?'

'No, only you.'

'Good. Keep it that way. Tell nobody else. Do exactly as Hank has stipulated. Leave the money at the summit of this mountain. Before you do so, write down the numbers of all the $100 notes and keep the list in a safe place. Place the letter from Hank and its envelope into a larger envelope and bring it with you when you fly in. Then post it to me at the address I gave you on my business card. Put the list of the numbers of the $100 notes into the same package. Be sure to send the package registered mail. Do you still have my business card?'

'Yes, I do have your card, and I'm happy to do as you ask, but I don't want to go through an ordeal like this again. What sort of a guarantee can you give me that all this is going to work out?'

'Jayne, I would be quite wrong to make any promises. We have a highly professional team and we rehearse long and hard for situations like this. We'll be ready. I want you to ring me as soon as you get to Orange. Do you know the place at all?'

'Never been there. The nearest I have been is Bathurst for the Bathurst 1000.'

'When you ring me from Orange let me know where you are staying. I also want to know which bank you will draw the money from.'

'That's easy. It will be the NAB.'

'Contacting me was the right thing to do. We will do everything we can here to catch the person or persons behind this and we are getting closer every day. I'm happy for you to ring me out of hours if necessary. The number is (08) 8392 2809.'

'Thank you, Inspector.'

'Bye Jayne, catch you soon.'

'Bye.'

With the call ended, Johansson swivelled round in his chair, clenched his fist and excitedly exclaimed, 'Yes, this is great. Just as we were wondering how to proceed next, events determine the next course of action for us.'

'I can't believe the blackmailer is so brazen,' remarked Tania. 'He certainly likes living dangerously. He has virtually set up a trap to catch himself.'

'Yes, but he is working on the premise that Jayne will be too scared to tell anyone. And that's his first big mistake. It always amazes me that criminals that are successful for a number of years in the end become so complacent. They think they are indestructible.'

'I'm going to see the chief ASAP to outline the situation to him and request additional resources be found from the NSW Police force to catch this character once and for all. But before I do, we need to have a strategy worked out to present to him. So, Tania, what do you propose?'

'Okay sir, off the top of my head, let's call this "Operation Everglades". The operation commences as soon as Jayne Prescott arrives in Orange and goes to her motel which will be booked for her. She is under constant surveillance from the time she arrives at the motel until the operation is successfully concluded. Successful conclusion means full recovery of the money and the arrest of the blackmailer or blackmailers. So we have plain-clothed police watching her every move; when she goes to the bank, if she leaves for a walk, goes out to a restaurant, picks up her rental car, anything that takes her out of the motel. For Jayne's peace of mind, we will tell her she is being shadowed at all times.'

'Sounds good so far, keep going.'

'At a prearranged time, Jayne will drive to the top of Mount Canobolas to deposit the money as requested by Hank on the night of the deadline. I would suggest around nine in the evening after dark. An armed policeman will be hiding in the back of her car but will only reveal himself if there's trouble. Other armed police will be hiding up in the bush lying in wait for the blackmailer from 9:00 pm onwards. It all sounds too easy!'

'You're right there. Now a couple of other things. Because all this is happening in Orange, it falls under the NSW police jurisdiction, so they will have to provide all the resources and conduct the whole operation. The most we can expect is that I will be granted permission to be present as an observer-come-advisor. Once the culprit is arrested, we will seek to have him extradited back to Adelaide to be tried in South Australia.'

'So, all the detailed planning will be done by the NSW strike force. They will know the best motel and even the best room to reserve for Jayne. This will be the room they can best maintain under careful twenty-four-hour surveillance.'

'Exactly. Our chief will have to do all the top-level nego-tiating with the top brass in NSW to set this up. Our role will be to keep in touch with Jayne and pass on all her travel details to the officer appointed to lead Operation Everglades. So, unless you can think of anything else, I'll give the chief a ring now and arrange to discuss this matter in depth. I will need to convince him that we have done all our homework and to provide the evidence to back it up. Could you please gather up all our reports, the eight letters and anything else I may need?'

'Certainly sir. I think I can have everything together within the half hour.'

¶

Forty minutes later Tania knocked on the Inspector's door to deliver the necessary papers.

'Good work. The chief wants to see us both at 4 pm. When I mentioned your participation in this case, he thought it best that you attend as well. Have you met the chief before?'

'No, never. I have rarely even seen him in the three years I've been a policewoman. He was the guest speaker at my police graduation though, so I suppose he presented me with my certificate and shook my hand.'

'Well, be warned. He has a military bearing, can't stand waffle and comes over as domineering. He is sharp as a tack and often intimidating. Best to let me do the talking and you can chip in if I get something wrong.'

A few minutes later Tania and the Inspector drove out of the carpark and headed for police headquarters to meet with the police commissioner, Nigel Parkes. They were just ahead of the rush-hour, so they made good progress arriving with ten minutes to spare. Parking in the "visitors" car park they strolled through the main entrance, were checked by security and reported at the receptionist's window. The police head-quarters accommodated all the heads of departments, the deputy commissioner and of course, Nigel Parkes, together with their respective personal secretaries.

The top brass occupied suites of rooms on the third floor. Coming out of the lift, they both noticed the thickening of the carpet, the plush furnishings and tasteful decor. A second receptionist, even more smartly dressed than the one down-stairs, looked up from her desk and gave them a welcoming smile. 'Welcome. The commissioner is on the phone at the moment but will be ready to see you shortly. May I get you a cup of tea or coffee while you wait?'

Johansson declined, so Tania felt she should do the same. She was feeling nervous. Most serving police never have an audience with the commissioner and those that did were sometimes there because of misdemeanours and so dreaded the encounter. Nigel Parkes had a fearsome reputation for tearing miscreants apart, limb by limb. Tania was relieved such a situation did not apply to her first appearance before the commissioner.

Tania jumped when a red light sitting on the receptionist's desk suddenly lit up and beeped. The receptionist stood and requested them to follow her. Tania noticed the smart suit she was wearing and the slight swing of the hips no doubt for Johansson's benefit. They moved silently across the foyer to where the receptionist held the door open. 'The commissioner's private secretary, Mrs Weatherall, will look after you now.' With one more parting smile, she closed the door behind them. Mrs Weatherall exuded efficiency, a much older woman with greying hair and deep blue eyes. She stood and shook their hands and repeated that the commissioner would see them now. She tapped gently on the adjacent door and waited a moment.

'Come.'

'Commissioner, may I introduce Detective Inspector Mike Johansson and Senior Constable Tania Markovina?'

'Thank you, Valerie. Please be seated.'

Mrs Weatherall closed the door gently behind her after collecting a couple of papers from the commissioner's out-tray, and left Johansson and Tania to settle into their comfortable straight-backed chairs.

The commissioner was large and rotund. He peered keenly at them through a pair of thin framed spectacles. His face was rather too red for a healthy man and his thinning hair reflected his age as somewhere between sixty and sixty-five. There was already some conjecture as to when Nigel Parkes might call it a day. A thin military style moustache sat above his upper lip and a double chin hung loosely below a still firm-set jaw. Two chubby hands were interlocked and resting on a massive desk. The fingers reminded Tania of the bag of pork sausages she had taken out of the fridge last night to cook for their dinner.

Three small flags sat in a wooden block on one side of the desk; the Australian flag in the middle with the Aboriginal flag on one side and the flag of South Australia on the other. In the centre were the ubiquitous three trays; IN, OUT and PENDING. A framed photograph occupied the other end of the desk but its content was not visible to the two visitors. Behind the commissioner, a large framed photograph of a youthful Queen Elizabeth II looked down on proceedings.

'Righto Inspector, convince me that I need to involve the NSW Police Force in this Hank case.'

Johansson and Tania spent the next quarter of an hour outlining the case from the discovery that Charles Frederic Allsop had been poisoned through to the last blackmailing attempt by the mysterious Hank, which had now moved the action to Orange in NSW. The Commissioner listened attentively interjecting only a couple of times to clarify some points.

'Thank you for an excellent summary. Do you have any suggestions as to how we might request our colleagues in NSW to handle this?' Johansson invited Tania to take the lead.

A few minutes later the Commissioner cleared his throat, leant back comfortably, paused a moment and then responded.

'We clearly have two major crimes here, murder and blackmail. It would seem that there are at least two dangerous people still out there somewhere who are likely to reoffend. They must be caught and face trial. The best chance of achieving a breakthrough appears to be this next attempt at blackmail on the mountain outside Orange. I am happy to accede to your request and to talk to my counterpart in the NSW Police service and ask for his assistance.'

There was a barely audible sigh of relief. 'Thank you, sir.'

'Some details; I shall request that you, Inspector, are to stay in close touch with Orange throughout the duration of this operation and I will expect a full written report from you within a week of the conclusion of the exercise. You both need to understand that once I hand this matter over to the NSW Police, they will take charge and carry out the operation. We have little say in the proceedings. It is imperative we maintain our excellent working relationships with our interstate colleagues. You, Inspector, will be an advisor only, but with reporting responsibilities directly to me. Constable, you will remain in Adelaide covering any issues at this end. Any questions?'

'Expenses, sir?'

'Your flights to Sydney and possible sojourn in Orange will all be covered by SA Police of course. Ask Valerie for the requisite claim forms as you leave. Anything else?'

'No thank you sir, we are delighted to have your support.'

'We still have to have NSW's agreement remember. Valerie will be in touch as soon as everything is agreed and will arrange any flights. I shall request NSW to have you booked into the same motel as Jayne is booked into.'

The Police Commissioner rose to his feet revealing what a bear of a man he was and shook hands across his desk. 'Good luck.'

CHAPTER 19

The Trip to Orange

Jayne Prescott stepped elegantly from the pool at her luxury home in Western Samoa. With a slight adjustment to her bikini she picked up her towel, had a quick rub down and lay back seductively on her li-lo. She blew a kiss at the hunky man watching her from the adjacent li-lo. 'Can you mix me another drink please, darling?'

'Sure.' Jayne's current male companion wandered casually over to the bar and returned a few minutes later with the concoction that was his speciality.

John Sandringham was Jayne's latest lover, happily accepting her invitation for free board and lodging for a week in return for making Jayne feel young, virile and still irresistible to men.

John found the weather too hot and sticky for his liking but couldn't find fault with anything else. The food was great, the scenery something to die for and the sexual activities each night in such an exotic setting, sensational. He felt honoured that Jayne had selected him from her numerous male acquaintances to spend this week with her. He knew it was important for Jayne's ego to have a man about the place and appreciated that next week he would be on his way home and some other lucky bloke would take his place. Jayne recycled men like plastic bags for as long as they were willing, and rarely did she have to survive a week alone.

John wondered what the servants made of this sexual roundabout. Western Samoa was a deeply Christian country and it was almost unheard of not to attend church every Sunday morning. The tight-knit village community nearby that provided the domestic staff for Jayne's establishment remained discreet and never openly criticised Jayne. She purchased all her groceries, fruit, fish and vegetables from the village store and the little family stalls along the side of the road. She was good for business.

One night, towards the end of John's week in paradise, as they lay naked together across the queen-sized bed, Jayne rolled over to face him and asked what he was doing next week. The question surprised John as he was booked on the Friday night flight out of Apia en route for Sydney. He also knew that his replacement would be arriving that evening on the incoming flight. Had Jayne found him so hot in bed that she had changed her mind and wanted him to stay a second week? If so, had she cancelled the replacement? Much as he relished the sex with Jayne, he drew the line at a threesome.

Something warned him to be cautious. 'Why darling?'

'I have to go to a place called Orange next week. It's in NSW. It's about 250 kilometres west of Sydney.'

John resided in Hunters Hill close to the centre of Sydney, and had been to Orange a couple of times. He knew the city to be an attractive place with a blossoming wine industry developing on top of a highly productive agricultural base of fruit and vegetable growing. Situated more than 700 metres above sea level it enjoyed a cool, damp climate. Indeed, it shivered with many frosts in winter and snow falling two or three times every year. It owed its prosperity to the rich soils that had developed as a result of volcanic activity many millions of years ago.

'Yup, I know the place. Lovely little city.'

'Well, I'm not going there for pleasure, but I would greatly appreciate your company John if you are free next week?'

'I thought for a beautiful moment you were going to invite me to hang around here for another week.'

'No such luck, lover boy. But you never know your luck if you come with me to Orange on Friday night.'

John was still on long service leave next week so he had no real binding commitments. A trip down to Orange might be a pleasant way to spend a few days.

'Why do you want to go to Orange?'

'Private business.'

'How long do you want to stay?'

'I expect to go back to Sydney on March 1st.'

'Okay, count me in. How about you come back to my flat in Hunters Hill on Friday night and then we drive down Saturday. We can make a day of it. If you like we can say hello to the Three Sisters near Katoomba on the way.'

'What? Have you got three bloody sisters to visit?'

'No, no. The Three Sisters is a famous geological feature in the Blue Mountains. You folk from Adelaide are an ignorant lot.'

'Just as well then. Putting up with the likes of you is bad enough without all your sisters around too.'

John laughed. 'I know what you wild Adelaide women like best.' He smacked Jayne lightly on the bottom, pushed her gently over onto her back and started fondling her breasts.

¶

Friday came all too quickly. The flight from Apia was uneventful and they landed at the Sydney International Airport at dusk. Hunters Hill boasted a number of excellent eateries and they settled on a sushi bar just off the main street. Back at John's flat they threw a couple of loads of washing through the machine, enjoyed a night cap and retired to bed.

For the first time in the week Jayne declined any sexual activity. 'Is something worrying you?'

'I suppose. I'm a bit concerned about these few days coming up in Orange.'

'Anything I can do to help? I'll not have much to do in Orange, so just say the word if you think there is anything useful, I can put my mind to.'

'Thanks John, I appreciate that. To be honest I'm not sure what is going to happen. I expect that I will have to be dealing with things on my own though, so you may have to go off and entertain yourself.'

'That's okay by me. Where will we be staying?'

'In a motel.'

'Have you booked?'

'No need.'

'It might be wise to make a booking.'

'No, someone will be doing it for us.'

Strange answer, thought John. In fact, he did not feel Jayne had been quite herself these last few days. She seemed preoccupied. Something was bugging her and she clammed up as soon as he tried to uncover what it was. She had provided no clues about this business interest in Orange. Perhaps she was off to meet another bloke? If so, why did she want him to drive down to Orange and stay with her? And who would have booked their motel room for them? Plenty of questions that he hoped would be resolved tomorrow.

Jayne was restless. She complained she couldn't get to sleep. Two or three times she got up and walked about his small apartment. Eventually, annoyed that he wasn't getting any sleep either, John retired to his spare bedroom where he finally dozed off.

¶

Saturday morning brought rain. A southerly buster had come through overnight bringing welcome respite from the heat that had hung over Sydney the last couple of days. John rose with the dawn and fussed around organising some breakfast. Jayne was finally sleeping reasonably peacefully so he left her undisturbed. He popped out with his umbrella to get the paper and some milk and fruit from his friendly Italian-run convenience store at the end of the block. By the time Jayne emerged, around half past eight, he had finished his cereal and fruit and was making toast with dark wholemeal bread accompanied by generous serves of butter and Rose's chunky marmalade.

Jayne was still wearing a thin, silky negligee that was deliberately revealing of the more interesting parts of her anatomy, but she seemed tired and nervous. Whatever it was that was going to happen in Orange today, it was clearly stressing her. This was not the usual Jayne who normally presented a fun-loving, live-life-to-the-full persona. John was worried but determined to put on a cheerful face.

Jayne picked at her food and remained quiet. Around 9:30am they were ready to leave. He locked up, stowed the bags in the boot, rang his mate next door to mention he would be away in Orange for a few days and opened the garage door. The rain was still belting down and the drains were struggling to cope. A couple of hardy runners sloshed their way past the garage door as he was pulling out. If this weather kept up, they could expect to be in fog as they climbed up to Katoomba and it would not be pleasant to get out and explore the Three Sisters.

Their conversation was limited to a few polite comments as they negotiated the Sydney traffic heading west towards the Blue Mountains. 'When do you think we will get to Orange, John?'

John did a few quick mental calculations and responded, 'Allowing for this lousy weather, and a stop for some lunch and a morning coffee somewhere, probably about 4 pm. Why?'

'I promised to let them know when we expect to arrive.'

'Who is "them"?'

'Sorry, can't say. Could you pull over at the next telephone box you see please so I can call them?'

'Only if you tell me what this is all about.'

'Oh, don't be so bloody difficult John. I promise to tell you everything in a few days when it's all fixed up.'

'I do care about you Jayne. I'm just trying to help. You've got your knickers in a knot about something and it doesn't make you good company.'

'I know, but it will work out okay. Just hang in with me for a few more days please.'

'Are you doing drugs?'

'No way! I've never touched the things and never will.'

'Are you dealing then?'

'Just shut up John and concentrate on the driving.'

The mood in the car remained strained. The rain eased somewhat but visibility was still poor. 'Pull over John, there's a phone box coming up.' He did as he was bid and parked. 'Do you have any coins please John? I may need a few more.' He fished around in his pocket but could offer only a fifty-cent coin and two twenty-cent coins. 'Stay in the car John. I don't want you listening to my phone call.'

'I'm getting out to have a stretch, but I can promise you I won't come near you in your precious bloody phone box.'

Jayne glared at him and scurried through the rain to the phone where she hunted in her purse for the number she needed, all the while keeping an eye out for John. John meanwhile headed for a row of small shops with verandahs where he could wander up and down out of the rain, stretch his cramped legs and speculate again on what Jayne was up to. Whatever it was, he felt uneasy about it. Had he been conned into being the driver for some criminal activity? Was Jayne organising something at this very moment with the boss of a criminal gang or an accomplice? Perhaps Jayne was the boss! She was rolling in money. Was her wealth the result of criminal activity and not an inheritance from her husband as she had explained to him? Had he been luxuriating all week and having sex with a leading criminal?

His thoughts were rudely interrupted by a yell from Jayne who was standing out in the rain unable to get back into the locked car. As John fumbled for the key to open Jayne's door, he inquired whether she had got through okay. 'Yes, thank you,' was the curt reply.

They began the long ascent up into the Blue Mountains passing through attractive little towns and winding their way ever upwards. Jayne had vaguely heard the names of some of these towns when living in Adelaide; Leura, Medlow Bath and Blackheath. When they finally arrived in Katoomba it was blanketed in fog and everything was cool and damp. There was no point trying to see the Three Sisters or the

Grosse Valley so they found a little cafe and snuggled in for some early lunch. Fish and chips, followed by a pavlova did for John, but Jayne, ever conscious of maintaining her hourglass figure, chose a Waldorf salad. By one o'clock they were on their way again and keeping to their schedule for a 4.00pm arrival in Orange.

¶

The NSW task force assigned to Orange for a special mission had arrived aboard their Toyota Cruiser bus on Friday afternoon. There were twelve of them. At 5 pm they had assembled in the conference room at the Orange Police Station for a background briefing. Here they had met and been addressed by a Detective Inspector from the South Australian Police by the name of Mike Johansson. He had been well received by the team who had appreciated his presentation that was clear, informative and laced with humour.

The detective had thought long and hard about this presentation and had only finalised its format when he stepped from the Cessna that had flown him into the small Orange Airport that morning. Much of the police work that he and Tania had been engaged in over the last few weeks was not relevant to the NSW task force who were here to do a very specific job. Johansson had limited his talk, therefore, to the bare bones, outlining the blackmailing and murder of Mr Allsop and the subsequent blackmailing of Jayne Prescott. He concluded by informing the group of the planned hiding of $30,000 under the trig station on the summit of Mount Canobolas. A couple of questions followed his briefing before he resumed his seat.

Next to speak was the leader of the NSW task force, Inspector Bruce Farley. He came equipped with two rolled up sheets of butcher's paper on which he had drawn maps of the motel where Jayne Prescott was going to be staying and the area around the summit of Mount Canobolas. Using the maps as visual aids the group discussed how best to keep guard of Jayne at her motel and how to execute an ambush and arrest at Mount Canobolas if Hank, or one of his stooges, should appear. Next, a timetable of duties and rosters was established. Jayne would require twenty-four-hour surveillance wherever she went and a two-person team would be needed on top of Mount Canobolas every hour from now on. Three eight- hour shifts a day were organised. The task force had been accommodated at another Orange motel and two additional police vehicles had been made available. All was set for the arrival of Jayne Prescott and her partner.

The third and last speaker was the policeman in charge of the Orange Police Station, Chief Inspector Norman Sheldon. He was keen to make the team feel welcome and to assure them that he and his forty or so police serving in the Orange district would do all they could to support their mission. He finished with a recommendation of a couple of the best wineries they must visit before they returned to "the big smoke".

The group broke up and the three speakers retired to the canteen for coffee and cake and a final session to ensure that they had not missed anything. Johansson agreed to get in touch as soon as he heard from Jayne Prescott about her expected time of arrival on Saturday.

¶

Saturday morning in Orange was chilly, the overnight rain clouds had departed as the welcome cool change embraced everyone. All that remained were the woolly clouds still scudding across the sky blown by the south westerlies. Johansson was stuck at his motel waiting for the call from Jayne to alert him to her arrival time in Orange. It was a relief to hear from her at about 11 am with the news that she and her current partner, John, were aiming to arrive around 4 pm. He rang the head of the Orange Police Station and Bruce Farley, head of the police task force, to pass this information on and to advise that if they needed him he would be squeezing in nine holes at the Orange Country Club but would be back at the motel in time to welcome Jayne and John by 3:45pm in case they fetched up ahead of time.

Johansson enjoyed every minute of his nine holes. It was a beautiful golf course with spectacular deciduous trees, almost as green as Ireland and the stately mansion that had been partially converted into the Club House was an architectural delight. He scored poorly, however, which was hardly surprising since he didn't know the course, had to manage with hired golf clubs and had competed against a strong southerly wind. He grabbed a pie and takeaway coffee before he left the golf club and was showered and ready at Jayne's motel dressed as a civilian by the allotted time. Here he introduced himself to the receptionist as plain Mike Johansson and explained he was meeting one of their guests, Jayne Prescott. He presumed that the motel was already under surveillance.

The time ticked by. The Swiss cuckoo clock hanging on the wall opposite him suddenly sprang to life as its door opened and a cheeky looking cuckoo emerged and cuckooed loudly four times. A couple of guests checked in. By 4:30 pm he was feeling rather peeved that they were running late. The receptionist was kind enough to offer him a cup of tea or coffee, and was about to make it for him, when her phone rang again. She looked across and inquired, 'Excuse me, did you say your name was Mike Johansson?' When he replied in the affirmative, she beckoned him over, 'It's the police, they want to speak to you.'

Johansson jumped up and took the phone. 'Johansson here.' The message was short. There had been a major car accident at a small place called Lucknow which was just a few kilometres from Orange on the Great Western Highway. The road had been closed in both directions and diversions had been set up. It was believed that Jayne and her partner had been delayed in a long line of traffic and would now be coming into Orange via the much longer diversionary route. The police, ambulances and the fire brigade were attending. The detective resigned himself to waiting longer and gladly accepted the cup of coffee and the two chocolate biscuits that kept it company.

The cheeky cuckoo jumped out at him again when it was five o'clock. Still no sign of Jayne. He asked the receptionist if she would mind if he rang the police station to find out what was happening. She welcomed the idea as two or three of her other guests had not yet checked in either and she was hoping they were not involved in some way. His call was answered by the duty policeman who was very cagey about releasing any information about the accident over the phone to strangers. Johansson decided to pull rank. 'This is Detective Inspector Johansson. If you won't tell me anything then put me through to the Chief Inspector. And do it now.'

'But sir...'

'Do it now or I'll have your guts for garters.'

'Yes sir.'

A moment later he was connected. 'Chief Inspector Norman Sheldon speaking. Is that you Mike?'

'Sure is. What's happening Norman?'

'Bloody awful pile-up at Lucknow. Three cars involved. The road's closed and the major crash unit is out there now trying to sort out what has happened. Five ambulances were called. Latest report says we have one deceased and four injured, two critically. Emergency services are using the jaws of life to get a couple of them out. God knows what has happened to Jayne. The diverted traffic is only now beginning to arrive in Orange as it's about twenty extra kilometres all up. Sorry Mike. I suggest you sit tight at the motel a bit longer. They should be there soon.'

'Thanks Norman. By the way, the young fellow answering

your phone just now did the right thing. I had to get quite abusive before he would transfer me.'

'Yup, he's a good lad. Talk to you soon.'

Ten minutes later the motel's phone rang again and this time it was the Chief Inspector.

'Mike, the emergency crew boys have just rung in to say they have an initial ID for the two who they had to extricate from the vehicle down in the culvert. The driver is in a critical state. His driver's licence gives his name as John Sandringham. The deceased woman in the passenger's seat was Jayne Prescott. You had better come over to the station straight away.'

¶

As Johansson drove to the Orange Police Station a hundred thoughts scrambled for his attention. How did this accident happen? Was it an accident? Was there some criminal intent? Did someone wish to kill Jayne or perhaps her partner? What would happen now with regard to the blackmailer? Would the blackmailer hear about this accident? How were they going to find the blackmailer now? Was it possible that the Ernstein family were somehow implicated? If anyone was to benefit from Jayne's sudden demise it was the Ernsteins who would now inherit.

Arriving at the police station he had to push his way through a number of reporters and concerned locals wanting to know what had happened and who had been killed or injured. The detective flashed his ID and was bundled in through the main entrance by one of the three uniformed police guarding the entrance. A moment later he was in Chief Inspector Norman Sheldon's office.

'Terrible business this. I've just finished preparing a short statement to read out to the crowd of reporters out there. You have to be so careful what you say and to get the facts right. Do you mind if I read the statement to you first Mike and you can tell me if it sounds okay?'

'Certainly, go ahead.'

'Statement issued by Chief Inspector Norman Sheldon, officer-in-charge, Orange Police Station, 1800 hours, February 28th, 1979. The police advise that at approximately 3:40 pm today a major accident involving three vehicles occurred on the Great Western Highway one kilometre east of the small township of Lucknow. Police, the fire brigade and five ambulances attended. The highway is closed to all traffic and will remain closed until major accident crews have completed their work. Expect lengthy delays as all traffic is being diverted.

'One vehicle travelling west rolled down an embankment. The male driver was critically injured and has been flown to Sydney. His passenger, a woman, died at the scene. Two cars travelling east were also involved. The male driver of one of these vehicles is critical and has been air-lifted to Sydney. His passenger, and the occupant of the third vehicle, are both in a serious but stable condition and have been taken to the Orange Base Hospital. A further bulletin will be released tomorrow morning.

'How does it sound? I can't release any names yet until we have ID confirmation and the next of kin have been informed.'

'It sounds good, Norman.'

'Thanks. Wait here while I go downstairs and read the statement. I won't be taking any questions so I'll be back in a few minutes.'

The Chief Inspector's phone rang three times whilst Johansson waited for his return. Major accidents often seemed to happen at weekends when secretarial staff were not on duty. A few minutes later a slightly flustered Chief Inspector walked back in, 'Bloody reporters, they are never satisfied. I reckon they asked thirty questions all at once. Who was in the accident? What model of vehicle? What happened? I can't answer these questions correctly yet. One cheeky bloke even asked when the police were going to do their job properly. It's not pleasant having to attend these kinds of incidents. First responders are spared nothing and can have sleepless nights for weeks afterwards. Sorry Mike, just letting off a bit of steam.'

'I quite understand Norman. As a detective I'm spared this kind of thing, but we do have our grizzly episodes too.'

'I'm sure you do. Now, let's put our heads together and decide where we go from here. Looks like this whole blackmailing business is stuffed?'

'Yes, I agree. I guess the task force can be dismantled immediately and everyone can return home. However, I still have a very strong interest in Orange because all the letters from this Hank guy have all emanated from here. Every letter has had an Orange postcode on the envelope. I had my assistant go through your electoral rolls for the last twenty years trying to trace Hank. We found a few but none of them could be the Hank we are after. I would really appreciate your continued assistance in trying to identify who has been sending these letters.'

'Mike, there are 30,000 residents in Orange, and if I include all the people living in the outlying villages, we number over 40,000. How do you propose I find your Hank? Had it occurred to you that the name Hank may be a nom de plume? If I was intent on blackmail, the last thing I would do is sign my blackmail letters with "Norman". I think "Hank" is a pen name. Furthermore, "Hank" has led you up the garden path for weeks and consequently you are getting no closer to finding him.'

'I'm beginning to think you are right and we may have to switch our focus elsewhere. My bet is that now Jayne has been killed and the bounty all goes to the Ernstein family, the whole blackmail thing will stop. However, we must find the perpetrators and bring them to justice.'

'I couldn't agree more. I am more than happy to assist you in any way I can, but for now I can't see how.'

'Thanks Norman, and we have really appreciated all your help to date. I'm just sorry it has had to end this way.'

'Okay, I have to get on and finally confirm the identities of all involved in this accident. I will ring Sydney shortly and ask permission to scrap the task force and send the twelve boys back home. At least they will be pleased.'

Mike Johansson returned to his motel where he dined alone. He rang his wife and Tania Markovina to tell them he would be home tomorrow. He would be back in his Adelaide office first thing Monday morning. The more he thought about it the more he felt Norman was right. Hank was not the name of the person sending the blackmail letters. Perhaps someone living in Orange was doing the bidding of the black-mailer? Maybe there were two people involved. The mystery lady who had arrived twice in her red Austin Healey Sprite must surely be one of them. Perhaps Chris Allsop was the other? He looked forward to bouncing these ideas off Tania.

CHAPTER 20

The Chase Begins

For good reasons Detective Inspector Johansson had a serious attack of "Mondayitis" the next morning. The flight home on Sunday evening had been tedious and when he arrived home his wife was out with her friends tenpin bowling. He couldn't blame her because he was coming home unexpectedly early. She had left him a hastily prepared salad in the fridge.

Disturbingly, they were not getting much closer to solving this murder/blackmail case. Around 8 pm Norman had rung from Orange to say that it had been confirmed that it was Jayne Allsop who had died and that all the evidence from the major accident guys pointed to her driver, John Sandringham, causing the accident. It was still too early to say why he had suddenly swerved into oncoming traffic. The most likely reasons were that he had fallen asleep at the wheel or had had some kind of severe medical episode.

Tania also was suffering Mondayitis but not as severely as her boss. With very little notice, her mother had descended on their small apartment and invited herself to stay for the weekend. Mrs Markovina was of the opinion that couples do not sleep together before matrimony. The fact that Tania had decided not to follow her mother's advice put a constant strain on their relationship and these tensions were exacerbated whenever her mother came to stay. In deference to her mother, Tania had felt obliged to ask Tony to vacate their bed for the weekend and to sleep on the sofa. Naturally, this did not go down well with Tony who growled about the apartment all weekend.

In a way it was a welcome relief for both Johansson and Tania to have to meet for their early morning review as it offered a different scenario. They could forget the disappointments of the weekend and focus instead on police matters. The detective detailed the events of the last few days and expressed his frustration that a promising series of events with regard to the blackmailer had been thwarted. He was convinced that the best option now was to question Christopher Allsop a second time, to try and ascertain what had happened at Charles Allsop's apartment so many years ago and had led to Christopher's intense animosity towards his father.

'So, what's the strategy this time, sir?'

'We bring Christopher in for questioning here at the station this time and really put the wind up him. He can have a solicitor if he wants one. We were too kind to him the first time. I'm also going to try a bit of bluff on Christopher. Anything to get the truth out of him. Let's get that tape we recorded only a few days ago of our first interview and listen to it again and also check over that excellent profile you compiled. We need to have all the known facts at our fingertips. That sound okay to you, Tania?'

'Certainly. Do you want me to set up the interview for some time tomorrow?'

'Yes, in the late morning sometime please. At the same time, I want you to do some more digging. Contact his manager at work again to find out where Christopher banks and then check his bank accounts. I want to know whether there are any spikes appearing in his bank account that coincide with the payment of blackmail moneys by Mr Allsop over the twenty years that this racket was going on. I also want to check Christopher's fingerprints against those we found on the blackmail letters. Christopher has been in strife with the NSW Police at least three times so they should be able to help you. We will also photograph Christopher when he arrives this time and get more details about the car he drives. If the bank asks for a police clearance in order to release Christopher's account details, get back to me. Any questions?'

'No sir. I'll try to have all this ready in time for the interview tomorrow morning.'

Mike Johansson eased back into his executive's chair. Tania was an excellent copper, keen, sharp as a tack, perceptive and so pleasant with it all. Just what the SA police force needed. Amazing to think that only a few short years ago, the fairer sex was not even permitted to join the force. The best they could aspire to was an office job. If he ever got the chance, he would tell her young Tony to stop faffing about and put a ring on Tania's finger.

While he was checking through his in-tray the phone rang. 'Johansson here.'

'This is Tania. We think Christopher might have done a runner, sir. He didn't turn up for work today. He rang in to say he was sick. So I traced the call back and you'll never guess where he was calling from.'

'Surprise me.'

'Orange.'

'Orange! Right, leave it with me. Do you have his car's registration number? I'll alert Orange Police, Highway Patrol and the airports in case he tries to leave the country.'

'The manager had the number. Apparently he has a reserved parking spot at work. It's a South Australian number; S467 AUU. He drives a blue Holden Commodore. I think it best to first check whether he took his car sir, because Adelaide to Orange is one hell of a long drive. He could have decided to fly or hire a car.'

'Good thinking. Check to see if he made any flight bookings to Sydney, and from there, on to Orange. Get 'round to his place to see if the car is still there and sound out the neighbours to see if they know what his movements were over the weekend. It has just occurred to me that Christopher Allsop may have been the person who was to collect the money at the top of Mount Canobolas after Jayne Allsop had left it there. The more we learn about Christopher, the closer we seem to be getting to unravelling this mess. We must bring him in as soon as we can.'

'Okay sir, I'll ring you back in about half an hour.'

Detective Johansson didn't wait until Tania got back to him. The adrenaline was starting to pump. In quick time he contacted Chief Inspector Norman Sheldon to ask him to alert his officers to the possibility that Christopher's blue Holden Commodore could be there in Orange and to detain Christopher if they found it. Johansson also contacted Interpol and had Christopher Allsop put on their wanted list. Interpol would alert officials at international airports and seaports. Finally, Johansson rang his chief to update him on developments.

Next the detective made a quick dash down to the canteen to grab a coffee and one of those delectable cream buns that were there only on Mondays, and had only just managed to get back to his office after two mouthfuls and got himself a handful of sticky fingers, when his phone rang again. How dare Tania ring at such an indelicate moment. With his mouth half full, and smearing cream over the handset, he offered a somewhat indecipherable sound which was meant to be 'hello'.

'Are you all right, sir? You sound a bit strange.'

'Yes of course. What's the news?'

'I've been 'round to Christopher's place. The old lady who lives across the road says he left straight after work on Friday in his car but he hasn't been back since. He told her he could be away for several days and asked her to feed the cat. Left her three tins of cat's meat which he said is enough for six days. Sounds as though he expected to be away for a few days at least.'

'Thanks. Anything else?'

'Yes sir. It would take him two days to drive the 1,000 plus kilometres to Orange and another two days to get back. My guess is that he flew. I'll get on to the airlines next. Do you realise sir, he could have flown in or out of Orange on one of the flights you were on?'

'True, but he must have been on a flight either the day before or after me because I never saw him and it is only a Cessna so I couldn't have missed him. There is only one flight into and out of Orange each day. The other possibility is that he is still in Orange waiting for things to quieten down a bit before flying back.'

'Do you think Christopher knew we were planning to intercept the blackmail money?'

'I have no idea. After we interviewed him a few days ago, he must be as nervous as hell though. Perhaps his plan was to get this last cache of money from Jayne and then try to disappear off the face of the earth.'

'Sounds feasible, sir.'

'Now that I have the details of Christopher's car, I will send uniform out to the Adelaide Airport to look for his vehicle. If we find it, I will leave it in situ but immobilise it. I'll also post someone to watch the vehicle so that when he comes back to collect it, we can arrest him.'

'Sounds good, sir.'

Later in the day Tania was back in contact with her boss. She had checked with the manager at Christopher's workplace again to find out which bank his salary cheques were being sent to. Unfortunately, this didn't help because Christopher always collected his cheques in person from the accounts office and had never divulged his bank details. He must have had an account at a bank somewhere though in order to have his cheques honoured. Christopher certainly wasn't making life easy.

Next Tania contacted the hotline at each of the major banks to see if they had any accounts in Christopher Allsop's name. Success at last. He had opened an account at Westpac about three years ago when he began work as a senior storeman. The bank reported no sudden large deposits though. Prior to the opening of Christopher's current account with Westpac, Tania could not trace any other bank accounts in his name. Perhaps he was using an alias previously? This line of inquiry had gone cold too!

Crosschecking Christopher's fingerprints with the fingerprints found all over the eight blackmail letters and envelopes indicated no match either. Nearly all the fingerprints on the letters belonged to one person, but a person who was unknown to the police. Another line of inquiry that led nowhere.

Detective Inspector Mike Johansson was becoming increasingly frustrated. He was convinced that Christopher Allsop was their man but so far, he was eluding them. There was still no real evidence. They had set a trap for him when he tried to get back to his car at the airport and the police in Orange were looking for him. Interpol had swung into action to prevent him leaving the country by sea or air. The only other avenue open to the detective was to search Christopher's home. He rang his chief and made the case to carry out a search the next day. Permission granted; Johansson jotted down the items they would look for:

1. Previous banking details (old statements, cheque books, cheque butts).
2. Personal letters, particularly any correspondence with Orange or his father.
3. Information about his previous marriages and divorces particularly involving Rochelle Joan Brooks who was married to Christopher at the time of the incident in Sydney back in 1955.
4. Address books.
5. Telephone numbers.
6. Any other interesting items.

By the end of the working day arrangements were in place for Tania and himself, with the assistance of two uniformed police, to undertake a thorough search of Christopher's home and garden at 10 am the next morning.

CHAPTER 21

The House Search

The search team assembled the next morning at 9:30 am. The forecast was most disagreeable. The Bureau of Meteorology was expecting temperatures in Adelaide to reach forty-plus degrees by mid-afternoon with no cool change in sight. Extreme fire danger warnings had been announced for most of the state. The police station was air-conditioned but could barely cope with excessively hot conditions like this. The team anticipated there would be no air-conditioning available at Christopher's house and that they would be uncomfortably hot there. Before leaving they sat around the desk in Johansson's office.

Tania was her usual delightful self, vivacious, fun, and eager to get started. Sitting next to Tania was Constable Maureen wearing her rather too tight uniform. Maureen had been based at the station for barely two years, but Johansson had been struck by her tenacity and quiet determination to complete any task assigned to her with an unusual degree of devotion. She was thorough, thoughtful and happy to work overtime if a job required it. She had a wicked sense of humour and could have the station laughing in very quick time when she did one of her impersonations. Johansson wondered if he was sometimes the subject of her satirical comments. It didn't really worry him, because he found Maureen good to work with and quite reliable.

On the other side of Tania sat "Shorty" George, swinging one of his lanky arms about as he told the story of what he nearly did to some poor soul on his way to work that morning. "Shorty" George was highly intelligent and Johansson already had him short-listed for a plain-clothes job in the future when a vacancy arose. A gaunt-faced basketballer, he reminded Johansson of a daddy-long-legs as his arms and legs seemed to spread out all over the place. He was said to be six foot seven and a half but the joke at the station was that nobody knew for sure because no one could reach up that far to measure his height correctly. "Shorty" was blessed with an astute brain and was forever curious about everything he came in contact with. He relished a challenge.

Johansson opened proceedings by outlining the job for the morning and possibly into the afternoon. The operation would be carried out with the minimum of fuss, quietly and respectfully. They would knock on the doors of the neighbours prior to entry to explain what was happening so as not to frighten them. If one of the neighbours had been given a key this would prevent a forced entry and unnecessary damage. Gloves and protective suits were to be worn throughout the search. As far as possible, everything was to be inspected and then put back in its place exactly as it had been found. Anything they unearthed that was evidential in nature was to be carefully bagged and its precise location noted.

Johansson ran through the list of items he had jotted down the evening before which he'd expected to be of most interest. They would work intensively for sixty minutes then have a break of fifteen minutes and this scheduling of their time would continue until the job was done. Johansson even had a thermos of coffee, cups, and a couple packets of biscuits to make the breaks a little more enjoyable. Their first job on entry would be to pacify the cat as best they could.

Shorty jumped in quickly. 'What do we do if the phone rings or someone comes calling while we are doing the search?'

'Good question. Leave the phone alone. If someone comes to the front door leave it to me to handle. Anything else?'

'What if I want a pee?'

'You can use the bathroom as if you are a guest, Maureen.'

'Okay, if there is nothing else, we can get down to the car. By the way, I will be writing up a search report at the end and will ask you each to countersign it as being an accurate account of what transpired.'

Stepping outside onto the concrete carpark was like walking into an oven. It was hot enough to cook egg-on-concrete. 'I'm stripping down to my undies before I don the protective gear,' threatened Maureen. There was a titter of laughter as they opened all the doors to let the intense heat out of the car and climbed aboard.

It was barely a ten-minute drive to Christopher Allsop's

home. Although the house was small it was located in one of Adelaide's more delightfully leafy suburbs. You needed to be reasonably well-heeled to live in this location. They pulled up under a mature jacaranda tree that afforded plenty of shade and Maureen and Shorty went off and visited the near neighbours as planned. Shorty was able to retrieve a front door key from the little old lady who had informed them earlier that she was looking after the cat. The cat, she assured them, was not permitted in the house and spent half the night howling or catching birds. She was not overly impressed with her feline neighbour.

The house itself was circa 1920s and needed a paint job. A rusting bull-nosed veranda provided shade for a couple of pot plants that were not enjoying life squeezed into pots too small for them. A hose lay spread-eagled across a small grassy patch that harboured weeds as much as grass. Nondescript bushes, needing pruning, hid the wooden fence that surrounded the property. It was potentially a lovely house but somewhat neglected. They donned their protective gear.

The interior of the house was, by contrast, clean and tidy. Johansson surmised that there was a cleaning lady who maintained standards. They checked the house for rooms. The entry porch led down to a spacious living room from which you could enter an office and two smallish bedrooms. The master bedroom and en suite were on the left of the passageway before you reached the living area. On the right was a formal dining room. At the back of the house, through the living room, was a large entertainment area with the ubiquitous BBQ, outdoor tables and chairs. The backyard looked as unkempt as the front garden although there was a grand old oak tree spreading its branches all over the place. A Hills clothesline fought for a place in the small patch of sunlight that might've reached the backyard by midday. There were still clothes on the line suggesting Christopher had left in a hurry.

It was almost 11 am when they all split up to commence their work. An hour later they reassembled in the living area to relax, enjoy a coffee and discuss anything promising. Tania had been assigned the master bedroom and en suite and had found some of the storage areas occupied by a woman's clothing. There was, however, nothing like a full wardrobe of female attire as you would expect if a woman was residing there permanently. *A casual visitor who stays occasionally,* she speculated.

She could find no sign of any contraceptives so the female visitor was possibly post-menopause. This fitted well with the style of clothing she had found which resembled what a middle-aged woman might wear. It would be worth talking to the neighbours who might be able to shed some light on who the female visitor was. In the en suite she had come across hand gels, creams, a shower cap and even some perfumes. Johansson, recalling that the eight blackmail letters all had traces of a perfume on them, instructed Tania to package these perfumes for fingerprint crosschecking.

Maureen had drawn a complete blank in the two small bedrooms. 'Boring, boring, boring,' she'd reported. She had even looked for trapdoors, hidden compartments and anything secreted away. Constable Maureen insisted on devouring at least two extra biscuits to make up for her total ennui.

Shorty had been allocated the back porch and the backyard and arrived in a lather of sweat. 'It's got to be over forty degrees already,' he exclaimed. He had spent some of the hour looking for signs of anything buried in the so-called lawn. He had become excited once when a patch of soil appeared to be looser than the rest of the backyard at one particular spot. Finding a spade, he had dug down only to find the skeleton of what appeared to be another cat. No doubt it was the unfortunate predecessor of the howling cat that the neighbour had complained about. So Shorty also had drawn a blank.

Johansson had spent his time in Christopher's office, a more productive zone he'd hoped. In the top right-hand drawer of the office desk he had found Christopher's personal telephone book and had spent some time going through the pages and listing any numbers he thought might be useful. The book contained numbers from many years ago but there was no way of knowing whether Christopher was still in touch with any of the people listed in the book. As you would expect, all his family seemed to be there and Johansson noted that Rochelle Joan Brooks, who was Christopher's wife back in 1955 when the Sydney incident involving Charles Allsop occurred, appeared with several telephone number changes against her name. Most had been crossed out indicating that Rochelle Brooks had moved about.

Was Christopher still in contact with her? Could the clothes that Tania had found in the master bedroom be hers? An intriguing thought. Christopher and Rochelle had divorced in August 1955, a month or two after things had gone badly wrong in Sydney. Perhaps they were reunited?

There were a couple of other intriguing phone numbers listed. The single word "Orange" appeared but without a person's name against it. *This must be Christopher's contact in Orange and, even more tantalising, this might be the number of the person responsible for sending out the blackmail letters. Perhaps, if they ring this number, Hank will reply,* thought Johansson. Other interesting inclusions were the phone numbers for Dr Peters' home and workplace as well as Jayne Prescott at The Everglades. With these phone numbers there was some promising homework to be done once they returned to the station.

Next Johansson looked for an address book but without any luck. Perhaps Christopher had taken it with him, or he didn't even bother to keep one? In the corner of the room there was a simple brown cardboard filing system. It was bulging with papers and almost ready to explode. Clearly, Christopher was not particularly conscientious with regard to filing away his important papers. The detective rummaged through them alphabetically being careful to put everything back into its correct place. When the coffee break had been called, he had reached the letter M which looked promising. In this compartment were papers and certificates of marriage.

It was too hot for second cups of coffee, so they all resorted to drinking cold water instead. Maureen had made sure that the biscuits had not been neglected and was much relieved to hear that there was another packet, so far unmolested, that could be devoured at the next break in an hour's time.

Johansson reorganised his team. He and Tania would continue going through anything of interest in the office, and Shorty was to check the remaining parts of the house, namely the garage, the kitchen, and the second bathroom. Maureen was despatched to speak to the neighbours again to see if they recalled seeing visitors to Christopher's home and could furnish any other details of interest. She was then required to order pizzas to be delivered by 1:15 pm when they were due for their next break.

The pizza delivery boy was ten minutes late arriving, so when he did finally appear, they ravenously descended upon the three pizzas that Maureen had laid out on the kitchen table; Neapolitan, Vegetarian and Hawaiian. Their stomachs well on the way to satisfaction, Johansson called for reports on what had emerged from the last hour of the search.

Maureen had circulated around the homes within sight of Christopher's front door, six houses in all.

The occupants of two of the houses reported seeing a slim woman arriving occasionally and staying for a few days but had never been introduced to her so had no idea what her name was. Again, it was the elderly lady, charged with the task of feeding the cat, who was the most forthcoming. 'A good-looker she was, and turned up once in a flashy red car,' requoted Maureen who had recorded this snippet of information in her notebook.

Johansson and Tania exchanged looks. 'This is very helpful information,' exclaimed Johansson. 'It links in with previous sightings of a red car. She didn't by any chance have further details about the vehicle or the woman?'

Maureen had her mouth full of her favourite Hawaiian pizza and had to swallow before answering in the negative with a shake of her head.

'What about you, Shorty? Anything exciting to report?'

'Absolutely zilch,' was the response. If it wasn't for the tasty pizzas, Shorty would have dismissed the day so far as a complete waste of time. He was hot and had so far found nothing to help the case.

'Tania, how about you tell the folk what we found?'

'Well, we have been looking through Christopher's rather untidy filing system full of old stuff, much of which should have been ditched years ago. He has been married and divorced twice and we found proof of these events by way of certificates and court orders. Nothing we didn't know, but useful confirmation of the facts as we believed them to be. We also found a pile of bank statements going back over three years to when he apparently returned to Adelaide. Cunning sod seems to have got rid of his bank statements any further back that might have shown us any large sums of money coming in, if he was ever the recipient of large blackmail moneys. A couple of Telstra bills came to light that could be useful because they itemise his long-distance phone calls. We can check to see if there are any Orange numbers.'

There was a short pause as Inspector Johansson

endeavoured to dislodge an annoying piece of olive skin from between two molars. 'Good work everyone. Do we have any other parts of the house to check over still?' The three younger police, still grabbing slices of pizza, shook their heads. 'Okay, as soon as you are done here, check around the house and make sure everything is back in place. I want everything to look as though we never came here. Maureen, be sure to return the key. Then we will head back to the station.'

¶

The detective and Tania spent the remainder of the afternoon compiling their search report. Johansson was a great believer in getting any paperwork done as soon as possible after an event. This got the tedious work out of the way speedily but also ensured the paperwork was reasonably accurate. From experience, Johansson knew that the longer you leave the paperwork, the more is forgotten. Before they knocked off late that evening, one report sat in the Chief's in-tray, one was sent to archives and they both retained an individual copy. Two more copies were on Maureen and Shorty's desks for them to countersign. For Tania, the highlight was the final section entitled, "Recommended Follow-up Action." The list included:

1. Crosscheck type and make of the perfumes found in the house with that found on the blackmail letters.
2. Crosscheck fingerprints.

3. Contact Telstra to ascertain in whose name the Orange phone numbers were listed. Request addresses.

4. Check with Telstra to determine if the telephone number listed as belonging to Christopher's last wife, Rochelle Joan Brooks, is still her phone number. Request this address.

5. Ask Christopher's neighbour responsible for feeding his cat to contact the police immediately when she hears from him again or sees him return to the house.

6. Request NSW Police and SA Police to detain Christopher Allsop if sighted.

Both Inspector Johansson and Tania went home for the weekend well pleased with their efforts. At last they felt they were closing in on the most likely suspect.

CHAPTER 22

Escape

Was it a woman's intuition, a premonition, instinct or just luck that convinced Christopher and Rochelle to leave Orange that night? They certainly had a strong sense that the noose was tightening as they hastily consumed a meal of baked beans, a couple of eggs and sausages. The normally calm and composed Rochelle was a bag of nerves sensing that something was brewing. She couldn't put her finger on it or explain why she felt such unease. She had not heard anything that might explain her nervousness, nor had she seen anything that threatened her usual imperturbable self, yet she was frightened.

Christopher watched her nervously. She was still a fine-looking woman despite being close to fifty. He loved the strong lithe body, tanned and fit from working out at the gym regularly and taking early morning runs up into the hills around Orange. Unlike some of her friends, who over-did the exercise thing and became skinny and boob-less, Rochelle appreciated the balance needed to keep reasonably well-endowed and still looking gorgeous. She could dress to kill too. Working for Email White Goods factory as their senior research scientist paid well and her salary had been handsomely subsidised from the successful blackmailing of the despicable Charles Allsop.

For many years Rochelle had lived quietly in her home in Orange. She had built up a reputation as a model citizen, attending local events and joining clubs and associations from time to time. She was well-liked and enjoyed the company of several girlfriends. Suitors had come into her life for short times and then moved on. Occasionally she had slept with one of them but had never wanted to marry or have children. The typical mother-come-housewife scene had never appealed to her. Besides, she was still in love with Christopher Allsop, her husband, all those years ago. True, they had divorced in August 1955, but that was a deliberate ploy designed to conceal what the two of them had been successfully doing for many years; blackmail.

Rochelle never quite understood what it was that attracted her to Christopher. They had met when she was a first-year student studying a science degree at the University of Sydney. Coming from a home with domineering parents and attending exclusive private schools, she had been overprotected during her childhood years. Suddenly, university had allowed her to escape the oppressive influence of her parents and the stifling school environment. She went wild, drinking to excess, doing drugs, partying every weekend. Somehow she still managed to front up for most of her lectures and submit assignments. About a week before major exams were due, she behaved herself and devoted her energies to serious study so that she somehow scraped a pass in almost every subject.

Christopher worked at his father's transport company and was never a university student. This didn't stop him turning up at student parties often uninvited. They fell madly in love. As they say, the chemistry was there, and within a month of first meeting they were sleeping together. She found Christopher a loveable larrikin and a wonderfully refreshing contrast to the stuffy life she had led until coming to university. He was great fun to be with, quite irreverent and highly intelligent. At the start of her second year at university they married. Christopher was twenty and Rochelle only just eighteen. Her parents despaired of her and declined to come to the wedding that was hastily contrived at a registry office. Christopher's father attended though and welcomed Rochelle enthusiastically into the family.

Two days before their marriage, Christopher had presented her with an envelope that his father had asked them to open together. Inside was a fortnight's honeymoon, all expenses paid, in Japan. Flights were included as well as accommodation in five-star hotels. It was this generous wedding gift that made Rochelle finally realise that Mr Charles Allsop was a formidable multi-millionaire. On their return from the honeymoon they moved into a luxurious apartment next door to Christopher's father. Mr Allsop was happy to pay the very substantial rental. As it turned out, occupying the next-door apartment proved a disastrous move.

Christopher had unexpectedly turned up at Rochelle's home in Orange a few hours ago. He had let himself in and was awaiting her return after her day's work. She was thrilled to see him again; it was so typical of Christopher to just turn up unannounced. This was one of the reasons she adored him. He was a master of the element of surprise which contrasted nicely with the more mundane, comfortable life she had settled into over her many years in Orange. They had not had intimate relations for well over a month, since she had visited him in Adelaide, so they hastily undressed, showered and fell into bed ravishing each other. Even in bed Christopher could surprise her and they experimented with a new position for intercourse which was exciting if not particularly fulfilling for Rochelle.

As they lay together enjoying the afterglow, she got around to asking what had brought him to Orange this time. 'You, of course,' he had responded, '... and the luscious sex.'

'Oh yes,' she replied, 'and where are my flowers or box of chocolates may I ask?'

He laughed. 'Since when have you needed flowers or chocs to drag me into your bed, sweet Rochelle?'

She chortled and slipped her hand down his leg to see if he was still erect. 'Steady on, give me half an hour to recharge,' he grinned.

But the second coitus never happened because Christopher began to outline all that had happened to him over the last two or three weeks. He detailed the interview he had had with Johansson and Tania and how they suspected him of being involved in the blackmailing of his father. He was worried that they were planning to arrest him, although, if they had any definitive evidence they would have done so already.

So he had left Adelaide and driven for two days to Orange, which he felt remained a safe haven. He was sure the police knew nothing about Rochelle and that the two of them could live for a time quietly in beautiful Orange. Christopher promised to keep a low profile, leaving the house only at night, and if it was absolutely necessary. He planned to sell his car as soon as possible, because, with its South Australian number plates, it could eventually lead the police to his whereabouts.

There is nothing like stress and tension to spoil any romantic thoughts and Christopher's revelations had an immediate impact on Rochelle's mood. Surely, after all these years they were not going to be found out. They had been successful for so long, first with the blackmailing, and then, regrettably perhaps, with the murder of the loathsome Charles Allsop. She needed time to think. This was all so sudden. How had the police got on to Christopher? She was the one who had despatched the blackmail demands, not Christopher. She was the one who had administered the poison so cleverly three and a half years ago. Certainly, Christopher had been complicit all along, and it had been his idea to blackmail his father in the first place. Who, even in their wildest dreams, would believe that a son would do such a thing?

Rochelle's head was spinning. It was all too much to absorb. Christopher must be really naïve if he thought he could hide out with her in Orange and not be discovered. If they are after Christopher, then it would only be a matter of time before they would connect the two of them and see them for what they were, partners in crime. The more these thoughts hit home, the more convinced Rochelle became that they were in deep trouble and that staying here at her home was crazy. The police were far more sophisticated these days and were probably looking for Christopher's car this very minute. The police could be on their way to arrest them both this very evening!

'Get dressed Christopher. We are leaving. The bloody police could be here any moment. Do you really think they don't know where you are? They have probably been tracking you all the way from Adelaide to Orange. And your car is sitting out there on my bloody driveway. Grab a couple of cardboard boxes from the garage so I can throw some non-perishable food in. I'll knock us up a quick meal and then we'll get the hell out of here. Step on it!'

'Oh, come on Rochelle, you are overreacting. I drove past a police car on my way from the city centre to your place only two hours ago and they made no attempt to stop me. If I am a wanted man, they would have nabbed me there and then.'

'Don't be so sure. They probably used a bit of nous and followed you at a safe distance to see where you went. Now hurry up and get those boxes. I'll have a meal organised in ten minutes. I want to be out of this place in half an hour.'

Christopher never liked it when Rochelle was in one of her organising moods. There was no point in trying to resist. She became bossy, stubborn and sometimes quite irrational.

Reluctantly he traipsed off to the garage to find sturdy cardboard boxes. As he did so, he looked out onto the road apprehensively. Was there anyone suspicious out there on the road? A police car perhaps? All was quiet, so he busied himself looking for boxes that were suitable and then returned to the kitchen where cooking odours were already permeating. Onions had browned in the pan already and eggs, tomato and baked beans were about to be added.

'Those are the things to pack in the boxes. Then go and grab any clothes you have up in the cupboard together with anything else you might need. Throw in a couple of towels. Anything you might want for a few days.'

'Are you sure all this is necessary, Rochelle? You might be panicking about nothing.'

'Better to be safe than sorry. We can always come back if there is no sign of danger. We'll go in my car, it will be more reliable than yours, and the police won't be looking for mine either.'

Rochelle dished up their meal and poured them each a glass of locally produced red wine. 'Go and get some petrol in my car while I pack some things – it's nearly empty. Forget the washing up. I want out of here quick time.'

Christopher went off feeling like an obedient lapdog. A short time later he returned with the petrol, and had the water, air and oil checked. 'Where the hell are we going?' he asked.

'A good friend's place,' she snapped. 'We can stay the night there and then move on tomorrow.'

They loaded up and left Rochelle's comfy home around 9 pm.

Connections

It had been a brilliant weekend for Mike Johansson. Not only had he won his round of golf but finally managed to lower his handicap. To cap it off, he won the meat tray at the golf club afterwards which put him in good stead with his wife, Lynda, when he finally arrived home a little bit the worse for wear near midnight. Sunday had been recovery day and he had spent the afternoon collecting umpteen bags of sheep manure for Lynda's new garden bed, that she assured him would be displaying prize-winning roses within a couple of years. Adelaide is well known for its roses and Lynda was determined to show the rest of the street that she was up there with the best of them.

Tania also had relished her weekend. Tony had surprised her on Saturday night with tickets to the Adelaide Symphony Orchestra's concert. Tony was not particularly fond of classical music, which made this gesture even more special. He knew, however, that she had played violin in youth orchestras at school and for a time afterwards. At one point, Tania had even considered trying to qualify for the Adelaide Music Conservatorium. The concert program included one of her favourite violin concerti, Max Bruck's Violin Concerto No. 1 in G Minor. She was worried that Tony might fall asleep during the concert, but he actually admitted to 'quite enjoying it' when they dined out afterwards. Sunday had been a beautiful lazy day just right for recharging her batteries.

So, both Johansson and Tania bounced into the police station on Monday morning ready for action. Within the hour, the five lines of further inquiry they had identified on Friday evening were under way. Forensics was analysing the perfumes that they had bagged up in Christopher's bedroom to see if there was a match with the fingerprints and scents emanating from the blackmail letters. Telstra had agreed to investigate the Orange telephone numbers and to report back with names and addresses later in the day. With the chief's authorisation, the NSW Police and the SA Police were actively on the lookout for Christopher Allsop and his car and had instructions to detain him if found. The international airports and seaports had extended the period during which they would detain Christopher if he attempted to leave the country. Even Christopher's next-door neighbour had been instructed to look out for his return and report on this immediately. For the time being it was a waiting game. Telstra was the first to report back and their findings were indeed most fruitful. The phone number in Orange that Christopher had in his phone book turned out to be that of his ex-wife, Rochelle Joan Brooks. This finding posed a whole new set of possibilities.

Were Christopher and Rochelle working together in the blackmail plot? Was it Rochelle who had sent all the blackmail letters from Orange using the name Hank to confuse everyone? Was Rochelle the mystery woman with the red Austin Healey Sprite who had visited The Everglades at least twice before Charles' death by poisoning? Was Rochelle the woman who occasionally turned up at Christopher's Adelaide home? Were they still in a relationship, despite being legally divorced? Was the divorce also a smokescreen? If Rochelle was so heavily involved, how had she been drawn into this nasty business in the first place, and what was her motivation?

Johansson moved quickly. He alerted the Orange police to keep a watching brief on Rochelle's house but to do so discreetly. He anticipated that Christopher would turn up at her house and that the police could then quietly detain him without alerting Rochelle. Then it struck him that Christopher may already be there hiding in Rochelle's house. Perhaps the two were holed up there together? The detective next instructed Tania to do some background work on Rochelle and to get back to him next morning with anything useful she had turned up.

Late in the afternoon, forensics sent one of their staff around to speak with Johansson. They had confirmed that there was a definite match. Traces of Chanel No. 9 was the perfume detected on all the blackmail letters. One of the three perfumes Tania had discovered in Christopher's bedroom was also Chanel No. 9. This match, of course, was not conclusive proof to implicate Rochelle to any of the crimes, but it was certainly another small piece of supporting evidence. Chanel No. 9, one of the perfumes promoted by the fashionista, Karl Lagerfeld, was a popular perfume amongst the well-heeled who could afford such luxurious adornments.

Tania had spent the day researching Rochelle. Two fascinating facts had emerged. Rochelle had graduated from Sydney University with a degree in Biochemistry and throughout the time that the blackmail letters were landing in Charles Allsop's in-tray she had been living in Orange where she held a position as a research scientist at the well-known Orange Email White Goods factory. Once again, connections were being made. A qualified biochemist would have both the knowledge and the skill to be able to concoct a poison that might be very difficult to detect. Charles had been poisoned, and she had been seen near his premises only a day or so before his demise. The blackmail letters had all originated from Orange where Rochelle had resided for nearly twenty-five years since her divorce.

Once Johansson had been briefed by Tania, he agreed there was now sufficient evidence to also detain Rochelle Brooks. With the chief's permission, he gave the order for Rochelle to be arrested and Rochelle's house in Orange to be subjected to a full search. It seemed definite now that Rochelle and Christopher were partners in crime jointly responsible for the blackmailing and murder of Charles Allsop. They had to be apprehended as soon as possible. The chief, however, warned against involving the public in any way at this stage, as it was unknown whether the pair, if cornered, might be dangerous.

So far, they appeared to have been responsible for a cruel, premeditated murder, and there was nothing to suggest that they were carrying arms or weapons. The search of Christopher's home had yielded nothing dangerous. Nevertheless, it was wise to be cautious.

In the wee small hours of the next morning, two police vehicles drew up a short distance away from Rochelle Brooks' home in Orange. Quietly, befitting a well-drilled team, the eight officers encircled the house and took up their positions to cover any attempts to escape from the building. The officer-in-charge carried out the normal police procedures at the front door calling for the inhabitants to open up and allow the police in to conduct the search. There was no answer. He tried again and then a third time. Still no response. He nodded to his second-in-command who used the battering ram to smash down the front door. Still no sound, so they entered, commando-style, checking each room one at a time before declaring it safe. Within a few minutes the team commenced the search leaving just one of their number to watch at the front entrance.

One of the team was a fingerprint expert. She was assigned the kitchen as this was where Rochelle was most likely to have left her fingerprints; on cupboards, cooking utensils and the hundred and one jars, packets and Tupperware containers found in almost all kitchens. The remainder of the team scoured the house looking for the usual items; personal phone numbers and addresses, bank statements and anything to link Rochelle to Christopher. Next, they searched the garage and backyard. Two hours later, their work completed, they cleaned up and returned to the Orange Police Station for a debrief.

The sun was struggling to show itself as the two police vehicles pulled into the police compound. It was early Autumn and there was already a sharp chill in the air. Orange, located 250 kilometres inland, and at a relatively high altitude, recorded over a hundred frosts a year and the first one of the year felt as though it was not far away. Early autumn leaves lay scattered about the ground whilst others occasionally drifted down from the deciduous trees that surrounded the station. The team scurried through the doors and into the meeting room where they were greeted by Chief Inspector Norman Sheldon. The Chief had done the right thing by coming in early to conduct the debrief and had the urn boiling and a plentiful supply of coffee, hot chocolate and teas available. Even more impressive was the pile of freshly baked croissants the Chief had picked up from his local bakery on his way to the station.

'Grab yourselves a plate and some refreshments, sit yourselves down and we'll start the debrief in five minutes.'

The Chief Inspector had high expectations for the forty or so police under his command in the Orange district. He was well respected however, as a fair man, decisive but considerate. Not all chiefs would have thought to welcome their charges back from night duty with hot drinks and croissants.

'Thank you, ladies and gentlemen, your attention please. First, I want to thank you for taking on this arduous night duty. I have arranged for you to all have an extra day off in lieu. Your verbal reports will be recorded and I expect to see the full written report in my office by 14.00 hours. Now, if you are ready Sergeant, as the officer-in-charge, please get us under way.'

'Thank you, sir. I jotted down notes as the search was conducted but I'll confine myself now to the most important matters. Others may wish to add to my comments when I've finished.'

'Go ahead, Sergeant.'

'Entry went according to standard practice. The residence was found to be unoccupied but there were signs of a hasty exit. There were clothes in the washing basket that had been washed but not hung out. They were still wet. Most of the clothes belonged to a woman but we also found a man's shirt, pants and socks there. We also found a man's electric shaver in the bathroom. The shaver has been bagged for the fingerprint experts to inspect. We found two sets of dirty plates, cutlery and other things in the kitchen sink together with wine glasses and a half-emptied bottle of red. It appears as if there were two people having an evening meal together last night when something alerted them to a possible police raid, so they left in a humongous hurry. There was even a dessert in the fridge untouched.'

'That's infuriating,' remarked the Chief. 'We must have missed them by only a few hours.'

'I'm afraid so, sir. We have plenty of fingerprints and these should be checked and identified by this afternoon. There was very little of use that we found inside the house. We found

Chanel No. 9 in the bedroom, as we expected, and a Telstra bill that included calls to Christopher Allsop's number.'

'And what about outside?' an impatient Chief Inspector demanded.

'Very interesting indeed, sir. Behind the garage was a rusting, unroadworthy, red Austin Healey Sprite with its registration plates removed. We could find no paperwork proving the car belonged to Rochelle Brooks. No doubt the papers have all been destroyed and the plates dumped somewhere too. The sticker on the windscreen indicated it was last in use in 1976. In the garage we found Christopher's blue Ford so it looks as though they both took off in Rochelle's current car. We will need to find out what she is driving.'

'Good work. We'll get on to the details of Rochelle's car as soon as we finish this debrief. Anything else useful?'

'Well, I'm not sure sir, but at the back of the garage is a sort of science laboratory that has been set up there. None of our team have a sufficient science background to know what all the stuff is being used for, but we think someone with the necessary know-how ought to go and have a good look at it. Perhaps she is creating poisons there. Who knows?'

'Righto, leave it with me.' The Chief Inspector cleared his throat before continuing, 'I'm going to get someone with a science background to check that garage out. In the meantime, I want the house cordoned off and declared a crime scene. We certainly don't want kids or anyone else wandering in there and playing with any chemicals they find. Keep the house under surveillance twenty-four/seven too.'

'Thank you everyone. I'm going to ring our friends in Adelaide to put them in the picture. Any final comments from anyone?'

There was a moment of silence. None of the team had anything else to add.

'Help yourselves to any remaining cold croissants.' And with that, the Chief Inspector jabbed at the recording device, got to his feet and was gone.

¶

The Chief Inspector waited until almost 1700 hours before he rang Mike Johansson in Adelaide. South Australia was on Central Australian time which meant they were thirty minutes behind Orange and he hoped to catch the detective before he left for home. During the day a considerable amount of additional information had landed on his desk and it was time to impart all of this to his colleague.

He began by outlining everything the sergeant had covered at the debrief and then followed up with the findings that had been forthcoming since.

Fingerprints had been found all over the house and were confirmed as belonging to Rochelle Brooks and to a far lesser extent, Christopher Allsop. The pair had left the house in a hurry some time during the previous evening in Rochelle's car, a white Mini Cooper S with an NSW registration number. These two were clearly the criminals they needed to catch he added. Everything has been connected up now.

The Chief Inspector ended his call by describing what the scientist from the Orange Agricultural College had told him after she had examined the makeshift laboratory at the back of Rochelle's garage. Dr Reinhart's Ph.D. was in chemistry, but for surety, she had suggested a second opinion was needed to double-check her assessment of what she felt was being developed at the back of the garage. In Dr Reinhart's opinion, all the materials required to produce explosive devices were present. She was unable to say whether some type of explosive was already available to Rochelle to use or whether she had taken the device, or devices, with her. Putting it bluntly, Rochelle and Christopher could well be in possession of one or more home-made bombs. They should be approached with extreme caution!

Needless to say, this news was not welcome to Johansson and Tania. The connections had now all been made between Christopher and Rochelle which was certainly pleasing, but the whole crime scenario had escalated to a far more frightening level. If the two fugitives were in possession of explosive devices, they now had to be regarded as extremely dangerous criminals. Nobody could possibly know exactly what it was they were carrying. Were they bombs or more like hand grenades? How many did they have? How trustworthy were these weapons? Had they ever been tested? How powerful were they? Did they contain toxic chemicals? To make matters worse, nobody knew where they were or where they were headed.

Johansson and Tania had come to work a few hours earlier on highs after wonderful weekends but they set off for home that evening in a far more subdued mood.

CHAPTER 24

Heading Eastward

'I'll just pull over at this phone box and give my friend a ring to tell her we are coming.'

'Won't she think it weird that we suddenly turn up at this time of night?'

'Yes, I'm sure she will. I'll tell her we have just had a burst water main at my place and have had to leave. She'll understand. I know her well. She's the Accounts Manager where I work.'

Rochelle pulled over and parked. Christopher sank down as low as he could in his passenger seat. He already felt a wanted man, a fugitive, someone in hiding and fearful of anyone he saw in the streets. There were few people about this late but he peered suspiciously at them all wondering if they might be plain-clothes police already out looking for him. He felt horribly exposed crouched in Rochelle's car. A powerful urge to flee gripped him and he longed to get out of Orange and away as quickly and as far as possible. Staying in Orange for the night was not his choice.

'Okay, all arranged. Tina is expecting us in about ten minutes, the time it takes to get to Lucknow.'

'Lucknow? Isn't that the place you said the car accident happened? You know, where Jayne Prescott was killed only a few days ago?'

'Certainly is. My friend lives near where the crash occurred. The road outside their place was closed for hours.'

They pulled away from the kerb and lapsed into an uneasy silence, both trying to process all that had happened in the last few hours and how serious potentially their position now was. A damp clinging fog was starting to roll in as they passed a "Welcome to Lucknow" sign and Rochelle swung the car to the left and stopped at the second house in the street. An outside light had been turned on for them and it cast an eerie glow through the trees in the front yard. *At least the car will be well hidden here, off the main road and under trees,* Christopher mused.

The front door swung open and a buxom woman emerged. 'Rochelle darling, what a horrible experience, water all over your place and plumbers splashing about in it. Do come in and get warm.'

They grabbed their bags from the boot and hastened in.

'Tina, meet my ex from about twenty-five years back, Christopher. He only turned up today and walked into a quagmire.'

'Hello Christopher, darling, you are most welcome. Anybody associated with Rochelle is my friend too. Now what do I do about beds, darlings? I guess you want your own bedrooms, don't you?'

'No, not at all, we'll be happy to sleep in the same room together.' Christopher responded with no hesitation. Tina was surprised by this reply and looked expectantly at Rochelle to see if the sentiment was reciprocated.

'No problem, Tina. We may be divorced but we are still good mates.'

'So it seems, darlings. Now, have you eaten? Would you like a drink?'

They declined the offer of food and a glass of wine and settled for a hot chocolate instead. Tina gushed on for half an hour or so, telling them about the awful car accident at the end of her road and how she had been very late home from work as a consequence. Christopher remained quiet and let Rochelle do all the talking.

'Tina, could you let the boss know tomorrow please that I won't be in? The house is in such a mess, and the plumbers will still be there. God knows when they will finish and then I have to do all the cleaning up.'

Christopher marvelled at Rochelle's ability to tell a pack of lies and to do it so convincingly. Clearly, she had missed her calling as an actor.

'Of course, darling, happy to help.'

Feeling well and truly "darlinged out" Christopher excused himself and retired to the bedroom that Tina had indicated was theirs earlier. He was exhausted not only because he had been on the road for two days but the stress was taking its toll as well. He clambered into bed and fell into a restless sleep almost immediately. Rochelle stayed up chatting to her friend for another half an hour or so and enduring snide comments such as, 'do you need any condoms, darling?' and, 'don't worry if you mess up the sheets, sweetie.' Rochelle had a lot of affection for Tina but sometimes she went a bit too far with her lewdness. Sex was the last thing on Rochelle's mind right now.

By 5 am Christopher could not contain himself any longer. They needed to talk. They needed to plan. Somehow, they needed to disappear. During the night he had pondered whether Rochelle had completely overreacted and that perhaps her premonition that the police would be calling on them during the night was unfounded. It was too risky to drive back into Orange to see if the police were at Rochelle's home. If they were already wanted by the police, they would surely know by now that Rochelle drove a gleaming white Mini Cooper S and such a car would stand out like a sore thumb. He caressed one of Rochelle's delightful breasts with immediate effect.

'Oh no, no, no, not now Christopher.'

'For once you are safe, Rochelle. I only want to talk. You know NSW far better than I, so what do we do? Where can we go? We can't stay here and we can't go driving around in your white Mini Cooper S. We have to plan and we have to move pronto.'

Rochelle allowed herself a yawn and a stretch before answering. Her perceptive mind began to analyse their predicament. When she finally spoke, she surprised Christopher with the audacity of her thinking.

'Do you think you can steal a car? We can't use my car

because it's too obvious, we'll be spotted straight away. If we go out west into the outback somewhere the locals will wonder who we are and get nosey and ask questions so it would be better to head east for the big smoke of Sydney. We have a good chance of melting away there amongst three million people.'

'Okay, going to Sydney makes sense. Perhaps we could tell Tina that we are going to go out west for a couple of days whilst the house gets fixed up. This might throw the police off our scent.'

'Sounds good but we still have the problem of my car.'

'How about we trade it in and get something else? That might give us a couple of days leeway at least before the police get around to checking out what has happened to your car. I guess the police will try to spot it on the roads first and then when it doesn't show up anywhere, they will check out trade-ins.'

'Yup, that sounds far better than stealing a vehicle. As soon as the theft of a car is reported to police, they will be looking for that car so we would be no better off. There's a car sale place right here in Lucknow. They would take the car into the workshop to be detailed before putting it out on display so it will be almost invisible for a few days.'

'Where do we stay in Sydney?'

'We have plenty of blackmail money in our bank accounts, so finding a small apartment somewhere will not be a problem. The main thing is to stay away from anyone we know as they may be tempted to dob us in if they know we are wanted by the police.'

'We could also sell the trade-in car when we get to Sydney and just use public transport. That would help to cover our tracks.'

'Good thinking, Christopher. Let's get up and have some brekky. Tina told us to help ourselves to what we want and when we want it. She leaves for work around eight-ish. The car sale place won't open before 9 am. Should be easy to then drive the 250 kilometres to Sydney today.'

'How about we go overseas, Rochelle? We have heaps of money. I brought my passport with me.'

'No way, the police are bound to have alerted the airports to be on the lookout for us.'

So, with a definite plan in place, and enough money to execute the plan, they both felt far better about their immediate prospects. Fear of the unknown is a highly stressful situation to be in, but now that they had discussed and agreed to a plan of action that stress was lessened. They showered, dressed and wandered down for some breakfast.

Tina was already up and tinkering about in the kitchen. She gave them a knowing look and with a twinkle in her eye inquired whether the darlings had both had an enjoyable night. They smiled in return but declined to comment on the level of enjoyment they had experienced, which of course was interpreted by the ever-inquisitive Tina as a "yes".

'It must be a bit unusual for a divorced couple to be still sleeping together twenty-five years later,' observed Tina, persisting with her obsessive fascination in their sexual affairs.

'Oh, I don't think so,' ventured Rochelle. 'Some couples still get along very well despite not wishing to stay married.'

'Well good luck to you darlings. Now, what do you want for brekky? Would you like me to cook you up something?'

'Thanks Tina, but we are happy to do our own thing.'

Rochelle and Christopher had both noticed that a television was positioned in one corner of the kitchen in full view of anyone who sat at the small breakfast table. Tina had The Morning Show on and they kept a watchful eye on the television to make sure there was no news item that might implicate them. They were relieved that nothing to do with Orange appeared.

Half an hour later Tina was grabbing something out of the fridge to take to work for lunch and Christopher and Rochelle thanked her most profusely for taking them in at such short notice. 'Think nothing of it, darlings, anytime. It has been lovely to have you here, even if it's only for one night.'

'If the house is still half under water and it's going to be a couple more days being fixed, we might head out to Dubbo and visit the zoo and look around there for a couple of nights,' Rochelle lied. Once again, Christopher was full of admiration for her ability to be deceitful and completely convincing. He nodded and mumbled something incoherent in support.

'Well, I must go, darlings. Make yourselves at home. Do give me a ring Rochelle when everything is sorted, and I'll see you back at work next week.' With that, Tina waltzed out, and they watched her leave in her car a moment later.

¶

The Lucknow car dealer was reasonably cooperative when he finally turned up a quarter of an hour late.

'Why the heck do you want to trade in a near new Mini Cooper S?' the car dealer queried.

'Decided I don't like it after all. It's a bit cramped and the sump is so low that it could scrape the road,' responded Rochelle.

'Okay, it's your decision. These Minis don't have any problems tearing around the Bathurst Race Circuit though, sump or no sump.'

Less than hour later Rochelle and Christopher left in a second-hand Mercedes, having signed all the transfer papers and paying with a cheque. Rochelle handed the key to Christopher as she was nervous about taking an unfamiliar car out onto the main road until she had some practice on country roads.

'Beautiful smooth drive,' Christopher remarked, as he put his foot down after leaving Lucknow.

'No speeding Christopher, you have to be a model driver. The last thing we want is to be picked up by the police for some kind of traffic infringement.'

'How long do you think it will take the police to find out we have changed cars, Rochelle?'

'At least two or three days. By which time we will have disappeared without trace in the Sydney metropolis.'

'What the hell are we going to do about our respective houses? My Adelaide house is nearly paid for now and I want to keep it.'

'So is mine,' replied Rochelle.

'Now that we have both lost our jobs as well, we are going to have to sell the houses to keep afloat financially. But how the heck do we do that when we are not living there?'

'Easy. We'll employ an agent to do the work.'

'And I left my cat in Adelaide. Poor fellow. The dear old lady next door will probably jack up about feeding him and then get rid of him.'

'I have a freezer full of meat and other perishables,' sighed Rochelle. 'I guess it will all be wasted.'

They continued on in this vein, gradually becoming more and more morose and depressed, as they realised the extent of what they were having to give up. The blackmailing of Charles Allsop had realised well over $200,000 which had helped both of them get established. However, they were now in danger of losing far more than this, without any employment and having to pay for accommodation and living expenses in Sydney.

'They say that crime never pays,' remarked Christopher.

'Rubbish! Crime pays if you are clever enough.'

Christopher gave this some thought. Some of the pirates of the high seas had probably made their fortunes. The Vikings, who had raped and pillaged their way through parts of Britain, may have been successful. What about the Mafia? He concluded that crime was like everything else. It was the survival of the fittest. The criminals who were the strongest and cleverest could retire in luxury but most would fall by the wayside and end up in prisons, impoverished or dead. The real question now was whether he and Rochelle were survivors.

Could they get away with cheating society? Like it or not, it was him and Rochelle now against everyone else. Society did not condone blackmail and murder.

They had passed through Bathurst, the oldest town west of the Blue Mountains, and stopped off in Lithgow for a coffee and a stretch. Next stop was the Three Sisters near Katoomba. Here they purchased hamburgers and coke, and were sitting down in the cafe relishing their first bites, when Rochelle suddenly turned almost 180 degrees in her seat and looked at the floor.

'What's up?'

'It's my bloody dentist. He's at the counter. We can't let him see me,' exclaimed Rochelle.

There was a moment of panic. Rochelle wanted the floor to open up and swallow her. It was not a large cafe and there were only about a dozen people eating there. How could she avoid her dentist?

Christopher looked behind him as casually as possible and watched as the one man at the counter put in his order for lunch. Then, a stroke of luck. The man sauntered off to the men's toilet and Christopher was able to declare the coast clear. As unobtrusively as possible, they picked up their hamburgers in their paper serviettes and grabbed their cokes beating a hasty retreat.

'Oh God, that was close. If he had seen me... no more stops now until we hit the big smoke.'

They reached the outer suburbs of Sydney later that afternoon and booked into a motel for the night under the name of Mr and Mrs Kennedy from Broken Hill.

Back in Adelaide

It was 9 am and Tania and Inspector Johansson had arrived in the office each armed with a mug of coffee. They discussed a couple of other cases they were working on and then focused on the main business, the blackmail and murder of Charles Allsop. It was now four days since Christopher Allsop had fled his home in Adelaide and driven to Orange in New South Wales to stay with his partner in crime, Rochelle Brooks. And it was two days since these two criminals had literally disappeared from Orange.

'Okay, what more do we know and what more can we do?' queried the detective.

'Frustratingly, the trail seems to have gone cold, sir. I have had someone watching Christopher's home day and night but there has been no sign of him. The dear old soul who lives nearby, and has been feeding Christopher's cat for him, has had enough of it, so I had the cat taken down to the local pound. They will keep the cat for a few days and then make him available to anyone who would like to take him.'

'Paying a security company thousands of dollars to watch Christopher's house twenty-four/seven is no longer feasible. It's burning a nasty big hole in my budget. When you chatted to the neighbours, did you come across anyone who is likely to be able to keep an eye on Christopher's place and could advise us if there are any signs of his return? I'd be prepared to pay them police informant rates.'

Tania laughed. This was the first time she had ever heard of "police informant rates". She suspected no such rates existed. However, there was a likely candidate for a position as a "police informant" living across the road from Christopher's abode. The lady, only in her early fifties, was wheelchair-bound as a result of a stroke some months earlier. When Tania had been asking questions of Christopher's near neighbours, she had felt a real affinity with this lady because her own father had been struck down by a stroke that had ended his working life and left him with moderate aphasia and confined to a wheelchair. The lady across the road had lost nothing intellectually but had to endure low-level aphasia. With the help of speech pathologists, she hoped to be speaking normally again within twelve months. When Tania mentioned this good lady to Johansson, he asked her to go and visit her and offer thirty dollars a day for the next ten days. He reasoned that if Christopher was desperate to collect certain items from his home, he would attempt to procure them sooner rather than later.

Johansson was contemplating a second cup of coffee when his phone rang. It was Chief Inspector Norman Sheldon, the officer-in-charge at the Orange Police Station. The detective switched to loudspeaker phone so that Tania could participate.

The Chief Inspector was in a buoyant mood because they had had a minor breakthrough. The Orange Police had concentrated their efforts in and around the city, hunting for Rochelle's white Mini Cooper S, and yesterday afternoon they had found it. The vehicle was about to undergo detailing at the Lucknow Car Sales and the police had spent an hour or so carefully examining the car and interviewing the proprietor. On the floor of the boot they had discovered traces of a grey powder which this morning had been identified as a highly volatile substance used in explosives.

The proprietor had described in some detail the two people who were with the vehicle and it was undoubtedly Christopher and Rochelle. The proprietor had not suspected anything, but he was surprised they had wanted to trade in a very new car and had remarked that they did appear to be a bit on edge and wanted to get going. The transaction had gone smoothly enough and they had let slip that they were travelling west to Dubbo to stay for a couple of days and then out into the outback. The Dubbo Police had been alerted but there had been no sightings of the 1970 cream coloured Mercedes in which they were known to be travelling.

The Chief Inspector went on to confirm that the Federal Police were also looking for the Mercedes but that overall control of this case still resided with Johansson since the crimes had been committed in South Australia. Tania couldn't help but feel that Norman Sheldon's cheerful call was, at least in part, because the problem had now moved off his patch elsewhere. The only responsibility that remained with the Chief Inspector in Orange was to maintain a watch on Rochelle's house which he promised to do. With assurances that he would ring again if there were any further developments, the Chief Inspector ended the conversation.

'They'd be crazy to go out west. It's far more difficult to remain incognito driving around in a cream coloured Merc out in the sticks,' Johansson commented.

'So, what do you think they are doing?'

'Gone to Sydney probably. If you want to disappear, head for a big city. They both worked there remember? And Rochelle studied at Sydney University, so they know their way about.'

'Makes sense.'

'It's going to be difficult to track them down though. I'm presuming they have plenty of money so they can survive for a time. Eventually however, they will either have to sell their respective homes, find jobs or turn to crime for a living. Unless they make a serious mistake, they can lie low for many months and remain undetected.'

'So, is there anything we can do, sir? It feels a bit stupid just sitting about waiting for them to stuff up.'

'I agree. Sadly, many crimes stay on hold for years. Eventually, many of the crims become over-confident and get careless, so that many years later they are finally caught. By then, of course, some key witnesses have died and details have been lost so it is more difficult to prosecute. We just have to remain positive and wait for them to blow their cover.'

'What about some publicity in Sydney, sir? If we can get on to a good journalist, he or she might write up an article and include photos of the two villains in the local Sydney papers. It might be worth a try. Somebody is bound to have seen them and might come forward.'

'That's not a bad idea. I know a couple of journos in Sydney that are trustworthy. These guys have worked cooperatively with police in the past. Its quid pro quo. We give them a story and they give us the exposure we want. We have plenty of information we can feed them. Getting decent up-to-date photos might be hard though.'

'If you can arrange the journo sir, I'll chase up photographs.'

'Okay, let's give it a try. Meet as per usual tomorrow morning and we can work on the draft story. See if you can get any photos faxed to this office.'

Lying Low

Mr and Mrs Kennedy from Broken Hill turned in early that night, not because they were tired, but because after sharing a reasonable bottle of red wine, they had other things on their mind. They were well pleased with their escape to Sydney and felt relaxed and safe at their motel. The motel proudly proclaimed that they had waterbeds in all units which was the recent craze to sweep Australia. Neither Rochelle nor Christopher had ever slept on waterbeds and certainly had never made love on one. It was a fun challenge but clearly a practiced art. They managed in a clumsy way and vowed to improve their performance in the morning.

Christopher woke first, and seeing Rochelle still in a deep sleep, crept out of bed and silently opened their door to sample the early morning air. Traffic was already streaming noisily up and down the main road. He contemplated an early morning swim in the motel's pool but then remembered he didn't have his swimming togs. Underpants? No, that might be risky. He returned and showered instead.

As he emerged from the shower, Rochelle appeared stark naked.

'Time for your advanced lesson on the waterbed,' she purred.

Christopher needed no more encouragement. He dried hastily and joined his lover. She gave him seven out of ten this time.

Breakfast was a casual and relaxed affair in the motel's dining room. This was a far better option than having breakfast delivered to your room and being disturbed at an inconvenient time. They gorged on a full cooked breakfast, backed up by wholemeal toast with lashings of New Zealand butter and Rose's Chunky Marmalade. Two cups of coffee and a quick skim of the morning's papers completed their repast.

Mr and Mrs Kennedy from Broken Hill paid for their night's accommodation in cash. Seeing where they were from, the receptionist took a special interest in them. It transpired that she had lived in Broken Hill for several years and had loved it there. Did they know Alfred Thomas? Was the fishmonger still there? And how's the water now? For the third time, Christopher was grateful to Rochelle for the way she handled the questions with such aplomb.

As they cleaned their teeth, he asked her when she had last been to Broken Hill.

'Never.'

'So how did you know how to answer her questions?'

'I didn't, I just bullshitted.'

¶

Many years ago, Rochelle, when a student at Sydney University, had lived in digs in Glebe. Here you were within easy walking distance of shops, cinemas, the city centre and trains and there were appealing areas to exercise along the harbour shores. It was a crowded suburb, but had a lot to commend it, including many cool restaurants and eating houses. Their plan was to sell the car and in future rely entirely on public transport. They decided they would spend the day looking at reasonably priced furnished apartments and put down a deposit if they found something suitable.

The Glebe real estate office Century 21 was their first port of call. They had five small vacant apartments in the Glebe environs on their books that were reasonably priced. As a monetary precaution, Christopher and Rochelle had decided they could make do with a one-bedroom place, but it had to be a class above a bed-sitter. They found a suitable small flat at the back of one of the few remaining mansions along Glebe Road and there and then put down a deposit of $300 in cash. Rochelle completed all the forms in her name, Rochelle Joan Brooks.

That evening they were in possession of the key and moved in holding a minimum lease of three months. The furnishings were rather antiquated and worn, but they could cope. There was no garage, but they were permitted to park the car at the back of the main house on a concrete slab. Here it was not visible to anyone using the main road. In any case, they planned on selling the vehicle within the next few days.

The landlady, apparently, was the elderly lady who lived in

the mansion on her own. Christopher and Rochelle thought it prudent to get into her good books, so around 6 pm they walked around to the front of the building and rang the handsome brass bell. The front yard was overgrown since the trees and shrubs had not been pruned back for years. Christopher made a mental note to offer to do some work in the garden if the owner wanted it done.

One ring of the brass bell was not enough. They liked the chime of the bell which was a copy of Big Ben's opening stanza in London. It rang out a second time and was then followed by a crackly voice, 'Coming, coming, I won't be long.' There was the rattle of keys in the lock and a moment later the heavy wooden front door opened a few inches. The safety chain was still in place. They could just make out a small lady with snowy hair and spectacles peering up at them suspiciously.

'Yes?'

'Good evening. We are your new tenants and would like to introduce ourselves.'

'What are your names?'

'I'm Rochelle Brooks and this is Christopher Brooks.' *There she goes again*, thought Christopher, who had been on the verge of correcting Rochelle and telling the little lady that his name was really Christopher Allsop.

'Yes, the agent rang me to say a couple named Brooks would be moving in. Let me undo this chain and you can come in.'

At first, they could discern very little as the entrance hall was in darkness. Christopher almost bumped into the head of what appeared to be a tiger mounted on the wall. On the opposite side the head of a grizzly bear eyed him menacingly. The little lady had yet to introduce herself and was prattling away as they felt their way cautiously down the long hallway. 'Here we are.' And she heaved open another large door and ushered them in.

At first, they thought they had entered a museum. The room was huge and full of antiquities. Four or five angle poises provided small arcs of light around the room whilst two massive candelabras high above them remained in the dark.

'This was the ballroom,' the little lady announced. 'Tea?'

The Brooks couple were uncertain how to respond to this invitation. On the one hand they were intrigued by the strange world they had just entered and wished to see more, but at the same time they were concerned about the hygiene of any "tea" that emerged.

'Sit,' she demanded. They gravitated towards one of the arcs of light where the little old lady picked up a hand bell and shook it vigorously. A moment later the door opened and an elderly man dressed like a butler appeared. 'Tea for three please Simon.'

'Now, why are you in Sydney renting my place?'

Somewhat taken aback by the little lady's abrupt way of speaking, it was Rochelle who was first to think of something vaguely plausible. 'We are looking at business potential.'

'What kind? Not prostitution I hope?'

They both laughed politely and Rochelle, never lost for words for long, came out with a story about how they were apiarists and wanted to explore possible Sydney exporters for their honey.

'Can't stand the stuff myself,' their unknown host declared.

'What a pity, I could have given you a sample.'

At that moment Simon, the butler, reappeared pushing a tea-trolley fully laden with all the crockery required, a large teapot with a cosy over it and a plate full of rather delectable looking cakes. Simon proceeded to dispense cups of tea and cakes as required and quietly left the room.

'Been with me nearly thirty years,' she observed. 'My husband employed him a couple of years before he carked it. We were in India and other places through Asia. George was a diplomat. Great life if you could take it. Malaria got him in the end.'

'So is that how you built up this amazing collection?' Rochelle inquired.

'Some of it. This is really three collections. My father's, George's father and our own. It's from all over the world, you know.'

'Have you ever had it valued?'

'Had most pieces looked at. Antique dealers are always trying to get in here. They annoy me. That's why I keep a loaded shotgun handy. If anyone ever tries to get into this place, I'll blast their heads off. Another cake?'

Rochelle and Christopher didn't doubt her declaration of war on anybody unwise enough to try and break and enter.

'I've got a top security set-up too,' she added, just in case her guests were entertaining any ideas.

'Must go. Have a meeting of the local history group tonight.'

The Brooks' took the cue and thanked their still unknown host. Simon was summoned again to see them off the premises and Rochelle and Christopher retired to their humbler abode.

The next morning, they called in at the Century 21 office again to discover that the name of their landlady was Mrs Diana Doveton.

¶

Rochelle and Christopher spent most of the day visiting car dealers. By late afternoon they had accepted the best offer for their Mercedes and went on to a Chinese restaurant. Christopher was keen to go nightclubbing but was dissuaded by his partner who stressed the need to lie low. She was worried that he might drink too much and make a scene.

As they shared a bottle of red from the Orange region, they discussed how they might fill in their days. Essentially, they had joined the ranks of the unemployed. Now that they had organised their accommodation and sold the car there was nothing more left to do. Work and owning a house had kept them both busy for many years and they had led fulfilling social lives at weekends. But all that was finished. Living the life of a layabout might be enjoyable for a few days, or even a week, but after that boredom was likely to set in. Rochelle, in particular, claimed that if she didn't find something satisfying to occupy her time, she would go crazy. Perhaps they could find casual employment? Or get involved in charity work? Rochelle even suggested they enrol in a course at the University of Sydney as mature-age students. After all, the university was within easy walking distance and she had often dreamt of going on to do her Masters. An excellent idea, until she realised that she would have to complete an application form, and thereby reveal all her personal details.

'Well, I'm going to adopt a disguise,' laughed Christopher. 'Watch my beard grow and watch my stomach grow as I become a beach bum.'

'Don't be so stupid, Christopher. A beard maybe, but you need to stay fit. In fact, you don't do enough now to remain trim. That's one excellent thing you can do, increase your fitness level, feel better and that in turn will improve your sex life.'

They both giggled. Rochelle helped herself to another helping of beef in black bean sauce and Christopher refilled their glasses. By the end of the meal they had decided to buy more clothes, since they had come away with the barest minimum, and Christopher had resolved to volunteer to fix up Mrs Diana Doveton's front yard. No harm in "getting-in" with the landlady. He would start tomorrow.

¶

The next morning the sun was reluctant to show itself, preferring instead to lurk shyly behind threatening clouds. After a leisurely breakfast, Rochelle went shopping for clothes and, true to his word, Christopher rang Mrs Diana Doveton's big brass bell with his sleeves rolled up and a smile on his face.

'What, you again?' snapped Mrs Doveton.

'Good morning Mrs Doveton. It's a cool Saturday morning and I don't have to go to work, so I thought I would volunteer to clean up your front yard for you.'

Mrs Doveton eyed him suspiciously. 'Why, young man? Do you want me to pay you?'

'Oh no, no, no. I enjoy physical work and I don't want any payment.'

'Is that so? I'm always getting people ringing my bell and wanting a gardening job. I hate gardening and haven't done anything in the garden since my husband died many moons ago. However, if you are keen to get some exercise, and don't want payment, I'll get the key to the shed and show you where the tools are kept. George did all the gardening.'

Christopher had ulterior motives that he hadn't discussed with Rochelle. If he could ingratiate himself with Mrs Doveton, and be invited into her house again, he could have a better look at the incredible antique collection in her possession. Years ago, he had flirted with the idea of becoming an antique dealer himself and had worked occasionally at weekends with a friend who owned an antique dealership. He felt he knew a bit about what might be valuable. It had even passed through his mind that Mrs Doveton might not miss a few of her smaller objects. There was such a clutter of items in the ballroom that he was sure she would not notice a few disappearing. He also wanted to poke about the mansion and check the garage out. Did Mrs Doveton own a car? When you are a wanted person, it is good policy to have a car handy in an emergency.

Christopher did not perceive his thoughts as wrong or criminal. He preferred to view them as "forward planning" or "strategic planning" as his boss was fond of saying, when he wanted to impress the employees. If things went wrong, easy access to a car could be enormously helpful.

A few minutes later Mrs Doveton reappeared at her entrance clutching a couple of keys. 'Now one of these is the shed and the other is for the garage,' she announced. 'I don't use the car much nowadays, but it's there if I need it,' she assured him.

'Do you get the car serviced regularly, Mrs Doveton?' Christopher inquired.

'Not enough really. It must be a couple of years since I had it done,' Mrs Doveton admitted.

'Would you like me to have a look at it for you? I always do my own servicing. I might have to ask you to pay for the engine oil, but I can check the vehicle over for you quite easily.'

Mrs Doveton stopped for a moment and looked up at Christopher inquisitively. Was this young man for real, she wondered? 'Well, one thing at a time is good hunting young man. Let's see how we go with the gardening first.'

Christopher felt he was off to a flying start. Take things carefully and his highly devious plans might come to fruition faster than he had expected. He toiled hard and worked up a sweat. After an hour and a half, he needed a drink. He had hoped that Mrs Doveton would invite him in for some morning tea, which would give him a chance to have another stickybeak at her possessions, but nothing had happened yet. He decided he would ring the bell again and ask Mrs Doveton to come and see what he had done so far. If she was impressed, she would surely invite him in.

His plan was thwarted, however. As he raised his hand to ring the bell, Simon, the butler, appeared with a tray on which was a jug of lemon juice, a glass and a couple of rather ordinary looking Arnotts biscuits.

'Mrs Doveton has asked me to tell you, sir, that when you are finished, please ring the bell and she will give you the key to lock up the shed.'

'Thank you, Simon.'

Christopher downed two glasses of the juice, left the biscuits and decided another half hour of work would be more than enough. About midday he was back at the front door, all smiles and oozing charm.

'Would you like to see what I have done, Mrs Doveton?'

'Not just now thank you, I like to listen to the ABC News at midday. Here's the key and thank you for all your help today. Leave the key under the mat and I'll pick it up after the news has finished.'

The midday news on the ABC was a long bulletin; fifteen minutes to be exact. Christopher might not have managed to get an invitation into the house, but he was now in possession of the keys to both the garden shed and the garage.

Promptly he returned the tools to their rightful places and hurried across to the garage.

The garage was a late addition to the property and had probably replaced the original stables, Christopher mused, as he inserted the key and pulled the garage doors open. It was gloomy inside, but there was a cobwebby light switch to the left of the door, and pleasingly it worked. In front of him was a Land Rover dating back probably fifteen years. It needed a decent wash but seemed to be in working order. The tyres looked sound and the sticker on the windscreen was evidence that it had been registered nine months ago which could only have happened if it had passed its road worthiness test. Christopher had driven one of these vehicles a couple of times and knew they had a reputation for being reliable and capable of managing rough terrain. No doubt the Land Rover had been the choice of Mrs Doveton's husband. An excellent escape vehicle for Rochelle and himself, if required.

Christopher switched off the light and was closing the garage door when he heard a noise behind him. He swung round, like a naughty boy caught pinching a cream bun, to see Simon, the butler, closing the garden gate. Their eyes met. The butler bowed his head slightly and walked off.

'Bugger,' Christopher spat out under his breath. Everything had gone so well this morning until now. What would the butler do? As he returned to the front door to place the keys under the mat, as directed, Christopher was already thinking how he would explain himself should he be challenged.

Wanted!

——————————

Johansson stretched and stifled a yawn.

'Oh, sorry, I stayed up late last night finishing off writing up the story on Christopher and Rochelle. Then I faxed if off to my journo mate in Sydney. He promised to jazz it up a bit. Apparently, a group of the local daily and weekly newspapers all around Sydney often publish some of the same stories. Saves them a heap of time and money if they work together. These papers have a regular feature that comes out on Wednesdays under the heading WANTED in which they highlight some recent criminal activity and ask the public to cooperate with the police if they know anything that might help solve the crime. They get quite a good response, although the great majority of the callers really don't offer anything useful. They do occasionally get some strong leads however, and apparently in the few years since they started the WANTED column, they have even made half a dozen arrests. So it's certainly worth a try. Those photos you dug up of the pair will be terrific. In fact, my mate said that photos were mandatory or they won't publish.'

Tania licked her fingers to be sure she didn't leave even a trace of chocolate from her Tim Tam and commended her boss for getting the story away so quickly. 'Do we know when the story will appear in the local Sydney papers?'

'If all goes well it should be out next Wednesday. We are too late for this week.'

'I have been checking with Orange, sir. Nobody has been near Rochelle's house yet. Surely she will need to come back and collect mail, pay bills, pick up personal belongings soon?'

'Yes, you would expect that to happen. There is no sign of Christopher returning either. All we can do is wait patiently. I have arranged for out of sight closed circuit TV to be set up at both houses front and back. If they are going to try to re-enter their homes, it will most likely happen under the cover of darkness.'

'How dangerous do you think Rochelle and Christopher are sir? We know they are capable of murder and we also know that Rochelle took away bomb-making materials.'

'Yes, that is worrying. In my article I stressed that they should not be approached or challenged in any way. Members of the public should report sightings, or suspicious behaviour, to the police and let us deal with it.'

'Fair enough. Why did they take explosive materials with them though? Do you think they are seriously planning to attack someone or blow up a building?'

'I doubt it. My bet is that they will only use explosives if they are cornered and in a desperate situation.'

'I hope you are right, sir.'

'Now, if these stories are published in Sydney simultaneously on Wednesday week, we are going to be bombarded by hundreds of callers. The public will be given an 1800 number so the calls are free. I want you to find five reliable people to receive these calls from 7 am Wednesday morning until 3 pm. They will need to be fully briefed so they know exactly what we are looking for. At 3 pm another team of five will take over and stay till 11 pm. We will then set up an answer phone service overnight and bring in the same teams again on Thursday as well. By Friday everything should be calming down a bit and we can probably just keep one or two people on. Can you handle all that Tania?'

'No problem, sir. I'll get onto it straight away.'

'You will also need to set up extra phone lines. I suggest you use the police archive building where it is reasonably quiet and they won't be constantly disturbed. You will need to have a roster system so the receptionists can have meal breaks. Develop worksheets for them to use so we have details of every caller, where they are from, phone numbers, what the information is and so on. We ran a similar exercise a couple of years ago so you can use their worksheets as a model.'

'Whew, anything else sir?'

'That should keep you out of mischief for a day or two Tania.'

Tania devoted three whole days to recruiting appropriate casual staff and organising for what she hoped would be a crazily busy Wednesday and Thursday next week. She rooted out the original worksheets, redesigned them, and then set up a room in the archives building. Everything was finally set up for the anticipated telephonic bombardment.

Johansson received a call from his journo friend in Sydney on Monday morning confirming that the eight local papers in the consortium would be running with their story, as planned, on Wednesday.

'Watch out Allsop and Brooks. You are wanted!' muttered Johansson.

CHAPTER 28

Lives of Leisure

Christopher and Rochelle soon settled down to their respective lives of leisure. The secret, they discovered, was to remain active, stay out of trouble, and live quietly.

They were enjoying a most fulfilling sex life, finding intimacy almost every night and sometimes even during the day. The flames of passion, first kindled so many years earlier when they were married for a short time, had excitingly reignited. They both wondered why they had stayed virtually apart, except for occasional visits, for so many long years and had not fully reunited years before. At least they were doing their best to make up for lost time now.

Rochelle felt she was occupying herself usefully, if not profitably. She had found a gym that offered the first month's membership for free. She was now into her third week there and was sufficiently hooked so she had decided to extend for a further six months. She went almost every day and, in addition to the gym workouts, ran several kilometres daily, whatever the weather was doing.

Likewise, Christopher was looking after his physical self far better. Frequently he ran with Rochelle but found it quite challenging keeping up with her. On one of the side streets coming off Glebe Road he had discovered a boxing club. Most afternoons he had a workout there which was doing wonders for his upper-body strength. He had paid his subs for six months. After nearly three weeks, his beard was also slowly taking shape, and he hoped it would be respectable soon.

Other forms of entertainment had attracted their attention also. Together they had been to the greyhound races that were held nearby and had had a couple of bets. A cinema complex, closer to town, had featured some interesting films, although finding a film that they both wanted to see sometimes presented a challenge. They relished the Sunday markets and had found a couple of pubs they really liked where they ate regularly and sometimes had a flutter on the pokies.

One evening they were dining in one of their favourite pubs when Rochelle raised a concern.

'Now that we have been here for almost three weeks, there is a danger that we will become too well-known around the place. We eat here quite often, for example. Many of the staff know us now by name. It's the same at the other pub that we frequent. Even the manager knows us there.'

'So what? Nobody in Glebe realises why we are here. We are open and friendly with everyone and behave normally. We are accepted. Nobody suspects us of doing anything wrong. It would be quite different if we slunk about trying not to be seen and behaving secretively. If we did that, people would still notice us probably, but would likely want to know who those two weirdos are who sneak in and out and don't join in with the rest of us.'

'You may be right, but we did agree to lie low and try to melt into the local community as it were. I'm just a bit nervous about becoming too well-known around Glebe. Perhaps we should think of moving on somewhere else? It's much harder to hit a moving target.'

'Quite unnecessary, Rochelle. There's no need to worry, so forget about moving on somewhere else. We have a good life of leisure here, why spoil it?'

'I guess I'm just sounding a warning about becoming too complacent, that's all.'

Christopher reached across the table and gently caressed Rochelle's hand. 'Finish up that beer sweetheart and I'll get us another one.'

¶

One of the reasons Christopher did not share Rochelle's concerns was his success in gaining Mrs Doveton's trust. Rochelle was aware that her lover had been spending some time helping the dear old lady, but she did not realise Christopher's malicious intentions. Christopher had not confided in Rochelle, so she remained blissfully unaware of his nefarious plans with regard to Mrs Doveton.

Christopher did not see his manipulation of Mrs Doveton as something untoward. He preferred to regard his actions as a kind of insurance policy for the future, should things suddenly go wrong. Whereas Rochelle viewed Mrs Doveton as an eccentric with whom it was wise to stay on friendly terms, Christopher saw an opportunity for ruthless exploitation.

Since the first time he had volunteered to help clean up Mrs Doveton's front yard and inveigled himself into the garage to view her Land Rover, he had steadily increased his standing in her eyes.

On the very next day he had finished the pruning and cutting back of the natives that had spread-eagled themselves all over the front garden. Their branches lay untidily and abandoned everywhere. When he rang the brass bell once again to let Mrs Doveton see his handiwork, she was full of appreciation and quite animated.

'Oh, that's made such a difference,' she exclaimed. 'Do come in and have a cup of tea, you must be hot after all that work.'

'Are you sure? I have rather dirty shoes on?'

'Take them off, young man.'

Once again, they retired to the ballroom and Simon, the butler, was duly summoned to provide morning tea. He did not disappoint. He reappeared some ten minutes later with a trolley with all the tea-making facilities along with a mouth-watering mudcake. Just in case mudcake was not to their liking, a bowl of raspberries backed up by a container of fresh cream completed the repast.

'Now, how did you tell me you like your tea, young man?'

'Milk and two sugars, please.'

'What did you say your Christian name was? Now that I am getting to know you, I think I should call you by your Christian name?'

'Christopher.'

'Here you are, Christopher. Help yourself to something to eat. I'll risk a small piece of that mudcake.'

Christopher did the duties and helped himself to a not entirely meagre helping of mudcake surrounded by a lavish helping of raspberries and cream.

'Now what are you going to do with all that mess you have made in my front yard?'

'I'd like to pick it all up and take it out to the tip. There's probably two trailer loads there, maybe more.'

'My friend next door has a trailer and there's a tow-bar on the Land Rover. Do you think you could take it all out to the tip for me? I'd be happy to pay you.'

'Oh no need for any payment. I'd be happy to get the job done for you. I can manage it tomorrow if that's convenient?'

'Excellent, shall we say 10 am? I'll arrange things with my neighbour.'

9

Christopher presented himself at Mrs Doveton's front door right on time. The good lady was ready for him armed with the 1977 edition of the UBD so she could show him where the closest council tip was. Christopher estimated that he would need at least two hours for each round trip by the time he had loaded up, driven there, unloaded and returned. He explained this to Mrs Doveton so she wouldn't worry.

'I should be back here by about midday ready to pick up the second load, Mrs Doveton.'

'I do appreciate your help, Christopher. When you get back, I will have Simon make up some sandwiches and we can eat them in the conservatory.'

Christopher pricked up his ears at the mention of a conservatory. Was it possible that there were even more treasures in Mrs Doveton's mansion? Lunch would reveal the truth.

He collected the key for the Land Rover and the garage key, both of which were on the same key ring, attached the trailer, loaded up and strapped his load down securely. He moved out into the traffic but instead of going to the council tip via the most direct route shown to him by Mrs Doveton, he diverted and headed for the nearby shopping centre. Parking with a loaded trailer proved a nightmare but eventually he found a double parking spot. Grabbing the keys, he hurried into the mall where he had only a few days ago noticed a small shop called Mr Minute. Mr Minute was one of those excellent craftsmen who could do any small odd jobs for people from fixing their watch straps to repairing shoes and everything in between. Christopher was after duplicate keys for Mrs Doveton's garage and the Land Rover.

'I'm in a real hurry, mate. If I pay you an extra ten quid can you do these two keys straight away. Please?'

Mr Minute lowered his head and looked at Christopher sternly over the top of grimy glasses. 'Planning to steal a car, are you?' Somewhat taken aback, Christopher laughed nervously and for once was lost for words. This was precisely what he was contemplating! How did this geyser know?

'Ha ha, very funny. Actually, I'm just helping an elderly lady who lost her spare keys.'

'That's what they all say,' Mr Minute observed, as he set up his grinding gear. 'Give me ten minutes and I should have them done for you.'

Realising that when people quote a time to a customer, they inevitably underestimate, Christopher gave Mr Minute fifteen minutes to finish his tasks and was pleasantly surprised to find the job had indeed been completed when he re-entered the shop. He handed over an additional ten dollars, as promised, and wished Mr Minute a pleasant day. Christopher was now in possession of his own garage door key and the key for the Land Rover. He and Rochelle could escape in a matter of minutes if the need arose. The keys were an excellent insurance policy.

The rest of the trip proceeded without a hitch, but it was close to 1 pm before he finally drove back into Mrs Doveton's driveway. He apologised profusely for being so late and explained that he had become lost on the way and then had to queue up at the tip. Mrs Doveton had however, waited for him. Christopher sensed that she was beginning to enjoy having him around and that his company helped to pass the time.

The conservatory did not boast any particularly interesting antique items and served more as a sunroom than anything else. On cool days, like today, it warmed up like a glasshouse and was a pleasant space to sit. Simon, the butler, excelled again with his cuisine. Christopher and Mrs Doveton shared a bottle of Cabernet Sauvignon so that the warmth, the wine and the good food combined pleasingly to relax them both. Christopher seized the opportunity to press Mrs Doveton further about her antique collection.

'You must be very proud of your antique collection, Mrs Doveton?'

'Well, I take it for granted I suppose. When you live with so many beautiful and valuable objects all around you, one can become blasé, and forget to appreciate how very fortunate you are.'

'Have you ever catalogued the collection?'

'Of course. I did most of it myself, but then I hired a reputable antique dealer to come and verify my listings. I know quite a lot about antiques you know Christopher. Nevertheless, the expert was able to correct me on quite a number of items.'

'Did you have the collection valued?'

'I did.'

Christopher resisted the urge to probe further and ask what the collection was assessed as being worth. Instead he excused himself on account of needing to despatch the next load of green rubbish to the tip before they closed. He promised to return the trailer and keys at the end of his day's work and bade Mrs Doveton farewell. He packed the trailer neatly and tightly so that one more trip out to the tip was all that was needed.

That evening Christopher and Rochelle celebrated three

weeks of their lives of leisure together quietly in their apartment. They cooked a meal on the small but adequate stove, and, fortified by a couple of extra drinks, made passionate and satisfying love before collapsing into bed. Christopher never told Rochelle that he was now in possession of the keys to the garage and the Land Rover.

Hundreds of Calls

It was Wednesday April 1st, April Fools' Day. True to his word, Johansson's journalist friend had submitted an article to the consortium of eight local newspapers based on the details supplied to him by the detective. It made for fascinating reading.

BLACKMAIL LEADS TO MURDER!

Many of our readers will remember the sudden death of millionaire Charles Frederic Allsop on January 18th, 1975. South Australian Police have recently announced that they now have good reason to believe that his death was murder. According to forensic analysis, the famous transport magnate died from poisoning.

Police investigations have been underway for some weeks now and the evidence suggests that Mr Allsop was also being blackmailed for some twenty years before his death. Apparently, Mr Allsop eventually refused to continue making huge payments to his blackmailers who then threatened him with death unless he made one last payment. Tragically they carried out their threat.

Three people have been identified as being behind this heinous crime. One is a doctor who was persuaded to falsify Mr Allsop's death certificate to make it appear that he died of natural causes. The doctor confessed to his part in the plot on his deathbed. Photographs of the two other people that the police are anxious to locate are provided at the foot of this article.

The first person is Christopher Allsop, the younger son of Charles Allsop, who recently resided in Adelaide. Christopher Allsop is 49 years old and has held a number of jobs over the last 25 years. About three weeks ago he suddenly left his position as a senior storeman in Adelaide and travelled to Orange in NSW.

The second person is Rochelle Brooks, a research scientist who has been working for many years with the White Goods factory in Orange. Christopher Allsop and Rochelle Brooks were married many years ago but divorced in 1955. They are believed to be travelling together in a 1970 Mercedes and to have possibly moved to Sydney, a city they both know well.

Police are warning members of the public not to approach the pair as they may be carrying dangerous explosives. If you have seen either of these two people recently, please report the sighting to the Police immediately on this specially designated free 1800 number: 1800 641 982.

The Police are appealing for your help!

'Well if anything is likely to flush out our pair this should do it,' remarked Johansson.

'If our hunch is right, and they did in fact move to Sydney,' Tania replied. 'I'm going down to archives to see what kind of a response the girls on the phones are getting.'

The archives room was busy when Tania arrived. The five women were flat out receiving calls and putting others on hold. If they had an additional line available Tania would have gladly joined them.

Yesterday Tania had run a training session for the ten women working across the two eight-hour shifts. They had been carefully instructed to be patient and polite at all times, but if they were convinced that the caller had nothing helpful to offer, then the caller was to be politely, but firmly, thanked and the call terminated. Tania concluded her training by providing a series of role plays which created much amusement but also reinforced the messages and helped raise discussion points. The receptionists recorded details of each caller on a separate sheet of paper and after each call provided one of three ratings.

D – Definitely to be further followed up. Highly likely to be helpful. Report this call to Tania ASAP.

P – Possibly worth following up. Store this for future follow-up work if none of the D ratings are successful.

T – Terminated call. Clearly of no use.

The telephone receptionists had been working for almost two hours already and were starting their rostered fifteen-minute coffee breaks with one or two girls going off at a time leaving the remainder to continue working the calls. Between them, the women had already taken nearly a hundred calls, the great majority of which had been terminated. Four had been rated 'P' and there was one 'D' ready for Tania to follow up.

Sue, the girl who had listed the single D of the morning, was excited as she left for a coffee. Tania joined Sue as soon as she had poured her coffee and began to quiz her.

'Okay, Sue, tell me about this call please.'

'Tania, I'm sure this is going to be a help. It was a middle-aged lady who works as a receptionist at a small motel on the outskirts of Sydney. She told me that one afternoon, a bit over three weeks ago, a middle-aged couple turned up and said they wanted a room for the night. The couple said their names were Mr and Mrs Kennedy from Broken Hill. The receptionist said that she used to live in Broken Hill herself but when she started asking them about how Broken Hill was these days, they gave her silly answers that she knew were bullshit. She booked them in anyway and didn't think any more of it until she saw their pictures in the newspaper today. She said she was sure it was them. They left the next morning and were driving an old Merc. She has the date of their stay, the rego number, and would be very happy to talk to the police again if required.'

'Great work, Sue. I'll collect this lady's phone number from you and ring her straight away.'

¶

Tania appreciated her conversation with the motel reception-ist and was quickly convinced that this was a positive sighting of Christopher and Rochelle. The only problem was that it was well over three weeks ago that they had checked in and out of this particular motel. Who knows where they might be now? However, three useful pieces of information resulted from this sighting; the fugitives had headed for Sydney as the police had expected, they were driving a Mercedes, and were calling themselves Mr and Mrs Kennedy.

The next call to be rated D arrived at the start of the evening shift, by which time Tania had left work and was headed for home. Tony welcomed her with the news that the telephone crew had been trying to contact her urgently. This second call had come in from a young lass who served drinks in the bar of a pub called the Dog and Whistle in Glebe, Sydney. Tania rang the number provided and was relieved to discover it was the bartender's night off, so the young informer was able to chat without being hassled or interrupted.

'Hello, Libby here.'

'Hi Libby. This is Tania Markovina ringing you from Ade-laide. I'm a policewoman working with the South Australian Police Force. Is this a convenient time to have a chat with you about the 1800 call you made earlier today?'

'Yup, now is as good as ever.'

'Would you mind running through what you reported earlier one more time please?'

'Sure. The pub always gets a few copies of the local paper for our customers, and I was thumbing through it before the evening got busy, and I saw this photo of two people who I'm sure have been here in the pub several times over the last few weeks. To make sure I was right, I checked with Rachel, who is on duty with me on the same evenings, and she agreed.'

'Wonderful Libby. Could you describe them to me please?'

'Well the bloke's name is Christopher and he's a bit flirty. He comes in here with his wife, or partner, or girlfriend, I don't know which it is. If he thinks she's not watching, he gives me the eye over and sometimes he makes a bit of a crude comment. We get lots of that stuff from some of the men here. We just put up with it. The boss always tells us to ignore the rude ones and just be pleasant to everybody all the time.'

'What does he look like?'

'Middle-aged with thinning brown hair. He's quite slim, likes a beer or two. He's growing a beard which looks a bit of a mess but is slowly getting better.'

'And what about the lady?'

'She's nice, well-educated I'd say. I guess she's about the same age as Christopher but is really fit and good looking. She has a lovely smile and is the quieter one of the two. They order an evening meal and often sit at the same table in the corner of the bar. I reckon they have been here half a dozen times over the last month.'

'Do you know what her name is?'

'Oh, golly, I don't know. It's something like Rosie or Renee or something. She doesn't come up to the bar much because Christopher does the ordering. I think it starts with an R though.'

'What about Rochelle, could that be it?'

'Oh yeah, I think that's it.'

'Libby, this information is a great help. Thank you so much. Now please rack your brains as hard as you can. Can you think of anything else about this couple? What they wear, any peculiarities? Anything they talk about?'

'No, not really. I work behind the bar all the time. I don't take the meals out to the customers.'

'Do they always come in on the same night each week?'

'No, they don't seem to have any pattern. I only work at the pub four nights a week. Sometimes they are there, sometimes they're not. You never know.'

'Libby, if they come in again would you please ring the police at the Glebe Police Station? Whatever you do, don't challenge the couple. Just behave as you always do. I will be ringing the Glebe Police Station tomorrow so that everything is arranged. Are you happy to do this?'

'I think I would prefer to tell the boss and then let him ring you.'

'Fair enough. Whatever you do, don't let Christopher and Rochelle know you have seen their picture in the paper.'

'I won't.'

'Thanks again for all your help. We rely on clever members of the public like you to help us catch the baddies.'

'Good luck.'

Tania replaced the receiver. 'Great,' she exclaimed. 'I think we have a definite ID.'

'I'm pleased to hear it. Now no more talking shop. Dinner's ready.'

¶

Tania awoke on Thursday morning to the welcome sound of rain pattering on the roof. April was usually the month that the weather changed in Adelaide. After a long hot dry summer akin to the Mediterranean climate, the cooler southerlies began to push up into South Australia more forcefully during the winter months. Tania loved this cooler time of the year and jumped out of bed at the same time as recalling the valuable phone call she had had with Libby yesterday evening. As soon as she arrived at work this morning she would get in touch with Johansson and ask him to contact the officer-in-charge at the Glebe Police Station. The next time Christopher and Rochelle fronted up at the Dog and Whistle for a meal they would be arrested. Tania took it upon herself to telephone the manager of the pub to put him in the picture and warn him what will eventuate the next time the couple turned up there.

Things were at last beginning to happen. This second definite call had narrowed the search area to a small part of Sydney in and around the suburb of Glebe. It seemed only a matter of time now before the fugitives would be caught and the long and tedious process of proving guilt would finally get under way.

By midmorning Tania had cleared her desk of paperwork and decided to visit the telephone reception team again to encourage their efforts and see if anything else of significance had come in. She grabbed her umbrella, as it was still spitting, and made her way over to archives, stopping en route to buy a plateful of doughnuts for the workers.

The pressure had eased considerably. Calls were still coming in, but hardly anyone had to be put on hold any more. The team appeared relaxed and welcomed the doughnuts enthusiastically. The total number of calls received had grown to 346. Only two had been rated D with the P list now expanded to fifteen. Tania cast her eye over the P list and determined that at this stage only two or three were worthy of following up. She would check again how many calls were still coming in later in the day and subsequently reduce the teams from five to two or three people for Friday.

On Friday morning they hit the jackpot. Tania was called into archives to be told that another D had just been answered. It was a Mrs Doveton from Glebe who had reported that the "wanted" couple were living in her apartment at the back of her house. She was very frightened and wanted to know what she should do. The receptionists had advised Mrs Doveton to do nothing but to stay in her home and make sure all her doors and windows were locked. The police would be ringing her back very soon. She should remain close to her telephone.

Tania returned to the comparative quiet of her office, notifying Detective Johansson of the call she was about to make to Mrs Doveton as she passed his office. She rang the number provided, and when an elderly lady answered, switched the phone over to loudspeaker.

'Good morning Mrs Doveton. This is Tania Markovina from the South Australian Police.'

'Why are you ringing me from South Australia? I live in Sydney.'

'It's okay, Mrs Doveton. The South Australian Police are in charge of this investigation. As soon as I have checked some information with you, I will contact the police at the Glebe Police Station and then they will look after you.'

'This is awful and I'm scared stiff. Are you sure you are chasing the right people? They have been good tenants and have helped me in the garden. I can't believe they have done all the things you claim.'

As before, Tania requested Mrs Doveton to describe her tenants. She listened carefully and there was no doubt that it was Christopher and Rochelle.

'When was the last time you saw your tenants, Mrs Doveton?'

'Oh, I'm not sure. They live at the back of my place and can come and go without my seeing them. I don't see her much, but Christopher is often around. He and I share an interest in antiques you see.

I think he had morning tea with me on Tuesday, or was it Wednesday? I can't remember.'

'Mrs Doveton, do you know what kind of a car they have?'

'Oh dear, I'm not very good on cars. Now I come to think of it I don't remember them having a car. There's a place for tenants to park a car at the back of my place but I don't remember seeing a car there. Perhaps they don't have one.'

'Do you have a back window or a door you can look out of to check whether there is a car there now, Mrs Doveton?'

'Oh yes, would you like me to look out of the window?'

'Yes please.'

'I won't be long.' There was a loud clatter as Mrs Doveton put down the receiver. A moment later she was back. 'There's no sign of a car and there's no washing out on their line.'

'Thank you, Mrs Doveton. Do you think they are in their apartment right now?'

'Oh, I don't know. I don't go prying about you know. I leave my tenants alone. I remember now, the last time I saw Christopher was definitely Wednesday morning. He came around to ask if I wanted my car to be serviced.'

'Now listen carefully, Mrs Doveton. As soon as we finish speaking on the phone, I will ring the Glebe Police and report this matter to them. No doubt they will contact the specially trained Police Response Team who will then surround your apartment in the hope that Christopher and Rochelle are still there and they can arrest them. You must appreciate that potentially this will be a highly dangerous operation as we believe Rochelle is in possession of explosives. Do you have someone you can go and stay with today so you are out of the danger zone?'

'Oh, that's awful news! Yes, I suppose I do. I have a younger sister living in Hunter's Hill.'

'Good, contact her and leave as soon as possible. Don't return until you have been given permission to by the police. Is that clear?'

'Yes, this is all very upsetting you know, Officer. I don't like to leave my home. I have a lot of valuable antiques and artefacts stored here.'

'I quite understand Mrs Doveton and I apologise, but your tenants are believed to be dangerous criminals and we have to respond accordingly. Order a taxi to get you across to your sister's place and keep the receipts. Glebe Police should be able to fork out a refund for you. Anything else you would like to know?'

'I don't think so. I had better give you my sister's phone number so you can contact me.'

'Thank you for your cooperation, Mrs Doveton. The police will be in touch again as soon as the coast is clear.'

CHAPTER 30

Escape

The damning article about Christopher Allsop and Rochelle Brooks had appeared in the eight local Sydney newspapers on the morning of Wednesday, April 1st. However, Christopher and Rochelle remained blissfully unaware of the publication throughout most of Wednesday. They went about their normal daily activities unperturbed. Rochelle enjoyed a run and a workout in the gym during the morning and even spent half an hour having a coffee and a chat with a couple of the women at the gym's cafeteria. The talk was all about ridiculous April Fools' jokes and pranks. Apparently, and fortunately for Rochelle, nobody she met had yet seen the article.

Christopher had a lazy morning and then decided to progress his plans with Mrs Doveton and her Land Rover. His thinking was to offer his services in getting the Land Rover serviced, thereby ensuring that if ever they needed to avail themselves of its use, they could be sure it was in tip-top working order. It would be a win-win for all concerned. He waited until 10:30 am to give Mrs Doveton plenty of time to get organised for the day, and then rang the brass bell.

Simon, the butler, was off sick, so Mrs Doveton pottered about in the spacious kitchen to get a pot of tea made for them both and even managed to find some lamingtons that were still edible. The good lady thought that having her Land Rover professionally serviced was an excellent idea and was more than happy for Christopher to make the necessary arrangements. She felt blessed to have such a pleasant couple of tenants living next door. One of Simon's morning jobs was to pick up a copy of the local paper on his way to her place in the morning. Because he was off sick, Mrs Doveton had not yet seen the WANTED article.

Christopher booked the vehicle in for its service for Friday and promised to have the Land Rover at the premises by 8:00 am. He then wandered down to meet Rochelle at the shopping centre for a bite to eat and to take in a movie. Around 6 pm they sauntered into a Chinese restaurant that advertised takeaways and placed an order for boiled rice and a couple of their favourite dishes. While they waited for their meal to be prepared, Rochelle picked up a somewhat tattered newspaper that several earlier customers had obviously also perused. Thumbing through the pages she suddenly froze. 'Good God!' she exclaimed, turning to Christopher, 'Look at this!'

Across the top of the page was a headline: "Blackmail leads to Murder!" At the foot of the article were photographs of Rochelle and Christopher. Together they scrambled to read the short article and then flicked back to the front page to find the date the paper had been published. 'It's today's paper,' hissed Rochelle not wishing to draw attention to herself.

'Let's get out of here,' Christopher responded just as their takeaway appeared. They did their best to look outwardly calm, but inside their stomachs were churning and Rochelle felt a migraine start to gnaw at her brain. They grabbed their takeaway and hurried out.

'What shall we do?' demanded Rochelle.

'Easy, we get out of Sydney. That article will only be seen by people living in Sydney, so we are safe if we get out of town.'

'But we don't have a car.'

'Yes, we do.'

'What car?'

'Mrs Doveton's of course.'

'She's not going to let you borrow her car.'

'Yes, she is, although she might not realise it.'

'What are you saying, Christopher?'

'I took the precaution of getting spare keys made for Mrs Doveton's garage and her Land Rover. We can get out of town as soon as we get packed. It's as easy as that.'

'Oh, Christopher… more bloody crimes. The list is getting longer and longer; blackmail and murder and now break-in and theft.'

'It's still not as bad as what happened to you all those years ago.'

When they reached a set of traffic lights they stopped talking whilst they stood waiting with other pedestrians for the lights to change and they could cross over. They both felt awkwardly self-conscious wondering if anyone nearby would recognise them. But Sydneysiders, like most people living in large cities, seldom looked at who was near them and automatically assumed an air of disinterest in their fellow travellers. Once across the road they felt it safe to resume their conversation.

'So, where are we going to head for, Christopher?'

'With any luck we can get away tonight without Mrs Doveton even knowing we have taken her car. The police can only find us if they set up roadblocks because they don't know what kind of a vehicle we will be driving. I reckon the Blue Mountains is as good as anywhere. A friend of mine, down in Adelaide, used to hike all over the Blue Mountains and he says there are heaps of deserted houses and huts about that you can shack up in for days without anyone knowing.'

'So, we are going to rough it then?'

'Seems so, unless you have a better idea?'

Rochelle's migraine had started to clear. It must have been the awful shock of seeing their pictures so brazenly displayed for all to see that had brought it on. She reasoned that after a week or two everything might have blown over and anyone who had seen their photos in the paper would have forgotten about them. The only people who might ring the police would be those with whom they had interacted closely during the month they had been hiding out in Sydney. She passed these thoughts on to Christopher.

They were nearing their apartment now and decided to eat their takeaway before they packed and left.

Around 7 pm, as the sun was setting, they stole quietly around to Mrs Doveton's garage carrying their meagre belongings. They also had a cardboard box filled with groceries that would travel well and a large container of drinking water. The materials needed for the explosives remained untouched and no longer wanted in the apartment. Mrs Doveton's curtains were drawn so they could make their escape unseen. They both felt some minor pangs of remorse for clearing off in Mrs Doveton's vehicle for they had grown to like the dear lady. Christopher drove out onto the road then jumped out and locked the garage door. With any luck, their theft would not be realised for a day or two since Mrs Doveton seldom used her vehicle.

They drove along Glebe Road and headed out towards the Great Western Highway en route to the Blue Mountains.

¶

Christopher's walking friend had explained that trekking in the Blue Mountains was different. Most people drove to the top of the range or caught the train up and then started their walks by descending into the steep gorges. After enjoying walks along the leafy valley floors the walkers were then faced with exhausting hikes back up the cliff face to finish their day's exertions. This was the opposite to what most walkers expected.

The mountains became a Mecca for Sydneysiders wishing to escape the heat and humidity of the coastal plains during summer. As the mountains opened up, people with an artistic bent settled there, and tourists flocked to the area even in wintertime when it was often enveloped in mountain mists or even snow. Because of its beauty, it was considered by many as an ideal romantic getaway.

Rochelle had often driven through the Blue Mountains on her way to Sydney, but amazingly, had never stayed or even hiked there. One night she had encountered a heavy snowstorm on her way back to Orange and thought she might be forced to abandon her journey and have to stay the night in Katoomba. Just in time however, the weather had cleared and she was able to continue.

Now Rochelle felt a bit ashamed that she had not explored the famous Blue Mountains more thoroughly during all the years she had lived in Orange. A working knowledge of the area would be handy in their present predicament. The only useful information she possessed was where you could usually get a decent meal in some of the small towns along the highway such as Leura, Lawson, Blackheath and Mount Victoria.

It took them three hours to reach Katoomba near the top of the range driven on by the need to get out of Sydney as quickly as possible. Tired and hungry they pulled into a service station to refuel and buy a couple of hot pies. It was after 10 pm and probably too late to look for somewhere to stay the night. There was a sharp nip in the air, not frosty, but not far from it. The thought of staying the night in the Land Rover without blankets did not appeal.

'Know anywhere we can get a bed for the night, mate?' Christopher asked the guy who was manning the service station.

'Nope, you're a bit late for the motels I'm afraid.'

'It's too bloody cold to sleep in the Land Rover. If I give you twenty quid could you let us stay in the service station for the night?'

'The police often call in during the night to get a bite to eat. If they find you asleep in here, they'll kick you out or throw you in the cells.'

'We are down on our luck, couldn't you just let us bunk down in your back room for a few hours? The police won't see us there. Here you are, make it thirty. Please, anything to stay out of the cold for the night.'

Christopher and Rochelle watched the young man as he thought about the easy thirty dollars on offer. Unbeknown to them, the young man was saving up to get married and this would be a welcome addition to his savings.

'I ain't got no beds. You'll have to kip on the floor. The boss takes over at 7 am so you have to leave before he arrives.'

'That's okay. Wake us up at 6:45am and we promise to be gone before the boss arrives.' Rochelle handed over the thirty dollars and the young man took them through to the back room that was comfortably heated. There were two old and tatty lounge chairs there and after using the toilets and parking the Land Rover around the side of the service station, they settled down for their first night on the run. At least they had been able to escape from Sydney.

¶

Not surprisingly, sleep did not come easily to either of them that night. They pushed the two lounge chairs together so they could lie snuggled up in a sort of half foetal position and spent the night turning over simultaneously. The young man looking after the service station only disturbed them twice to go to the toilet and left them to their own devices the rest of the time. By 6 am they had had enough and arose to stretch their cramped joints and use the ablutions.

Few customers came in at this early hour, so they bought some sausage rolls and coffee and chatted to the young man. They told him they didn't have the money to stay in motels or pubs and were looking for a deserted house where they could hang out for a few days. They enquired whether he knew of anywhere.

'You want to be bloody squatters then?'

'What else can we do?' replied Christopher.

The young man was tired and anxious to get home to bed. This couple had already created problems for him by staying the night and he wanted rid of them. Besides, the boss would be arriving soon.

'Just drive down any of the roads that come off the main drag and go along the ridges and you'll find places that have been abandoned. Most of them have probably been vandalised but you might be lucky. It gets bloody cold up here, so you'll need a roof over your heads. Now you'd better scarper before the boss gets here.'

And scarper they did. They took the young man's advice and began exploring the mostly dirt roads that tongued out along the ridges into the gorges and valleys north and south of the highway. The lukewarm sun was rising slowly but the air remained bitterly cold. Whenever they stopped to check out a place that looked unoccupied, they were welcomed by kookaburras that seemed to be competing with each other to determine which could sing the loudest. The valleys were filled with a dense layer of fog that crept up and over the ridges.

They had nothing better to do all day, so they went about their search for a place to squat meticulously. Christopher drove slowly and Rochelle was the spotter. Most occupied houses had smoke rising from their chimneys, a TV aerial, and signs of gardening. The presence of a vehicle was a giveaway too. Rochelle had a pen and paper with which she carefully noted the name of the roads they traversed and the location of any likely squats. At this stage they were just spotting. Once they had a better understanding of the roads and the potential squats, they would return and make a more thorough inspection.

There was a surprising number of roads to check out and it took until early afternoon to cover them all. Some roads snaked their way through the bush for many kilometres and then ended up at a magnificent lookout where rugged-up tourists were to be seen wandering about with cameras. They decided to eliminate these popular tourist roads from their search, preferring instead the quieter and less travelled roads.

Christopher and Rochelle spent the rest of the afternoon doubling back on their tracks to visit the dozen or so places marked out as potential squats located on quiet back roads.

Most were too dilapidated to provide adequate shelter, and three, to their surprise, already were occupied by squatters, who reacted badly to their nosing about. At one place they were even confronted by an old-timer brandishing a shotgun. Two places still remained possibilities, however.

The one they finally selected had all its windows, exterior stone walls and roof intact. It sat roughly 100 metres back from the dirt road completely surrounded by natural bush. The front door was partially off its hinges but could be forced closed. There were a couple of bunks, even a wooden table, and two chairs. They surmised it still served as a bushwalker's retreat. A large water tank sat on one side of the building and was connected to a tap in the kitchen that still gurgitated water. They would need water purifiers they noted. Most pleasing was the large fireplace in the living area. Since they were surrounded by bush, finding wood would be easy. The cistern in the toilet wasn't functioning so the bush would have to suffice. This place, they decided, was going to be their home for a week or two, at least until things quietened down.

They raced back into Katoomba before the shops closed and returned with two Arctic sleeping bags, a portable cooking stove, basic camping plates, mugs and cutlery, Puritabs, a pile of books from a second-hand bookshop, toilet paper, a small hand axe, a couple of bottles of cheap wine and a few other necessities. There was no power connected any more so they would have to manage by the light of the fire and adopt the natural rhythms of daylight and night.

Soon they had a fire blazing and Rochelle was discovering

the joys of working on a small cooking stove. The Land Rover was safely parked behind the stone house out of sight from the road. The meal was basic, but wholesome. As they sat finishing off their bottle of wine in front of the glowing embers of the fire, they heard possums scampering around on the roof and, both feeling snug and well-fed, their thoughts turned to romance; an interesting challenge with single sleeping bags.

The Hunt Continues

Events moved speedily following Mrs Doveton's involvement. Tania, quite correctly, passed the matter of contacting the Glebe Police Station over to her superior, Johansson. Within a few minutes he had convinced the senior police officer at Glebe that two dangerous criminals were residing on his patch, and that they should be approached with extreme caution. It was believed that Rochelle Brooks, a biochemist, was in possession of explosive materials and might use these if cornered.

Glebe Police Station agreed with Detective Johansson that this was a job for the Special Incident Squad and contacted them immediately. The sergeant commanding the Special Incident Squad sent a man around to Mrs Doveton's apartment to reconnoitre the building and report back before the squad was sent in. He returned within the half hour. Although he could not be sure, he believed the criminals had already fled. Nevertheless, the sergeant sent his squad in fully armed. Better to be safe than sorry. Finding no sign of

Rochelle and Christopher, the sergeant cordoned the apartment off to allow forensics to do their work unimpeded. Mrs Doveton was advised that it was safe for her to return but on no account was she to approach the apartment.

Anxious not to be away from her home and its valuables any longer than necessary, Mrs Doveton returned in a taxi that evening. She had ignored her sister's pleadings to stay the night. She allowed herself a peek around the back of the house and noticed the police cordon encircling her apartment.

Muttering to herself, she hurried back indoors relieved to be back with her beloved antiques. Her sister rang later to check all was well.

Shortly after Mrs Doveton had convinced her sister that she was shaken but quite capable of looking after herself, Simon appeared at her sitting room door. It was a great relief to know that Simon would be staying in the house tonight and she had to admit to feeling nervous. It was still difficult to believe that for a month she had happily played host to criminals. The double-dealing that Christopher had been engaged in she found particularly upsetting. She asked Simon to knock up something simple for dinner, an omelette followed by some fruit would suffice.

Mrs Doveton sat back in her favourite easy chair feeling tired and was delighted when Simon anticipated her need for a sweet sherry a few minutes later. She sipped the first relaxing glass and was contemplating a second when a nasty thought struck her. Several times Christopher had been her invited guest in the ballroom where all her antiques were displayed. He had shown a measure of interest in her collection and had mentioned at one stage that he had worked in a friend's antique shop. Now that she knew Christopher to be a criminal, she wondered whether he had been tempted to steal anything? She got to her feet and began a hasty survey of her impressive collection of hundreds of items all carefully numbered, labelled and dated.

Mrs Doveton had only just begun the process of checking the collection when Simon arrived and announced that dinner was served. She retired to the dining room and enjoyed her meal. She was so exhausted though that she decided to go to bed straight away after her meal and worry about her collection tomorrow morning when she was feeling refreshed.

¶

Mrs Doveton rested in the arms of Morpheus, as she liked to describe sleeping, far better than might be expected. She was up and about by 6 am and ready for breakfast that she normally sat down for by 6:30 am accompanied by the newspaper. As always, Simon was awaiting her appearance and inquiring what she would like to break her fast.

'Do we have any kippers, Simon?' Simon was unsure, but promised to check. He returned ten minutes later with the much-anticipated kipper and a spare plate on which to deposit the tricky bones you needed to remove. Black coffee and two rounds of toast followed. A good breakfast was important today, as Mrs Doveton had set herself the task of scrutinising her antiques from one end to the other to check nothing was missing. She requested Simon's assistance once he had completed his morning's chores.

Using her collection inventory, Mrs Doveton began the tedious task of checking off every one of her pieces. Half a dozen she knew were missing, lent to trusted friends or to the local museum. She was at a loss, however, to explain the absence of a small Indian stone figurine (catalogue number 568) that had been valued in the order of $500 if offered at auction. With Simon double-checking as they laboriously ticked off each item in the collection, they had to conclude that it was definitely missing and unaccounted for. Valuable, and small enough to fit into a man's pocket; Mrs Doveton suspected Christopher.

After lunch she rang Glebe Police Station to report the suspected theft. It was a Saturday and the policewoman on duty promised that a detective would call in to see her on Monday morning.

¶

Mrs Doveton was pleasantly surprised to find a female detective on her doorstep shortly after 10 am Monday morning. She felt more at ease with a woman, and they shared a friendly cup of tea while she explained how she and Simon had methodically checked her collection on Saturday morning. The detective examined the place where the Indian figurine had stood, looked at the inventory and took down some notes. She was aware of the drama that had unravelled at the apartment at the back of Mrs Doveton's home and was full of sympathy. A standard question at any investigation of theft is, 'Are you aware of anything else that is missing?'

Mrs Doveton shook her head, but Simon interjected. 'Have you checked the garage? I saw Christopher nosing about in there a couple of times.'

'Well, I did let him use my car to take tree trimmings out to the tip. That is why you probably saw him there.'

'May we go and check just to be sure please, Mrs Doveton?' the pleasant detective asked.

'Yes, of course, here's the key.'

A few minutes later Simon and the detective returned with the bad news. Mrs Doveton felt faint and was obliged to sit down. Once the detective was sure that Mrs Doveton was feeling a little better, and that the butler would stay with her, she went back to the police station and organised forensics to visit Mrs Doveton's home and garage as soon as possible. The only good that had come from the discovery that the Land Rover was also missing was that the police now possessed full details about the vehicle they were looking for.

Police stations throughout the country were alerted to the details of the stolen vehicle. Unfortunately, the criminals had departed three days ago and could be almost anywhere in Australia by now.

A Pact

Christopher and Rochelle's first night, in what they now referred to as Stone Cottage, passed peacefully enough. At one point Rochelle heard what she thought might be a rat snuffling about but she wasn't game to get out of her warm sleeping bag to investigate. She was relieved when the morning light came and there was no sign of droppings.

Christopher was still asleep, so she cleaned out the hearth, reset the paper and kindling wood and lit the fire. Moving into the kitchen she fired up the cooking stove and managed to produce a tasty breakfast of bacon and eggs. The smell wafted into the bedroom and proved irresistible to Christopher who appeared at the table just in time for his portion. They considered making toast by poking a stick through a piece of bread and holding it as close to the hot embers of the fire as possible, but then realised that they had no butter or marmalade so it would be a waste of time.

The sun was up and gave promise of a pleasant day once the air warmed up. They decided that they should spend part of the day exploring the bush around them. They had passed another house about a kilometre back, but as far as they could tell, they were the last house at the very end of the road since the road deteriorated into a track past Stone Cottage. Being at the end of the road had been another reason for settling on this place for a squat; there were no inquisitive tourists travelling through.

For now, they felt safe, but both realised that the future did not portend well. As a couple they were being hunted down for blackmail, murder and theft. Nowhere in Australia was totally safe. For the rest of their lives they must live by guile and cunning, staying one step ahead of the law, constantly moving on, planning their every move and avoiding making any mistakes. Leaving the country was impossible, unless they did so illegally. How were they to survive financially?

They made a cup of coffee and sat outside in the sunny clearing behind the cottage. A couple of blue wrens were flitting about nearby and the smell of eucalypt scented the air. It was a beautiful and peaceful setting.

'I think we need to talk about our situation,' Christopher announced.

'Sure.'

'We may be able to squat here for a few days, perhaps a bit longer, but if we keep the Land Rover we are bound to be recognised eventually. All the police have to do then is follow us out here and then it's curtains for us.'

'Yes, I agree Christopher. If we are arrested, how many years are we going to get?'

'Life probably, whatever that means.'

'I think we would be lucky to get out of prison in under twenty years, by which time we will both be about seventy bloody years old.'

'That's a situation I am not prepared to accept,' Christopher responded.

'You might have to, mate. If we are caught there will be no leniency, even if we cooperate and confess to all we have done.'

'What about those explosives you brought with you, Rochelle? We could use them to blow ourselves up.'

'I didn't bring them. I left it all at the Sydney apartment.'

'So why did you bother to bring them in the first place?'

'I don't know really. In the heat of the moment, as we fled my house, I thought they could come in handy. God knows why.'

'Well they might have done. Given a choice of twenty years in the clink or a quick exit, I would have been very tempted to use the explosives.'

'I can offer you a better option, Christopher.'

'What's that?'

'During the second world war, and in a number of theatres of war since, spies and key personnel were supplied with small vials of deadly poison that killed anyone who ingested them within seconds. Rather than give away vital secrets, spies had the option of self-administering these deadly vials. In some cases, they did. I have two such vials with me. I haven't told you about them before, because they are so incredibly dangerous, but now you know I have them.'

'Good God! You are saying that we could have a joint suicide pact?'

'I am.'

The reality of what Rochelle was saying shocked Christopher into a long silence. He had to agree that this would be a better way to end his life than mucking about with explosives. He was relieved to know that this option was open to both him and Rochelle but earnestly hoped it would never be necessary. Christopher considered himself a fighter and had no intention of being arrested for his wrong doings.

'Coming back to our present predicament, we are stuck out here fifteen kilometres out of the small township of Mount Victoria. We have to keep the Land Rover to get us in and out of town whenever we need supplies. We will just have to take the risk of having the vehicle spotted by the police. We can plan things so that we are in and out of Mount Victoria really fast. That's all we can do, unless we get another vehicle.'

'Changing vehicles won't help us much. In fact, it might be a stupid thing to do because someone will report the transaction and then the police will locate the Land Rover and know where we are.'

'Yes, you are right, Rochelle. Now, how about we check out our surroundings around this cottage. It might be helpful to know if there are any easy escape routes we can take on foot if we have to.'

¶

Christopher and Rochelle washed up their meagre dishes and set off to explore. They were not equipped with any bush-walking gear and had to walk in sandshoes and the everyday clothes they were wearing. They had no compass or water containers. Wisely, they decided not to go far from Stone Cottage, as there was every chance of getting lost in the bush. Rochelle remembered many years ago, when she was in the Girl Guides, that their leader had told them that if they didn't have a compass in the bush, they could use a simple system to avoid getting lost. Locate a particular object that stands out about 100 metres away. It might be an unusual kind of tree, an ant-heap, or a fallen tree. Walk straight to the object and stop there. Look for the next special feature about another 100 metres away and proceed towards it. As long as you take careful note of each feature, you can use the objects again to find your way back. This way you might string together as many as ten features which will take you about a kilometre away and then get you back. Rochelle knew it was not a fool-proof system, and you needed a good memory, but it was far better than just wandering about vaguely. Rochelle decided there and then to try out her crude navigating skills.

She explained the system to Christopher and asked him to help identify the features they would target and to then commit these to memory. Two heads were better than one she told him. The sun was getting up high in the sky but still was at a sufficient angle that they could steer a path walking broadly eastwards towards the sun. They headed off and found their system worked surprisingly well over a short distance.

They had only reached the fifth feature when they suddenly found themselves looking out over the lip of a frightening precipice. Without warning they had emerged at the edge of the bush to peer into a gorge that hurtled down at least 400 metres. It was typical of the places where they had seen tourists congregating to admire the views except that this spot was way out in the sticks. No protective fences here. The sheer sandstone wall extended as far as they could see in both directions forming an insurmountable barrier to any attempt to escape.

Christopher couldn't resist a comment.

'Well at least this gives us a third option; death by explosives, poison vials or jumping!'

Rochelle ignored Christopher's poor attempt at humour. 'You have to admit that gorges like this are spectacular. Did you know that Charles Darwin journeyed to the Blue Mountains? It is said that the numerous layers of rock strata he saw here helped to convince him that his ideas of evolution were correct. You know, all that stuff he wrote in *The Origin of the Species*. When you look out at scenery like this you can understand how gob-smacked he must have been.'

'Okay, madam philosopher. Let's see how your navigating skills succeed in getting us back to Stone Cottage.'

The journey back was uneventful and they found their five landmarks easily enough. At one point two wallabies, alarmed at their presence, broke cover and bounded off through the scrub. Rochelle wondered who was the most scared, the fugitives or the wildlife whose sleep had been so rudely interrupted? On another occasion they heard the deep guttural roaring sound emitted by a male koala somewhere above them. Try as they may, they failed to locate the animal.

Back at Stone Cottage they considered their next trip into the bush. The sound of a chainsaw floated across to them from further back along the road where the last home was that they had passed. No point going in that direction to seek an escape route. So this time they walked westward virtually following the access road to their temporary home. At the broken-down gate, at the entrance to the property, they paused. On the other side of the dirt road was a six-foot high newish fence running parallel to the road for as far as they could see. Barbed wire was coiled along the top of the fence making it virtually impossible to climb over. There were no clues to indicate why this forbidding structure had been erected. Perhaps it bordered a shoot-ing range or an archery club? Clearly there was no escape in this direction.

Only one other option remained as a possible escape route and it was the track that led off into the bush from the end of the road. There were no signs to tell the casual walker whether the track had a name or actually went any-where. There was no letterbox or gate. It was simply a rough four-wheel drive track heading north directly into the bush. They decided to follow the track for an hour and then turn around and head back to their cottage. The average walker can travel four kilometres an hour across normal terrain, so they should've been able to find out what the area was like in that time and whether there was any chance of escape in this direction.

It was midday and high cirrus clouds were starting to move slowly across the sky from the south gradually lessening the intensity of the sun. Walking was easy as they had a track to follow. In places there were deep ruts on the sides of the track where a vehicle had spun its wheels in wet weather. They passed several pretty, wild blue orchids and once Christopher, who was leading, jumped when he disturbed a wallaby that suddenly bolted for cover barely three metres in front of him. The bush was eerily quiet now that they were beyond the range of the sound of the chainsaw.

'Looks like the track is used quite often,' observed Christopher, after they had walked in for about half an hour. 'Perhaps people come in here to collect wood?'

'Why come in this far though when you can collect wood virtually on the side of the road?' Rochelle queried.

'Perhaps it's a witches' coven?'

'Don't be so stupid, Christopher.'

'Or there's a gang of armed criminals hanging out here.'

'You're just trying to scare me but it's not working.'

'How about aliens then?'

Rochelle laughed, although she did admit to herself that as they disappeared farther and farther along this gently undulating track, she was becoming a little nervous.

'We should have driven the Land Rover down here instead of walking all this way.'

The track, that had until now been heading more or less

along a straight line, now began to take a wide sweep round to the left. They continued on, dropping down to cross a shallow creek bed with but a trickle of water running through and up the bank on the other side. Suddenly, all hell seemed to be set loose. Barely a hundred metres away two huge Rottweilers, startled by their sudden appearance, stood barking ferociously and straining desperately at the chains that held them. Behind the savage beasts stood a wooden shack. Before they had time to turn and run back along the track, a man appeared from the hut brandishing a gun that he put to his shoulder as if to fire.

'Quick run for it!' Christopher shouted, 'before those bloody dogs break their chains!' Rochelle needed no urging. The two of them turned together and ran slipping and sliding down in to the creek bed as a couple of shots rang out.

'Good God, it's a madman!' yelled Rochelle as they scrambled up the other side of the creek and out of sight of the man and his guard dogs.

'Keep running. If that idiot decides to follow us in his four-wheel drive and with those bloody dogs, we're in trouble.'

'What do we do if he comes after us?' shouted Rochelle.

'Pray,' was Christopher's only retort.

They continued running for another fifteen minutes or so by which time they were both getting tired and incapable of keeping up the pace much longer. Sweat poured down their faces and they gasped for breath. 'Thank God we kept reasonably fit in Sydney,' Rochelle remarked.

'I think we are safe now,' Christopher answered. 'Looks

like that maniac has decided he doesn't need any more meat for his dogs tonight.'

They slowed to a brisk walk, occasionally glancing back to be sure the salivating Rottweilers were not tearing after them.

Christopher and Rochelle separately came to the conclusion that Stone Cottage might be a safe haven, but if surrounded there was no escape route except to get in their Land Rover and drive like hell back along the road.

Perhaps the pact they had made to use their vials may have to be realised after all.

CHAPTER 33

The Waiting Game

Inspector Johansson and Tania were annoyed that all the action was in New South Wales. Responsibility for this case still rested with the South Australian Police, and specifically with Johansson, yet he and Tania were physically far removed. Glebe Police had been cooperative, as had the Orange Police earlier, nevertheless, it was deeply frustrating learning everything secondhand. They both wanted to be at the coalface where the action was.

In an attempt to brighten up her boss's mood Tania asked, 'Okay sir, if you were in Christopher and Rochelle's shoes right now, what would you do?'

'Good question Tania. It's always good practice to try to anticipate a criminal's moves.'

'Well, what do we know sir?' It was a rhetorical question and Tania went on. 'The two of them escaped in a Land Rover with NSW number plates and got away three days before anyone realised they'd even pinched the car. They also have a valuable Indian figurine stolen from Mrs Doveton's collection, which they will probably try to sell, because they must be worried about money by now. They know their story has been published all around Sydney and if they stay there, they, or their vehicle, might be spotted and reported to the police.'

Johansson joined in. 'We can also surmise that they may try to sneak back to their respective homes to pick up passports and other essentials if they are planning to leave the country. Another possibility is that they may contact family or close friends to ask them to hide them. They will know for sure that they are high up on the "wanted" lists throughout the country and so must lie low.'

'So, sir, where do you think they have fled to?'

'Out of Sydney for sure. They would stick out like sore thumbs if they go to the outback, so my guess is that they will try and find somewhere in NSW that isn't Sydney or the bush which leaves all the parts in between. With a NSW number plate, they will probably not attempt to leave the state. So that brings it down to the coastal strip north and south of Sydney and up into the Blue Mountains.'

'They stole a valuable antique Indian figurine and may need to sell that to an antique dealer somewhere. Mrs Doveton says she had it valued about twenty years ago and way back then it was worth at least three hundred pounds, which is around $500. But taking inflation into account, it's present day value would be more in the order of $800. A nice little nest-egg.'

'So, we need to think of the antique dealer hotspots. Every other town has an antique dealer or two but where do we find heaps of them located closely together to attract the serious collectors?'

'Easy sir, it's the Blue Mountains. My nana is a nutcase about antiques and she has spent at least two holidays in the Blue Mountains "doing the antiques" as she calls it. I can't get interested myself, but her house is chock-a-block full of antique stuff. She has done her darnedest to stimulate my interest but so far without success. It must be good in the Blue Mountains though because she flies from Adelaide to Sydney and then takes the train up to a place called Kabumba.'

'I think you mean Katoomba, not Kabumba!'

'Yep, that sounds better.'

'Righto, there are two actions we can take. Get on to all Christopher and Rochelle's rellies and closest associates who might be tempted to assist them in some way either with money or perhaps hiding them. Warn them, in no uncertain terms, that aiding and abetting a suspected criminal is an indictable offence and that the full force of the law will come down on them if they do not immediately report any sort of contact from Christopher or Rochelle. The second thing we can do is to ask the NSW Police to scare the wits out of the antique dealers throughout the Blue Mountains. If someone then comes into one of their shops wanting to flog an Indian figurine, the police must be advised as soon as it's safe to do so. I'll get on to the NSW Police straight away and you worry about all the rellies.'

'Sounds good sir. My job won't be too difficult with regard to Christopher. I'll get in touch with his brother, David, at the

University of Sydney and his sister, Joanne Ernstein and her family here in Adelaide. I don't think there is a strong connection, but Dr Peters' family, the guy who falsified the death warrant, will need to be contacted as well. Is there anyone else on Christopher's side we should warn off?'

'Yes, contact the boss at his workplace and put the wind up him and tell him to pass the message on to all Christopher's workmates.'

'So far sir, we know very little about Rochelle's family.'

'True. You will need to do some research there. Two people you can start with are the CEO at the Orange White Goods factory where Rochelle was the research scientist and her best friend with whom she and Christopher stayed on the first night they fled from Rochelle's place. What was her name again?'

'The best friend's name was Tina Smith.'

'That's it. When you speak to Tina, try to ascertain whether Rochelle has any close family she might try and approach. I'd be surprised if there are no brothers or sisters. Perhaps Rochelle has offspring somewhere? Let me know what you find out tomorrow please.'

'Tomorrow is Saturday sir.'

'Hell, so it is. Make it Monday instead, Tania. Club championships tomorrow and I'm teeing off at 8 am.'

Tania also had an exciting weekend to look forward to. Her nana, of antique fame, was celebrating her eightieth birthday on Saturday and the family was putting on quite a show. A marquee had been erected in the backyard and over a hundred guests were expected. Tania was officer-in-charge of desserts and her boyfriend, Tony, was helping on one of the two large BBQs they had hired. It was all expected to end by about 6 pm and she and Tony were then off to stay the night at a romantic Bed and Breakfast at Aldgate in the gorgeous Adelaide Hills. Perhaps this was going to be the ideal opportunity for Tony to pop the question? She had been waiting for so long now. If he didn't get around to it soon, she would break with convention and ask him to marry her!

By the close of business, the NSW Police had telephoned about half of the antique dealers in the Blue Mountains and had promised to contact the remainder on Monday morning. Most of the antique dealers were accustomed to receiving similar threats from the police when some antique item was running hot, and so just took it in their stride. Basically, they were an honest bunch though, and certainly did not wish to create problems for themselves with the police.

Tania also had had a fruitful day. She had been able to make contact with everyone on her list and did her best to terrify them all. The consequences of non-compliance were dire, she promised. She had even had success tracking down Rochelle's close family. Apparently she had never had children. Her parents were dead, and only one brother remained, who lived in the United Kingdom so was most unlikely to become involved.

The net was closing. Family and close associates had been warned not to cooperate and a trap was being set with the antique dealers of the Blue Mountains. Now, it was just a waiting game.

Easy Money

B y dusk, heavy storm clouds were rolling in from the south, the temperature was dropping and the wind started a frenzied attack on the gums that surrounded Stone Cottage. Realising rain was approaching, they hurriedly collected armfuls of dry wood which they stored undercover. They estimated they had enough dry timber to last for at least two or three days.

Boredom was rapidly dispiriting them. With no electricity, they had insufficient light to do anything useful after dark. There was no radio, television, only a few books, no magazines or playing cards. They decided to observe nature's bidding and climb into their sleeping bags once darkness fell and try to sleep through until the light of dawn.

Ablutions were becoming a serious problem also. The best they could muster from the shower was a trickle of cold water and the cistern didn't work. To relieve themselves they were forced to venture outside and find a tree. There was an old copper out the back where they could wash clothes by hand in cold water, carried in laboriously from the shower, and then hang out the garments over a wire that ran along what remained of the back veranda. A horribly slow and arduous business.

'I'm going to go mad here if we don't get something more to occupy us,' Christopher exclaimed.

'Agreed, but we only have a few dollars left and we need that money to buy food.'

'I guess it's time to flog the Indian figurine then,' countered Christopher.

'It's a risk. We will have to drive into town and then go around a few of the antique dealers to get best price. We, or our vehicle, might be spotted but we just have to take the risk. If we want to stay out here, we have to replenish our basic food rations. How about we also get a small radio and a pile more books to read? A pack of cards would be great too. Do you play chess?'

As they planned tomorrow's trip, the first heavy drops of rain began falling on the corrugated iron roof making listening to each other difficult. Within minutes the sound of the raindrops began to change. It was hailing. The noise of hail stones, the size of golf balls, crashing onto their flimsy roof was deafening. The wind howled and moaned all about them as if it wanted to suck them out of their humble abode. They clambered into their sleeping bags grateful that the roof wasn't leaking. The storm blew itself out within a couple of hours and an eerie silence followed. When Christopher went outside to relieve himself in the early hours of the morning, he was met by flurries of snow falling silently. It was too wet for the snow to settle but the air was bitterly cold. Christopher had rarely seen snow falling and for a moment or two stood transfixed by this unexpected delight.

It was tempting to remain in their snug sleeping bags and not face the biting cold. They didn't have decent warm gear to put on and so winter garments was added to their growing list of purchases in town. They shivered through breakfast with two cups of hot coffee and double eggs and baked beans doing little to relieve their near numb hands and feet. They decided against lighting the fire as the day would be spent in town. Better to save their precious dry wood for when they returned. Still shaking with cold, they grabbed the small Indian figurine, car keys and what little money they still had left and ran out to their Land Rover. Jumping in, they moved off slowly with the heater on high.

The snow had stopped and broken nimbostratus clouds raced across the sky driven by the cold southerlies. Smoke rose from their next-door neighbour's house. The dirt road was slippery after last night's heavy combination of rain, hail and snow and Christopher drove carefully. The few horses they passed stood stoically, backs to the icy wind, and in the paddocks, cattle huddled together under the shelter of the few trees the farmers had spared. Their hearts went out to newborn lambs bleating with the cold and staying close to their mothers. After about ten minutes they began a slow thaw and their hands and feet gradually came back to life.

When they reached the little township of Mount Victoria

they turned left onto the Great Western Highway and travelled east towards the larger towns of Katoomba, Leura and Blackheath where they had spotted most of the antique dealers. It had clouded over again and a few flurries of snow filled the air. Hopefully the cold weather would discourage the locals from going out so that they were less likely to be spotted.

Arriving in Katoomba they circled about looking for the dealers who had spurned the main commercial part of town and established their businesses where rents were less ruthless. The Indian figurine had to be sold first so they had the cash to buy everything else they desperately needed. Christopher, with his limited knowledge of the value of antiques, opined that $800 would probably be a reasonable return. He admitted that this guestimate was largely based on Mrs Doveton's evaluation of 300 pounds some twenty years ago. They parked the car in the centre of a carpark surrounded by other vehicles which they hoped would provide some sort of cover and headed for their first antique shop.

The antique shop had an atmosphere all of its own. Essentially dark, and poorly heated, they entered a strange world of time gone by. Usually a bell, near the entrance, would warn whoever was lurking somewhere in the depths of the gloomy establishment, that somebody had ventured in. Floors creaked, the air was musty and the occasional lamp lit up an item considered to be of particular interest to the shopper. You could get lost in these places wandering about between rows of period pieces, nude statues and glass display cabinets crowded with dining sets, Toby jugs, tea sets, badges, thimbles and even teaspoon collections. These halls of nostalgia always evoked memories of one's past, 'Grandma used have one of these… oh look, there's an old Singer sewing machine like your parents once had.'

Once their eyes had adjusted to the dim light, they noticed an elderly, bespectacled gentleman sitting hunched up behind an ancient desk on the side of the shop.

'Good morning, may I help you with anything?' the gentleman wheezed.

'Yes, quite possibly you can,' Christopher smiled, sensing that being nice to antique dealers might elicit more generous offers.

'We have decided to sell off a few items that my parents collected. I have one of them here and wondered if you might be interested?' Rochelle delved into her bag and passed the Indian figurine across to the elderly man.

There followed a few moments silence, punctuated by the occasional 'ahum' or 'mmmm' as the gentleman studied this object d'art. 'Well, I can tell you it's genuine for a start. Probably eighteenth-century Kashmiri. Sadly, there's not much demand for this sort of thing these days. Not many collectors here in Australia I'm afraid.'

This didn't sound too promising, but Christopher persevered. 'How much would you be prepared to offer me for it?'

'Well it's not really the type of antique I'm interested in, so my offer wouldn't be to your liking,' the gentleman smiled.

'All the same sir, it would be useful to have your evaluation please?' Rochelle flashed the gentleman a smile.

'You would be wise to find a dealer who specialises in oriental and middle eastern artefacts and that's not me,' the gentleman advised.

'Well, what sort of price would a specialist dealer offer us do you think?' persisted Christopher.

'I wouldn't want to hazard a guess,' the elderly man smiled.

'Okay, thank you for your time.'

'Cagey old bugger,' Christopher whispered to Rochelle as they left the store.

Rochelle swung around and went back in. 'Could you recommend any antique dealer up this way who specialises in something like this?'

'I'd suggest you try Raj Krishna and Sons over in Medlow Bath. Their place is close to the Hydro Majestic.'

'Thanks again,' Rochelle was able to muster up one more of her lovely smiles as she left the shop for the second time.

¶

Christopher and Rochelle tried another three antique dealers en route to Medlow Bath. If possible, they wanted to get some sort of a fix on the value of their object d'art before descending on Raj Krishna and Sons. The next place they visited also declined to disclose a value. The second and third dealers were more helpful, however. One suggested their figurine would be worth up to $1000 at auction while the other suggested it might be possible to sell it for $500. At least they now had some inkling as to what to expect at Raj Krishna and Sons.

A colourful sign on the side of the road invited them to visit: "Raj Krishna and Sons, Purveyor of Antiques and Good Books. Tea and Coffee Always Available. Come in and Browse."

'Great, I could die for a coffee,' exclaimed Rochelle, as they pulled off the highway onto a short side street where half a dozen more signs ushered them into the inviting kingdom of Raj Krishna and Sons.

What a contrast this place was. A teenage girl dressed in a stunning sari and her face beautifully made up, welcomed them at the door. 'Good morning sir. Good morning madam. Welcome to the famous business of Raj Krishna and Sons. Please feel free to wander around at your leisure.' Rochelle responded warmly to the young lass with a lovely smile, while Christopher found himself admiring the shapely figure and attractive smiling face of this exotic young woman.

Here there was no shortage of lighting. Many of the glistening items on display were seen at their best in a bright light and the use of so much power warmed the place up too. Their need for a coffee fix was becoming intense, so they headed straight for the equally well-lit side room which contained Indian wooden furniture (all for sale) and colourful woven carpets on the floor, also for sale. There were about a dozen people enjoying elevenses with two Indians sitting cross-legged on one of the mats. They found a table and had barely sat down when another sari-clad girl smilingly handed them each a menu.

'Indians don't drink coffee, they drink tea,' announced Rochelle, running her eye down the list of teas available, 'Let's get a pot of Darjeeling, Christopher?'

Christopher was still getting over the shock of seeing two beautiful young Indian women in the space of only a couple of minutes and merely nodded his agreement.

'This is more like it,' he responded. 'If you want to sell antiques, open the place up, have sexy young women serving, get the place well-lit and put on refreshments. I don't know where the sons are, but the daughters are something to behold.'

'Okay, calm down, Christopher. See how enchanted you are with the place when we ask what they will pay for the figurine.'

Before Christopher could reply, the sweet young lass had taken their order. A few moments later they were enjoying the light clean flavour of Darjeeling tea with the aftertaste of muscatel. There was a fire blazing in the room and its warmth, together with the incense-like aroma of the place, lifted their spirits. They had used their last few remaining dollars on their pot of Darjeeling tea so now they simply had to sell the figurine or starve.

As they finished their second cup of tea, a coach pulled up outside their window and began disgorging a seemingly endless line of Indians of all ages. Several of the men wore turbans and the women colourful saris. Feeling the blasts of wintry cold as they exited the coach, the Indians wasted no time moving into the warm and welcoming ambience of Raj Krishna's.

They all crowded into the restaurant. Clearly this was the morning tea stop for these Indian travellers and it prompted Christopher and Rochelle to get a move on with their sale.

They were greeted at the desk by two well-dressed young men who were presumably Raj Krishna's sons. They unveiled their figurine and explained their business. The taller of the two men looked the figurine over, confirming that it was genuine, and asked whether he could take it through to his father who was the expert assessor. Receiving Christopher's positive response, he disappeared into a work room carrying the figurine with him.

About ten minutes later Raj Krishna himself emerged from the work room. Raj was impeccably dressed, including a bright red cravat, so that he looked more like a member of the British aristocracy. He spoke BBC English too, with no hint of his Indian origins.

'Good morning sir, good morning madam,' he bowed his head gently as he greeted them. 'I am Raj Krishna. It is a great pleasure to have you join us today.'

This is a smooth bastard, thought Christopher, *the ultimate business man and as sharp as a tack.*

'I understand that you are interested in selling this figurine?'

'That's the general idea,' Christopher responded.

'May I ask where, and how, you procured it?'

'It belonged to my aunt,' Christopher lied.

'And do you know how it came into her possession?'

'No idea.' Christopher was feeling nervous about this line

of questioning. He just wanted Raj Krishna to get on with it and make a generous offer so they could collect their money and get the hell out of the place.

'Excuse my asking, sir, but the provenance of items like this is always of interest to me,' Raj Krishna continued. 'You see, some items like this were stolen by the British when they occupied India.'

Christopher was not at all certain what "provenance" actually meant and he was feeling more and more uncomfortable as this conversation went on. Now Raj was talking about theft which was a worrying trend.

Raj smiled knowingly. 'It amuses me that so many of my customers are like you sir and have no idea how these treasures came into their possession. It's a pity, isn't it?'

Christopher gladly picked up on the use of the word "treasure" but merely nodded his agreement. Although he was not warming to Raj Krishna, he needed to remain polite and respectful if he was going to successfully conclude a deal. Rochelle came to his rescue. 'I'm sorry we can't furnish you with more details Mr Krishna. We have been recommended to come to you as we have heard you are an expert on these matters.'

Everyone enjoys being flattered including the likes of Raj Krishna. He smiled dutifully towards Rochelle, 'Thank you madam, very kind of you.'

'So, what do you think?' Christopher persisted.

Despite the blunt question, Raj Krishna remained unflustered and professional.

'I am a successful businessman sir, and I put that down

largely to my being totally honest with all my customers. As always, I will be honest with you both.'

Christopher's patience was running low. The longer they hung about in Raj Krishna's antique store, the greater the chance that somebody would spot them, or their vehicle, and dob them in. Raj droned on.

'I have examined your figurine carefully. It is a lovely piece, delicately carved in high quality teak, which is very hard to find these days. It is in excellent condition. There is not a great demand for this sort of thing in Australia, but the market is steadily improving as more and more Indians make Australia their home and want to collect small items such as this. Being successful in business means anticipating future demand. You are indeed fortunate that high quality figurines such as this one is just starting to become popular among the wealthy Indian collectors here and overseas. I'm happy to offer you $900.'

This was more than Rochelle and Christopher had expected. Christopher was quick to respond. 'Thank you, Mr Krishna, but we had hoped for a bit more than $900.'

Raj smiled. 'Indeed sir. $950 and that is my final offer. Take it or leave it.'

Rochelle was a softy when it came to bargaining, and disliked the whole nasty process. 'I think we can accept that price Mr Krishna.' Christopher was all for pushing again to see if he could get up to a neat $1000, but Rochelle had trumped him. He didn't wish to start an argument with Rochelle and $950 was considerably better than he had hoped for anyway, so he kept his mouth shut. After all, this was easy money.

Raj was speaking again. 'If you will excuse me for a moment, I will need to go to my safe to get the cash for you.' He gave another of his measured smiles, and a nod of the head, and left them at the desk.

Behind them a cold blast of wind blew in, signalling the arrival or departure of customers through the main entrance. They both turned. To their horror, two burly policemen from Highway Patrol entered. They headed straight for the desk where Christopher and Rochelle stood, trying to look and act as if they were happy to see members of the police force going about their duty. Was this it? Were they here to arrest them? Had Raj somehow alerted the police? Why was Raj taking so long to return with their money? Had they been cleverly trapped?

One of the policemen came up to them. 'Bloody cold out there. They reckon there's a bit more snow on the way. Could be heavy enough to close the highway.'

Rochelle and Christopher's emotions violently reversed from instant panic to huge relief in the space of a couple of seconds. They both managed to smile weakly but could find no words with which to reply. They may have mumbled something incoherently, but they couldn't recall what when they finally escaped from Raj Krishna's a few minutes later. The two policemen obviously knew Raj well, and after a brief joke, retired to the restaurant for some sustenance.

With $950 now safely stowed in Rochelle's handbag, they headed for Katoomba where they re-stocked and purchased warm clothes and all the other necessities they had listed. As they drove back to Mount Victoria, and along the dirt road out to Stone Cottage, the snowstorm hit. This time the snow was settling but was falling so thickly they could barely see the beautiful snowscapes building up all around them. They made it back, but only just. The bottom of the Land Rover was working like a snow plough as they finally approached Stone Cottage.

A Sighting

By late Monday morning all known family, friends and close working colleagues of Christopher and Rochelle had been telephoned by Tania. Not one of those contacted had heard a whisper from the two fugitives. Some expressed concern for their wellbeing and all assured Tania that they would report any attempts to make contact. Tania's efforts appeared to have drawn a total blank.

Detective Inspector Johansson's efforts to alert all the antique dealers in the Blue Mountains was to prove far more helpful. The NSW Police had faxed all the dealers during Friday which happened to be the same day that Christopher and Rochelle were trying to sell their Indian figurine. It was a stroke of luck for them that the antique dealers they had visited on Friday morning, either hadn't received their faxes, or had received them but not had the time to read them.

It was one of the attractive young women serving in Raj Krishna's shop on Friday afternoon who eventually picked up a fax from the fax machine. This was one of the jobs assigned to her. The fax was from the NSW Commissioner of Police so she felt obliged to read it. From time to time, similar faxes would arrive, and they usually warned of stolen goods that the police suspected criminals would try to sell. In fact, the illegal sale of stolen antiques was a serious problem that had existed for many years. Try as they may, the police were powerless to stamp out the practice completely.

This particular fax, the young lass noted, went a step further than most they had received in the past because it included two grainy photographs of a middle-aged man and a woman both wanted by the police. The faxed photographs were of poor quality, but she had a feeling she had seen these two people come into the shop this very morning. She could not be sure of the man. The photo showed a clean-shaven gentleman, whereas the man who visited today sported a beard. But the woman's face certainly looked very familiar.

The young lady read the fax through a second time. Her father, Raj, had always stressed the need to be scrupulously honest at all times. Regard the police as your friends he had always impressed upon his children. Look after them, and they will look after you. Her father enjoyed friendly banter with all the police who dropped by sometimes to purchase a coffee or have a short break. She had noticed that she could even tell how well the India-Australia test cricket matches were faring by the number of police visits they received. Whenever India was being trounced, the police turned up more frequently just to stir Raj and his family up. But if India was in the ascendency, the police, strangely, were too busy to call in.

The young lady went to the office to show the fax to her father. Raj was on the phone speaking to someone from the Bureau of Meteorology about the heavy snowstorm that was expected to hit Medlow Bath and the upper Blue Mountains in an hour or two. Apparently a severe weather warning had been issued at noon, and schools and businesses in the upper Blue Mountains were being advised to close early so everyone could get home before the forecast heavy snow arrived. It was just after 1 pm and ominous grey clouds were already sweeping across the sky.

'We need to close the shop my dear. There's a really bad snowstorm heading our way and they are predicting white-out conditions and road closures. Would you please put up the "Closed" sign and politely ask anyone in the shop to leave as quickly as possible? I'll let the staff know they can all have an early mark.'

'Dad, a fax has arrived about a couple of criminals and I think I saw them here this morning.' She passed the fax to her father.

'I'll have a look at it in a moment. Right now, it is more important to get everyone off home before this storm hits.'

Raj placed the fax on his desk and set off around the store to speak to his staff. Ten minutes later the wind was picking up and light snow started falling. Raj raced back to his office to grab his hat, coat and scarf and checked that the lights and heaters were off, except for the security lighting.

'Come on my dear, no time to waste.'

They locked the door, and carefully negotiated the slippery

snow that was already an inch deep. In a moment they were on their way home as the snow swirled about them.

The fax lay unheeded on Raj's desk.

¶

The snowstorm was unseasonably early in the year and lasted only a couple of hours. Slightly warmer air drifted in behind it so that by dawn the thaw was on. The highway remained closed until nearly 8 am Saturday morning when the police declared it safe to re-open.

Raj Krishna enjoyed a relaxed breakfast at home and left at precisely 9:46 am, allowing himself the usual fourteen minutes he needed to drive to his much-loved specialist antiques store in Medlow Bath. On the stroke of ten he rattled his keys in the lock, swung the "Closed" sign around to "Open" and was ready for business. It was only as he headed for his office that he remembered the fax that his daughter had shown him yesterday as they were hurrying to leave. There it was on his desk.

Raj studied the fax closely together with the two photographs. Halfway through, he let out a choice Indian expletive. According to the fax, he had paid out $950 to two criminals for that beautiful Indian figurine. If only he had received the fax a few hours earlier, he could have done something to prevent the criminals getting away with his hard-earned money. He dialled the police number provided on the fax and described what had transpired the day before. The policeman on duty thanked him most profusely for his assistance and noted down all the details of his encounter with Christopher and Rochelle. The information was duly passed on to the senior officer on duty.

Sergeant Robertson, senior officer on duty at the Katoomba Police Station, ruminated on what course of action he should take. The sighting had taken place nearly twenty-four hours earlier, before the big snowstorm hit. Who knows where the criminals were by now? Whereas he already had the details of the vehicle they were thought to be driving, he had little else to go on. It was far too late to set up road-blocks. Robertson did the only two things he thought might be helpful; he contacted his superior, and a Detective Inspector Johansson based in Adelaide, to report the sighting and alerted all personnel at the Katoomba Station to be extra vigilant and watchful for the two fugitives and their stolen vehicle in case they were still in the vicinity. Finally, he put his feet up on his desk and enjoyed the last few mouthfuls of his cup of hot chocolate accompanied by one of his wife's tasty lamingtons.

The snowstorm had delayed the reading of the fax, which in turn had enabled Christopher and Rochelle to escape safely back to their hideout.

Luck Turns

Rochelle and Christopher were well pleased with their shopping expedition. They now had sufficient food supplies to last them several days, meaning they could lie low at Stone Cottage and not have to take their vehicle to town until sometime next week. Boredom should now be alleviated by a pile of decent second-hand novels they had purchased, together with a chess set, a pack of cards, a battery-operated radio and a couple of puzzle books containing crosswords and Sudokus galore. They planned to keep fit by walking and running every day along the dirt road that led from Stone Cottage towards town. They certainly would not risk exercising anywhere near the madman with his two Rottweilers.

As they lay warm and snug in their respective sleeping bags, with the first light of day beginning to filter through the windows, they fell to discussing their longer-term plans. Stone Cottage would suffice for a week or two until things quietened down, but hanging out in this remote place for any longer did not appeal to either of them. They would have to move. Winter was near and already the weather was horribly cold. With regard to their longer-term plans, the two questions they wrestled with were, where would they go, and how could they find the money they needed to survive there?

Rochelle's house in Orange, at current market value, would probably realise around $200,000. Christopher still had a mortgage on his place in Adelaide and would be lucky to raise $150,000. But how could they proceed with the sale of these houses without exposing themselves to arrest? The authorities would be watching their respective homes like hawks ready to swoop as soon as they began sale proceedings. It was just too dangerous. Even trying to sell secretly through an agent was too risky. Tragically, they concluded that they would have to abandon their homes and seek substantial assets elsewhere. Inevitably they believed they would have to resort to more crime to acquire the money they needed.

They did allow themselves to dream, however, about where they might settle. Assuming they were successful in pulling off a major heist, where would they go? It was too risky to return home to collect their passports so they must settle somewhere in Australia. Rochelle was in favour of Tasmania. She had visited the Apple Isle several times and adored the fabulous scenery, the bush walking, the cool climate, the wines and the whole feel of the island. Rochelle imagined a small holding in the countryside where she could run an agribusiness growing and selling herbs, flowers, berries and with a small orchard as well. With hard work, and Christopher's help, they could make a go of it. They were still young enough to support such a venture for another twenty years or so.

Christopher, on the other hand, dreamt of tropical Queensland up on the Atherton Tablelands somewhere. Here you would seldom need heating and could exist like a hippie, Nimbin-like. As long as you had a small patch of land you could practise subsistence farming and sell any surplus products. It would be a quiet but idyllic existence. He had heard there were several communities you could join nowadays that worked cooperatively. Pangs of hunger eventually forced them to brave the cold and organise some breakfast. They would have to re-visit the questions of where and how to spend their future lives together some other time.

About an hour after their meal they set off for a run. The idea was to run for thirty minutes towards town and then turn around and run back. The air was crisp and invigorating and each time they exhaled they could see breath blowing out behind them. Christopher dropped in behind Rochelle and couldn't help but admire the slim, neat figure of his partner in crime.

At the thirty-minute mark they stopped for a short breather. They estimated they had covered nearly five kilometres and felt comfortably warmed up. In the distance they saw a vehicle coming towards them. It had to be either the madman with the two Rottweilers or their next-door neighbour who they had yet to meet. No one else lived at this far end of the road. Seeing the two runners, the driver pulled over, dropped his window and leant out.

'What are you two doing out here?'

'Just having a run,' Christopher replied.

'Are you the folk who are shacking up at Charlie's old place?'

Rochelle assumed that "Stone Cottage" must have once belonged to someone called Charlie and responded cautiously. 'We wanted to go camping out in the bush and stumbled across this rather lovely deserted old house so thought we might stay there for a few days.'

The farmer allowed his eyes to run up and down this attractive looking woman before he continued.

'You bloody camping or squatting there?'

'It's been so cold we decided to move into the house so we could have a good fire going,' Christopher responded.

'Do you realise that bloody squatting's illegal?'

'Well yes, but it's only for a few days and we are really looking after the place. We have cleaned it up, aired it out and we are taking great care of it,' Rochelle replied, feeling somewhat vulnerable as the man continued to leer at her sparsely clad body.

The farmer sniffed, corrected the angle of his ancient hat and diverted his attention to Christopher. 'How long are you planning to stay out here, mate?'

'Maybe a few more days.'

'Suppose I dob you in when I get into town then?'

'Oh, please don't do that,' Rochelle decided to try and appeal to his better instincts if, in fact, he had any. 'You see, we are just married, and this is like our honeymoon because we don't have enough money to go to a hotel or anything. We just want to have a few romantic days together and then we will be on our way.' Realising she wasn't wearing a ring, Rochelle put her hands behind her back which accentuated her nipples that had already firmed up in the cold.

The farmer couldn't keep his eyes off her breasts. With a knowing smirk he said, 'Have fun then,' and engaged gear and accelerated away towards town.

'Bloody pervert,' offered Christopher.

'Yes, but I think he will leave us alone now. Do you think he has a wife? How about we call in for a few minutes on our way back and find out? If he's living next door on his own, I would be worried he might do something silly like try and visit us. If we spin the same story about us being on our honeymoon to his wife, we will be much safer.'

'Okay, that was a clever idea of yours to say we are honeymooning. Watch out tonight though!'

They started trotting back, their minds preoccupied with the scene that had just played out with the far from pleasant farmer. Before long they reached the driveway leading to their neighbour's house and kept running up the gradual slope to the front door. A couple of chained kelpies at the side of the building announced their arrival and they were relieved to see smoke spiralling up from the chimney. Somebody must be home.

They didn't need to knock. The row the dogs were making had alerted whoever was inside. As they approached the door it opened wide to reveal an equally wide woman with chubby red cheeks and a mop of hair busily wiping her hands on a pink apron with various fruits emblazoned all over it.

'Good day. We are living next door and thought we should come and introduce ourselves,' panted Rochelle.

'Well I never!' The large lady was clearly surprised to discover a pair of half-naked strangers on her doorstep and in such cold weather. She recovered quickly though. 'You'd best come in before you freeze to death.'

'Thank you,' they chimed in unison.

'You timed that right. I've just made a batch of scones. Sit yourselves down and you can try the first ones.' Gratefully, they sat at her kitchen table savouring the smell of fresh cooking and enjoying the warmth of the room. 'My name's Hazel.'

Christopher stood, extended his hand and told Hazel that his name was Tom Ellis. 'And this is Mary Ellis, my very, very new wife.'

Hazel giggled. 'Don't tell me you are out running on your honeymoon?'

'Well actually we are,' blushed Rochelle.

'Well I never,' was all Hazel could offer. 'Can I see your ring, Mary?'

'Oh, I never run with my ring on. It could fall off and that would be just terrible,' she said, looking lovingly at her new husband, who nodded enthusiastically.

'Here you are...' Hazel placed a plate loaded with hot scones in the middle of the table followed by a generous bowl of cream and a jar of strawberry jam. 'Sorry they aren't proper strawberries.'

'Oh, this is just wonderful. Thank you so much,' smiled Rochelle.

'So, when did you get married?'

'Thursday evening,' Rochelle congratulated herself on remembering that they had arrived at Charlie's place on Thursday.

'How unusual getting married on a Thursday,' Hazel remarked.

'It's a second marriage for us both so it was a quiet affair. It's much cheaper during the week.' Christopher wondered how much longer Rochelle could keep up all the drivel she was coming out with. 'You see, we have very little money and couldn't afford to stay anywhere, so we are camping next door in Charlie's place.'

For the second time Hazel appeared almost lost for words. 'Really, at Charlie's old house?' Hazel still wasn't sure if she was hearing correctly. 'But the old place is almost falling down. Charlie died four years ago now.'

'We just wanted somewhere to go to start our married life together. It's not too bad.'

'Oh, my dear, we could put you up here for a few days. Have another scone. They came out okay, didn't they?'

Christopher and Rochelle assured Hazel that they were indeed excellent scones and supported their approving comments by helping themselves to another generous portion of cream and jam.

'That's very kind of you but we are fine. We are used to roughing it.'

'But you don't even have hot water, do you?' inquired a concerned Hazel.

'No, we don't.'

'Well go and get your towels and come over for a hot shower. It's the least we can do for you,' offered Hazel.

Christopher and Rochelle exchanged glances. A hot shower after three days and nights without a decent wash would be a most welcome treat.

'Well, that does sound lovely,' replied Rochelle.

'Righto, Mary and Tom. Go and get your gear. The shower's all yours. My husband won't be back for a few hours.'

They needed no more encouragement.

An hour or so later, showered and in clean clothes, they were ready to return to Stone Cottage.

'I think we met your husband when we were out running this morning, Hazel.' Rochelle mentioned casually.

'If you were out on the road you couldn't have missed him.'

'He didn't seem very happy about us staying at Charlie's place,' Rochelle continued.

'Oh, he's a bit of a crusty old bugger, my Bert. Don't worry about him. His bark's worse than his bite. He was off into town to get some feed for the lambs and then he'll call into the pub for his weekly game of darts. You'll probably hear him when he gets home tonight. He'll be as drunk as a turkey. At least he only hits the booze once a week. He used to take old Charlie in with him until Charlie got too sick. I used to have to get the two of them back into their beds. At least I only have Bert to worry about now.'

'Well thank you so much for letting us use your shower, Hazel. We really did appreciate it.'

'Come over any time in the morning when you want another one. Bert always leaves his shower until he gets back from working on the farm. So don't come afternoons or evenings.'

With that proviso, they made their farewells, and headed off. It was amazing how delicious they felt having rid themselves of three days of dirt and grime. They made love to celebrate. After all, they were on their honeymoon!

¶

As Bert drove off, leaving the two just-marrieds on the side of the road, he wound up his mud-splattered window, powered up the heater and started thinking. Bert was a man of simple tastes and he tended to see things as either black or white. These two characters had shacked up in his old mate's house, without asking anyone's permission, and in Bert's book, that was being disrespectful to Charlie. Bert missed his old friend and had taken it upon himself to keep an eye on his property. A couple of times he had caught blokes on Charlie's land pinching timber and had given them the flick quick time. On another occasion two young idiots had gone on to Charlie's place to shoot roos. He'd sent them on their way too with a flea in their ears. Perhaps he should dob these two characters into the police? They were trespassing. There was no two ways about it. All this bullshit about being on their honeymoon. So what?

Bert was still mulling the matter over as he approached the outskirts of Mount Victoria. Perhaps he would erect a sign at the entrance to Charlie's to stop people trespassing in future. He'd seen a beaut sign recently that said:

TRESPASSERS WILL BE SHOT
SURVIVORS WILL BE SHOT AGAIN

He pulled up in the yard at the back of the grain store that stocked the food concentrate he wanted for the lambs. His mind was made up. He'd get his supplies and then call in at the police station in Katoomba and report the two trespass-ers. After that it would be down to his local for the weekly darts comp followed by a few beers.

¶

Parking for customers at the Katoomba Police station was never easy. Driving in, Bert could see no vacant places, so he thought again about dobbing the two trespassers in. He did not want to be late for the darts competition. He turned his vehicle around and was just about to leave the carpark when a lady close to the entrance started backing out. He grabbed the spot and trudged into the station.

'Morning Officer.'

The young man on duty rose from his chair and walked over to the reception desk. 'Can I help you sir?'

'I want to report a couple of squatters.'

'Certainly sir. Please wait a second while I find the correct form.'

The constable returned with a pad of forms marked SQ/3/R and a pen. 'Now sir, I first need your personal details please.'

'I hope this is not going to take all day, Officer? I've got places to go.'

The young constable sighed quietly to himself. This looked like being one of the more difficult customers that called in to the station to report things.

'Would it help if you tell me what to write on the form, sir?'

'Yup. I left my glasses in the truck anyway.'

The young policeman dutifully recorded what details Bert was able to provide. It was all a bit sketchy. Apparently, a couple of honeymooners had shacked up in the deserted house next door. Bert didn't know their names and couldn't reveal any more about them except that they were middle-aged runners and he had met them trotting along the Mount Victoria road. Not much to go on. Bert reckoned they had been squatting there about three days and they had claimed they did not have enough money to go for a proper honeymoon.

The young constable debated whether to do anything about this matter. He was in a serious relationship with a lovely lass down the street and felt some sympathy for a couple wanting to have a quiet, undisturbed honeymoon out in the bush. If they didn't have any money to spare, and were not doing any harm, he was of the opinion that it might be worth turning a blind eye. If they were planning to stay for weeks, then that would be a different matter. He signed off on the form and placed it in the "POSSIBLE ACTION" tray. He would leave it to his superiors to decide what, if anything, to do.

The form lay in the tray until the next morning when Sergeant Thelma Stephens clocked on at 8 am. Sergeant Stephens was "on the ball" as they say. Ambitious and highly intelligent, she had made it to sergeant in almost record time, but this was only the start. Thelma had set her sights higher. It was more difficult for a woman in a man's world to move up through the ranks but she felt she had the drive to make it at least to Chief Inspector. The patrol car was already out on a call, so Thelma picked up the forms in the "POSSIBLE ACTION" tray. There were three forms there but the one that interested her most was the SQ/3/R.

Sergeant Thelma Stephens had always made it her business to carefully read all the reports that came in for noting. These reports ranged across a host of topics; flood, fire, road repair warnings, missing persons, lost items, important coming events, road accidents, major crimes and wanted persons. All serving police were obligated to 'read and inwardly digest' all these reports but Thelma knew there were a number of slack officers who only glanced over reports. In her opinion, the amount of attention given to the reports coming through the office distinguished a truly effective officer from the rest. And she was about to prove this once more.

Last week, a report had come in from SA Police about a couple wanted for multiple crimes including one case of murder, blackmail over a twenty-year stretch and serious theft.

Thelma had taken particular heed of the report because the miscreants were thought to be heading for the Blue Mountains to sell an Indian figurine at one of the many antique shops. That these two people came to the Blue Mountains was confirmed only three days ago when Raj Krishna, who owned a well-known antique shop in Medlow Bath, had reported that he had given a couple $950 for a high-quality Indian figurine. The couple had then simply disappeared just before a severe snowstorm had hit the upper Blue Mountains. Some had speculated that the couple and their vehicle could have become disoriented and driven over the edge of one of the many precipices in the district or perhaps they had decided to carry out a double suicide. *Could it be,* Thelma wondered, *that the middle-aged squatters brought to the attention of the police yesterday by this man, Bert, living at the end of the Mount Victoria Road, is the couple wanted for multiple serious offences?* Thelma moved form SQ/3/R from the "POSSIBLE ACTION" tray to the "ACTION" tray. She was in charge today at the station, and this might be another ideal opportunity for her to demonstrate her policing skills and attention to detail.

Katoomba was a relatively small police station. During normal daytime hours, only five police were on duty consisting of the officer-in-charge, two juniors in the office handling inquiries from the public, and two other police assigned to outside duties who made their presence known by cruising about in the patrol car and responding to calls wherever they happened within their designated area of responsibility. A second patrol car was available, if required, and other back-up off-duty police officers were "on call".

Thelma retired to her office with the SQ/3/R form and quietly began to formulate a plan of action.

Actioning Thelma's Plan

Reaching for a pad of writing paper, Thelma started jotting down a few notes. She found her thought processes usually benefited by committing her ideas to paper. Her first note simply said, 'quiet surveillance by call and visit.' This was her shorthand way for saying she would telephone Bert at his home to confirm his story first and try to ascertain more about the alleged squatters. Thelma believed that some careful probing would help her decide if in fact the squatters were Christopher and Rochelle. If her phone call proved positive and she was sure she had the right target, she would then conduct on-the-ground surveillance by sending in two of her police posing as bushwalkers. It would be their job to do a thorough recce of Charlie's house and its environs in preparation for a full assault by the police leading to the arrest of the suspects.

Next, Thelma ran through the list of police based at the Katoomba Station. She wanted two young police who could convincingly be recognised as genuine bushwalkers. This was easy. A romance had recently developed between Senior Constable Rodney Thompson and Constable Ruth Knowles. Relationships between officers at work were frowned upon, but everyone at the station knew about this budding romance from attending various social events. To cap this arrangement off, Rodney and Ruth actually enjoyed walking in the mountains and possessed all the proper walking gear. They could legitimately claim to be bushwalkers.

Thelma noted down two more points; 'discuss with the station chief' and 'contact SA Police and NSW HQ.' These she would enact only if her phone call to Bert convinced her she had found the fugitives. Clearly, she needed the boss's blessing. She was also cognisant of the fact that it was the SA Police who had charge of this whole operation so she would require their permission before proceeding.

Thelma poured herself a strong black coffee, informed the two police in reception that she did not wish to be disturbed for the next ten minutes, and returned to the office. She rang the number that Bert had supplied. No answer. She tried the number again and this time the phone was answered by an out of breath woman.

'Hazel here.'

'Good morning, this is Sergeant Thelma Stephens from the Katoomba Police Station.'

'Good morning. Sorry to be panting. I was out feeding the chooks and had to rush in when I heard the phone.'

'That's fine Hazel. I apologise for disturbing you.'

'That's okay.'

'Actually, I want to talk to Bert Entwistle. Is he there please?'

'Oh God, what's he done?'

'Nothing serious. Yesterday afternoon he called in at the station to report on two squatters illegally staying at the house near your place. I just wanted to get some more details from him please.'

'I have to admit, Officer, that he got home blind drunk late last night, early this morning to be precise, and he is dead to the world right now sleeping it off.'

'May I ask what your relationship to Bert is please?'

'I'm his wife.'

'Have you seen the two people who are living next door?'

'Oh, yes. They called in yesterday morning to introduce themselves. A nice couple they are. Ate half my scones and then came back for showers. Are they in trouble for squatting? I suppose squatting is breaking the law nowadays?'

'Well, rather than disturb Bert, may I ask you a few questions about the two squatters?'

'Yes, of course.' Hazel's panting by now had subsided into deep breathing.

'Did your two visitors give you their names?'

Oh yes. Let me think now. Um, …oh, I remember. It was Mary and Tom. I can't remember their surname now but they had only just got married last Thursday would you believe? That's why they were squatting. They didn't have enough money, they said, to go somewhere nice. They said they saw the house and wanted some peace and quiet. A bit of slap and tickle too I expect,' and Thelma descended into another of her mischievous giggles.

'Hazel, you are being most helpful. Could you describe the couple to me please? What did they look like?'

Hazel was rather enjoying this experience. She was lonely living at the end of the road and welcomed a good old natter over the phone even if it was to a policewoman. Bert was a quiet old codger and did not engage her in much conversation, or anything else for that matter.

'Well, when they first came in, they had been out running along the road and were all sweaty. They looked much better after they had showered and changed their clothes though. They are middle-aged, at least in their forties, but fit. Mary had a figure to die for. Like a model she was. Very nicely endowed if I might say so. She did most of the talking and seemed to be a well-educated woman.'

'And what about the gentleman? What was he like?'

'Well, he was slim too, going a bit bald but he had quite a large beard.'

'Anything else?'

'Not really.'

'Have you seen what they are driving, Hazel?'

'No. They walked up to our place both times.'

'Can you see their place from yours?'

'Oh no, there's a lot of bush between our places. They are about a kilometre away.'

'Well thank you again for all your help, Hazel.'

'Any time, Officer.'

Thelma replaced the receiver and sat thinking. She had the fax in front of her with the grainy photographs of Christopher and Rochelle. It was quite likely to be them but she wasn't sure. If she called out the big guns and raided the place and it turned out to be somebody else altogether, she would never live it down. It would be disastrous for her next promotion. She concluded that she must send in her two "bushwalkers". If nothing else, they could confirm that the vehicle's registration number was the one they were looking for. In Thelma's mind that would seal it and she would then go flat out to apprehend them. This could turn out to be excellent for her promotion chances.

Thelma reached for the phone and dialled Senior Constable Rodney Thompson's number.

'Hi Rodney, Thelma here. How would you like to take Ruth for a romantic bushwalk this arvo on police pay?'

Rodney needed no more encouragement. Within the hour, he and Constable Ruth Knowles were knocking on Thelma's door kitted out in their bushwalking gear and enduring the wolf-whistles of their colleagues in reception. Thelma sat them down and gave them a full briefing using a map to orient them.

It was agreed that Rodney and Ruth would take the back-up patrol car and proceed along the Mount Victoria Road until they reached Bert and Hazel's property. There they would park the car and continue on foot. Thelma meanwhile, would ring Bert and Hazel to explain what was happening in case they became nervous seeing a police car parked outside their gate. The two walkers would then walk into Charlie's place on the pretext that they were heading for the cliffs directly behind the house looking for a rare orchid that was thought to prosper there. Their main task was to locate the squatter's vehicle to check the registration number. If it was the vehicle they wanted, and they had the opportunity, they were to quietly disable it. On no account were they to arouse suspicions that they were not genuine hikers. Further instructions included: If the occupants appeared, engage them in polite conversation and then walk on through the bush. Don't go far. When safe, drop down to the ground and observe the house for half an hour before re-emerging from the bush. Use this time to draw a more detailed map of the house and its surroundings. Return to the police car and report progress to the Katoomba Police. Wait for further instructions.

Rodney and Ruth called in at the deli next door and bought hamburgers. Thus fortified, they collected the patrol car keys and set off. It was a bit more than a half hour drive. The weather had improved, although still cold, but the skies had cleared. There would be a sharp frost tonight. Arriving at Bert and Hazel's property they parked on the side of the road. Hazel could be seen at the side of the house hanging out washing and she gave them a cheerful wave which they returned. They put on their backpacks and Ruth collected the small camera they would use covertly. Locking the car, they set off along Mount Victoria Road heading for Charlie's place.

They certainly looked the part. They were both wearing thermals and Rossi hiking boots. Rodney carried a map, contained in a clear plastic pouch, that hung from his neck and had a compass and Swiss army knife attached to his belt.

They were not expecting trouble, but as a precaution Ruth had a revolver safely stowed in her backpack together with the camera and paper and pencils should they need to take any notes or draw maps.

They walked steadily for about fifteen minutes, enjoying the sounds of the bush, until they came across a rough driveway to their right that led up to an attractive looking early sandstone cottage. The cottage had certainly seen better days. Any remnants of a garden were long gone although a couple of what looked like ancient peach trees still grew on either side of the front door. All was quiet, but intriguingly, smoke was rising straight up from the chimney. Whoever was living here appeared to be home and enjoying a warming fire. There was no sign of a vehicle out the front except for tracks along the driveway and disappearing round the side of the house.

They paused at the ramshackle gate deciding what approach to take. One option was to sneak in, walk around the house paddock and take photos of the vehicle and the immediate surrounds and sneak back out, hopefully unobserved. Alternatively, they could brazenly walk up the driveway, pass the cottage and on into the bush behind. This was not what bushwalkers would do, however. Respectful of property owner's rights, the typical bushwalker would endeavour to walk around the property. In the end they decided to behave like bushwalkers and circle the cottage but stop somewhere in the bush on the other side of the cottage and take their photos from there.

¶

Inside the cottage Christopher and Rochelle were living as luxuriously as a tumbledown old building would allow. A fire was roaring in the grate and most of the smoke was now escaping up the chimney. Earlier attempts had been less successful until Christopher risked his life climbing onto the roof to dislodge a sizeable abandoned bird's nest sitting atop the chimney. Being a bright sunny day, the light streaming through the window afforded ample light to read or play chess. Christopher had boiled up a couple of cans of Campbell's hearty beef and vegetable soup for lunch accompanied by chunks of wholemeal bread with butter and vegemite. Apples were in season so they completed the repast. Now, with steaming cups of hot chocolate in their hands, life felt pretty good.

They had decided that they could probably safely stay in Stone Cottage for another week or two and only go into Katoomba to re-stock food supplies once a week on Thursday evenings when it was late night shopping, and, more importantly, dark. They were terrified that they, or their Land Rover, would be spotted if they appeared in public more frequently.

Increasingly they were aware that if they were ever to realise their dream of settling down in Tasmania or Queensland, they needed to develop detailed plans to carry out a major robbery. They had reviewed a range of ideas several times without settling on anything. Part of the problem was that they did not move in elite criminal circles so were not party to the latest thinking, or indeed opportunities. Apart from executing highly successful blackmailing over a period of twenty years, they had absolutely no experience of how to commit crimes. They were green, naive and sadly ignorant of the more daring criminal initiatives that, if successful, might earn millions of dollars in one event.

Christopher had found a book in the second-hand bookstore entitled, "Fifty of the World's Most Successful Robberies". He devoured the book quick time, but it lacked detail, and did little more than give him a run down on the basic facts for each heist. He read about successful bank robberies, hold-ups of various forms, of transports conveying wealth, embezzlement, break-ins at jewellery shops, theft of famous artworks from art galleries and valuables stolen from the homes of multi-millionaires. Two things stood out for success; top class planning and access to high quality criminal colleagues. So far, he and Rochelle had not even decided what they were going to target; a bank, a home, a train, a jeweller? They needed to select their target first, then start planning and finally co-opt additional members to their group. Becoming a successful criminal demanded prior knowledge, dedication, skills and the time to plan effectively. Christopher was starting to feel they fell short of the mark in all these areas and it was worrying him.

Rochelle, on the other hand, was beginning to hatch up her own plan. She had not yet shared it with Christopher as the plan was still in its very early stages, but she felt it had potential. Essentially Rochelle's strategy was to return to Mrs Doveton's home in Glebe and to steadily sell off her collection of antiques. $950 for one small Indian figurine had been such easy money. Why not, she reasoned, sell an antique item each week or so, and in this way gradually accrue a few thousand dollars? It might never be enough to purchase a property in Tasmania or Queensland but it would certainly allow them to live a comfortable life for some years. There was, of course, the problem of what to do with Mrs Doveton and her butler, Simon. Until Rochelle felt she had solved this part of the equation she wasn't going to sound Christopher out on her ideas.

And so it was that Christopher and Rochelle occupied themselves quietly in Stone Cottage during the afternoon alone with their thoughts. Around three o'clock Christopher announced that the supply of dry wood was being used up faster than he had anticipated and he needed to go out and find more. It took at least three days for the wet wood he was collecting to dry out sufficiently to burn. One of the spare bedrooms served as their wood storage area which worked well except for the unwelcome creepy crawlies that sometimes came scampering out of the wood pile. They had lost count of the number of insects they had had to despatch. Slaters were the most common invaders but they were closely followed by assorted spiders, ants and millipedes. The occasional cockroach had also been seen and once a giant centipede. Rochelle was particularly intolerant of this creepy crawly invasion and reminded Christopher again to shake all the wood out well or bang it up against a tree trunk to knock out all the nasties, before bringing fresh timber into the house.

¶

About a hundred metres back, the remains of a fence ran into the bush dividing Charlie's property from Bert and Hazel's. The two bushwalkers headed back to this landmark and began to pick their way along the fence line staying on Bert and Hazel's side. There was no track here and they had to push their way through undergrowth and dodge low leaning branches from the gum trees. In places they came across rabbit holes. Miss one of these and you could do yourself a nasty injury. They took their time. They were too far away from the cottage to be heard, provided they kept their voices down.

Soon they were adjacent to the cottage and Ruth pulled out her camera and took a couple of shots of the space in front of the cottage and behind. Parked discretely under an ancient pine tree at the rear of the cottage was a greyish-coloured Land Rover.

'There's the vehicle we need to check out,' whispered Rodney.

'It's the right make of car,' Ruth replied, 'but we need to get a bit closer to check the numberplate.'

'How about we go on about another hundred metres and then get across this fence and head for that bunch of blackberry bushes? From there we should be able to get a good gander on the back of the house and be able to clearly see the car's rego.'

'Sounds good, Rodney.'

The bush thinned out a little, making progress easier. They found a break in the fence at the same time they disturbed a couple of grey kangaroos that must have been camped nearby.

The beautiful animals charged off through the bush making plenty of noise. They were now on Charlie's property. They continued carefully, negotiating their way through the bush towards the blackberries, when suddenly a door slammed and a man appeared on the back porch. Instinctively they fell to the ground and kept still. The man carried a small tomahawk-like weapon and was heading in their direction.

'Oh shit,' hissed Rodney.

'What do we do if he finds us?'

'Easy,' retorted Rodney. 'We have a passionate roll in the grass and make out we are lovers, which we are!'

Ruth wasn't game to answer because the man was now only about thirty metres away but had stopped and was chopping off some dead branches. Very slowly she focused her camera and photographed the woodchopper. Apart from the beard, he looked similar to the Christopher they were seeking. They lay still, afraid to move or make a sound. Even their breathing sounded loud to them.

After what seemed an eternity, and Ruth could feel the back of her left leg beginning to cramp-up, the man stacked up his pile of branches and moved off slowly towards the house.

'Okay, quick Ruth. It will take him at least two or three minutes to take that wood inside. Let's go.'

They arose from their hiding place and headed for the blackberry bushes. Here they were close enough to photograph the vehicle and its numberplate. Ruth took a couple more shots of the back of the cottage and then gave the thumbs up to Rodney. Without a word, they moved stealthily on, past the blackberries, towards the other side of Charlie's property glancing back frequently as they did so.

'Down.' The urgent call came this time from Ruth who had spotted the same man emerging again from the back porch. They were still too close for comfort and would be easily visible should the man decide to come their way. They watched as the man cast his eyes over the array of trees across the back of the cottage. He was looking for the right sized deadwood that was easily accessible. He scanned over in their direction but thankfully strolled instead towards the blackberry bushes where they had been hiding only a couple of minutes before. He resumed his chopping.

Once again, they waited until the man had loaded up and was on his way back before they silently broke cover. There was no fence to follow on this other side of the cottage so they had to crash their way through the bush. Their movements seemed unbelievably noisy but they decided they were probably far enough away to be unheard. At one point Rodney tripped, fell clumsily and swore loudly. They hurried on and in minutes reached the road undetected. There they assumed the appearance of genuine bushwalkers and walked on past the cottage and back to their patrol car.

As they approached the car another man appeared mounted on a horse.

'Gooday. How did yer's go?'

'Are you Bert Entwistle?' inquired Rodney.

'That I am. I knew those two were up to no good,' Bert confided. 'They fooled the missus though. She fed 'em bloody scones and all, and then turned around and let 'em have bloody showers.'

Fortunately, the two young police had been well-briefed by their sergeant and knew what to expect from Bert who had a reputation for being brusque.

'Well, we have you to thank sir, for raising the alarm. You calling in at the police station to report the squatters was hugely helpful,' offered Ruth.

'So, do I get a bloody reward or what?'

'Sorry Bert, no rewards. Rewards are very rarely offered and no reward has been offered for these two.'

'Bloody stingy lot you are. A man does his civic duty and there's no bloody recognition,' Bert grizzled on.

'That's the way it is Bert but thanks again.' The two of them jumped into their patrol car since there was little point trying to reason with Bert, and set off back to the Katoomba Police Station.

CHAPTER 38

The Noose Tightens

Senior Constable Rodney Thompson and Constable Ruth Knowles congratulated each other enthusiastically on the way back. Posing as bushwalkers they had achieved what they had been asked to do. They had confirmed that indeed the car parked behind the cottage was the one everyone was looking out for. The man they had seen collecting wood answered the description of Christopher Brooks, except that he had grown a handsome beard. They had not sighted Rochelle but they could safely assume she was there too. Ruth had captured photographs of the man, the vehicle, the cottage and its surrounds, all in readiness for the specially trained assault squad to use as soon as they came up from Sydney. It had been a highly profitable afternoon.

They parked the car in the police compound at the station and hastened in. Sergeant Thelma was still in her office waiting patiently for their return. It took them less than five minutes to fully brief Thelma and for her to ask a couple of questions. She congratulated the two young officers, assured them that they would be paid an additional four hours pay for their efforts, and sent them home. The negatives were sent down to the dark room for immediate processing.

Speed was now of the essence. Thelma needed to enact the remainder of her strategic plan. First, she rang her boss with the good news that she had located the criminals and that they should be reasonably easy to arrest where they were, living deep in the bush and out of the way of the public. There was no doubt in Thelma's mind. Her boss trusted her judgement and there and then contacted the chief of the assault squad based in Sydney. The chief locked in an assault to take place around 3 am in the morning under the cover of darkness and with the element of surprise. He requested Thelma be on duty from 2 am to assist. Next the Chief rang Detective Inspector Johansson in Adelaide and briefed him. Johansson asked for another call once the arrests had been carried out and expressed his intent to get to Katoomba as soon as possible to take charge of the interrogations. If Johansson could get an early flight, Adelaide to Sydney, he should be in Katoomba shortly after midday.

All was set. The Bureau of Meteorology was forecasting a clear, frosty night in the mountains with a gibbous moon so the assault team would be assisted by a helpful amount of moonlight. Thelma left for home, cooked up a quick meal and was in bed by 7 pm. Her alarm was set for 1 pm giving her time to get dressed and down to the station to meet the boys from the assault squad when they arrived circa 2 pm. At least she would get some sleep which was probably more than the assault team would get. She would love the excitement of serving with the assault squad but appreciated that the job was not only dangerous, but highly demanding, since you were on call twenty-four/seven.

¶

The eight-strong assault team arrived at the Katoomba Police Station on time shortly after 2 pm and rolled into the reception area looking tired and cranky. Thelma was ready with the urn boiling and a choice of chocolate, tea or coffee together with an ample supply of cake and biscuits. The refreshments were enough to liven them all up and the chief availed himself of the photos of the site. He then called for quiet and briefed the group. Nothing out of the ordinary, standard procedures he told the group. Each member of his team had specific tasks and they had undertaken scores of similar assaults. They were a well-rehearsed team.

In this case it was thought that the woman involved, Rochelle Brooks, might be in possession of some form of explosives, but if the assault was conducted, literally in seconds, there was no way she could organise anything. The chief turned to Sergeant Thelma to ask if she could escort the team out to the location in the local police wagon in which the two alleged criminals would be placed for the return trip to the Katoomba lock-up. She was happy to do this but requested that she drive approximately fifty metres in front of the assault vehicle all the way back just in case there was any trouble and that one member of the team ride with her up front in the passenger seat. 'No problem,' the chief agreed.

Both vehicles left shortly after 2:30 pm on the half hour drive to the end of Mount Victoria Road. Everyone by now was in good spirits. One of the guys, who had taken a bit of a shine to Thelma, joined her for the trip out. The Bureau of Meteorology was spot-on with their forecast and the clear night allowed Thelma, who was leading the way, to easily see and dodge a couple of roos as they negotiated a bend. They reached their destination shortly after three hundred hours. It took a further ten minutes to prepare, check weapons and have a final briefing. This done, the eight team members moved silently along the driveway up to the cottage and took up their positions. Thelma was instructed to remain with the vehicles.

Thelma was feeling elated. As a result of her good work, the assault team was just minutes away from making two significant arrests. It was not often that she was involved with criminals who had committed such serious crimes. The bread and butter work at the Katoomba Police Station revolved around the usual drunks, idiotic young teens speeding and the occasional theft from shops or private homes. Sometimes the police would be called out for a domestic row or a party that had got out of control, but major crime was rare amongst the usually law-abiding denizens of the Upper Blue Mountains. It must have been at least five years since the last murder case.

At the prearranged time, the chief gave the signal. Eight men moved quietly into position. There was no sound from inside the cottage. They waited for a minute or so and then the chief gave the action signal. Suddenly all hell let loose, the door was smashed in and the men poured into the old cottage yelling and screaming. They covered off as they went methodically through the building room by room with their guns drawn. Within half a minute the exercise was completed. Nobody was there.

The remnants of a fire still smouldered in the living area and the house remained relatively warm but its occupants were nowhere to be seen. The chief called his team together. Two men were instructed to go through the building a second time to double check any possible hiding places including underground cellars or attics that were quite common with buildings of this age. The rest of his men he ordered outside to carry out a search of the immediate vicinity. Armed with torches and still carrying their weapons they methodically combed the bush on all sides. Almost immediately they discovered the vehicle was missing. Around forty minutes later the team reassembled out on the roadway and asked Sergeant Thelma to join them. The birds had flown. Who had tipped them off? How had they known the assault team was coming? Where had they gone? Were they coming back?

So many questions and no answers.

¶

About the same time the assault crew were entering Stone Cottage, Christopher and Rochelle drove into Mrs Doveton's garage in Glebe, Sydney. Here they planned to stay the rest of the night curled up in their sleeping bags. If they were lucky, they might squeeze out three or four hours of sleep.

They had left Stone Cottage about 11 pm and driven through the night stopping only once to get a snack and to re-fuel at a twenty-four-hour service station. They had left their escape till late to lessen the chance they would be recognised en route.

When Christopher had left the cottage around 3 pm to collect more firewood he had been shocked to see two people lying on the ground watching him. He pretended not to have noticed them. Who were these people? He immediately feared the worst. He gathered up his supply of timber and nonchalantly wandered back to the cottage. He repeated the process. This time he didn't see the spies but they had definitely moved from where he had seen them the first time he went out. Staying as calm as possible – though inwardly near panic, he returned to the cottage to dump his next bundle and went out a third time. This time he saw the couple moving quickly through the bush on the other side of the house towards the road. They were dressed like bushwalkers but were behaving in a highly suspicious manner. He watched them until they reached the road and began walking towards town. He followed them, dodging between the trees and keeping under cover. His suspicions were confirmed when they rounded the corner that led to Bert and Hazel's gate. The two so called "bushwalkers", looking very pleased with themselves, climbed into a clearly labelled police patrol car.

Christopher hurried back to Stone Cottage to report to

Rochelle. She was all for leaving immediately, before dark, terrified that the police would be on their way as soon as the spies returned to the station and raised the alarm. Christopher was more reasoned, arguing for them to stay until late in the evening before setting off. They had a massive falling out. They both yelled and screamed driven by fear and anger that their hideout was no longer safe. Eventually Rochelle relented and reluctantly agreed to stay until 11 pm, grudgingly accepting Christopher's assertion that leaving late at night was the much safer option. They threw their belongings into the Land Rover and left for Mrs Doveton's home shortly before 11 pm.

It was a bittersweet journey to Sydney. Rochelle was enormously relieved that Christopher had discovered the imminent danger they were in so that escape was possible. On the other hand, she was still furious that she had bowed to his wishes. She half expected a convoy of police cars to pull them over as they journeyed into Mount Victoria late that night.

As they travelled down the highway towards Sydney, they began to feel a bit safer. The immediate danger had passed and Christopher had proved correct. Now they began to contemplate what they would do at Mrs Doveton's home. Just past Lawson they encountered a Highway Patrol car parked on the side of the road booking any late-night speed-hogs. It was too late to avoid being seen. They were well within the speed limit but feared that their registration number might have been picked up. For the next hour they kept glancing back behind them, but nothing was following. Perhaps their car was now off the wanted list?

Christopher had already made plans with regard to their stay at Mrs Doveton's home. Again, Rochelle resented the way Christopher was becoming the decision-maker. She felt her opinions were being devalued. They had the key to Mrs Doveton's garage so they could park there for the remainder of the night and try to get some shut-eye. The next part of Christopher's plan was far more troubling, however. He planned to hide in the front garden for Mrs Doveton to return from a shopping expedition and, as she opened her front door, he would suddenly appear and push his way in. Once in, he would try to calm her down but explain that she was now a prisoner and that he and Rochelle would be living in her house for an unspecified time. Next, they would seek out Simon, the butler, and somehow subdue him also. Over the weeks they stayed there they would start selling off the antiques so they had money available for day by day living. It was a deeply worrying plan, not properly thought through, but Rochelle was so exhausted she could not think of a better alternative.

CHAPTER 39

Anger All Around

The noose had tightened but the neck was missing. Now there were a lot of angry people. The Sydney assault team, which had driven over 150 kilometres during the night to reach its target was less than impressed to discover their quarry had vanished. The chief had been matter-of-fact about it to Sergeant Thelma though, telling her that around twenty percent of all the assaults they carried out ended up this way. They returned to Sydney.

Thelma was upset. She felt horribly embarrassed that the fugitives had given them the slip. If only she had been less careful and had arranged for an arrest the moment she heard from her bushwalkers that the fugitives were holed up at Charlie's place. Had she moved quickly then she would now be up for special commendation and perhaps a promotion in the near future. Instead she had been shamed. Her boss was unimpressed that the assault had been such a waste of time and effort. He hoped ardently that the press would not hear about the disaster. To cap it all off, the spunky young member of the assault team who had taken a liking to her on the way out to the cottage declined to travel back with her. That said it all! She returned alone.

Matters were no better in Adelaide. Johansson and Tania were having their 9 am meeting when the phone call came from Thelma's boss at the Katoomba Police Station advising that the pair had escaped and nobody had a clue where they had gone. Johansson was particularly angry as he had been advised only the day before that Christopher and Rochelle would be arrested overnight by the Sydney assault squad. What had happened? How could they have been allowed to get away? Why weren't they kept under twenty-four-hour observation? Heads needed to roll at the Katoomba Police Station. They had allowed serious criminals to evade them.

Tania did her best to console her boss but was feeling equally irate about the disastrous outcome. She volunteered to cancel the detective's flights booked for later in the day.

They discussed the matter for another ten minutes or so. There was little they could do from Adelaide. Johansson agreed to contact the Orange police again to advise them to continue their surveillance of Rochelle's home. Likewise for Christopher's place in Adelaide. The close relatives would have to be contacted again to inform them that the pair were still on the loose. Finally, Australian Customs must be advised to extend the overseas travel bans for the couple and to arrest them if they attempted to leave the country.

There was frustration all around.

Desperate Times

Sleep was almost impossible. Around seven in the morning Rochelle and Christopher climbed out of their sleeping bags, stretched their cramped limbs and took it in turns to sneak out into the garden to relieve themselves. Despite their fatigue, they were hungry and decided to risk walking down to the eateries that served breakfasts. They would carefully avoid any places they had frequented previously in case they were recognised.

Rochelle was starting to question whether she wanted to continue living the life of a fugitive. She had not confided these nagging doubts to Christopher but her concerns were deepening like a cancerous growth. Was there really any point in trying to evade the law anymore? They were living in constant fear of detection and resorting to increasing criminal activities to survive. Now Christopher had some crack-pot idea about physically overcoming Mrs Doveton and the butler and keeping them prisoners in their own home, and flogging off all their antiques in order to buy food. Even if they were successful in somehow subduing Mrs Doveton and Simon, how long would it be before one of them escaped to raise the alarm? It was all becoming too difficult. Wouldn't it be easier to admit defeat and face up to all the shocking things they had done over more than twenty years? They would probably get life imprisonment, but Rochelle knew that so called "life" was usually reduced to fifteen years or so, if you behaved. These thoughts were rolling around in her mind as they entered a small cafe promising a full Aussie breakfast.

A hearty cooked breakfast, accompanied by black coffee, lifted their spirits somewhat but Christopher remained silent about just what he was planning. They were about to commit a house invasion, yet another crime to add to their shameful list. Christopher did not appear too concerned about what was about to happen however, and all but ordered Rochelle to do as she was told when they broke into Mrs Doveton's home. 'Treat this like a military operation,' he said. 'Let me take control. Please promptly do whatever I ask you to do.' Rochelle was becoming more and more resentful of playing second fiddle to a man she increasingly saw as a desperate hardened criminal rather than the man she had loved. She tried in vain to get Christopher to outline what he planned.

They walked back towards Mrs Doveton's home as light rain began to fall. It was just after eight o'clock and they knew that Simon, the faithful butler, arrived promptly at 8:15 am every morning. Christopher told Rochelle to stay in the garage while he attended to Simon. 'Don't come out till twenty past eight and then come and join me inside the house,' he instructed.

Christopher took up his position behind one of the bushes he had trimmed. It afforded him excellent cover. Almost to the minute he saw Simon approaching. The latch on the gate clicked open and then closed. Simon, sheltering under his umbrella, walked past. Christopher charged him using a rugby tackle and knocked him to the ground winding Simon in the process. Before the stunned butler could say anything, Christopher had gagged him using two serviettes tied together that he had pinched from the cafe after breakfast. Simon was a slight man and could offer no resistance. Once gagged, Christopher concentrated on tying Simon's wrists together using a pair of Rochelle's stockings. The whole operation had taken place without a word being uttered and out of sight of the road where people were still making their way to work. Mrs Doveton's trees and bushes had provided all the cover Christopher needed.

He yanked Simon to his feet and frog-marched him up to Mrs Doveton's front door. Rummaging through Simon's pockets he found the key and pushed it into the lock. 'Do exactly as I say and you won't be hurt,' Christopher whispered menacingly. The door opened. All was quiet. No sign of Mrs Doveton. She was most likely in the kitchen getting herself a cup of tea. If she had heard the door open, she would have thought it was Simon who always arrived right on time. Christopher pushed the terrified butler towards the kitchen. Mrs Doveton stood at the kitchen sink with her back to them.

'Sit down on that chair and don't move,' barked Christopher. Alarmed, Mrs Doveton turned towards the voice and at once realised what was happening. She paled instantly and her knees buckled. She slumped to the floor where she remained not moving.

At this moment Rochelle appeared at the door. 'See to Mrs Doveton,' he demanded. 'Get her up on a chair and tie her to it.'

'What with?'

'I don't know. Find something. Hurry up Rochelle. Don't just stand there.'

Gathering her wits together, she noticed that Christopher had used a pair of her stockings to tie Simon's wrists. She removed her shoes and took off her last remaining pair of Razzamatazz and approached Mrs Doveton, who was still lying on the floor but now moaning quietly. The poor old lady must have fainted. Rochelle helped her up onto a kitchen chair, speaking kindly to her as she did her best to tie up her wrists. Meanwhile, Christopher had used the ends of the stockings tied around Simon's wrists to attach him to one of the uprights in the back of the kitchen chair he was obediently sitting on.

'Right, listen carefully you two. You are prisoners. As long as you do as I say and don't do something stupid, you can stay here with us. You will both sleep in the same bedroom so we can keep a watch on you. Simon, you will cook all the meals and do the housework but must never go anywhere without one of us following you. Even if you want to go to the toilet. The same applies to you Mrs Doveton. You are not allowed to leave the house or to use the telephone. If the telephone rings, Simon you will answer it but only when I give you the OK. If anyone comes to the house you, Simon, will go to the door and behave absolutely normally. I will be standing right behind you listening. No visitors will be allowed to come in. Is that all clear?'

The two prisoners were still too stunned to offer a proper response. Mrs Doveton looked quite ill and appeared drowsy. Simon sat, looking from one to the other of his aggressors, apparently unable to speak. He was clearly concerned for Mrs Doveton.

'Do you understand?' shouted Christopher. Simon nodded. Rochelle stood by the door still unable to believe what was happening.

'Who's living in the flat out the back?'

'Nobody,' Simon mumbled.

'Is anybody booked to come in?'

Simon shook his head.

'Righto, you will both stay in Mrs Doveton's en suite at night. As far as possible you are to carry on with the same daily routines, but remember we are watching you all the time. Make one wrong move and you will both be locked in the en suite until further notice. Cooperate with us and we will treat you well.'

'I'm worried about Mrs Doveton,' Simon had at last found his voice.

'Take Mrs Doveton to her bedroom Rochelle and make her lie down. Get her a drink if she wants one.' Rochelle sheepishly followed Christopher's orders and the two of them left the room.

Christopher untied the stocking that held Simon to the chair and stuffed it in his pocket. 'Now, go about your normal duties.'

¶

And so it was that an uneasy peace endured in Mrs Doveton's home. Christopher was on edge and constantly watching the prisoners. He had checked through the house to make sure no windows were visible to anyone outside. Fortunately, trees and bushes all around made this a perfect sanctuary. During the first week there were only a few deliveries of goods to the house and the telephone had rung only four times. He was satisfied that neither Mrs Doveton nor Simon had been able to send out any messages of distress. Once each day Christopher escorted Simon when he went to collect the mail.

Mrs Doveton recovered quickly. It was the shock that had caused her to faint. She had slumped to the ground like a sack of potatoes but was unhurt. Not bad for an 81-year-old. Simon appeared to have accepted his lot without rancour. As the faithful butler, he concentrated on looking after his boss but at the same time managed to feed them all well and to carry out all his normal housework duties.

Christopher was worried about Rochelle though. She had become very quiet and seemed depressed. If he asked her to do something she obeyed, but not graciously. Sometimes he noticed her silently watching him. She only nibbled at her food and seemed listless. In bed she was unresponsive, allowing him to have his way with her, but there was no love or warmth anymore. He tried to discuss what it was that was bothering her, but she just shrugged her shoulders and walked off. Rochelle seemed to prefer the company of Mrs Doveton and Simon. Was she turning traitor? Was she empathising with the prisoners? Could he still trust her?

After roughing it at Stone Cottage they were now living in the lap of luxury. Excellent meals were provided and there were no chores. Christopher spent a lot of time with the antiques. He checked through Mrs Doveton's catalogue and at times would invite her to join him so that he could learn more about their provenance or history. Rochelle had discovered that Mrs Doveton had a fine collection of classical music records and would spend hours listening to her favourite symphonies. Beethoven, Mozart and Haydn were hard to beat. Occasionally, for a change, she would listen to Tchaikovsky, Schubert or even Prokofiev. Mrs Doveton often joined her and they would take it in turns to select the next symphony and together read from the accompanying notes. In the evenings the four of them sat around the television set. Christopher always decided what they would watch. It was a strange kind of disunited family.

And so, the first week passed tolerably well. Apart from a few snarls from Christopher, who was still intent on stamping his authority over the other three, they managed to live together peacefully. By the end of the week however, they were all feeling horribly confined. Nobody had even put a nose out of doors except to collect the mail or put out the garbage. Imprisonment in a dark mansion was unhealthy. They all longed for fresh air and exercise. Christopher toyed with the idea of running a keep fit class for the four of them every morning. He didn't dare let anyone out to exercise. He refused to allow any windows to be opened for fear that a message for help would be tossed out.

By the end of the week Christopher had decided which of Mrs Doveton's antiques would be the next to be sold. Although he had not told Mrs Doveton his intentions, he suspected she had guessed what was going to happen. He had selected a magnificent piece of silverware called the Jaipur Cup. It was another Indian piece displaying wonderful craftsmanship. Mrs Doveton had had it valued at around $1000. His problem was that he might need all morning to go around the antique shops seeking the best price and would have to leave the other three home on their own. He did not trust any of them now. Rochelle, in her present depressed state, could easily be persuaded to let the others go. If he sent her out to do the selling, she might never return. She was no businesswoman either and would probably end up being swindled by dealers. Christopher was not sure how to proceed.

¶

Across the road from Mrs Doveton's mansion was another one designed and built by the same architect. This second house belonged to a retired couple, Dr and Mrs Nankivell, who had lived there for almost twenty years and were now in their early eighties. Over the years they had gradually become good friends with Mrs Doveton and occasionally would invite each other over for morning tea or even dinner. Dr Nankivell had been Professor of Statistics at the nearby University of Sydney.

The Nankivells were creatures of habit. Some would put it less kindly and say they were "stuck in a rut". Nevertheless, being long retired, they had developed certain daily routines that helped them cope with the stresses and aches and pains of old age. One of these routines led to a series of unexpected and surprising events.

The Nankivells treasured their front lawn. They insisted that it be manicured which involved constant watering, fertilising, mowing and weeding. The heavy work was done by their gardener, but every morning, at exactly the same time, Dr and Mrs Nankivell would don appropriate apparel and totter out to inspect their front lawn. Near the road stood a majestic old eucalypt that even pre-dated the construction of Glebe Road. The Nankivells loved Old Sammy, their one and only eucalypt. They would never dream of having it lopped or removed.

Old Sammy had one nasty habit though. Every day, without fail, it dropped leaves and the occasional twig onto the sacred green lawn. Consequently, every day the Nankivells would each carry out a handsome red bucket into which went all the offensive leaves and twigs that had dared overnight to litter the lawn. There was a bigger bucket for the good doctor who concentrated on the larger twigs.

The only event that disturbed this daily routine was the arrival of Simon, the butler, at precisely 8:15 am every morning, except Sundays, at Mrs Doveton's home directly opposite. Being statistically minded, Dr Nankivell loved to follow horseracing and always had a bet if any horseracing was happening on that day. Nearly twenty years ago he had discovered that Simon was also an enthusiastic punter. Each would study the form early in the morning and Simon would always stroll over to where Dr Nankivell was picking up his leaves and sticks to throw him his tip for the day, 'Top Hat for the 2:15 at Rose Hill' or 'Snodgrass for the first race at Wagga today'. Dr Nankivell would return the compliment and offer one of his statistically ranked favourites for the day.

Now, a week ago, this comfortable daily exchange abruptly stopped. Simon no longer turned up to swap tips and unlatch the gate to Mrs Doveton's home. At first the Nankivells assumed that Simon was indisposed or on holidays. After five days had passed sans Simon, Dr Nankivell thought he had better ring Mrs Doveton because she might need some extra assistance with Simon away for so long. It was a good neighbourly sort of thing to do.

Dr Nankivell was most surprised when his phone call was answered by the butler himself. When he inquired if all was well, he received a most peculiar response. It was a sort of muffled, hesitant sound, certainly not the confident, professional Simon he was accustomed to. For some reason Simon had changed his morning routine. Perhaps he was now entering via the rear of the building or perhaps he was living-in full-time and not returning to his little flat every evening? How peculiar that Simon had not mentioned that their brief exchange every morning would no longer be happening.

Two days later, whilst on his morning's leaf and twig duties, Dr Nankivell saw Simon bringing out the garbage bin. 'Hello Simon!' he called cheerfully, relieved to see his fellow-punter was looking okay. Again, a very odd reaction. The butler ignored his greeting, dumped the bin and retreated quickly to the gate and was gone. The doctor was perplexed. A couple of seconds later he thought he saw a second man in Mrs Doveton's front yard. Perhaps he had imagined it. His vision was certainly not as good as it used to be.

He discussed his concerns with his wife as they munched their way through their Weet-Bix at breakfast. She suggested he ring again or call in at the house. He chose the former. He waited till midmorning and rang Mrs Doveton's number. This time he would ask to speak to the dear lady herself. As before, the phone was answered by Simon. This time the butler pattered out his usual response, 'Good morning. You have rung Mrs Doveton's residence. May I help you please?'

'You certainly can. This is Dr Nankivell speaking,' the doctor replied, 'May I speak to Mrs Doveton please?'

There was a short delay, most unlike Simon, who usually answered promptly. 'I'm afraid she is unavailable at the moment,' he finally mumbled.

'Are you okay Simon? You don't sound your usual happy self,' the professor inquired.

'Yes, thank you. I must go. Thank you for calling.' Simon abruptly rang off. This weird behaviour was totally out of character for the usually impeccably polite butler. Something was seriously wrong at Mrs Doveton's. Gone was the confident and more than competent Simon. Never before had he denied him the opportunity to speak to Mrs Doveton. Putting it all together, the good doctor decided that the number of peculiar events was now "statistically significant". He needed to do something.

It was time for his cup of cocoa which Mrs Nankivell made for him in the middle of the morning. Once they were sitting comfortably, he broached the subject of Simon and Mrs Doveton again. He recalled the odd way Simon had behaved when he rang the second time. Encouraged by his wife, he determined he must approach the police. It was all too difficult to get the car out and drive down to the Glebe Police Station. Besides, the parking was impossible at this time of day. He didn't like using the telephone much but it would be easier. He dialled 999.

'Police, ambulance or fire brigade?'

'Umm... police please.'

'Connecting now.'

'New South Wales Police, how may I help you?'

'Um… this is Dr Nankivell here.'

'Good morning doctor, what seems to be the problem?'

'Well, I'm worried about my neighbour across the road.

Some strange things seem to have been happening there for the last week or so.'

'What sort of things, sir?'

The retired professor of statistics spent the next ten minutes explaining, answering questions and doing his best to be helpful, while the policewoman at the other end probed and queried his observations. Finally, she asked, 'Is this the same house where we sent in the assault squad a few weeks ago sir?'

'Yes, yes, it is. The squad moved in on Mrs Doveton's flat at the back of her house. She rents it out.'

'I remember the case now sir. Thank you for bringing this matter to our attention. Please leave it with me and I will make further inquiries.'

'Thank you. I hope I haven't been a nuisance?'

The young policewoman who had taken the professor's call realised this matter needed following up. She asked her assistant to contact the assault squad to get the details of the previous squad outing at the home of Mrs Doveton. She soon learned that it was Christopher and Rochelle Brooks, wanted for a string of crimes, who had twice successfully escaped before the assault squad arrived, once at Mrs Doveton's and then again in the Blue Mountains. Was it possible that the pair had returned to Mrs Doveton's house and were now holding her and the butler captive? Such an audacious move. The assault squad chief agreed to investigate.

CHAPTER 41

Sydney at Last!

Tania, and a police colleague, had been responding to a call for assistance at an apartment in Kent Town, Adelaide, where a woman had alleged her partner had attacked her physically. There was no evidence of such an attack, so the two police officers had written up their report stating that the incidence was merely a domestic argument. They were just driving off when Tania received an urgent call from Inspector Johansson.

'Tania, I want you to catch the 1830 hours flight this evening for Sydney. The New South Wales Police believe they have found our two fugitives. There is going to be action and they want me there. Since you have been so closely involved with this case all the way, I think it wise for you to come as well. It would be an added advantage to have you there especially if we have to interview Rochelle Brooks. Can you be ready in time?'

'Certainly sir. I'll meet you at the airport.'

'Excellent.'

Tania made her way back to her apartment as soon as she could, grabbed what she needed and ordered a taxi to get her out to the Adelaide Airport. At the airport she rang Tony to apologise for her sudden departure, briefed him on what he might find in the fridge to eat and ended her call by saying she had no idea when she would be back in town. She felt a bit mean clearing out so quickly and unexpectedly on her boyfriend, but this was the life of a policewoman. He might as well get used to it if he was ever going to marry her.

Tania checked her baggage in and headed for Gate 22 to find Johansson already sitting there thumbing through some photocopied papers about Christopher and Rochelle. Within a few minutes they had boarded and had politely asked the passenger sitting next to the detective if he would mind changing seats so that Tania could be fully briefed during their flight. The gentleman was most obliging, and they didn't even have to show their police IDs to convince him.

According to the latest briefing from Sydney, Rochelle and Christopher were believed to be holed up at Mrs Doveton's abode having taken her and the butler, Simon, captive in their own home. The police were still not a hundred percent certain however, and were trying to confirm the situation. Apparently, they were close enough to being sure that they had requested Johansson to fly in and take charge of the case. Accommodation had been found for them at a nearby hotel and there would be a police car and driver awaiting them when they arrived in Sydney. The assault squad was on standby but would not be deployed until sometime tomorrow and only when Johansson gave the order. It was difficult to believe that finally the two fugitives might be about to be apprehended.

The excitement of the chase, and its possible imminent conclusion, meant that neither of the two police slept well; Tania because this was the first time she had been involved with the apprehension of two major criminals; Johansson because he was wrestling with the problem of when he should give the order to go ahead and send the assault team in. The detective realised that an elderly lady living in a house and finding the place suddenly under siege, would find it a terrifying experience. He could well imagine that the sight of a squad of eight fully armed and highly trained men, wearing full protective gear and making a heck of a lot of noise, bearing down on a building would be petrifying. Ideally, he would like to warn Mrs Doveton and the butler well before such an attack.

Another concern was haunting Johansson. Nobody knew for sure that Christopher and Rochelle were actually in the building. It was supposition. They had not been sighted or heard from. The whole case rested almost entirely on the information provided by an elderly man who lived across the road. How reliable was this witness? Dr Nankivell's evidence was paltry at best, and was largely based on what he had not seen. He had not seen his friend for a week or more nor had he spotted Mrs Doveton. True, the two phone calls the doctor had made evinced some strange and uncharacteristic responses from the butler. Nevertheless, the combined evidence appeared flimsy at best. If Johansson gave the order for the squad to assault the house and he was wrong, he would be in deep trouble. He could see the headlines now, "Cop Stuffs Up" or "Elderly Lady Terrified by Brutal Police Attack". The detective knew the media would be merciless and unforgiving in its condemnation.

The day began with a meeting between Johansson, Tania, the senior officer at the Glebe Police Station and the chief of the assault squad. They reviewed the evidence again. Johansson was not convinced and ordered no action be taken until he had tried one more tactic. He had an idea but first wanted to talk to Tania about it privately. He thanked and dismissed the other two officers, promising to be in contact again in an hour or two.

'Tania, what are your acting skills like?'

'Acting skills? Why sir?'

'I cannot order the assault crew to go in until I'm absolutely certain we have got this right. So, I'm suggesting we do a bit of hamming up to try and glean more information.'

'I'm not with you sir.'

'I want you to collapse on the front path of Mrs Doveton's house. I will pretend to be a passer-by who sees you there and will bang like mad on Mrs Doveton's door to raise the alarm and ask for help. All you have to do is stay comatose, as if you have fainted. Do you think you could do that?'

Tania giggled. 'Don't I even get a speaking part?' she teased.

'No, not this time. Next time perhaps, if you do this well.' Johansson smiled.

'Okay, I'm in. There's one problem though.'

'What?'

'Christopher knows us from our previous interviews with him. If he recognises us, he will realise we are onto them and they will escape again.'

'I have already thought of that. If I bash on the door like hell, they will send the butler out to deal with it because they won't want to be seen themselves. But just in case, I will also post a couple of undercover police near the gate posing as passers-by. If Rochelle and Christopher do try to make a run for it, they will nab them. These police will stay there till the Assault Squad arrives or I call the whole thing off.'

Once again Tania's analytical skills came to the fore. 'So how do you see this little bit of drama playing out? Do I make a sudden recovery? Are you going to ask to get into the house?'

'Good question. If we are entirely wrong about this whole thing then we can expect both the butler and Mrs Doveton to come out and try and help you. If this happens, we can ask them quite simply if everything is okay. We will be able to tell from the way they react.'

'My guess is that if they are there, they might open the door and then slam it shut again. They are not likely to let the butler come out and help for fear we will grab him or ask him questions. If they suspect a trap, we will be able to tell by what happens at that door.'

'Agreed' replied Johansson. 'So, are you game?'

'All in the line of duty sir.'

¶

By 1300 hours all was in place. A police car was parked a hundred yards away from Mrs Doveton's house and two undercover police were stationed near the entrance gate doing their utmost to look like casual neighbours. A second police car was parked around the back of the house out of sight. This car disgorged two more plain-clothed undercover police, to protect the rear of the house, as well as Inspector Johansson and a nervous Tania. Tania had had her face made up to look pale and sick. 'A walking zombie,' quipped the Inspector.

Tania unlatched the gate and began walking along the path. At the foot of the three steps that led up to the front door she made her dramatic collapse. Here was a gorgeous young woman, spread-eagled on her back, eyes closed looking a ghastly colour and seemingly unconscious. Johansson waited a couple of seconds before jumping up the steps and thumping desperately on the oak door. He thumped and thumped, wondering how much longer he could keep it up, until what seemed minutes had elapsed, and the door finally opened. In front of him stood a rather slovenly looking man dressed as a butler but not playing the part well.

'What's up?'

'This woman needs an ambulance. She's collapsed and looks awful. May I come in and ring for the ambulance please?'

The butler peered anxiously at the distressed woman but didn't leave the top step.

'Come on man. You can see she's unwell and needs assistance. Please can we ring for help?'

The butler stood rooted to the spot and seemed incapable

of making a sensible reply. He was looking at Johansson with a mixture of fear and pleading in his eyes. Somewhere behind the butler, Johansson distinctly heard a man's voice saying, 'No, no, no' repeatedly.

The butler at last seemed to find his tongue. 'I'm very sorry, sir. It is not possible for you to come in. You will have to get the lady to the road and call for help from there.' And with that the front door was firmly closed.

The distressed woman started to come around and made a remarkably quick recovery, aided by the handsome man who had valiantly come to her rescue. The pair of them kept up their dual act back along the pathway and a few metres down the road until completely hidden from Mrs Doveton's house by the trees.

'An Oscar winning performance,' joked Johansson.

'I think I need a Bex and a quick lie down.'

The two undercover police wandered over, enjoying a chance to smoke whilst on duty. 'What's up sir?' they inquired.

'You can stay here and watch the house. I'm sure they are in there. If anyone comes out detain them. As soon as possible the assault squad will be here. When they arrive, keep the traffic and crowds away and be ready to assist in arresting the two people we want. You may also be needed to help the other two who have been virtually kidnapped in their own home. Meantime you can enjoy a few more smokes.'

'Sounds good sir.'

Johansson and Tania headed back to their car along the way alerting the other two undercover policeman at the back to what was happening. Tania had brought along a wet face washer and spent most of the trip back to the station trying to remove the white make-up that had been plastered over her face.

The whole piece of drama had taken only a short time and the assault squad was ordered to go in at 1530 hours. Hopefully, the assault would be over and the criminals in custody by 1600 hours before the rush hour began which would cause major chaos along Glebe Road.

¶

'You're a dithering bloody fool!' yelled Christopher. 'I've told you many times to say no to anyone that comes to the door. If I hadn't been standing behind you saying "no, no, no" you would have let that idiot in to make his phone call. How do we know that was not a trap? Do as you're bloody told next time or else.'

Simon didn't wait around to be abused anymore and mooched off to the kitchen to get the afternoon tea. Despite the tensions within the house, they still retained the niceties such as morning coffee and afternoon tea. Keeping to these daily routines helped him and poor Mrs Doveton to remain passably sane. The butler felt dreadful that they had not been able to help the unfortunate lady who had collapsed on their front doorstep. It was shameful.

As he was preparing the scones, he could hear Christopher and Rochelle having a heated discussion in the living area.

'Who were those bastards?' demanded Christopher. 'What are the chances that some woman is going to come up our path and collapse and then some other dude sees her and wants to come and help. I tell you I think it was a trap. I think they are on to us Rochelle.'

'You are getting too uptight Christopher. Just calm down and look at things rationally. Think about it for a minute. If someone collapses in the street, wouldn't you go to their aid? That's all it was. This woman must have staggered up the path to call for help but didn't quite make it. You are making a mountain out of a molehill.'

'I still don't like it. I just don't know what to believe. If it was a trap and they are on to us they could be here any moment and we have no way of escaping. I reckon we should go now before they come back.'

'Rubbish Christopher. As usual you are exaggerating. If they know we are here they wouldn't be play-acting on the garden path, would they? They would come straight in and arrest us.'

Christopher remained unconvinced. He slumped into an armchair and yelled out to Simon in the kitchen. 'Simon, when you bring in the afternoon tea bring in a bottle of wine too please.'

The ever-obedient butler first served tea and scones to his employer, Mrs Doveton, who was reading in the conservatorium. He briefed her on what had happened at the front door. Mrs Doveton was holding up well but was distressed and angry about the antiques that Christopher had selected for sale. She knew they had almost run out of money for food and that any day now Christopher would be forced to leave the house to sell off the next lot of her treasures. She and Simon had on several occasions tried to plan their escape or think of a way whereby they could get a message out to someone to call for help. Mrs Doveton had had a letter written explaining their predicament a day or two after their imprisonment began, but so far to no avail. They were not allowed near any windows or outside doors unless they were being supervised and telephoning was forbidden. They were effectively isolated from the outside world.

Next Simon took scones, afternoon tea, a bottle of wine and glasses into the living room for Christopher and Rochelle. He hated having to wait on them but did his best not to show his distaste. He recalled a couple of movies he had watched when English butlers had continued to serve their masters even when their masters were highly unsavoury characters. These impeccably dressed butlers behaved like polite robots showing no emotion. Simon removed the cork and poured them both a standard glass hoping he was still perceived as a professional, high quality butler.

'Remember Christopher, that I have no intention of being arrested and spending the rest of my life behind bars. If the game is up, I will drink my vial and I'll be dead almost instantly. You have that choice too. All you have to do is take the cap off the vial and throw the contents back just like you are throwing back that wine.'

'Like you Rochelle, I'm tempted. It would be so easy to do

and that would be the end of it. No more worries, no miserable life eked out in a prison somewhere. I never thought it might end this way but I'm so relieved you have those two vials. Neither of us have any responsibilities with children, so nobody is going to be dependent on us. Have you made a will Rochelle?'

'No, have you?'

'No. If you die intestate what happens to any assets you own?'

'I think it goes to the government unless your family can argue otherwise. But I'm not too sure.'

The wine was having a calming effect, and Christopher was beginning to unwind. Little did he know that Rochelle was wrestling with a terrifying personal dilemma.

¶

The two vials that Rochelle had meticulously prepared several weeks ago, before leaving her home in Orange, still lay safely hidden in a pocket in her suitcase. They looked identical. The vials were exactly the same size and type and the liquid contained in each was the same light green hue. There was, however, one tiny detail that differentiated the two. Unless you knew it was there you might never see it. Under one vial was a tiny black dot. There was no black dot beneath the other.

Rochelle had taken great care to place this distinguishing mark under the one vial. Although both vials looked almost identical on the outside, their contents were totally different.

One contained devastating toxins that would kill in less than a minute, the other contained a totally harmless liquid.

Rochelle had earnestly hoped that the vials would never have to be used. She had always believed that she and Christopher would successfully evade the law and eventually settle down somewhere to live out their lives quietly and peacefully. That little farm in Tasmania was still her dream. After the dreadful crime she herself had had to endure so many years back, when still married to Christopher, she was entitled to end her days well. She readily admitted that she had taken advantage of old Mr Allsop by blackmailing him many times and finally murdering him when he refused to pay up one last time. But this was revenge for what Mr Allsop had done to her. He deserved it.

Rochelle was not prepared to be a long-term guest of Her Majesty. If there was no hope of escape, she would not hesitate to take the poison. Death would be a welcome release. She would sit down with Christopher, and together, they would drink their vials. She would die almost instantly but he would live. She still loved Christopher and would never take his life. And so it was that she had made up two different concoctions that looked the same.

Rochelle's dilemma was that she could not remember whether she had put the tiny black dot under the toxic vial or the harmless one. Which was which?

The Climax

Shortly before 1530 hours, the eight-man assault squad moved silently into position around Mrs Doveton's premises. A traffic diversion was in place along Glebe Road and nearby neighbours had been instructed to remain indoors until further notice. The weather was fine, barely a breeze blowing. Detective Inspector Johansson and Tania, along with the arresting police, a paddy van, three ambulances and a fire engine were assembled at a safe distance away. Journalists and photographers had somehow got word of the impending drama and were straining to get closer to the action but were being held back by the ever-patient uniformed police.

As assaults go, this one followed standard procedure to begin with. The assault chief called for Christopher and Rochelle to release their two captors and then to come out quietly with their hands up, through the front door, when instructed to do so. In these situations, care is always taken to ensure that first of all any captives are safely removed from the danger zone.

Within a minute or two, Simon and Mrs Doveton appeared

at the front door looking frightened and anxious. They were instructed to walk calmly along the path towards the gate and then turn right and walk on down the road towards the police waiting there for them. Mrs Doveton stumbled as she made her way slowly to safety and was glad of her butler's steadying arm. They were met by a doctor and nurse and conveyed to the first ambulance for initial assessments.

As soon as they were in safe hands, the chief barked out more orders to the two remaining occupants.

'On the count of three, one of you come to the front door with your hands up and stand there for further instructions. I repeat. On the count of three, one of you must come to the front door and wait there with your hands up until given further instructions. If you do as ordered, you will not be hurt. If you fail to do as instructed, we will come and get you. If we come in, we cannot guarantee that you will not be injured. It's your choice. Now, move to the door and one of you be ready to open it when I count to three.'

Without a word, Rochelle walked to the bedroom where she and Christopher had slept the last ten nights or so. She opened her suitcase and reached into the large pocket on the underside of the lid. She rummaged about for a moment and pulled out a small clear plastic bag. Inside were the two vials. The one with the tiny black dot she held in her left hand, the one without the dot she held in her right. She now had a fifty-fifty chance of getting this next move correct. One of them would die within a few minutes and she wanted it to be her. If she got this right, Christopher would live.

Rochelle walked slowly back into the living room holding the two vials and stood in front of Christopher looking calmly down at him. She was still hoping for a miraculous revelation. Would it come back to her at this vital last moment how she had used the black dot? Had she placed the little black dot on the vial she should take to commit suicide, or on the vial she should give to Christopher to save his life?

That wretched man outside was still bellowing away on his loudspeaker system. She caught snippets of what he was saying. 'This is your last chance... come out peacefully... you'll be rewarded...' She noticed that Christopher was laughing at her. He had downed the remainder of the bottle of wine that now lay abandoned on the carpet beside him. He was drunk; Dutch courage she reasoned. Whatever she did, she must not tell Christopher her awful dilemma. If he drank from the wrong vial he would die and she would be up on another murder charge.

Christopher looked up at his partner, ex-wife and lover. They had had some good times together and they had run a good race. He shared Rochelle's wish to die rather than face up to all the crimes he had committed. There was something almost romantic about dying together. He would suggest they sit together on the couch, arms locked around each other. Somehow it was important to be found this way. The media outlets would get a kick out of telling the world how they died in each other's arms. A double suicide, a pact.

'Come on Rochelle, we don't want them to come in before we drink those vials,' Christopher called out in a slurring voice.

'The toxins will work very quickly Christopher. In twenty seconds, you will be gone.'

'Give me mine now...' Christopher demanded, clambering to his feet and lurching unsteadily towards Rochelle.

The voice from outside droned on, 'We will be entering in thirty seconds. Come to the door immediately. I will start counting down now. Thirty... twenty-nine... twenty-eight...'

'Sit on the bloody couch with me, Rochelle.'

'Twenty-four... twenty-three...'

Rochelle moved back two or three paces, alarmed at how intoxicated Christopher was. As he approached her, he lunged for one of the vials but stumbled and crashed against her like a front-row forward tackling the opposition in a rugby match. They fell to the ground together in a jumble of arms and legs.

'Nineteen... eighteen...'

The impact of falling to the ground so hard caused Rochelle to drop both the vials which rolled away a few feet towards the sofa.

'You idiot Christopher.'

Stunned, they both looked about for the vials. Rochelle with her sober eyes saw them first and grabbed the one nearest her. She struggled to her feet and slumped on the sofa.

'Thirteen... twelve...'

'Hurry up Christopher, or you will be too late.'

'Never too bloody late,' Christopher mumbled as he picked up the second vial and, in his drunken stupor, struggled to find his feet.

'Eight... seven...'

Rochelle extended her arm and like a drowning man Christopher grabbed it and hauled himself up onto the sofa and sat up close to Rochelle.

'Three... two...'

Rochelle and Christopher removed the caps from their vials and facing each other, they crossed arms and raised the vials to their mouths.

There was an almighty crash as their window was smashed and glass sprayed all over the room. At the same time screaming men came charging in at the front door. The man on the loudspeaker was still yelling something about lying down on the floor.

Two of the squad stormed into the living room with guns at the ready. Facing them was a sofa with two people sitting on it in an embrace.

'In here, boss.'

The men kept their guns trained on the couple as their colleagues swarmed in from the other rooms. Suddenly, without warning, the woman lunged across the man sitting next to her and grabbed a small container which she put to her mouth and sucked on desperately.

A shot rang out and the woman slumped back against the back of the sofa screaming in pain.

¶

It was instinct. Any sudden movement required a split-second response. The members of the assault squad were trained to react instantly to any sudden moves. For all they knew this woman could have been reaching for a gun, a grenade or a knife. Take no risks. Shoot and ask questions later. In these kinds of critically tense situations it came down quite simply to shoot first or risk being killed.

It took a few moments for the team to sort out what had happened. There had been two vials. One contained a deadly nerve agent that the man had consumed, causing his death within a few seconds. The other vial, which looked the same, and was also empty, must have contained a harmless liquid. This one the woman had drunk. When it had had no effect on her, in a panic, she had reached across to get the one that contained the toxins, but what remained of the nerve agent hadn't passed her lips. Either it had already been completely consumed by Christopher, or the shot had hit her before she had time to ingest anything. It appeared to be an attempted double suicide that had gone horribly wrong.

The woman had suffered a nasty upper arm bullet wound and was bleeding profusely. Within a couple of minutes, the ambulance team arrived and stemmed the flow. The woman was in a seriously distressed state moaning, 'I was the one who was meant to die. It all went wrong. I should be dead, not him.' She was arrested on the spot by Detective Inspector Johansson and then heavily sedated. Still mumbling incoherently, Rochelle was stretchered out to the second ambulance. Christopher went in the third ambulance but under a white sheet.

Johansson and Tania, together with the chief of the assault squad and the police photographer, spent the rest of the day and evening assessing the crime scene. Mrs Doveton and the butler were refused entry for the night but were comfortably accommodated in a nearby hotel. They had spent a couple of hours with a police counsellor debriefing and giving evidence. They were advised that there would be more interviews the next day and that the broken window and any other damage would be repaired at police expense.

At 9 pm Tania and her boss finally found a small Malaysian cafe still open. They celebrated with an excellent meal and a decent bottle of wine.

EPILOGUE

Rochelle was admitted to North Shore Hospital where she underwent emergency surgery to remove the bullet. She remained in hospital, under police guard, for four days before being transferred to a special prison facility where she could continue her treatment and commence physiotherapy. Her recovery was normal, but she battled depression for years. The psychologist who worked with Rochelle eventually provided her with some coping skills that helped.

Rochelle faced trial three weeks after her arrest. She pleaded guilty to all charges and showed some measure of remorse. The judge, in summing up, noted that Rochelle had initially been motivated by revenge for what she had been subjected to as a young woman living in Sydney with her husband, Christopher. A court order vetoed the publication of the details of what had happened to Rochelle.

According to Rochelle, one night when she and Christopher were sharing their Sydney accommodation with Christopher's father, Charles Allsop, Christopher went down to the pub for a couple of drinks, leaving Rochelle and Charles Allsop alone together. When Christopher returned, earlier than expected, he found the music from a record player turned up very loud. Upon entering his own bedroom, he was horrified to find his father savagely raping his new young wife. It was brutal and depraved. It was this horrific event that prompted their joint decision to blackmail Allsop. One thing led to another, and when he finally refused to make any more payments, the hatred and contempt they still felt for him twenty years later was intense enough for them to carry out their threat. With Rochelle's expertise in biochemistry, they believed they would never be caught.

Rochelle was sentenced to twenty years with a non-parole time of fifteen years. Once she learned to handle her depression, she was a well-behaved prisoner and, at the age of sixty-four, was finally released. Her good friend Tina, from Orange, stood by her and visited Rochelle in prison every couple of months. Rochelle eventually went to live with Tina on her release, but was never happy returning to Orange, because so many of her past friends and colleagues were so unforgiving. Rochelle died of cancer a few days before she turned seventy.

A post-mortem was conducted on Christopher's body confirming death as the result of ingesting poisonous fluids. He was laid to rest in the West Terrace Cemetery in Adelaide. The short funeral service was attended by his brother, David, and his sister, Joanne Ernstein. Detective Inspector Johansson and Senior Constable Tania Markovina were also in attendance. Rochelle was too unwell to be there, although it was unlikely she would have been permitted to attend had she been fit.

Joanne Ernstein did everything she could to erase all

connections with her brother, Christopher, after his funeral. They had never got on well together. After a few years she was diagnosed with type 2 diabetes and end stage kidney disease. She died, aged sixty, a few months after commencing dialysis.

Detective Inspector Johansson continued with the SA Police until his retirement nearly twenty years later. He remained an ardent golfing enthusiast throughout, but eventually had to resort to using an electric golf buggy to negotiate the courses.

Six months after the case was closed, Tania finally became engaged. She and Tony eventually had three beautiful children. During her time as a young mother, Tania changed direction and trained as a primary school teacher. She remained in the teaching force until her retirement, ending her career as a school principal.

Harry Childs, who had moved into The Everglades Retirement Village especially to make Charles Allsop's life a misery, didn't live long. His health quickly deteriorated. He did, however, follow the story of Christopher and Rochelle's demise with much interest. Harry had had a remarkable life, overcoming his enormously disadvantaged upbringing and becoming a respected leader in his field and a multi-millionaire.

Mrs Doveton returned to her home with the faithful Simon still in her service. The unpleasant experiences she had endured when Christopher and Rochelle had forcibly moved in, hastened her decision to sell. The large block was purchased by a developer for a figure well above the price Mrs

Doveton thought it would fetch. There were twelve modern apartments that replaced her stately mansion. Mrs Doveton moved into a luxury three-bedroom apartment in Hunter's Hill taking only a few of her favourite antiques with her. Simon, the butler, continued to work for her in a part-time capacity until Mrs Doveton died suddenly of a heart attack. Her collection of antiques became known as The Doveton Bequest and was left to the Museum of Antiquities for all to enjoy.

If there is a lesson to be learnt from this story, it is that Mr Allsop's savage and brutal rape of Rochelle led to a string of events that adversely affected the lives of many others over several decades. As they say; one thing leads to another.

T H E   E N D